Praise for
DragonLight

"Engaging characters, enchanting locales, and perilous creatures await the brave soul who enters the realm of Amara. Donita K. Paul's DragonKeeper chronicles will surely delight fantasy readers with the kind of story that allows a reader to escape into it, but its powerful message lingers long after the final page is turned."

—WAYNE THOMAS BATSON, author of The Door Within Trilogy

"Donita K. Paul is amazing! *DragonLight* has the allegorical depth to satisfy the most discerning adult seeking spiritual depth, yet it is fun enough to fascinate a child. This book will enthrall, uplift, and, if allowed, change lives—as we are gently drawn to realize that each of us is flawed and must have patience with other flawed believers."

—HANNAH ALEXANDER, author of *Double Blind*

"*DragonLight* is a delight, but I wouldn't expect anything less from the marvelous Donita K. Paul. I heartily recommend her books to all ages who love inspirational fantasy and wonderful creatures. Ms. Paul not only supplies imagination and talent, she provides heart and soul. Another winner!"

—KATHRYN MACKEL, author of *Boost*

"Humans and dragons join forces in a quest that leads to a final confrontation with ultimate evil. This is rich, exciting, mythic adventure, told as only Donita K. Paul can tell it. I predict that *DragonLight* will be your favorite book in the DragonKeeper chronicles!"

—JIM DENNEY, author of *Battle Before Time* and *Lost in Cydonia*

"C. S. Lewis once said, 'A strict allegory is like a puzzle with a solution. A great romance is like a flower whose smell reminds you of something you can't quite place. I think the "something" is the whole quality of life as we actually experience it.' In *DragonLight,* Donita K. Paul captures the haunting fragrance that reminds us of a place we think we've visited—or did we only dream it? This book will transport you to a world that captures the whole quality of life, whether it's the delight of a tiny dragon's hiccups or the very portal through which we meet the one, true, living God."

—WENDY LAWTON, author of the Daughters of the Faith series

"Donita K. Paul's vivid imagery and startling plot twists will delight fans, as Kale and Bardon unravel the mysteries behind eerie unmapped villages, a hidden colony of meech dragons, and a dark presence threatening the land of Amara."

—KACY BARNETT-GRAMCKOW, author of The Genesis Trilogy

DragonLight

DragonLight

Donita K. Paul

DragonLight

Trade Paperback ISBN 978-1-4000-7378-8
eBook ISBN 978-0-307-44625-1

Published in association with the literary agency of Alive Communications Inc., 7680 Goddard Street, Suite 200, Colorado Springs, CO 80920, www.alivecommunications.com.

Published in the United States by WaterBrook, an imprint of the Crown Publishing Group, a division of Penguin Random House LLC, New York.

WaterBrook® and its deer colophon are registered trademarks of Penguin Random House LLC.

Library of Congress Cataloging-in-Publication Data
Paul, Donita K.
Dragonlight : a novel / Donita K. Paul. — 1st ed.
p. cm.
ISBN 978-1-4000-7378-8
1. Dragons—Fiction. 2. Religious fiction. I. Title.
PS3616.A94D726 2008
813'.6—dc22

2008006374

Printed in the United States of America

Like sonar, I send out a signal, and when it bounces back,
I know where I am. Thanks for being first readers.

Jessica Agius
Mary Darnell
Jason Harris
Hannah Johnson
Alistair and Ian McNear
Rachael Selk
Rebecca Wilber

Contents

Acknowledgments

You make me think, and think, and think. Then you make me laugh! What friends you are, and how invaluable you are to my creative process.

Nangie
Mary Agius
Evangeline Denmark
Michelle Garland
Dianna Gay
Cecilia Gray
Jack Hagar
Jim Hart
Shannon Hill
Beth Jusino
Krystine Kercher
Shannon and Troy McNear
Paul Moede
Jill Elizabeth Nelson
Robert C. Peterson
Faye Spieker
Darren Stautz
Stuart Stockton
Case Tompkins
Peggy Wilber
Elizabeth Wolford
Kim Woodhouse
Laura Wright

Cast of Characters

Artross—light dragon in Kale's keep

Bardon—o'rant and emerlindian knight in service to Paladin, married to Kale

Brunstetter—urohm, noble ruler of Ordray

Wizard **Burner Stox**—evil female wizard, married to Crim Cropper

Wizard **Cam Ayronn**—lake wizard from Trese

Celisse—Kale's black and white riding dragon

Crain—young, pink minor dragon who studies with Librettowit

Wizard **Crim Cropper**—evil male wizard, experiments with genetics, married to Burner Stox

Crispin—young red minor dragon, breathes fire

Sir **Dar**—doneel diplomat and statesman

Dibl—yellow and orange minor dragon, reveals humor in situations, lightens the hearts of his companions

Wizard **Fenworth**—deceased Bog Wizard from Wynd

Filia—pink minor dragon, enthusiastic about all things, collects knowledge, some of it quite trivial

Fly—hatchling minor dragon who rejects Kale

Garmey—marione farmer who listens to the Followers

Gilda—meech dragon, married to Regidor

Glaringtonover—tumanhofer head of tunneling crew

Granny Kye—Bardon's emerlindian grandmother

Granny Noon—emerlindian, friend of Kale, Bardon, Regidor, Gilda

Greer—Bardon's riding dragon, purple with cobalt wings

Gymn—green minor dragon, heals

Holt Hoddack—marione adventurer

Lord **Ire**—another name used by Pretender

Sir **Joffa**—Bardon's father

Kale Allerion—o'rant wizard and Dragon Keeper, married to Bardon

Sir **Kemry Allerion**—Kale's father, also a Dragon Keeper

Kondiganpress—tumanhofer artist of murals

Lee Ark—marione general in the service of Paladin
Leetu Bends—emerlindian in the service of Paladin, recently undercover in Creemoor
Librettowit—tumanhofer librarian in Kale and Bardon's castle
Lyll Allerion—Kale's mother
Merlander—Dar's red and purple riding dragon
Metta—purple minor dragon, sings
Mikkai—Bardon's blue and green minor dragon, strong in geography
Mistress Meiger—woman who raised Kale
Mistress Orcutt—Wizard Namee's doneel housekeeper
Mot Angra—legendary evil dragon
Wizard **Namee**—Paladin's right-hand man at court
N'Rae—Bardon's emerlindian cousin
Old Woman of Wust—wise woman of another time and place
Paladin—leader of Amara
Pat—chubby brown minor dragon, fixes things
Pretender—ruler of the evil populace of Amara
Regidor—meech dragon, in search of a colony of lost meech dragons, likes fancy things, married to Gilda
Wizard **Risto**—evil wizard killed by Fenworth
Sachael Relk—meech dragon with many children and skilled as a midwife
Seezle—female kimen
Seslie—one of the meech leaders of Bility
Sittiponder—blind tumanhofer child
Taracinabloo—toddler child of Taylaminkadot and Librettowit
Taylaminkadot—married to Librettowit, housekeeper for Kale and Bardon
Tieto—a blue and green dragon, discerns the aura around people
Toopka—doneel child, under guardianship of Kale and Sir Dar
Tulanny—meech hostess to Kale and Bardon in Bility
Woodkimkalajoss—old tumanhofer who had traveled in the Northern Reach as a young man
Wulder—the creator and one true, living God of Amara

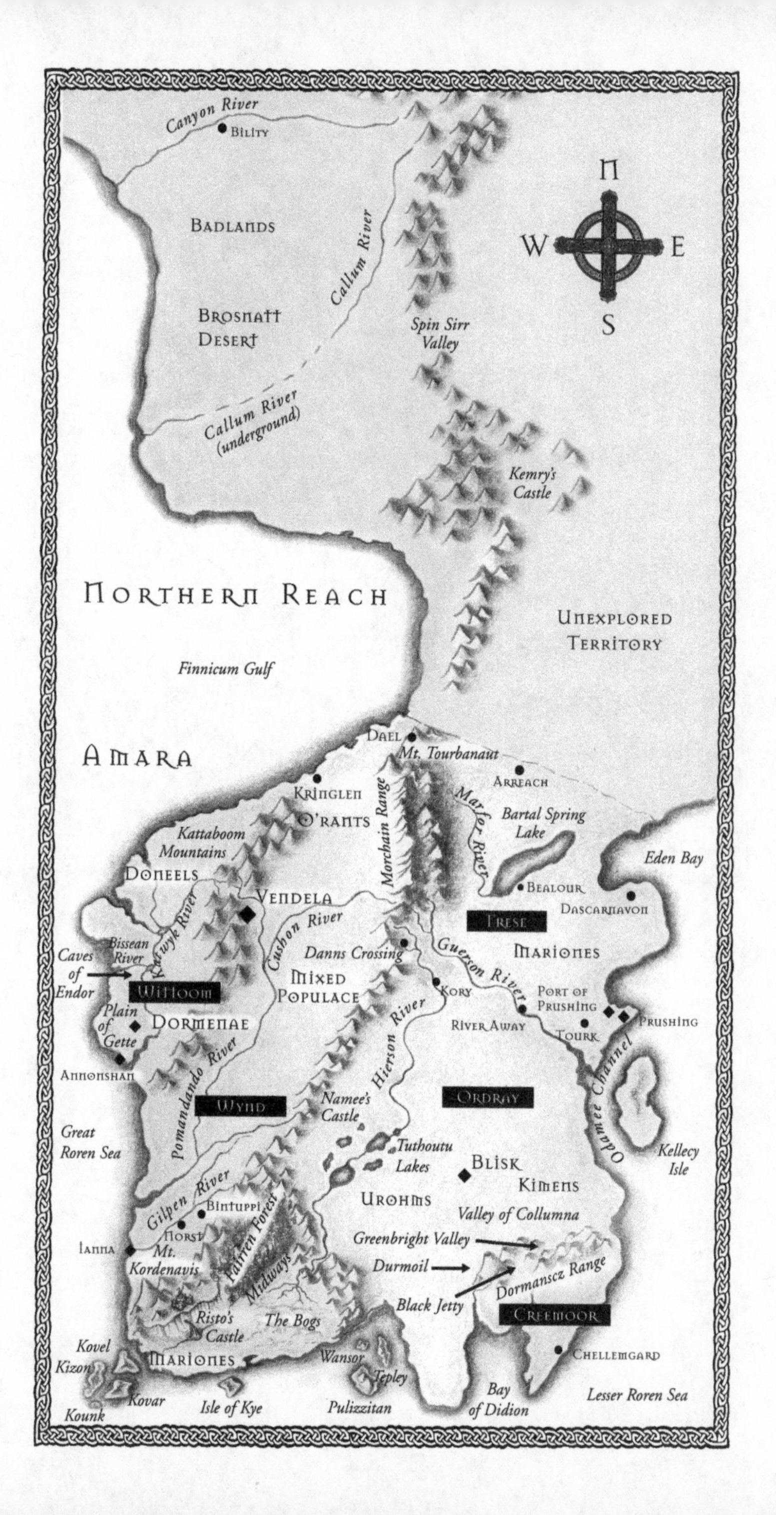

Canyon River
Bility
Badlands
Callum River
Brosnatt Desert
Spin Sirr Valley
N
W
E
S
Callum River (underground)
Kemry's Castle
Northern Reach
Unexplored Territory
Finnicum Gulf
Amara
Dael
Mt. Tourbanaut
Arreach
Kringlen
O'rants
Morchain Range
Marfor River
Bartal Spring Lake
Eden Bay
Kattaboom Mountains
Doneels
Vendela
Bealour
Dascarnavon
Cushon River
Frese
Karwyk River
Bissean River
Caves of Endor
Danns Crossing
Guerson River
Mariones
Wittoom
Mixed Populace
Kory
Port of Prushing
Plain of Gette
Dormenae
Hierson River
River Away
Prushing
Tourk
Annonshan
Pomandando River
Wynd
Namee's Castle
Ordray
Odamee Channel
Great Roren Sea
Tuthoutu Lakes
Blisk
Kimens
Kellecy Isle
Gilpen River
Bintuppi
Urohms
Valley of Collumna
Norst
Ianna
Mt. Kordenavis
Fairren Forest
Greenbright Valley
Durmoil
Midways
Dormanscz Range
Black Jetty
Risto's Castle
The Bogs
Creemoor
Kovel
Kizon
Mariones
Wansor
Chellemgard
Tepley
Kovar
Isle of Kye
Pulizzitan
Bay of Didion
Lesser Roren Sea
Kounk

I

Castle Passages

Kale wrinkled her nose at the dank air drifting up from the stone staircase. Below, utter darkness created a formidable barrier.

Toopka stood close to her knee. Sparks skittered across the doneel child's furry hand where she clasped the flowing, soft material of Kale's wizard robe. Kale frowned down at her ward. The little doneel spent too much time attached to her skirts to be captivated by the light show. Instead, Toopka glowered into the forbidding corridor. "What's down there?"

Kale sighed. "I'm not sure."

"Is it the dungeon?"

"I don't think we have a dungeon."

Toopka furrowed her brow in confusion. "Don't you know? It's your castle."

"A castle built by committee." Kale's face grimaced at the memory of weeks of creative chaos. She put her hand on Toopka's soft head.

The doneel dragged her gaze away from the stairway, tilted her head back, and frowned at her guardian. "What's 'by committee'?"

"You remember, don't you? It was just five years ago."

"I remember the wizards coming and the pretty tents in the meadow." Toopka pursed her lips. "And shouting. I remember shouting."

"They were shouting because no one was listening. Twenty-one wizards came for the castle raising. Each had their own idea about what we needed. So they each constructed their fragment of the castle structure according to their whims."

Toopka giggled.

"I don't think it's funny. The chunks of castle were erected, juxtaposed with the others, but not as a whole unit. I thank Wulder that at least my parents had some sense. My mother and father connected the tads, bits, and smidgens together with steps and short halls. When nothing else would work, they formed gateways from one portion to another."

The little doneel laughed out loud and hid her face in Kale's silky wizard's robe. Miniature lightning flashes enveloped Toopka's head and cascaded down her neck, over her back, and onto the floor like a waterfall of sparks.

Kale cut off the flow of energy and placed a hand on the doneel's shoulder. "Surely you remember this, Toopka."

She looked up, her face growing serious. "I was very young then."

Kale narrowed her eyes and examined the child's innocent face. "As long as I have known you, you've appeared to be the same age. Are you ever going to grow up?"

Toopka shrugged, then the typical smile of a doneel spread across her face. Her thin black lips stretched, almost reaching from ear to ear. "I'm growing up as fast as I can, but I don't think I'm the one in charge. If I were in charge, I would be big enough to have my own dragon, instead of searching for yours."

The statement pulled Kale back to her original purpose. No doubt she had been manipulated yet again by the tiny doneel, but dropping the subject of Toopka's age for the time being seemed prudent.

Kale rubbed the top of Toopka's head. The shorter fur between her ears felt softer than the hair on the child's arms. Kale always found it soothing to stroke Toopka's head, and the doneel liked it as well.

Kale let her hand fall to her side and pursued their mission. "Gally and Mince have been missing for a day and a half. We must find them. Taylaminkadot said she heard an odd noise when she came down to the storeroom." Kale squared her shoulders and took a step down into the dark, dank stairwell. "Gally and Mince may be down here, and they may be in trouble."

"How can you know who's missing?" Toopka tugged on Kale's robe, letting loose a spray of sparkles. "You have hundreds of minor dragons in the castle and more big dragons in the fields."

"I know." Kale put her hand in front of her, and a globe of light appeared, resting on her palm. "I'm a Dragon Keeper. I know when any of my dragons have missed a meal or two." She stepped through the doorway.

Toopka tugged on Kale's gown. "May I have a light too?"

"Of course." She handed the globe to the doneel. The light flickered. Kale tapped it, and the glow steadied. She produced another light to sit in her own hand and proceeded down the steps.

Toopka followed, clutching the sparkling cloth of Kale's robe in one hand and the light in the other. "I think we should take a dozen guards with us."

"I don't think there's anything scary down here, Toopka. After all, as you reminded me, this is our castle, and we certainly haven't invited anything nasty to live with us."

"It's the things that come uninvited that worry me."

"All right. Just a moment." Kale turned to face the archway at the top of the stairs, a few steps up from where they stood.

She reached with her mind to the nearest band of minor dragons. Soon chittering dragon voices, a rainbow vision of soft, flapping, leathery wings, and a ripple of excitement swept through her senses. She heard Artross, the leader of this watch, call for his band to mind their manners, listen to orders, and calm themselves.

Kale smiled her greeting as they entered the stairway and circled above her. She turned to Toopka, pleased with her solution, but Toopka scowled. Obviously, the doneel was not impressed with the arrival of a courageous escort.

Kale opened her mouth to inform Toopka that a watch of dragons provides sentries, scouts, and fighters. And Bardon had seen to their training. But the doneel child knew this.

Each watch formed without a Dragon Keeper's instigation. Usually eleven to fifteen minor dragons developed camaraderie, and a leader emerged. A social structure developed within each watch. Kale marveled at the process. Even though she didn't always understand the choices, she did nothing to alter the natural way of establishing the hierarchy and respectfully worked with what was in place.

Artross, a milky white dragon who glowed in the dark, had caught

Kale's affections. She sent a warm greeting to the serious-minded leader and received a curt acknowledgment. The straight-laced young dragon with his tiny, mottled white body tickled her. Although they didn't look alike in the least, Artross's behavior reminded Kale of her husband's personality.

Kale nodded at Toopka and winked. "Now we have defenders."

"I think," said the doneel, letting go of Kale's robe and stepping down a stair, "it would be better if they were bigger and carried swords."

Kale smiled as one of the younger dragons landed on her shoulder. He pushed his violet head against her chin, rubbing with soft scales circling between small bumps that looked like stunted horns. Toopka skipped ahead with the other minor dragons flying just above her head.

"Hello, Crain," said Kale, using a fingertip to stroke his pink belly. She'd been at his hatching a week before. The little dragon chirred his contentment. "With your love of learning, I'm surprised you're not in the library with Librettowit."

A scene emerged in Kale's mind from the small dragon's thoughts. She hid a smile. "I'm sorry you got thrown out, but you must not bring your snacks into Librettowit's reading rooms. A tumanhofer usually likes a morsel of food to tide him over, but not when the treat threatens to smudge the pages of his precious books." She felt the small beast shudder at the memory of the librarian's angry voice. "It's all right, Crain. He'll forgive you and let you come back into his bookish sanctum. And he'll delight in helping you find all sorts of wonderful facts."

Toopka came scurrying back. She'd deserted her lead position in the company of intrepid dragons. The tiny doneel dodged behind Kale and once more clutched the sparkling robe. Kale shifted her attention to a commotion ahead and sought out the thoughts of the leader Artross.

"What's wrong?" asked Kale, but her answer came as she tuned in to the leader of the dragon watch.

Artross trilled orders to his subordinates. Kale saw the enemy through the eyes of this friend.

An anvilhead snake slid over the stone floor of a room stacked high with large kegs. His long black body stretched out from a nook between two barrels. With the tail of the serpent hidden, she had no way of knowing its size. These reptiles' heads outweighed their bodies. The muscled section behind the base of the jaws could be as much as six inches wide. But the length of the snake could be from three feet to thirty.

Kale shuddered but took another step down the passage.

Artross looked around the room and spotted another section of ropelike body against the opposite wall. Kegs hid most of the snake.

Kale grimaced. *Another snake? Or the end of the one threatening my dragons?*

The viper's heavy head advanced, and the distant portion moved with the same speed.

One snake.

"Toopka, stay here," she ordered and ran down the remaining steps. She tossed the globe from her right hand to her left and pulled her sword from its hiding place beneath her robe. Nothing appeared to be in her hand, but Kale felt the leather-bound hilt secure in her grip. The old sword had been given to her by her mother, and Kale knew how to use the invisible blade with deadly precision.

"Don't let him get away," she called as she increased her speed through the narrow corridor.

The wizard robe dissolved as she rushed to join her guard. Her long dress of azure and plum reformed itself into leggings and a tunic. The color drained away and returned as a pink that would rival a stunning sunset. When she reached the cold, dark room, she cast her globe into the air. Floating in the middle of the room, it tripled in size and gave off a brighter light.

The dragons circled above the snake, spitting their caustic saliva with great accuracy. Kale's skin crawled at the sight of the coiling reptile. More and more of the serpentine body emerged from the shadowy protection of the stacked kegs. Obviously, the snake did not fear these intruders.

Even covered with splotches of brightly colored spit, the creature looked like the loathsome killer it was. Kale's two missing dragons could have been dinner for the serpent. She searched the room with the talent Wulder had bestowed upon her and concluded the little ones still lived.

The reptile hissed at her, raised its massive head, and swayed in a threatening posture. The creature slithered toward her, propelled by the elongated body still on the floor. Just out of reach of Kale's sword, the beast stopped, pulled its head back for the strike, and let out a slow, menacing hiss. The snake lunged, and Kale swung her invisible weapon. The severed head sailed across the room and slammed against the stone wall.

Kale eyed the writhing body for a moment. "You won't be eating any more small animals." She turned her attention to the missing dragons and pointed her sword hand at a barrel at the top of one stack. "There. Gally and Mince are in that keg."

Several dragons landed on the wooden staves, and a brown dragon examined the cask to determine how best to open it. Toopka ran into the room and over to the barrel. "I'll help."

Kale tilted her head. "There is also a nest of snake eggs." She consulted the dragon most likely to know facts about anvilhead vipers. Crain landed on her shoulder and poured out all he knew in a combination of chittering and thoughts.

The odd reptiles preferred eating young farm animals, grain, and feed. They did nothing to combat the population of rats, insects, and vermin. No farmer allowed the snakes on his property if he could help it. "Find the nest," Kale ordered. "Destroy them all."

The watch of dragons took flight again, zooming into lightrock-illuminated passages leading off from this central room. Kale waited until a small group raised an alarm. Four minor dragons had found the nest.

She plunged down a dim passage, sending a plume of light ahead and calling for the dispersed dragons to join her. Eleven came from the other corridors, and nine flew in a V formation in front of her. Gally and Mince landed on her shoulders.

"You're all right. I'm so glad."

They scooted next to her neck, shivering. From their minds she deciphered the details of their ordeal. A game of hide-and-seek had led them into the depths of the castle. When the snake surprised them, they'd flown under the off-center lid of the barrel. As Mince dove into the narrow opening, he knocked the top just enough for it to rattle down into place. This successfully kept the serpent out, but also trapped them within.

Kale offered sympathy, and they cuddled against her, rubbing their heads on her chin as she whisked through the underground tunnel in pursuit of the other dragons.

Numerous rooms jutted off the main hallway, each stacked with boxes, crates, barrels, and huge burlap bags. Kale had no idea this vast amount of storage lay beneath the castle. Taylaminkadot, their efficient housekeeper and wife to Librettowit, probably had a tally sheet listing each item. Kale and the dragons passed rooms that contained fewer and fewer supplies until the stores dwindled to nothing.

How long does this hallway continue on? She slowed to creep along and tiptoed over the stone floor, noticing the rougher texture under her feet. Approaching a corner, she detected the four minor dragons destroying the snake's nest in the next room. Her escort of flying dragons veered off into the room, and she followed. The small dragons swooped over the nest, grabbed an egg, then flew to the beamed roof of the storage room. They hurled the eggs to the floor, and most broke open on contact. Some had more rubbery shells, a sign that they would soon hatch. The minor dragons attacked these eggs with tooth and claw. Once each shell gave way, the content was pulled out and examined. No hatchling snake survived.

The smell alone halted Kale in her tracks and sent her back a pace. She screwed up her face, but no amount of pinching her nose muscles cut off the odor of raw eggs and the bodies of unborn snakes. She produced a square of moonbeam material from her pocket and covered the lower half of her face. The properties of the handkerchief filtered the unpleasant aroma.

Her gaze fell on the scene of annihilation. Usually, Kale found infant animals to be endearing, attractive in a gangly way. But the small snake bodies looked more like huge blackened worms than babies.

Toopka raced up behind her and came to a skidding stop when she reached the doorway. "Ew!" She buried her face in the hem of Kale's tunic, then peeked out with her nose still covered.

The minor dragons continued to destroy the huge nest. Kale estimated over a hundred snake eggs must have been deposited in the old shallow basket. The woven edges sagged where the weight of the female snake had broken the reeds. Kale shuddered at the thought of all those snakes hatching and occupying the lowest level of the castle, her home. The urge to be above ground, in the light, and with her loved ones compelled her out of the room.

Good work, she commended the dragons as she backed into the passage. *Artross, be sure that no egg is left unshattered.*

She received his assurance, thanked him, then turned about and ran. She must find Bardon.

"Wait for me!" Toopka called. Her tiny, booted feet pounded the stone floor in a frantic effort to catch up.

2

A Friendly Visit

"I think it's worth a short side trip, Greer." Bardon sat between the cobalt wings of his dragon, looking past the purple neck stretched before him. "It will only take a few minutes."

He scanned the countryside, looking for the village the kimens told him sprang up almost overnight, populated by strangers. "No, Greer. Kale doesn't know about the surprise, so she won't be agitated that we're late. Mikkai, quit fuming."

Mikkai sat on Bardon's shoulder, his small claws sunk into the material of the knight's jacket. His chirring reflected his indignation. The blue and green minor dragon's talent was geography. He'd stored in his mind each and every map he'd ever seen. Kale had inherited Wizard Fenworth's extensive library, and there the young dragon had soaked up a large amount of information. Bardon had encouraged Mikkai to travel with Regidor, who was in the habit of perusing cartographers' shops. According to Mikkai's memory, no village existed in this stretch of the Fairren Forest.

Greer relayed the information to Bardon that he had spotted a man-made clearing in the distance. The little dragon pitched a fit.

"Enough," said Bardon. "Instead of going off like a fizzle-pop, think how greatly appreciated it will be when you make note of the village and have it recorded. This is an opportunity, Mikkai, not an insult to your pride."

The little beast settled down, but his coloring darkened, as it did when he deliberately controlled his emotions. Bardon thanked Wulder that at least his little friend was trying to be calm.

Greer landed at the outer rim of the clearing. The houses sat closely in rows, so Bardon and Mikkai entered the village alone, leaving the large riding dragon behind. No children ran in the paths between the pale green buildings. Each structure looked much like the next, with doors centered in one wall, two windows on either side, then two windows on each of the three other walls. A carved stone provided a step into the house. In each flat doorway, an etching of a large bird was embedded in the slab of cold, gray granite.

"There are a few signs of life here," Bardon observed. "A bucket of clear water by one door, a broom leaning against the side of a house, an odor of porridge, and spotless curtains fluttering in an open window."

Mikkai chittered.

"Exactly," responded Bardon. "Not a person in sight."

They came to the center of the village and found the people they looked for. Bardon glanced around the semicircle of citizens waiting patiently and in silence. Their eyes focused on the front of a round building. The white stone structure had horizontal slits like vents near the roof and one doorway covered by a dark green curtain.

In the gathering, oddly dressed mariones and o'rants stood without touching. At least six inches separated them from one another. The gaps were too uniform to be a coincidence.

Men and women wore loose trousers that hung to their ankles. Sandals covered the soles of their feet but left the tops exposed under thin straps. A straight piece of cloth with a hole in the center draped over their shoulders and hung to their knees. Underneath, all wore a tight-fitting, long-sleeved shirt. These garments were in a variety of colors, but each person wore a single color and stood with those who wore the same shade.

Bardon kept to the rear of the small crowd, waiting and observing. *No young children. No babies. Where are they? Why are these people divided into their color groups? And how is the division made? It doesn't seem to be by age or race.*

A hand opened the curtain from inside, and five people, dressed in the same fashion as the other villagers but in a light purple, stepped out. Two mariones and three o'rants lined up in front of the villagers. Those who had been waiting outside stood taller.

Bardon didn't like the anticipation that rolled through the crowd. *Unnatural. Are they actually holding their breath?*

From the platform raised six inches off the ground, one of the o'rants in purple stepped out from the others. He scanned the crowd, then raised a hand. "I cannot speak. There is a stranger among us."

The whoosh of expelled air confirmed Bardon's belief that the villagers had been holding their breath. Their heads twisted as they searched for the intruder.

Bardon braced himself. What would their reaction be to his interrupting their meeting? But once the people located him, they merely turned their eyes to the ground and shuffled away, dispersing quickly into the village. He recognized a few unguarded reactions. Some gave Mikkai a speculative glance before lowering their gaze. Some frowned before covering their displeasure with a neutral expression. No one spoke.

The five came directly to him. They did not shuffle nor watch the ground.

"Greetings," said the one in the lead. He sounded friendly and undisturbed by the presence of a stranger.

"Hello," Bardon answered.

"I am Echo Marson. These are my brothers, Echo Hames, Echo Trox, Echo Feallat, and Echo Lowatter."

Bardon nodded but did not extend his hand. "You don't look much like brothers."

"Oh, not literally of course, but in our allegiance to Wulder and commitment to one another. In our society we have only brothers and sisters."

"I am Sir Bardon. I am magistrate over this district. If I can help you in any way…"

The men chortled among themselves, but the sound did not ease Bardon's apprehension. His shoulders tensed, warrior alertness rising. He scanned the area, taking note of who stood where and the options open to him if a fight broke out. Not a comforting sign that most of the men of the village had returned and stood idly just outside of the circle. He wouldn't let his guard down any time soon.

"No need to trouble yourself," said Echo Marson. He put a gentle hand on Bardon's shoulder and turned him toward one of the paths through the village. "Let me show you around."

Bardon missed the signal that dismissed the male villagers who lingered nearby, but they dispersed as quietly as they had assembled. Echo Marson dropped his hand from Bardon's shoulder and walked beside him. The four other echoes followed silently.

"We are a new order that has come out of Paladin's decree that the people of Amara be re-educated in the ways of Wulder. You realize that he sent teachers out from his palace and from The Hall to go from town to town and speak of Wulder's Tomes. Thousands of new copies of the Tomes have been published and distributed. Our village is made up of those who desire to be closer to Wulder. We seek to listen more carefully than most of those who are educated by Wulder to lead."

"Paladin knows of your dedication?" Bardon tried to keep the skepticism from his voice.

"Paladin initiated our group."

"I hadn't heard of it. Do you have a name?"

"Only the Followers. We don't wish to be glorified ourselves, but to point out that the way to happiness is to follow."

"I sit on Paladin's council and—"

"Prudently, it has been decided that this movement be separate from the ordinary governing forces of Amara."

"Are you not accountable to Paladin?"

"Of course, of course. And Wulder is our supreme judge, director, and guide."

Echo Marson's tone was meant to be placating, but Bardon found his hackles rising even as the man offered assurances. "Why is it I know nothing of the Followers?"

"Do not be chagrined. Only those most apt to succeed are given more knowledge."

Bardon bristled, meaning to interrupt. Surely this pompous leader didn't think Bardon felt offended by being overlooked by their group? But Echo Marson continued, exposing another odd idea.

"It would be unkind," he said, "to frustrate those who would never achieve the higher calling. So, we move slowly. We give our message, we watch the reactions of those who listen, and we approach the most likely candidates."

Bardon hesitated. His instinct was to take a stand, literally stop and challenge this absurd design. Wulder certainly never handed over the right to decide who should be His followers to a handful of representatives of the high races. And Wulder never refused anyone the chance to learn more about Him. Leetu Bends's friend Latho proved that concept. The bisonbeck tradesman had chosen to follow Wulder. But Echo Marson kept walking, and Bardon kept his peace. Gathering information was more important than entering a debate with this o'rant.

"Notice the clean lines of our architecture. This reflects the clean, direct purpose of our village. We seek to know Him better and serve."

"What is the name of your village?"

"Paladise. But each village is also named this."

"There are more than one?"

"Certainly. The movement will grow. It is Wulder's will. After rescuing us from the clutches of true evil, and annihilating the source of wickedness, He has commanded a new beginning."

Mikkai blurted a short sequence of angry chitters. Bardon mentally forbade him to continue. *Hush! I want to know more about these people. Where did they come from? Why does everyone shuffle except these five who are escorting us to the edge of the village? And since they are showing us the door, we don't have much time to learn more.*

"Do you teach that Wulder has extinguished evil?" asked Bardon.

"Yes."

"According to the Tomes, Wulder will not do that until some time in the future. Burner Stox and Crim Cropper have died—"

Echo Marson interrupted. "And Risto, don't forget Risto."

"Yes, but Pretender is still able to make trouble."

"Really? Has anyone seen him? Has he provoked a new war? Unleashed more mutant beings that are capable only of destruction?"

Before Bardon could answer, the man went on. "No, no, no. Wulder has thrown Pretender in the dark place and destroyed him. Of course, no one from the high races could have achieved this end, but

Wulder has protected us through His own power. And that is right and as it should be."

They approached the last houses at the edge of the village. Greer snuffled a greeting. He stomped a front leg and shook his head. Rarely did anything ruffle the riding dragon, but Bardon felt Greer's agitation and his desire to be away from the obscure village. The stream of thoughts coming from his dragon made it almost impossible to listen to the leader of the group.

"Thank you for dropping by." Echo Marson's head bobbed, and he smiled. "We will be sure to call on you if we need anything. But we are a self-contained group, and I really don't foresee an occasion arising—" He broke off and cleared his throat. "You are welcome at any time, and if you wish to learn more about what Wulder is revealing to our people, please ask. We are more than willing to carry out Paladin's decree to educate the populace."

At the condescending tone, shivers traipsed down Bardon's spine.

He faced the five echoes, bowed in farewell. "I look forward to that, Echo Marson. Good day."

He didn't tell them he would be out of the region for some time. He didn't tell them he suspected they had gone outside the bounds of Paladin's intention. And he didn't tell them he planned to send someone to infiltrate their little group to learn more about their ways.

3

A Vacation?

With Toopka on her heels, Kale rushed through the lower rooms of the castle, following the irregular path created by her parents. Up three stairs, forward a half-dozen steps, turn right, dash across a storage room, through a door, turn left, up one step, enter the creamery, weave through the vats, duck to exit through a short door, cross the platform, up six steps, turn right into the herb cellar, and out the door on the opposite wall. After two more twists in the long corridor, Kale and Toopka finally emerged in the kitchen.

A tumanhofer child squealed, lifted her arms, and wobbled on chubby legs toward Kale. She scooped the toddler into her arms and nuzzled the baby's neck. "Taracinabloo, you're a precious gal."

The child's mother looked up from stirring a pot on the stove. "Don't let her pester you, Lady Kale. She's bored and wanting someone to play with her."

"Don't worry, Taylaminkadot." She kissed the little girl on each cheek and then deposited her on the floor. "I'm on my way through to find Bardon. I'll leave Toopka here to tell you what we found in the cellars and to keep Taracinabloo out of your hair."

Toopka stuck out her lower lip and aimed a frown at her guardian. Kale strode to the door, ignoring the doneel's pout and the toddler's whine.

"Lunch smells delicious," she called to Taylaminkadot and passed through the doorway before Taracinabloo's protest could escalate to a full wail. Kale glanced back to see a smiling Toopka pull the small girl toward a pile of toys.

"Sing with me," Toopka said. "I'll be the farmer, and you be the animals." She picked up a wooden cow and placed it in Taracinabloo's hands.

Kale grinned and scurried down the hall. Her stomach had roiled at the smell of evil in her cellars, but fresh air and the scent of vegetable soup had blocked the nausea. *I wasn't cut out to be a warrior. Dragon Keeper is good enough for me.*

Her special bond with Bardon told her exactly when her husband approached, returning from a morning visit. She headed to one of the doors at the back of the castle. As she hurried through the maze of halls, she transformed her clothing into something more feminine than her fighting garb. Her sword bumped against her thigh. Without slowing her pace, she shortened it and its sheath to the length of a short dagger.

The large wooden door silently swung back as she pushed it open to reveal the equestrian stables. Bright sunshine flooded the cool, dark passageway around her. She stepped out and breathed in the aroma of the flowered meadow, sun-warmed stacks of hay, and fastidiously groomed horses. Kale paused, closed her eyes, turned her face upward, and soaked in the beauty of her surroundings.

"I love this life," she whispered. "Thank you, Wulder." Her eyes popped open. She blinked, rubbed her nose against a tickle, then briskly sprinted past the stable yard, the barns, and training ring to the sloping grassland beyond. Flowers dotted the hill, and bushes resplendent with colorful blooms marched up the knoll in uneven patches. She slowed her pace, a little winded but still anxious to get to the dragon landing. Above her, minor dragons swarmed in the air, circling their Dragon Keeper's head in a noisy greeting.

Kale returned their welcome with a laugh and a few friendly words, then told them to go about their business, which at this moment was to enjoy themselves.

A riding dragon approached, sailing through scattered, puffy clouds. Her contented smile stretched into a broad grin. Greer's wings flashed blue, and his purple scales glinted as he banked for landing. Bardon waved from the saddle as Kale lifted her skirts and ran to greet him.

As soon as the majestic beast folded his cobalt wings against his amethystine sides, Bardon swung his leg over the horn of the saddle and slid to the ground, grace and ease in his movements.

Thanks to Wulder, the treatment he'd received that morning had been successful. Kale carefully guarded her thoughts and feelings in order to not distress him. He'd groaned with pain most of the night. The herbal potion she had given him when they retired kept him asleep, but she knew the extent of his suffering.

For a moment, Kale took up again with Wulder the subject of Bardon's health. *Why stakes, my Creator? Why a childhood disease that could cripple him? He has seasons of health and then weeks of increasing pain. Why not increase the seasons of health and completely eradicate the stiffness and pain?*

Kale remembered the many times she and Gymn had eased Bardon's discomfort but never succeeded in pushing it completely out of his system. *We've failed, Wulder. Even when we feel closest to You, we have failed. This morning the suffering sent him to the kimens. And he looks better. But why not just cure him, Wulder? Is there anything I can do to bring this blessing to my husband?*

Kale forced a smile to her lips as Bardon strode forward. Mikkai rode on his shoulder but flew into the air as she approached. She ran into her husband's arms, and he swung her off her feet, spinning while she laughed with relief. His strength had been renewed.

He plopped her down and gazed into her eyes. "Guess who I saw at Minasterloan's castle."

Reading his mind, Kale shrieked, "Regidor and Gilda!"

He tilted back his head and laughed, then pulled her to his chest, rubbing his chin through her hair. He hadn't shaved before his brief journey, and the bristles tugged in a soothing way. Silver hairs streaked the black hair above his slightly pointed ears. Laugh lines spread out from his blue eyes, but deep creases accented his mouth where pain was often registered by his clenched teeth. Kale closed her eyes against the evidence of his struggle. She nestled her ear to his heart while she absorbed the details of his journey to their closest neighbor.

As he remembered, Kale joined his train of thought. She could see

Gilda's gown and cape, and Kale marveled at how elegant the meech dragon looked. Gilda belonged in the grandeur of a castle. Not in the rooms where work oiled the smooth functioning of the household. But in the formal rooms where discussions covered art, travel, spiritual enlightenment, expanding knowledge, politics, and fashion.

Through Bardon's memories, Kale heard Regidor's throaty laugh and watched as the meech husband and wife exchanged a look of understanding. In a rush of information, she learned the two dragons had determined to search for the hidden meech colony. She heard Bardon's voice enter the conversation. *"Kale and I will join you on your quest."*

She squealed, jumped out of his embrace to dance a jig, and then lunged forward to hug him again.

"Whoa!" he objected. "You're going to squeeze me in half."

She released him, all the excitement draining out of her.

Bardon placed his hands on her shoulders. "What's the matter?"

"I can't go. I'm busy all day long, and no one else can do some of the things I take care of."

Bardon chuckled. "The indispensable Dragon Keeper."

Kale pulled away, crossed her arms over her chest, and grimaced at him. "Don't you laugh at me."

"I'm not mocking, and you need a respite from your responsibilities." He held up a hand as she sputtered a "but." "I know you enjoy your work, but enough is enough. It's time for some fun, some adventure. It's springtime, and Amara is bursting with new life. Flowers abound. Little lambs are kicking up their heels in the fields." He waved his hand at a nearby trang-a-nog tree. "Birds are hatching and all that."

She giggled. "Yes, but we will have to enjoy all that in our own backyard. I have dozens of eggs ready to quicken."

"And that's why I sent for your father and mother."

Before she could ask how he had done that, he continued. "Actually, Regidor did the communicating." He grabbed her arm, pulled it through his, and started toward their home. "We'll just tell Librettowit and Taylaminkadot that we're on our way, and be off."

"Just like that?"

"Your parents will be here within the hour." He sidestepped to avoid a flock of heatherhens chasing an unlucky drummerbug.

"Doesn't my father have his own Dragon Keeper's castle to maintain?"

"He says his organization marches with such precision that he need only check in once in a while to deal with an odd problem or two."

"Oh, he does?" Kale bit the side of her cheek as she mulled over this bit of information.

Bardon squeezed her shoulders. "Which dragons will you bring with you?"

She answered promptly. "Gymn and Metta."

"Of course."

"Pat and Filia, Crispin and Tieto, Dibl and Artross."

"Artross may not like being taken from leader of his watch and put under Gymn's authority."

"I'll ask him, of course. He doesn't have to come if he doesn't care to." *And there's a big hint in there, dear husband, if you would only catch it. I don't mind going, but I don't like being rushed. It's not like you to sweep me into a plan without considering my situation.* She opened her mouth to speak, but Bardon spoke first.

"Artross will come. There isn't a dragon here who wouldn't jump at the chance to travel with you." Mikkai swooped over their heads and flew off again to mingle with his kind. "Of course, Mikkai will come. He'll be a great help." He winked at Kale. "Summon your choices now. It won't take but a minute to inform Librettowit and Taylaminkadot of our quest."

"Taylaminkadot has lunch ready by now."

"Umm..." Bardon rubbed his stomach, another sign that he felt better if his appetite had returned.

Kale breathed a sigh. Even when he exasperated her, she loved her husband and wanted health for him.

"We'll eat and then depart," declared Bardon.

Kale exhaled her frustration in a huff of forced air. What had gotten into Bardon? He usually deliberated and gave her plenty of time to adjust to any plans he made. Her shoulder and neck muscles tensed in rebellion. "I need to pack."

Bardon stopped and stepped away from her.

She frowned and felt the reaction within her husband. He wasn't chastised by her expression of disapproval. He thought she was cute. *Cute!*

He placed his hands on his hips and looked her over from head to toe. She squirmed under his gaze. She knew that expression. He was thinking of her attributes, not her attire.

He grinned. "You look ready to me. You just need to pick up your moonbeam cape."

"Bardon—"

"What? You change that outfit into anything you want to wear. You do the same for my clothes. The hollows of your cape hold everything from a toothbrush to ten gallons of parnot juice. You have books, herbs, jewelry, hats, food—"

Kale snapped her fingers. "Herbs and food! I should check to see if I have enough, and fresh food would be welcome. I haven't restocked those hollows in…"

Bardon cocked an eyebrow. "In?"

Kale shrugged. "Well, it was the end of last week, but I should check to see if I missed anything, and I need to tell Father some of the things he should know about—"

Bardon took her arm and started toward the castle once more. "Your father is a Dragon Keeper. He knows what to do."

"Yes, but he doesn't always use the same methods I do."

"And what would happen, lady of mine, if you waited to tell him the way you want him to do things?"

"He'd listen, agree to everything, and then do it his way as soon as I'm out of sight."

"Precisely. And will his way harm your dragons?"

"Not exactly."

"Not at all."

Kale sighed. "Right, not at all." She gripped his arm more tightly and gave it a shake. "But, Bardon, it isn't my way."

He didn't respond.

Why are you being so bossy?

"Why are you dragging your heels? Don't you want to see Regidor and Gilda?"

Of course I do.

He patted her hand clenched to his arm. "Everything will be just fine."

Kale tried to dampen her annoyance, but she only thought of more arguments.

"Who's going to do your duties? The school for the boys won't run itself. They need your training."

"Sir Grant has volunteered to come over."

The minor dragons came to greet him.

"Hello, Pinto. Hello, Fernan. You rascal, Jodi, have you been harassing these boys again?"

With Kale right beside him, he could mindspeak with any of the little dragons. Mikkai, who had bonded with him at birth, was the only one he could communicate with freely. These would pester him like a horde of children surrounding their favorite uncle.

"Shoo," said Kale. "Bardon and I are having a serious discussion." She almost blurted out her annoyance with her husband, but she knew the reaction she would get. She was the Dragon Keeper, but he was the head of the house. The leader's leader. They'd want to know details and then side with him. "Go on, go back to your games and snacks."

They flew off good-naturedly, not concerned with Kale's impatience.

"Where were we?" asked Kale. "Your crops. Who's going to take care of them? And your overseeing of the villages? And your role as magistrate? Someone has to be here to maintain the system you worked so hard to establish. And your council duties for Paladin? You can't walk off and leave that duty."

"Mort, Crownden, and Rasmiller."

"They're all coming to the castle?" She followed him through a back door, into a cool, dim corridor.

"Yes."

"It's a houseparty! I can't leave my mother to deal with all that. And Taylaminkadot is with child again. She doesn't need to be catering to guests."

"Both your mother and your housekeeper will be thrilled with the opportunity to show off their flair for hospitality."

You're suspiciously determined, Sir Bardon.

"I'm determined that my wife have some excitement instead of day-to-day drudgery for a while."

I'm not all that fond of excitement, especially when it involves armies of wicked bisonbecks.

"There hasn't been an army of wicked bisonbecks in Amara since you and your father took care of Crim Cropper and Burner Stox."

Whenever I've ventured from home, all sorts of evil pops up out of the ground, swoops out of the sky, and tramples down the grassy plains to get to me.

Once more Bardon gathered her into his arms and spoke as his lips touched the top of her head. "It won't be like that this time. Amara is at peace."

Kale leaned into Bardon, wanting to generate the same enthusiasm pulsating through him.

She lifted her head. "Toopka!"

"What about Toopka?"

She started off again as if she could outrun the disagreement. "I'm her guardian. I can't just abandon her. What kind of guardian goes off and leaves for who knows how long?"

"Sir Dar."

"Sir Dar?"

"Sir Dar. He's the kind of guardian who goes off and leaves for who knows how long!"

Ah! He's going to make this point, too, unless I come up with something. "Well, it's true that we have joint guardianship, but—"

"But, nothing. We'll take Toopka with us and drop her off with Sir Dar."

Kale stopped in the middle of the large entryway that faced the wrong side of the castle, having been built with much enthusiasm by a water wizard. She shouted to be heard over the many rivulets cascading from the walls. "Why are you in such a hurry?"

"Because," hollered Bardon, "Regidor is not going to wait for us. He's already gone, and we have to catch up."

"Why wouldn't he wait?"

"Because Gilda wants her egg to be presented at the meech colony and nowhere else."

⟻ 4 ⟼

Librettowit, the Librarian

Bardon left Kale to rush about doing the things she thought extremely important and sought out the company of Librettowit. Kale had transported her mentor's castle to this location, and her parents had joined it to the main building. Fenworth's home still resembled a massive group of cygnot trees. Most people got lost walking through the round corridors within tree limbs. Major parts of the rooms were dedicated to books. In a back room of this library built in a tree, the tumanhofer Librettowit sought sanctuary.

The creak of the door broke the silence as Bardon entered. The librarian raised his head from the book he was reading and gazed over his wire-framed glasses at the intruder.

"Hello, Master Librettowit." Bardon bounded into the room and pulled out a chair at the table piled with books. With a happy chirrup, Mikkai flew to an open book containing maps. Bardon moved two at the top of the pile in front of him so he could see the librarian. "We've new neighbors in Fairren Forest. A whole village of new neighbors."

Librettowit sighed, put a bookmark in his place, closed the book, and gave Bardon his attention.

Bardon leaned on a pile of books. "I'd like you to investigate." The books began to slide. He caught two and shoved them upright, then scrambled to keep them from falling the other direction. "But I fear you couldn't get in. There!" He settled the mixture of open and closed books in their precarious tower and met the tumanhofer's sharp gaze. "The citizens are made up entirely of mariones and o'rants."

"Harrumph! Totally against Wulder's principles."

"Oh, there's more. A suspicious lack of children under ten. Odd, regimented clothing. Leaders who dominate instead of lead. Doctrine that's been dunked in a fish barrel."

Librettowit took off his glasses and wiped them with a clean cloth from his pocket. "A faction?"

"I think so."

"Indeed, something must be done." He replaced his spectacles and shoved them up with one finger so that the bridge sat high on his nose. "How many are caught in the lie?"

"In that village, I would say under a hundred. Maybe sixty to seventy. But the leader, Echo Marson, said it was only one village, implying there were many more, and he said the movement is growing."

Librettowit pried himself out of the cushy reading chair and paced the room. "Who can we send?"

"I thought of Holt."

He stopped and frowned at Bardon over the glasses that had again slipped down on his nose. "Holt? That young man who hung around N'Rae years ago?"

"Yes."

"Why this ne'er-do-well Holt?"

"Because he hasn't been associated with us in eight years, and he is a ne'er-do-well as you say. Who would suspect that we would send him to uncover the truth?"

"Why should we trust him?" countered Librettowit.

"I think we can. He is more lazy than evil, and he is inclined to do heroic deeds if they are not too troublesome."

Librettowit went to his bookshelves and appeared to study the titles. Finally he returned his attention to Bardon.

"Do you even know where he is?"

"No, but I count on you to find him and give him the assignment, if his present circumstances indicate he will do well. In other words, if he isn't in the middle of chicanery of some sort."

"Me? I'm a librarian, not a director of espionage. Why don't you do it?"

"Kale and I are going on a quest."

Mikkai sat on a book in the shelves and demanded through a series of chirps to be listened to. Bardon got up, pulled the book from its place, and laid it open on the table at the top of one of the piles that seemed to be less wobbly.

Librettowit paced with his hands behind his back as Bardon returned to his seat and told him of his visit to Paladise.

"Paladise?" Librettowit harrumphed with even more vigor. "What kind of mockery is that of our Paladin and his role in preserving the Tomes, educating the people, exhorting and disciplining the followers of Wulder?"

"They present their society as more dedicated to Wulder than the average person."

"Better than the rest of us, huh? A sure sign of hypocrisy."

Bardon got up again to retrieve another book for Mikkai. "Another point of interest is the symbol they have on their doorsteps, a big bird with wings outstretched. I can't say it is a bird I recognized."

Librettowit stared at him as he pinched his bottom lip between thumb and forefinger. A light sprang to his eyes. He held up one finger and headed for the door. "I'll be right back."

Bardon sat down in one of the overstuffed chairs, put his feet on an ottoman, and leaned back. So far the day had been eventful in good and bad ways. The visit at Minasterloan's castle had relieved the constant pain of stakes, and he had learned from the kimens that this new commune had sprung up right under his nose. The opportunity to investigate and set wheels in motion before he left the region eased his conscience.

He didn't want to miss this important quest, and he wanted Kale to have some time to enjoy life. She worked so hard, and the fun-loving lady he married was often too tired at night to read or chat. When he played his flute for her, she went right to sleep. They'd turned into a very old couple when they should still be having a grand time. The stakes slowed him down, but he would make a concerted effort to allow his wife some lighthearted enjoyment. He'd been conspiring with Regidor to make it happen.

Librettowit returned with a scroll, which he put on the table and spread out over the peaks of book stacks.

"Look at this symbol and see if it resembles this bird you saw."

Bardon rose from the chair and came to examine the old parchment. "That's it. What does it signify?"

"That is a Sellaran, the bird Pretender rode when he first fled from Wulder's presence."

"I've never seen one like it."

"They are extinct. The eggs they laid rotted in the nests until they laid no more."

"And this *new* society uses this symbol to signify their allegiance to Wulder?"

Librettowit pursed his lips and furrowed his brow. "It is possible that they came across an etching of a Sellaran and did not know its significance. But somehow, I doubt it."

He rolled up the scroll. "I'll find Holt and put him on their trail. If I find him unsuitable, is there another we can send?"

"I'll ask Sir Dar when I see him tonight." Bardon placed a hand on Librettowit's broad shoulder and grinned. "Thank you, my friend. When I first located this hidden village, I thought my plans to take Kale away for a while would come to naught. But Wulder reminded me, 'A leader leads by entrusting those under him.' I am pleased to be able to entrust this problem to you."

"Ha!" said the librarian, blustering but with a smile on his lips. "I'd be pleased to get out of this if I could, but I see you are going to pull principles on me if I try. Where are you taking your wife?"

"To the northern reaches in search of the meech."

For a moment the old man's eyes lit with the yearning for adventure. Then he shook his head. "I'm a librarian, not meant for questing. Questing is a miserable business. I'll stay at home, thank you very much, in my cozy dens, with my lovely wife close at hand, and little Taracinabloo to make me feel young again."

"Sounds like a good plan." Bardon extended his hand, and the two men clasped forearms and shook. He started for the door and signaled

Mikkai to join him. The little dragon reluctantly left his books and flew to perch on top of the knight's head. Bardon called over his shoulder as he went through the door. "When Kale's father arrives, he shall have a new contraption to show you. I'll be in touch sooner than you would think."

5

SURPRISES

The chill air in a misty cloud tingled Kale's skin. She reached behind her neck and pulled the hood up to cover her head and the veil down to protect her face. Celisse soared through another shred of vapor, following Bardon on Greer. Toopka rode in a soft basket woven from strips of cloth. The contraption hung from Bardon's back as if it were a knapsack. And, indeed, the little girl inside already napped. While awake, Toopka chattered constantly, so Kale was glad for her husband's sake that the doneel snoozed as soon as the dragon reached a higher altitude.

Bardon's minor dragon curled up on top of the knapsack. But Mikkai wasn't sleeping. Kale suspected the dragon served as an alarm should the little doneel awaken.

Kale connected with Bardon's mind, hoping to ask a few more questions, but found rider and dragon deep in conversation. They discussed trade winds. *Trade winds! How boring.*

Kale let go of their thoughts and returned to her own musing. She muttered to herself, "How is Father going to handle both his castle in the Northern Reach and all the business of ours?" A breeze tugged at the hood. She held it in place with one hand.

She smiled at the thought of Regidor's wide grin. "I really want to see Regidor. Perhaps after we have a short visit, Bardon will be content to return home." She scowled. "Somehow, I don't think that's going to happen. Men like to go questing. It's in their nature. But I wanted to stay at home. I wonder if Gilda feels the same way."

Celisse lifted her neck, covered with ebony scales, and tilted her silvery-white head.

"You're listening to me puzzle this over, huh? Well, I don't mind. You won't tell anyone what a wishy-washy wimp I am. Really, I do well on my own ground, but I've never been all that great at questing. And I'm perturbed. Most of it is because of Bardon rushing me out of our home and not letting me be any part of his plans."

They banked, and Bardon pointed to a herd of chigot deer below. *"See the newborns. There must be a dozen of them. Amara is recovering very well from the years of war."*

Yes, I see them. They're cute. Too bad they grow up to smell like heaps of rotted cabbage.

She heard Bardon's answering chortle and turned her attention back to her conversation with Celisse. "Bardon's very excited about this journey. And if it will keep his mind off the possible deterioration of his health with the stakes, well…"

The minor dragons wiggled out of their pocket-dens in the moonbeam cape. They crawled to the opening, sniffed the air, decided it wasn't too cold, and scampered out to run over Kale's body. She recognized their mood. It would seem they rejoiced with Bardon at the chance to go adventuring.

Dibl jumped to Celisse's back behind the saddle. He tucked his wings close to his body to keep from being caught and tossed into the air by a draft of wind. He scurried up and down the prominent scales to perch near Celisse's tail.

Metta sat on one of the riding dragon's broad shoulders, and Filia on the other. They rocked to and fro in response to the powerful wing muscles moving beneath their feet.

Pat crawled forward to roost between the big dragon's ears. He held on to the ridge that formed a shield protecting his stout, round body from the wind. Gymn climbed to wrap around Kale's neck, under the moonbeam cape with only his head sticking out. Artross sat on one of her legs, and Tieto fastened his claws into the back of Kale's glove, where she rested her hand on the saddle horn.

Crispin emerged last from the protection of the moonbeam cape. His red skin glistened as patches of sunlight reflected off his scales. Young and inexperienced, he trotted forward, passing the horn and Tieto. With a jump, he landed on Celisse's black neck. He lost his footing and spread his wings to help regain his balance. The wind caught his kitelike frame and flipped him head over heels. He hit with a thud against Kale's chest.

The Dragon Keeper laughed and picked him up, being careful not to squeeze his leathery wings. She felt a twitch in his abdomen and turned him sideways just in time. The little dragon hiccuped, and a small flame shot from his mouth. He blinked in surprise, hiccuped again, and the fire spewed out once more.

"Oh, dear." Kale sighed. "I know you can't help it, Crispin. Don't fret."

The small red dragon kept up the fiery blasts with each rhythmic snag in his breathing.

"Try to breathe slowly," Kale suggested. "Try to breathe deeply."

The next explosion from his mouth outdid all those before it.

"Oh dear."

Her husband's voice came into her mind. *"Greer says not to start saying, 'Tut-tut.'"*

What?

"'Tut-tut' like Fenworth, your predecessor."

Bardon, this is serious.

She heard both her husband and his two dragons laugh.

Well, perhaps not life-and-death serious, but Crispin is most uncomfortable, and if he doesn't learn to control this…this side effect of—

"—hiccuping, sneezing, coughing, and even big sighs, he'll someday burn us out of house and home."

He has *learned not to sigh in full force.*

Kale caught the sense of where her other minor dragons were and quickly shielded her thoughts from the fire dragon in her hand. She felt Dibl inching up her back, using the moonbeam cape as if it were a vine to climb up the side of a building. She could see Pat approaching along Celisse's neck. She had no need to wonder who had initiated this attack on Crispin to surprise the hiccups out of him. Dibl would choose this way to do a good deed.

She tried to act just as nonchalant as the rest of the minor dragons who feigned ignorance of the plan. Tieto, Gymn, Filia, and Metta all ignored the progress of the two mischief-makers. Artross grunted occasionally, as if he could just barely keep either from laughing or giving out unwelcome advice.

Crispin inquired politely if Artross also suffered from the hiccups. As the white dragon struggled to answer, Dibl jumped over Kale's shoulder and slid down her arm. Pat synchronized his pounce beautifully, and the red dragon screeched out his shock at being attacked. A huge shot of flame accompanied his shriek but fizzled quickly.

Kale and her friends waited, hoping for the best and counting. When they reached twenty without another eruption from Crispin, they all cheered.

"What in all of Amara is going on back there?" asked Bardon.

A cure for the hiccups. I believe Crispin is all better now.

"Good."

Greer turned westward, and Celisse followed.

Bardon, where are we going? I thought Regidor and Gilda headed north.

"To visit Wizard Namee." He hesitated, waiting for her response.

Kale purposefully did not respond. She projected profound silence to her husband, knowing that would exhaust his patience.

Sure enough, he couldn't stand the wait and prompted for a reaction. *"You aren't going to ask why?"*

I am using my strength of will to force you to tell me without my asking.

Kale not only saw Bardon laughing as he looked over his shoulder but also felt the rush of joy as it swept through her husband.

You're having entirely too much fun, Bardon, and it makes me feel like you're up to something.

He shook his head. *"Regidor and Namee have been working on a special project. We're stopping at Namee's castle so he can demonstrate a weaving of a strange gateway, one that will come in handy on our quest."*

Kale raised up a bit in the saddle and leaned forward. *Tell me more.*

"No, you have to wait."

She heard the laughter in his voice and refused to be baited. She would not beg for details. With her lips pressed together, she scowled at him. He laughed even harder. *You wretched man.*

"You are going to have some fun tonight, lady of mine. And tomorrow, some surprises. Then off we go adventuring."

I can find adventure in our very own castle.

He picked up on the hidden meaning in her manner.

"What are you talking about?"

The snake.

"What snake?"

Oh, I forgot to tell you. You rushed me around so, and I didn't check… but Artross is here. I can ask him.

"Kale." The tone of his thoughts was as clear as a bell.

She giggled. *So it's all right for you to keep secrets, but not me.*

"If there is a snake in the castle, I need to know about it."

There isn't a snake now. At least, I hope we got them all.

"All?"

One mother snake and a nest of hundreds. Well, maybe only one hundred. Artross says ninety-seven eggs, and they were all destroyed.

"What kind of snake?"

Anvilhead.

"Oh, nice."

She thought back through the sequence of events. Bardon understood as clearly as if he had stood beside her during the search and rescue of Gally and Mince.

"I'll send a message to Librettowit to get one of his tumanhofer friends to inspect the lower regions of the castle."

Wizard Namee will have a messenger we can send. But Toopka told Taylaminkadot, and I'm sure she told Librettowit. She's no more fond of snakes than I am.

"Wizard Namee will not mind sending the message."

Kale caught a hint of humor in Bardon's statement, and then he shielded his mind from her. She wondered if he hid his thoughts because he was more concerned about the snake incident in their home than he wanted her to know. But that would not account for the ripple of laughter that accompanied his last thought. She sighed. Her husband would tell her in due time. He was not in the habit of being secretive for long.

The magnificent scenery distracted Kale. They were flying over the region called Tuthoutu. Supposedly, below them, two thousand and two lakes riddled the land, everything from big puddles to lakes too vast to swim across. The lush green vegetation and startling blue of the water made a spectacular view. The eastern slope of the Morchain Mountains swept up from the plains just beyond the wetland.

Namee's castle towered out of a chasm between two peaks. He had chosen a traditional architecture with nine towers dominating the roof line. Kale remembered it was Wizard Namee who constructed a formidable tower watching over one wing of their own castle. Daily she climbed to the turret at the top to survey the surrounding fields and observe the dragons.

The sun dipped behind the mountain peaks, leaving a ragged silhouette against streaks of orange, purple, and a greenish blue. The castle didn't hide in shadows, though. Namee had summoned what appeared like bursts of starlight perched on slender poles all around the grounds and on the palace itself. As they approached, Kale saw people scurrying about, some servants and some dressed in finery.

It's busy here tonight.

"Namee is having a ball. We shall dance. We haven't danced in years."

Excitement bubbled in Kale, suppressing her former complaints and ill-humor. *Bardon, this is a wonderful surprise. Thank you. Thank you very much.*

"You're welcome, my Kale. It was worth your fussing to bring you here for the surprises."

How many surprises are in store for me?

He hummed a ditty in his mind before he answered. The ploy made Kale more anxious. Just before she demanded he quit trying to drive her mad, he answered, *"Several."*

Bardon!

"'Patience rewards twice, once while waiting and once when waiting is no longer needed.'"

She growled in annoyance. If he was going to quote principles to her, she would give him patience in spades.

As they drew closer to the lighted castle, Kale saw more activity. She searched the area, pushing her talent to the limits, trying to identify guests and details of the events planned for the ball.

She met with frustration. Wizard Namee had cloaked the area so that his guests could maintain their privacy from prying mindspeakers.

"How inconsiderate of him," Kale muttered and turned her mind to designing the fancy dress she would wear to the ball.

6

Stopover

They circled the castle once, just to take in the extraordinary beauty of Namee's domain. Then Greer descended to the dragon field, with Celisse close behind. Kale fidgeted in her seat. Aware that she would get no results, she still stretched her mind to get a glimpse of those who had already arrived. Not knowing whom they would meet added to the thrill. Leetu Bends? Sir Dar? Granny Noon or Granny Kye? She could see spots of light moving among the promenades and knew they were kimens. Would some of her friends from former adventures be there? Unable to contain her delight, she turned to Bardon.

Wake Toopka. She'll be so excited. Remember how she danced down all the corridors at the urohm wedding?

"I remember you dancing with her."

Kale watched Mikkai plunge into the knapsack and heard Toopka's shout of glee when her head popped out from under the flap. Through Kale's mindspeaking ability, she heard the child begin a one-sided commentary on everything within sight. Greer and Celisse landed on a grassy foothill set aside for this purpose. Toopka finally stopped prattling when Bardon pulled her out of her traveling basket and set her feet on the ground.

Servants ran to greet them and, after the dragons were unsaddled, took the saddles from Kale and Bardon to store them in a tack house. Greer and Celisse moseyed toward a group of dragons whose riders had already entered the castle. Toopka dogged the workers' steps, asking questions and mentioning every ball she had been to before.

Kale only half-listened until she heard Toopka mention a ball in a pink palace.

"Where, Toopka?" she asked. "Where was this pink palace?"

The doneel child jerked at the question, blinked her big eyes, and then ducked her head. "I was just making that one up."

"It sounded very real. Your description of the music and the dance steps didn't sound like a made-up memory."

Toopka shook her head so hard her ears flopped from side to side. Then she looked up with sincerity fairly dripping from her serious eyes. "I have a very good imagination, and sometimes when people talk about things, I pretend they happened to me. And when I remember what they said, I pretend I was there."

Kale pondered Toopka's too-earnest expression. She tried to peek at her thoughts, but as she often found, the doneel's thinking lurked behind a hazy, noisy, and confusing curtain. Add to that the precautions Wizard Namee had made, and Kale didn't have a chance of deciphering Toopka's thoughts.

"All right, Toopka. I understand what you are telling me. Now, understand what I tell you."

Toopka's ears drooped, her whiskers quivered, and she dropped her gaze to the floor. Kale continued. "Misrepresenting the truth is lying. Pretending, when the listener doesn't know it is pretense, is lying."

Toopka nodded harder. Kale continued, even though she knew she had delivered this exact lecture many times before.

"If you lie to yourself, you can't help lying to others."

By now Toopka's head bobbed hard enough to rattle her poor brain. Kale wondered how much of this compliance was sincere.

"No lie will ever stand against even the slightest examination by Wulder. Explaining to Wulder why you chose to lie would be a very, very hard thing."

The doneel's head stilled, and a tear trickled down her cheek.

Kale turned away, exasperated with herself that even after all these years she still distrusted the little doneel girl and allowed her to unsettle her. Toopka presented a mystery she often ignored, but at moments like this, all the oddities of Toopka jumped to her attention. Where did the child come from? How old was she? Was she cunning or guileless? Why couldn't Kale penetrate Toopka's thoughts as easily as she did others'?

Bardon signaled for her to join him. An elegant coach had arrived to carry them the short distance to the castle.

"Come, Toopka." Kale removed the moonbeam cape and draped it over her arm as she strolled toward her husband. The minor dragons flew in a kaleidoscope of bright colors. "Someday we'll talk, Toopka, and you'll surprise me by giving me honest answers." She avoided looking at the girl's face, knowing the innocent expression that would be fixed there. And also knowing Toopka's childlike air would annoy her.

Bardon handed them into the waiting vehicle as the horses stamped their eagerness to follow the winding road up to the castle. Torchlights flamed along the way, and whimsical orchestra music drifted through the air.

Through the window in the coach, Kale admired the lighting of the drive Namee had designed. A small river stairstepped down a cliff, making a broken waterfall. Each segment gleamed with a different colored light. The display piqued her curiosity as a light wizard. She sighed with satisfaction as she untangled the spell in her mind and identified how it worked.

She started to share the discovery with Bardon but stopped short when she saw that Toopka had captivated his attention. At this moment the doneel's enthusiasm for her surroundings appeared to be genuine. Her large eyes sparkled, her ears perked forward, her whiskers twitched, and rather than the endless stream of nattering, Toopka let out soft gasps of astonishment. Kale's heart softened. If only she could get past the inscrutable veil that disguised this enthralling child, Kale was sure she could love Toopka without reservation.

She doesn't trust me with whatever she holds as her important, oh-so-carefully guarded secrets. I resent not being trusted. After all, haven't I always offered good and not evil toward this ward of mine?

She almost laughed when she remembered a plaintive line quoting Wulder and reported in the Tomes. *"Why should my creation accuse me of desiring their destruction? Why doubt the words I give them that would secure their happiness?"*

Wulder sounded as confused and aggravated as she did, yet Kale knew the great Creator was never puzzled. Bardon had explained that these quotes were given so that the seven high races could relate to the position, rather than the attitude, Wulder stood in when observing their disobedience, arrogance, and distrust. With this revelation, his followers could identify their impertinent mind-set.

Yes, that was it. Kale felt that all her good intentions had been disregarded by Toopka when the little girl denied sharing her confidences with her guardian.

She studied Toopka and wondered again if this demeanor was real or just a well-performed sham.

When they arrived at a castle portcullis at a side entrance, a servant in livery opened the coach door and arranged a footstool for them to use. Bardon stepped down first, then turned to give a hand to Kale.

She glanced around the darkened meadow, saw kimens gliding down pathways meandering through the garden bushes and servants carrying lanterns as they raced about doing their duties. The air vibrated with activity. Then Kale's gaze fell to her husband's upturned face, and love swelled in her heart. He had taken all her grousing in good stead and persisted in bringing her to this. All his efforts were to provide for her a surprise he knew she would appreciate. She placed her hand in his.

"I'm sorry," she said. "I've done nothing but whine at you and raise objections."

He kissed the back of her hand. "You're forgiven. Now, we're going to have fun, and not think about duties and pressing needs, and whether or not there is enough fruit in the orchards to provide nourishment over the winter."

Kale's face fell into an expression of dismay. "Isn't there enough fruit? Are the crops poor this year?"

Bardon shook his head. "Fun. We are going to have fun, pleasure, enjoyment. The crops are fine."

He winked.

She grinned saucily and stepped lightly out of the coach. Not only did she look forward to the ball and the promise of more surprises, but she had noticed the long ride had not caused stakes' stiffness to return to Bardon's joints. With this good sign, Kale allowed herself to hope the kimens' treatment would last weeks and maybe months. And she vowed to increase Bardon's enjoyment of the evening in any way she could.

Toopka hopped to the ground, took hold of Kale's skirt, and hovered behind her. The minor dragons scattered, perching on slanted flagpoles, onto the tops of other carriages, on the ornamentation of the portcullis, on piles of fancy luggage waiting to be taken in, and on the covered steps. A well-dressed doneel matron approached. The light wizard allowed her ward to hide, knowing Toopka's fits of shyness often occurred in the presence of her own race.

As the matron drew closer, Kale realized she must be an important servant. The string of keys dangling from her waist, the stiffly starched apron over her gown, and the mobcap clearly indicated she was the castle's housekeeper. In typical doneel fashion, her clothing was a bit showy for her position in the household.

The woman's black taffeta gown rustled as she walked. Shiny white silk peeked from beneath a cut-lace overlay on what should have been a simple apron. The floppy white hat sported more lace with a rainbow of ribbons woven through it. Kale grinned, thinking of the first doneel she had ever met. Much like Sir Dar, this doneel matron followed the prescribed standard of elegance common to their race.

The appearance of the housekeeper made Kale pause. *Oh dear, I wish I'd taken closer notice at what Toopka chose to wear.*

The doneel child had a flair for bright colors, but little regard for coordinating her choices. Without looking back and drawing attention to the half-hidden girl, Kale brought to mind an image of her often-scruffy ward. Orange pantaloons sticking out from under a green and purple striped skirt, an under blouse that almost matched the leggings in hue, a tunic of a clashing shade of purple, a dotted scarf wrapped around her neck, and a gray bonnet that had once been white hanging down her back with the strings hidden under the scarf. And wrinkled, of course. Toopka's clothes pleated around her in uneven creases. The child had been sleeping in a bag.

With only a bit of time to work and hindered by not being able to study the clothing as she changed it, Kale removed all the color from

Toopka's outfit to leave a sparkling white. She eliminated the wrinkles, took away the extra material of the bulky pantaloons, and lengthened the skirt. And then in a nod to Toopka's desire for fancy, Kale wove golden threads through the fabric, producing a design of shimmering leaves.

The housekeeper curtsied. "Lady Kale, Sir Bardon, I am Mistress Orcutt. Wizard Namee sends his welcome and will dine with you this evening. I have a bedroom ready. If you'll come this way…" She explained the particulars of the evening as she led them through the hallways lit with yellow, pink, and gold lightrocks. "Dinner is at eight, the ball begins at nine, a light repast will be served at midnight, and an early breakfast at three."

Kale took the moment to squeeze Bardon's hand and send him a message, promising to be exceptionally grateful for such a rare treat.

The housekeeper continued, "There will be a buffet in the main dining hall all morning so that you may partake whenever you arise. The noonmeal will be served at midday, of course."

"Mistress Orcutt," Kale spoke as they paused beside the open door to their chambers, "we have a doneel child with us, my ward. Is there someone to look after her while we are occupied?"

Kale reached behind her and took Toopka's hand to gently pull her into the housekeeper's view.

The woman's stern expression relaxed, and a sincere smile lifted her lips. "Oh yes, I have six little ones of my own. The oldest will be in charge, and your girl will be welcome to spend the night. They eat in a nook in the kitchen, then sneak into a hidden balcony to watch the dancing for a while. Eventually, my Gia will take them to our quarters to play games, hear stories, and sleep.

"My husband will retire early. He's head stableman, and his duties will be done long before mine. So he will be there if Gia needs him."

"That sounds like fun, doesn't it, Toopka?" Kale hoped the child would respond appropriately.

Toopka gave a cautious nod, keeping her eyes downcast.

"Fine, then." The housekeeper stretched out a hand. "Come with me now, and I'll introduce you to my young ones."

Reluctantly, Toopka released Kale's hand and took Mistress Orcutt's. She marched beside the matronly woman as though she were being led to an execution.

"Have a good time, Toopka," Kale called after her, then spoke quietly to Bardon, "Why do I feel like I've tossed her into a bubbling stew?"

"Because she usually plays with minor dragons." He put a hand on her elbow and steered her through the open door. "Relax, Kale. Remember, Toopka was once a street urchin. She'll have the time of her life."

"She's changed, Bardon. An odd sort of changed. She came to us as a scrappy alley cat, and she's become more timid, still curious, but somehow less sure of herself."

"She's Toopka." Bardon put his arm around his wife's shoulders and guided her toward their chamber. "Toopka is a mystery only Wulder could explain."

Kale nodded but kept her eyes on the little doneel until she rounded the corner with the housekeeper. "I believe we are going to be astonished when Wulder reveals Toopka's mystery."

7

Making Connections

Bardon kissed Kale's cheek. "Rest up a bit, consider your gown, and I'll be back before you know it. I've something to see to before the festivities begin."

He made a hasty escape down the corridor before his very astute wife could pin him to the wall with questions. His brain felt fuzzy from guarding secrets. He didn't want her to discover the pleasant surprises of the coming evening. And he certainly didn't want to spoil the surprises with worry over the Followers in the mysterious village of Paladise. Paladise! What a name.

Mikkai guided him through the castle without a problem. Apparently, the map dragon had seen somewhere the blueprints for many of the greater homes in Amara. The difficulty was finding Namee. They visited all the likely places for the host to be and found plenty of guests but not the wizard. Finally, a servant suggested they look in the kitchens.

Bardon's boots clattered on the stone steps as he followed Mikkai. As they got closer, he didn't need his guide. His nose could have led him to the cavernous rooms where chefs congregated with their minions around floured tables, bubbling pots, and red-hot ovens. Happy chatter flowed among the staff. Wizard Namee sat at a pastry table, eating bits and pieces of stolen dough in between slurps of hearty chukkajoop broth from a bowl.

The wizard raised his chalice to Bardon. "Come join me. Are you hungry? Better grab a bite now. Ten o'clock is an absurd hour to begin dinner, but it's tradition, you know. Tradition. How can we dance the whole night through if we start at a more seemly hour? It's tradition to dance till dawn. If we start at six, no one can last until the morning star appears. So we have to start at ten.

"My wife says it is because in the old days, before wizards cooled the air in the castle, dancers dropped dead from the heat. Now that would ruin the festivities, wouldn't it? But I say times have changed. I can cool the air. And she says it's romantic to start at ten and cool the air anyway. So I come to the kitchen to do a taste test. Wouldn't want to serve my guests something foul."

He raised a braised leg of a large heatherhen, laughed, then sank his teeth into the meat. "Besides, I get too busy mixing with the guests to sit down and have a proper meal. And it would seem that my stomach does not like a ten o'clock supper. I'm usually not hungry that time of night." He took a bite of a roll that the baker had just placed on his plate. "Hot! Ouch! Hot!" He drank and gestured for Bardon to sit with him.

Bardon chose a chair next to his host but waved away a servant's offer of a plate and bowl. He took the tankard.

Namee arched an eyebrow. "I deduce that you are not hungry."

"No sir, I'm not."

"Then it is me you seek out. The culinary arts of my fine staff did not lure you away from our fascinating guests above."

"Yes, that's right, sir."

He sighed, put down his chalice, and pushed his plate aside. "What is it?"

Bardon leaned closer. "Have you heard of a group of people calling themselves Followers?"

Wizard Namee pursed his lips, swirled the liquid in his chalice, then took a drink. "I have."

The simple answer perplexed Bardon. Wizard Namee sounded cautious, and caution was not one of the wizard's hallmarks. "What do you think of them?"

"I find them curious."

"I came across a group of Followers in a village in my district. What can you tell me about those you've encountered?"

"They seem harmless. A bit more intense than most folks, but I surmise that it is a pendulum swing. The citizens of Amara acknowledge their mistake in being too apathetic during our former troubles. Now this group has shifted to the other extreme. Time will balance it out."

"Nonetheless, I feel the need to report my finding to Paladin."

"He won't be here tonight."

"May I use your gateway?"

"Indeed." He signaled for a servant to come to his side. "Don't worry overmuch on this, Sir Bardon. This won't be a popular movement. Their ranks will be slim."

"Why do you say that, sir? Is there something you know that I can add to my report?"

"Only that these Followers aren't inclined to enjoy themselves. Odd clothing, dull food, and no entertainment. I also understand that one has to be enlightened in order to be given the privilege of producing offspring. Sounds anomalous to me."

Bardon rose. "Yes, strange and inconsistent with previous teachings from our scholars."

A tumanhofer bowed to Wizard Namee.

"This is Namutdonlowmack. He'll escort you to the gateway chamber. Be back in time for dinner, young man. It will be a feast worth tasting."

Once in the hallway, Bardon spoke to the servant. "It isn't necessary to escort me. Mikkai can direct me."

"Certainly, Sir Bardon, but I wish to speak with you." The tumanhofer glanced around at the many people wandering and socializing in the halls. "This way, sir."

Namutdonlowmack darted down a corridor and scuttled up a winding set of stairs leading to the top of one of Namee's towers.

"Would you mind sending your dragon to make sure no one lurks in the shadows? I do not want what I have to say to be heard."

Curious, Bardon nodded to the dragon who had perched in a window. With the signal, Mikkai winged off on his mission. As soon as he left, Bardon sized up the tumanhofer and determined from his frown that Namutdonlowmack was not going to spend the time in idle conversation. Bardon sighed, leaned against the window frame, and watched the skies. While they waited, two more large dragons landed in the field.

Mikkai returned. Bardon nodded in response to the minor dragon's chitter. "He says there is no one in the tower other than ourselves."

The tumanhofer hesitated.

"I have an urgent message to deliver, and I have little time."

"I'm aware of the nature of your message, Sir Bardon."

"You are?"

"Of course." Namutdonlowmack shuffled his feet. "I wasn't near enough to listen to your conversation with Wizard Namee until I moved a bit closer. It is important to know what is going on in the castle. I am one of his most trusted servants. If he had not wanted me to hear, he would have said so."

Bardon nodded. "The kitchen is not the best place for private conversation. But please, I must go."

"And Wizard Namee's control of sound included his knowing where sound is traveling, when it bounces off barriers, and in the case of conversation, who can hear."

"Yes, a very useful talent. The point, Namutdonlowmack."

"Wizard Namee wishes me to relay information that he did not feel he could speak of in the kitchen. About the people who interest you. Two things. First, there are representatives of the Followers here for the ball."

"I thought they spurned such activities."

"These men do not profess outwardly to be of this society. They are here seeking information and to look for potential converts."

"Converts? What a strange choice of words. How does one convert a person from one doctrine to the same doctrine?"

"You have already begun to suspect that their doctrine is not the same. That is why I chose to speak with you."

"Go on."

"So they look for recruits, if the term 'converts' does not please you."

"None of this pleases me. But I feel you have a personal quarrel with the Followers."

Bardon caught the slight jerk of Namutdonlowmack's head, and the fierce gleam in the tumanhofer's eye backed up the intensity of that affirmation.

"My brother's son, my nephew, thought the words these men spoke appealing. He followed. And got lost. We did not hear from him for six months."

Bardon waited. The tumanhofer cleared his throat and looked out the window. "He's dead. We know he's dead."

Bardon leaned forward. "But how do you connect his death with the Followers?"

"It's what we don't connect. He went with them to one of their villages. Only their villages have no citizens other than o'rants and marione. He owned a shop in Baranst. Now the shop is owned by another man who bought it from a marione."

"And his death?"

"We don't know, but when the family started making inquiries, we met with stony faces and false leads. Then one of them—pretending he wasn't one of them, but we knew he was—showed up and sadly presented us with young Forretpuranson's copy of the family principle, written on leather, wrapped 'round his music stick, and tied with the ribbon his mother had used when his father first made the keepsake. Told us a tale, which didn't ring true, and went off, expecting we believed the pack of lies."

"What do you want me to do, Namutdonlowmack?"

"Tell Paladin," he said between gritted teeth, "that it isn't just principles they're twisting. It isn't just controlling people's ways of doing things. They're lying, thieving murderers." The tumanhofer bowed his head after his outburst.

Bardon rested a hand on the servant's shoulder. "I will."

"Go then." Namutdonlowmack sniffed and gestured toward the steps. "The gateway's at the top."

Bardon bolted up the stairs and through the portal. He emerged in Paladin's palace courtyard. One of the two guards on duty escorted him directly into a chamber where Paladin was conversing with two emerlindian grands.

All three men rose as the footman announced their visitor.

"Good," said Paladin as he came to greet Bardon. "Now we have a warrior to send forth. Enough of our academic splitting of straws, gentlemen. Wulder has provided us with eyes and ears. Come in, Sir Bardon. Tell us what you have discovered."

"Do you know of the Followers?"

"Yes, and we are concerned. More than concerned. Ready to gather information so we might act wisely."

"They say you initiated their work."

Paladin gently shook his head as he guided his knight to a chair. "And you have reason to doubt, of course. We have yet to determine exactly where this offshoot sprang out of the main branch. We know these Followers have taken what was initiated from this office and forced it to grow in a direction not intended. They've grafted on a foreign branch and are trying to pass it off as the tree itself."

Bardon sat with Paladin and his two advisors. "What do you want me to do, sir?"

"I hear you're going on a quest to find the meech colony."

"Yes, but I can put that aside if you have another mission for me."

"No, this suits our purpose well. You will have a legitimate reason to be seeking information and to be away from your usual business. Go on your quest, Sir Bardon, but along the way, gather the facts we need to face our new enemy."

"Enemy? These are mariones and o'rants, our own people."

Paladin's eyes saddened, his face grew more solemn. "It is true that the enemy we face so often turns out to be ourselves."

8

Before the Ball

Kale came out of the side room to find Bardon alone in their quarters. "Where—?"

"I sent the minor dragons out to explore and perhaps bring back some tidbits of useful information."

Kale nodded and unbuttoned her blouse. She would hang up her clothes and give them a thorough cleaning before she rearranged the fabric and color to make her evening gown.

"That water closet is amazing, Bardon. Namee has a cylinder tank that holds water for a bath. The water is heated right there." She mumbled more to herself than to her husband as she continued to hang her clothes on the wall hooks provided. "Not all of his guests are wizards who can heat their own water. I've studied it and see the principle upon which it works but haven't figured out all the details." She draped her split-skirt next to her blouse.

Bardon lounged against a wall, arms crossed over his chest. "I'm not very interested in Namee's system for hot bath water."

"What?" Kale turned toward him and saw the look in his eye. "Oh."

"I am alone with my wife. Toopka is gone. The dragons are gone. I thought…"

"I know what you're thinking. Even with Namee's block on mindspeaking, I know what you are thinking."

"I'd like to kiss my wife."

"You are having a string of excellent ideas today, Sir Bardon."

"You're no longer grumbling against my plans?"

"Who, me? Grumble?"

An hour later, Kale stirred from a light sleep to sounds from the water closet. Bardon splashed in the tub, obviously having taken an interest in the water heated above the porcelain receptacle.

Kale pulled the covers close around her and gazed at her clothes. The material began to shake as dirt and oils were vibrated out of the individual threads of the fabric. After she freshened the cloth, she removed the color and infused the basic blouse and skirt with a soft yellow. That pleased her, and she attached the skirt to the bodice she transformed out of the shirt. She rearranged the waistband, making it a wide sash over a full skirt with an added swag of creamy white. She shook her head and dropped the added feature. The material tumbled to the floor.

"What color would you like me to wear?" she called.

Her lips moved to form the word *pink* just as Bardon answered, "Pink."

She sighed and, with a nod, changed the yellow to a pale pink. Since the ballroom would be crowded and hot, she chose a lighter fabric and spent some time loosening the weave of the material she worked with. She removed the buttons on the front and made a solid bodice with a scooped neck. She decided against sleeves of any kind as she got up to pull gloves from one of the hollows of her cape. By the time Bardon came out of the bath, her gown was ready, and she had cleaned his clothes and reshaped them into evening attire. She hadn't asked what colors he would prefer, because she knew he would answer green and black. He truly had no imagination.

"You should wear a tiara," he suggested.

"I hate wearing a tiara. It always sparks."

"It sparkles."

"It sparks, and you know it. I nearly caught a curtain on fire at the urohm wedding."

"The affair needed a little more excitement."

"I need a bath."

He stepped out of the doorway, made a bow, and swept his arm toward the water closet.

"I've used all the hot water."

"It's a good thing, then, that you married a woman who can heat her own bath."

When they were dressed and ready to go down to dinner, a tap on the window announced the arrival of a minor dragon.

Bardon unlocked the casement and pulled the glass panel open. Filia and Tieto flew in, gave Bardon a disgruntled glance, and landed on Kale.

"You locked them out?" Kale tried to look stern but barely hid her amusement.

He shrugged.

"Oh dear," she responded to a bit of news Tieto related.

"What is it?"

"He says he doesn't like the aura he sees around some of the guests."

"Pretender's people?"

Kale shook her head as she puzzled over the continued chittering of the unhappy dragon. "Tieto says the light contains threads that look almost identical to those surrounding teachers of Wulder's Tomes."

"Almost?"

"Yes, but the difference is so subtle, he can't discern the discrepancy. He wishes Regidor were here."

"That's one person I know will not be attending tonight." Bardon tilted his head, studying Tieto. "He matches your dress well enough. Bring him along, and maybe we can ferret out the underlying cause of his dislike."

Kale looked at the blue and green dragon and at her pink dress. They didn't clash, but the dragon would not blend in either. Filia came along, and as they walked down the hall, Kale allowed the dress to absorb the colors reflected off the pink and purple dragon. The original shade altered subtly to form a good backdrop for Filia clinging to her sleeve. For Tieto, Kale arranged a shoulder cascade of flowers, one of which was the blue and green dragon.

When they entered the banquet room, a servant ushered them to a partially filled table. Kale embraced Sir Dar, Wizard Cam Ayronn, and Lord and Lady Brunstetter. Leetu Bends, Lee Ark, and his lady wife greeted Kale and Bardon. Leetu went so far as to hug Kale and plant a kiss on her cheek. Bardon's father, Sir Joffa, blustered in his usual way and clapped both Bardon and Kale on the shoulders. His pride for his son shone through his gruff exterior. Shimeran and Seezle, two kimens she hadn't seen since her first quest, sat on the far side of the table on raised chairs.

Wizard Namee had worked some spell that subdued the sound in the crowded room. She knew she spoke in a normal tone, but the words floated softly to the listener, without disturbing those at other tables. And she heard distinctly any comment made to her. But the voices of all the guests together only made a soft murmur, not unlike the sound of the sea quietly advancing on a sandy shore and then flowing back.

A string quartet played dinner music, and each note drifted above the dining crowd without hindering individual conversations.

Kale soaked in the sight of so many dear faces and relished each bit of news, but the aroma of seared meat and the buttery sauces held no appeal. She visited with first one person and then another, discussed ideas with several people at once, and expressed joy at hearing the good news among them. She ignored her plate.

Bardon drew her attention by placing a hand on her arm and leaned in to whisper, "Are you all right?"

"Of course, why do you ask?"

He pointed to her untouched kitawahdo, a tumanhofer bean dish that she ordinarily devoured.

"I must be too excited to eat. My stomach is bubbling, and I have a tight place, like a muscle spasm." She placed her hand over the top of her abdomen. "Right here."

"Can you call for Gymn?"

She concentrated for a moment. "Horse feathers! What has Namee done here? I'll send Filia to find him."

The small dragon flew away, and Bardon put a piece of bread broken from a round loaf in her hand. "Here, eat this. You may just be hungry. You haven't touched your food."

Kale laughed. "I'm too busy talking. It is so good to be here. Thank you again, Bardon, for dragging me away. I think I could go back home and be content for years on this one evening alone."

"Nothing doing, lady of mine, we're off on a quest tomorrow."

Kale sighed, nibbled on the bread, and soon got interested in a story Sir Dar told of a castle being built by one of the mountain wizards.

"Perhaps a relation of mine," she whispered to her husband. "My mother comes from the mountains."

"Is that why she is seemingly ageless?" Bardon grinned. "As old as the hills, but beautiful in a majestic way?"

Kale narrowed her eyes at him but couldn't contain the twitch at the corner of her mouth that threatened to bloom into a smile. "My father is from the hills. My mother is from the mountains. A definite distinction is made among the families."

"Snobbery," said Bardon.

"Exactly," said Kale.

"Next, your relations will be looking down their noses at my ears."

She giggled. "I love your ears. A half-emerlindian is just what this stodgy old family needed."

"Your mother is not stodgy."

"And my father is?"

"Yes, but I didn't say it. You did."

Wizard Namee approached and claimed their attention. As host he walked from table to table, greeting his guests.

"I am particularly happy to see you, Lady Kale. Regidor and I have perfected a weaving of the old gateway spell that innovates—" he broke off, cleared his throat, and continued. "But that's a treat for tomorrow. Before you all leave, I will gather the wizards who have graced this evening's celebration and teach you the weave. Then you can teach it to those you meet as you travel."

"Celebration?" asked Kale. "I'm sorry. I don't know the occasion."

"Life! Life is the occasion. I envy your going on a quest, a peaceful quest, at that. I'm too old to be gallivanting around the countryside." He smiled, patted her shoulder, the one that didn't hold the flowers and Tieto, and wandered off to attend to his other company.

Tieto climbed out of his camouflage and nestled against Kale's chin.

"Bardon, Tieto says that Namee's aura is off, pushed to one side as if something was trying to get in from the outside."

"Odd." He watched the man as he moved away.

Namee now spoke to a gentleman urohm, and although the large man spoke with a booming voice, they could only make out a whisper of sound from the conversation.

Kale leaned against Bardon's side. "He doesn't look a bit different to me. Yet Tieto insists something is amiss."

Bardon placed his arm around her shoulders. "I don't detect anything in his manner that is untoward." He shook his head. "Now *I'm* wishing Regidor were here."

Filia returned with Gymn, who wrapped himself around Kale's neck. The little healing dragon was unconcerned that someone might comment on the Dragon Keeper bringing her entourage to the banquet. Truthfully, dragons didn't like to mix with the high races in their festivities. They thought the activities always overdone.

Kale's stomach settled immediately, but she still ate sparingly, giving more bites to the three dragons than to herself.

The musicians ended a song, packed up their instruments, and left the raised platform at one end of the room.

Moments later a chorus of trumpets heralded the beginning of the ball. The guests filed out through several sets of open doors and entered a dazzling white hall where shining alabaster walls glistened with pale yellow lightrocks. Pillars supported a towering ceiling too far above their heads to discern the structural design. Magnolias, gardenias, lilies, and sprays of snowdrops twined around each column. Minuscule, but brilliant, pastel lightrocks nestled in the green vines.

Wizard Namee led his lady to the center of the dance floor and bowed to the orchestra to begin. Kale was not educated in music other than tavern songs and ballads that the wandering minstrels sang. Bardon named the tune and the composer for her. The melody enchanted her. Gracefully, Namee and his wife twirled around the room. When they had completed one turn, others began to join them on the polished floor.

"Kale, would you like to dance?" Bardon bowed to his lady wife.

"Not yet. May we watch?"

"Of course."

They sat in dainty chairs set against the wall. Rows of seating encircled the dance floor in three tiers, the highest against the wall, the next level just in front of that, and the lowest level on a platform eight inches above the floor. The chairs were grouped in sizes so that kimens and urohms could each find a comfortable place to rest. Outside on the veranda, seats were clustered for socializing between the races.

After the third dance, the lights dimmed and the orchestra began to play a piece that reminded Kale of music she had heard Sir Dar play on his flute. The partners on the floor stood still. They couldn't see well enough to proceed. Between the dancers, shimmering lights began to appear.

"Kimens," whispered Kale.

The small creatures danced, twirling between their larger counterparts, circling couples, then spinning away and gliding in and out of the unmoving spectators.

Kale took Bardon's hand and stood. "I want to dance with the kimens."

They hurried to the floor. Bardon encircled her waist with one arm, held her other hand, and sailed into the midst of the others. Two by two, the couples shook off the awe of the beautiful kimens surrounding them. The colors of the kimens' lighted garb reflected off the shiny material of the dancers' clothing. "It's like being inside a kaleidoscope," Kale whispered. "The shifting colors could be disconcerting, but you know they're held together by a pattern even if we can't see the overall design."

"Very philosophical, but that reminds me of a principle." Bardon pulled her closer, laid his chin against her hair, and murmured in her ear. "Don't go analyzing it, Light Wizard Kale. Some things are meant just for us to enjoy."

"That's not a principle."

"Ah, but it is, an underlying principle that shows itself in many of the more formal wordings."

She felt him stiffen. "What is it?"

"I see evidence of Tieto's concern."

Kale's head swiveled so that she could look all around them. "I don't see anything."

"Our kimen friends are dancing freely among us, but there are those that they never circle, never come close to. I surmise that these are the folks that Tieto has identified as having an odd aura."

"Oh, dear." Kale sighed. "Things are never perfect, are they?"

9

Early Morning Conflict

Bardon slipped out of bed, dressed, strapped on his sword, and left his wizard wife for his rendezvous with Sir Dar, Lee Ark, Lord Brunstetter, and Wizard Cam. Mikkai came along to provide directions to the exercise field. Tieto chirred his displeasure over such a short night's sleep. He refused to fly, remained perched on Bardon's shoulder, and grumbled at being required to keep an eye out for tainted auras. He claimed all were skewed after so little sleep.

Bardon's footsteps echoed in the great hallways. He passed only a few people, mostly servants. They nodded in deference to a guest, but he grinned at their drooping eyelids and slow, shuffling steps. Most likely, no one eagerly jumped out of their beds this morning.

Sunshine greeted him as he stepped out onto a lawn that stretched over a rolling hill and ended at the base of a cliff. Those who had managed to rise that morning sparred in pairs or did forms in a line. Bardon unbuckled his belt, removed his outer jacket and boots, and laid them on a bench with Tieto and Mikkai standing watch over his possessions. He joined a group of men and two ladies who performed slow, dance-like stretches.

Bardon's body responded to the movements as if he had never burned with the fever of stakes. He breathed deeply and felt energy flow from his core to his fingertips. With the next measured lift of his right leg, he swung it easily to the side and down. A burst of vigor made it hard not to speed up beyond the required slow motion into a more energetic expression of pleasure. Perhaps this time the kimens' treatment would last forever. Perhaps he wouldn't return to that stiff condition that had almost paralyzed him.

He located Lee Ark with a group of men who were further along in the routine exercises. Sir Dar and Wizard Cam ambled onto the field a few minutes later. Bardon became engrossed in his forms and laughed at himself later when he saw that the giant urohm Brunstetter had somehow slipped into the activities unnoticed.

When Bardon finished his regimen, he joined Lee Ark to wait for the others. The men sat on benches along the castle wall. Servants brought them towels to wipe away the perspiration and tankards of cool well water.

"Ah," said Bardon as he took a slow draft and wiped his lips on the back of his sleeve. "Wizard Namee has a sweet supply."

"He does, indeed," answered Lee Ark. With military directness, he continued. "I'm anxious to talk over this matter of Followers with our comrades. My number of new soldiers has dropped in the past few months, and upon investigation, I find the young people are being lured away to improve their minds and souls."

"According to the Tomes, defending the old, young, and weak, providing stability in life, and assuring the land's ability to support us have always been a part of improving minds and souls."

Lee Ark crossed his legs so that one ankle rested on the other knee and leaned back against the bricks of the castle wall. "Apparently, that is no longer true."

Bardon snickered. "Someone has written another volume of the Tomes? I hadn't heard so."

"I've heard these people speak myself. At first I was impressed. They explained the principles with more wisdom and understanding than any teacher I've ever heard."

Bardon widened his eyes and paid closer attention.

Lee Ark nodded. "Until I heard one statement that struck me as out of place. Something about earning Wulder's favor. I kept attending their open-air meetings and made sure I prayed for discernment each time. In every message I found one speck of heresy almost hidden in the glowing rhetoric."

Over the clang of swords clashing in mock combat, a hum like the sound of swarming bees drifted across the lawn. The people on the exercise field ceased their forms and practice of various methods of defense.

All eyes turned toward the western corner of the castle. The drone drew closer and, as it became more distinct, Bardon realized it could not be small insects.

"What is this?" asked Lee Ark.

A tumanhofer boy came running around the corner. As soon as he saw the people, he yelled, "Dragons. Little dragons. They're attacking!" He ran on toward the stables, repeating his warning with increasing fervor.

Lee Ark took command. "Those who will not fight, return to the castle. Warriors, to your weapons. A line for defense. A second line behind, the distance of three yards."

Most of the servants and ladies disappeared into the castle. The remaining fighters hastened to follow Lee Ark's orders. Mikkai settled on Bardon's shoulder and clung steadfastly as his knight responded to the battle cry. Tieto chose to fly above the field. Wizard Cam stood beside Bardon on one side and Lee Ark on the other. They positioned themselves in the center of the front line. The men and a few women had just formed ranks when a hundred or more black dragons the size of a small lad's fist charged around the corner.

The black beasts stormed the defenders en masse without an apparent leader or a particular plan of attack. As they approached, the dragons blasted tiny streams of fire at the obstacles in their way but did not tarry to fight. Mikkai hunkered down on Bardon's shoulder and did not move. The swarm flew as if the people were merely an inconvenience in the way of their journey.

The small, quick targets were difficult to hit, but a score of dragon bodies littered the ground, a solid testament to the warriors' skills.

One man yelped when he attempted to pick up one of the black dragons. He shook his hand. "It stung me." He ran his sword point through the creature and lifted it. "In all of Amara, I've never seen the like of this."

Another defender crouched and examined a fallen dragon. "I mistook them for bats when they first rounded the corner, but the fire proved me wrong. These are dragons, peculiar, but dragons. The boy was right." The man stood and spit on the ground. "Dragons. I don't like any of them. Don't trust them, myself. Here's an example of how bad they can be." He strode off the field, glowering at all he passed.

Bardon lifted his eyebrows and glanced at Sir Dar. He shrugged, shook his head, and touched his singed hair. Bardon looked at Cam, but the old wizard was concentrating on something else.

Wizard Cam sniffed the air above the dead specimen before him. "I believe the spines along the back may contain toxins. Even dead, this venom could be released and cause pain. Since our friend over there is still standing, I doubt the venom is fatal."

Mikkai came out of a stupor and began a high-pitched squawk next to Bardon's ear. The knight cringed and forcefully removed the shrieker from his shoulder, peeling this little dragon's claws out of his shirt. He held shivering Mikkai next to his chest, stroking his back, and uttering soothing phrases. "It's all right. They're gone now. You aren't hurt."

When the little fellow quieted, Bardon asked, "Do you know anything about these dragons, Mikkai? Do you know where they came from?"

Mikkai shuddered, and Bardon heard the suggestion in his mind that Filia would be more likely to know. Bardon asked Tieto, who had come to find out what was wrong with his friend, about the tiny dragons. Through Mikkai, he found out the other dragon knew nothing more and didn't want to discuss such errant behavior in any species of dragon.

Sir Dar and Lord Brunstetter approached. The doneel fumed over the hair singed from his forehead. "Blasted beasts tried to set me on fire!"

"Hair will grow back, my little friend," said Brunstetter. "If the strike had been lower, it could have been your eye. You can't grow back an eye. It was a close one. Some of your eyebrow is black stubble."

"It is?" Sir Dar stopped short and glared up at the towering urohm. "How long does it take eyebrows to grow back? I'll be lopsided."

"As far as I can see, you've always been off-kilter." Brunstetter chortled, a deep resonating sound that vibrated the air.

Sir Dar ignored the dig and frowned at Lee Ark. "It doesn't seem we were the object of their attack."

"I assume we were simply in the way," interjected Wizard Cam. "There was no real need to defend the castle." He pointed at one of the dead beasts. "But the encounter gives us an opportunity to study this new threat. A good thing in the long run."

"A good thing?" The doneel huffed. "I suppose it is a good thing for those of us who still have two eyebrows and no bald spot between the ears."

Brunstetter snickered again. "So long as you don't have an empty spot between the ears where your brain should be."

"Brunstetter, you are annoying me."

"That's the plan."

Sir Dar squinted at his friend. "I bet you're hungry."

"We all are." Wizard Cam interrupted before Sir Dar could lead the conversation into another friendly barb.

Bardon stepped in as well. "I'll send Mikkai for Filia, and maybe we can learn more about these dragons. We can pool our thoughts over fried mullins and strong tea."

"Excellent idea." Lee Ark waved to a head servant who had stayed to join the battle line. "Have your men pick up the bodies to dispose of. Don't touch them directly. There's venom in those spines. Take one to Wizard Namee and inform him of what has happened here."

"Yes sir." The servant saluted and dashed away.

"An ex-military man," said Sir Dar. "No wonder Namee has put him in charge of the training field."

The men joined others in the room provided for washing away the sweat and grime of training. Bardon noted the lack of bantering between those who had participated in the confrontation with the black dragons. This jousting with words had been something he loathed as a child and had grown to love as a man. He shrugged, recognizing he didn't feel inclined toward lighthearted wit himself.

Mikkai returned with Filia after the five comrades sat down at a table away from the others. They desired to enjoy the morning's buffet and the privacy to speak freely.

"Mikkai says that Filia has some knowledge of an ancient myth that might be related to the black dragons." Bardon relayed the information to the others. "This is going to be arduous. Mikkai will have to interpret for me. I can't understand Filia's mindspeaking."

"I understand her well enough," said Wizard Cam. "Let me help, if I may."

Filia flew to sit on Cam's forearm as it rested on the table. She looked up at him and chittered away. The chittering always distracted Bardon but didn't seem to bother Wizard Cam as he listened to her mindspeak. He frowned, and the others leaned forward, anticipating his words.

"She says there are legends of a terrifying beast that was captured and put under a sleeping spell. This beast sheds these tiny dragons but is itself huge, as big as a mountain. While the evil dragon sleeps, it produces no vermin. The tiny black dragons we encountered this morning would be the vermin of the myth. When the horrible beast awakes, it sheds the small creatures like scales. As each one drops off, it takes flight."

Bardon scratched his chin. "So the legend must be based on fact."

"Not necessarily," said Sir Dar. "Myths often explain what cannot be explained by observation. If these creatures appear in a cycle—"

"This would have been a very long cycle," said Brunstetter.

Sir Dar nodded. "Yes, indeed. But if, in an ancient time, the creatures returned every ten years, every hundred years, whatever, the people may have made up the tale of the sleeping beast to explain the phenomenon."

Wizard Cam held up his hand. "This may be so. Filia says there is only one reference to the beasts, and it is chronicled in the writings of a scholar from the Northern Reach. She has never seen nor heard of any other record. An isolated, strictly regional, almost forgotten fable."

Sir Dar touched the spot of stubble on his forehead. "It would seem under present circumstances that it would be prudent not to treat this fable lightly."

Lee Ark put down his empty cup. "We shall know soon enough if we face a new danger. If this is a one-time occurrence, there will be reports from those who encounter the beasts, and then no more. If the accounts come from various directions and keep coming, then we have a problem."

10

After the Ball

The soft pillow cushioned Kale's head and invited her to stay cozy for a few more lazy minutes. But her nose twitched, and she turned away from Metta, who prodded her cheek with a wingtip and sang a cheerful tune.

"I don't want to get up, Metta." She twisted away and pulled the covers over her head.

The minor dragon hopped onto her head and sang a song full of trills and energy and high notes that raked over Kale's nerves.

"All right! All right!" She threw back the covers, knocking the laughing dragon off her perch. "I'll go join Bardon at breakfast, but I don't believe anything could be interesting enough to warrant getting up at the crack of dawn." She looked out the window and recanted. "Or before noon."

She swung her legs over the side of the bed. "Oh, my feet."

Gymn landed on her knee and ran down to sit on the arch of her foot.

"That won't do," she complained and carefully shifted her legs to lift her feet with Gymn to rest on the bed. "I didn't think I danced that much. But when they broke into the tavern songs, I couldn't help dancing one right after the other. The easiest was dancing with that urohm Stockton. My feet never touched the floor." She relaxed and stretched out on her back on the soft bed.

Gymn circled her feet, gliding over the skin and rubbing his scales against the places that hurt the worst.

"Ooh," sighed Kale. "That feels so good."

Metta trilled.

Kale rose up on her elbows. "I know. I know. I don't have time for this. Bardon wants me down at the breakfast board." She rolled over on her stomach and looked at her dress draped over the back of a chair. "I need time to change my ball gown into appropriate attire for the morning." She cocked an eyebrow at Metta. "Is it all right for Gymn to continue massaging my feet until I have it ready?"

The tiny purple dragon nodded and flew to the windowsill. She chirred and trilled until several songbirds came to perch beside her on the balustrade. Metta listened to their songs and then repeated them. When satisfied she knew the melodies, the musical minor dragon orchestrated a combined tune. Kale listened with a contented smile on her face. Metta bossed the birds just as she bullied Kale.

Kale's dress required simplifying, but that took much less time than creating the extravagant apparel for a ball. She modified the lines of the dress, took away the frill and fuss, and reworked the color from pink to a pale yellow.

The music stopped. Kale jumped from the bed before Metta could complain of her dillydallying. Gymn flew into the folds of the moonbeam cape and came out with a comb.

For the next few minutes her hair would look elegant, tied back from her face and cascading in large brown ringlets. After that, gravity would take its toll, and the curls would fall upon her shoulders in a tangled mess.

In moments, Kale descended the wide staircase to the main entryway. She'd left Gymn and Metta in the room. They had no interest in what the buffet offered, choosing instead to feast on insects in the extensive castle gardens.

In the dining hall, Bardon beckoned her to come directly to the seat beside him. He placed a finger to his lips and directed his gaze at two other guests deep in conversation. Tieto hopped from his shoulder to hers. Mikkai remained with his knight. Kale noticed the minor dragon was in an odd mood, hunching over, glowering around the table. He looked like a gargoyle from a book of foreign architecture she'd seen in the library at home.

Kale settled beside Bardon and gave him a morning smile that would pass for an ordinary greeting between husband and wife.

What's going on?

"Listen to those two. They've gone on to another topic now, but they have been circling back to the same odd interpretation of the Tomes as if the thought holds them captive."

Bardon reached for a biscuit from a platter piled high with them, broke it open, and buttered it. He put it on a clean plate in front of his wife. Then he speared a prickly gotza fruit and held it over a flame rising out of a small silver canister until he'd burned all the spines off. He put it in a bowl, sliced it in half and transferred one piece to another bowl. He gave Kale one and offered the other to the lady sitting at his other side.

The marione maiden leaned forward. "Your husband is such a gentleman."

Kale swallowed the bite in her mouth as she nodded, then drank from a cup before speaking. "He's a knight. They are trained to remember that in order to live in a comfortable environment, they must assure the comfort of those around them."

"Oh," the lady giggled. "I've never heard of such a thing. That must keep him very busy."

"Actually, it is a basic precept of the Tomes, but one not easily discerned without much study. A principle can be like a hidden riddle. Once you see the meaning, you start finding clues in many places."

"Still, following these principles must be hard to actually do. I mean, if you always have to see to others' comfort, when do you see to your own?"

Looking at the woman's fine dress, her manicured nails, the jewels on her ears, fingers, and around her neck, Kale almost dismissed the question. But the sincerity in her voice and the puzzled expression in her eyes led her to attempt the explanation.

"When you have a household running on this principle, the work spreads out. Sir Bardon demonstrates the implementation of the standard, and we as a family follow suit."

"Oh, you have children?"

Kale blushed. "No, I didn't mean that. I meant our household."

"You treat your servants as family?"

"Yes."

"Hmm." The woman turned away.

Kale knew the last concept was too much for her to take in.

Scowling, Mikkai moved across Bardon's back to the other shoulder. He stretched out with his tail hanging down Bardon's sleeve and his chin on the collar of the jacket.

Kale grinned at him and then turned her eyes back to the woman she had been talking to. Sometimes Kale felt like glowering at the world as well.

Bardon put his hand on his wife's arm. *"Give her time."*

I wish that when I was a village slave, the townspeople had treated me like a member of their families.

"Of course, but you cannot change the past. You can only influence the future. 'Moving a rough rock from the bank changes not the history of the ground surrounding it. But place it in the river, and the future is changed for the rock, the river, and the world downstream.'"

What have I told you about quoting principles before breakfast?

Bardon chuckled, leaned forward, and pecked her on the cheek. *"I have something to tell you later. Right now I want you to concentrate on our fellow guests."* Ever so slightly, he nodded toward the two he wanted her to note.

She busied herself with the food in front of her but kept her attention on the other people at their table.

She identified one man as a tumanhofer architect and the other as an o'rant merchant from Ianna. The conversation centered around the tumanhofer's need for a specific wood and the merchant's list of contacts that might be able to supply the need. Her ears perked up when she heard the mention of a truthteller speaking on a street corner near one of the shops the merchant recommended.

"I heard it again there," he said. "Among all the truth I am familiar with in my own study of the Tomes, the concept of forward forgiveness came to light."

"The truthtellers come from Paladin's palace. Surely their teaching is accurate." The tumanhofer pierced a sausage with his fork and took a bite.

"Do they all come from Paladin?" The o'rant merchant shook his head thoughtfully. "I'm not so sure. There are so many. A dozen or more in the small towns, two or three in every village, and scores in the cities."

"I didn't mean that they all came from the palace." The architect swallowed hard, wiped his lips with a napkin, and met the other's gaze. "The truthtellers came out from under Paladin's mentoring, spread out through the country, and trained more truthtellers to further Paladin's plan to reeducate the citizenry. It has been a great boon to our people. Groups have formed in every community to bring back the principles of Wulder."

The o'rant scowled. "The porridge has lumps in it."

"My porridge is fine."

Kale lifted her eyes to look at the food before the men. The merchant had no bowl of porridge before him, but the architect seemed oblivious. He turned the subject to the different types of food he'd experienced in his travels.

Kale looked at Bardon, who cocked an eyebrow.

"What does Tieto say?" he asked.

Kale listened to the minor dragon. *"The o'rant's aura is fine. The tumanhofer's contains several dents and a hole."* She looked her husband in the eye. *"What's going on, Bardon?"*

"A group of people who call themselves Followers are slipping in dangerous ideas while they pretend to be espousing Paladin's teaching."

"It shouldn't be Paladin's teaching at all. It should always be Wulder's."

"Exactly." Bardon shifted his chair in order to stand. "I wish to talk to Sir Dar about this and see if I can persuade him to come with us on the quest."

Kale squeezed his arm. "That would be wonderful. I'd go with you to convince him, but I have a meeting with Wizard Namee and the others."

"Having him on the quest would make you happy, wouldn't it?"

She nodded.

"Then I'll be very persuasive when I talk to Sir Dar."

Laughing, Kale stood. "And I'll go see about this mysterious new weave of a gateway."

Bardon winked at her. "Oh, you are going to like this new contrivance derived from two brilliant wizard minds."

11

The New Gateway

As soon as Kale entered the chamber where the wizards gathered, she heard talk of capturing sound. That didn't surprise her because Namee was a talented sound wizard. And according to Bardon, Regidor collaborated. Kale had long ago decided that Regidor had no distinctive trait to his wizardry, but his talent encompassed them all. She had no doubt he had developed skills that would put her light wizard ability in the shade.

She looked around the room, hoping this protégé of hers was present. It would be like him to make an unannounced appearance. The room held only four wizards—Cam, herself, and two others she knew slightly.

"Of what use will it be?" asked Sora, a plains wizard. She stood with her back to Kale, deeply involved in her debate with another wizard. "If he's captured sound, then does he let it go later?"

"Now, Sora," said Vog. "Namee is, above anything else, a sensible wizard. I'm sure there is some practical value to this new gateway."

Sora huffed. "Yes, but that fellow Regidor was involved in these shenanigans, and I've never trusted the meech wizard. Why isn't he off with his own kind?"

Vog looked over Sora's shoulder and nodded. "Welcome, Kale Allerion."

Sora jerked and turned abruptly. A quick smile took the place of a confused expression. "Oh, call me an ill-mannered wretch. I'm afraid my foot is in my mouth. I'm sorry, my dear. I don't know your meech friend. I'm just a prejudiced old fool."

"She is, at that," said Vog. "She's always rattling on about how things don't suit her. It's all those years with the wind whistling about her ears."

Sora gave Vog a disgusted look, but before she could toss back an answer, Namee entered the room.

"Good, we're all here. Take a seat, take a seat." He stood at the side of the room where an empty fireplace provided a backdrop. "Make sure you can see. Get comfortable. This will take a couple of hours."

Kale heard Sora mutter but didn't catch the words. She grinned as she deduced the wizard didn't care to be detained long enough to observe sound being captured.

"First, we'll have a demonstration with a gateway that has already been constructed."

The wizards glanced around the room.

Kale saw nothing unusual. She concentrated harder. Gateways usually could be detected without too much trouble, especially ones freshly made or frequently used. She found nothing. Observing the other wizards' expressions, she realized they were equally puzzled.

Namee chuckled. "I'm carrying it."

Kale leaned forward, her interest caught.

The sound wizard reached into his robe and pulled a round object from a hollow. The sphere had one flat side and was no bigger than his hand. He set it on the table.

"This isn't the gateway but a receptacle for containing the portal while traveling. The small portal is fragile." He touched the top of the sphere and two sides fell away. With thumb and forefinger he pulled out a shimmering cord circlet. The item stretched and opened to a circle two feet in diameter. "This is the gateway."

"It's too small to go through unless you're a kimen," observed Sora.

"You can't go through this gateway."

"Then what use is it?" asked Vog.

"You deposit something in it. That something travels to another gateway made like this one."

Sora sat forward. "Could you send a letter through? That would be useful."

Vog nodded. "A tool or an ingredient you want to share with someone."

"No, no, no." Namee looked pleased. "You've heard the rumors, haven't you? It's sound. Mostly. An image too if you construct the thing just right."

"But—" Sora stopped short in response to Namee's upheld hand.

"I'll show you."

Kale watched as Namee carefully maneuvered the strands of the gateway. At first she thought he was adding to the weave, but then she saw he was opening the portal. The air rippled within the circle. Rainbow colors shimmered across the surface from the center to the outside, then disappeared. Kale gasped as a face became clear. Regidor!

He blinked and smiled. "Hello, you probably think I am talking to you, but I am not actually speaking at this time. I inscribed this message before I departed from Namee's castle. My voice and image have been stored in the gateway. Namee and I will try another experiment soon, and you shall be the witnesses. Hopefully it will work, and Namee and I won't look like nincompoops."

The image disappeared. The center returned to an undisturbed calm. Kale could see right through to the blackened bricks in the fireplace wall.

"In answer to your first question," said Namee before anyone could speak, "yes, I can make that same image appear over and over should I want to."

He clapped his hands together and rubbed vigorously. The sound amplified with his enthusiasm.

Sora's face twisted at the harsh, grating noise. "Tone it down, Namee. You're going to have us all running from the room with our hands over our ears."

Namee ceased sliding one palm against the other. "Oh, sorry. Now look at this." He moved one strand making up the gateway and then another.

The center shifted and rippled. Kale no longer saw through to the other side. In a moment Regidor appeared again, wearing his black cape and the round-brimmed black hat he favored.

"If you are seeing this, the second part of our experimentation has been successful. Again, I am not really speaking to you. Instead, I have stored this message in the gateway, leaving it for Namee to unravel. At the time of this deposit into the portal, Gilda and I were in a small hostel in the city of Kory. I spoke to my gateway this morning and have since left on my journey. I can leave a message at any time in the gateway, directing it to another portal. It will remain until that gateway is opened."

Regidor shifted position to reveal the view behind him. Gilda pulled away a curtain over a floor-to-ceiling window, unveiling a large lake dotted with sailboats.

Regidor addressed the portal once more. "Kale, tell Bardon to hurry. Gilda and I are traveling north on the east side of the Morchain Mountains. This incredible weave has allowed you to know of my intentions, even though we are too far away to communicate. Namee will now show you a message left at another gateway. I hope you are enjoying our little device. Namee and I had a great deal of pleasure in putting theory into practice. Wizardry, what a superb occupation!"

Regidor flashed his toothy grin, and the image disappeared.

"Yes, yes, quite!" Namee rubbed his hands together again, remembering to keep the volume at a reasonable level. He fingered the weave of the gateway, and this time Kale understood a little bit more of what he was doing. He didn't open the portal clear to the other side but merely inched the interior wall backward, creating a shallow space in front. With her eyes trained on Namee's fingers as they worked at the edge of the weave, she missed the appearance of her mother and father in the portal's center.

"Morning, Kale." Her father's voice made her jump.

Framed by the circling weave, her mother and father peered out. Kale recognized her own sitting room in the background.

"Hello, Namee." Her father looked around as if he could peer right into the room. "Cam, Sora, and Vog. No, I can't see you. Namee told us who would be invited to this unveiling of the new gateway. Handy, wouldn't you say? Kale, this is how I can keep tabs on both my castle and yours. Hurry and construct your own portals, friends. We can communicate daily—hourly—if we want to."

The depiction faded.

Sora stood up. "Me first! I must have one of these."

Vog chortled. "You want to capture sound, Sora?"

"Sound, images, details, history, and even gossip." She put her hands on her hips and glared at Vog, who had bent over laughing. "Gossip can be very useful."

Lake Wizard Cam looked down at a puddle around his feet. "Oh, bother! I've sat too long." He stood up and shook droplets from his sodden slippers. "Only if you're discerning," he said, glancing up at the plains wizard. "Otherwise, gossip can be a trap." He raised his hand as Sora sputtered an objection. "And we all know our Sora is discerning."

Namee called them to gather around a table he had set up at the back of the room. The first steps of drawing dimensional threads from the air mimicked the beginning of building a conventional gateway. But Kale soon had to give all her attention to the intricacies of weaving a portal so much smaller than those she easily made. These new gateways also required the detail of layering from front to back.

Several hours later, she left a message for her parents in her own version of the gateway. Then Namee showed her how to fold it, and he gave her a cylinder in which to keep her new toy.

Wizard Cam lifted his sphere in the air and examined it. "We should give these gadgets a name. It's awkward saying, 'The new gateway invented by Namee and Regidor.' "

Sora held hers up. "The Nagidor? The Regimee? The Meedor?"

"I like the Meedor," said Vog.

"Humph," said Cam. "That's a rather silly name. I was thinking more on the lines of the message portal."

"How dull," said Sora.

"Descriptive," said Cam.

"We could shorten it to MP," suggested Vog.

"MP?" Sora scowled. "Mounted Patrol. Male Parrots. Magnificent Pottery. More Potatoes. I don't like MP at all. MP could be almost anything. Massive Pimples."

Namee took a step toward the plains wizard. "You've proved your point, Sora."

"Monkey Poop."

"Sora!"

She squinted her eyes and glared at Namee. "Mean People."

Namee sneered. "Missing Propriety."

"Silence," bellowed Cam. Water sprayed from his arms and shoulders, dousing the disputing wizards.

He glared at Sora as she opened her mouth. She pressed her lips together in a firm line.

"We shall call it, if Regidor and Namee concur, the talking gateway." He moved his pointing finger around the room as he scanned the faces of the other wizards. "Are there any objections?"

The four other wizards shook their heads.

Cam lowered his arm. "Fine. Let us take these talking gateways out into Amara and share them with our fellow wizards. I foresee they shall be a great convenience."

12

Buzz

The clamor of nine minor dragons in full alarm woke Kale with a start. She threw aside her blankets and jumped to her feet, grabbing her sword. The empty campground didn't give her a clue. When they left Namee's castle, Toopka had gone with Sir Dar to find Sittiponder. They'd meet up again farther along on the quest. Bardon was nowhere in sight, but he'd stirred up the fire in preparation for cooking. She glanced at the stream and surmised he'd gone fishing.

Greer and Celisse still grazed in the meadow some distance away. As she watched, they lifted their heads and stared off toward the mountains.

Kale tried to decipher the urgent calls from her dragons, but the noise would not separate into distinct words or images. The best she could envision from their thoughts was a swarm of big bees. She lowered her weapon. Her sword would be of little use swatting insects.

The minor dragons fell silent. Kale heard the drone of the approaching horde and gave the command, "Fly."

She dove under the blanket and made sure none of her skin was exposed. At first her covering muffled the sound of the swarm, but then she heard the buzz distinctly. The slam of what felt like a rock against her leg surprised her completely. Kale jerked but remembered in time to keep herself swathed in the blanket. She was pelted again and again. Some of the hits stung and some burned. She rolled away from the campsite, hoping to reach the stream.

Kale tuned in to the commotion outside her cloth shell and recognized that her dragons had engaged this enemy in battle. She heard Bardon's battle cry and knew he had joined them. The smell of smoke alerted her to another danger. She realized the strikes that felt like burns were exactly that. Bits of fire dotted the blanket. She quit rolling and struggled to free herself from the tangled cocoon.

A sudden calm enveloped her as her mind connected to her fighting husband. He swung his sword with practiced ease and batted small flying creatures from the air. She knew he had fought these black dragon-things before, and recently.

Dragon? These things are dragons? How—? Where—? Putting aside the questions that bombarded her, she tore away the last of the shroud and rose to her feet, expecting to fight beside her husband. The black dragons abandoned their squabbles with the other dragons and Bardon, changed focus in unison, and dive-bombed the Dragon Keeper.

Kale shrieked as a dozen flying missiles battered her arms, back, and legs. A score more of the creatures flew by, hurling tiny jets of flame at her hair. She held her arms straight in front of her, crossed them at the wrists, and lowered her hands so that her outstretched fingers pointed down to the earth. Quickly, she built an energy charge.

Protect your eyes! she warned, then flung her arms in a circle above her head.

Heeding the warning, Bardon and her fighting dragons turned their heads as soon as they saw what she was going to do. A blast of light issued from her body.

The black dragons had no forewarning. The explosion bounced the closest ones backward. They fell to the ground, lifeless. Others were tossed away, stunned. The remaining veered off and circled above.

Kale brought her arms down in front of her and again gathered energy. Some of the dazed dragons recovered quickly enough to join another onslaught. The black beasts gathered in the air, then plummeted downward. Kale's minor dragons flew above the cloud of attackers and spit. Their caustic saliva knocked several dozen out of their formation, and Crispin's spit fried the wings of others, causing them to drop out. But the majority of the black dragons continued their assault as if nothing had happened to their comrades.

Out of the corner of her eye, Kale saw Bardon pick up the blanket and race toward the center of the fight. She let off her blast of light right before he tackled her. She fell to the ground enveloped once again by a thick, scorched layer of cloth. Inexplicably, her husband slapped her head through the protection.

"What are you doing?" she screamed.

"Your hair is on fire."

The muffled reply startled her. She felt hot. What little air she could pull into her lungs stank. But burning?

"Let me out!" She thrashed against the shroud once more.

Bardon released his wife, then gently lifted her to her feet and took her to the stream. "Bend over."

She knelt beside the water, and he cupped his hand to splash the spots that still smoldered.

"Where are they?" she asked.

Bardon paused to look around. "Gone."

"What were they?"

"Tiny black fire dragons."

Kale sat back on her heels. Water streamed down her shoulders from her wet hair. She glared at what was their campsite, but now looked like a battleground.

The minor dragons lined up on a fallen log, all silently watching her. They didn't look any worse for the battle. Greer and Celisse stood nearby with char marks on their scales. She hadn't seen them join the fight. Her husband had red welts on his face and neck. He held one hand with the other as if to protect an injury. She felt the first prickles of pain on her scalp and her arms and legs. She'd been burned repeatedly.

"I'm a Dragon Keeper," she said. "There are horrid black dragons I know nothing about, and they attacked me. They left fighting all of you and attacked me." Her voice broke, and she shuddered. "What's going on? And why do you know about these beasts? Why haven't I been informed?"

Celisse stretched her long neck across the campsite and picked up the moonbeam cape from where Kale had used it as a pillow. She laid it in front of Kale. Gymn and Metta dove into the hollows and pulled out small brown jars of ointment.

Kale sniffed. "Let me see your hand."

"The stings on my face hurt more than my hand."

"I can see the welts. I want to see the hand." She took hold of his wrist and pulled. "Oh, Bardon, you got burned helping me."

He moved to sit closer to her as she relaxed into a more comfortable position. "It's nothing." His eyes examined her scalp. "Like I said, the stings are worse."

She grabbed a jar, read the label, and picked up another. After looking at several, she found the one she wanted. "Here, this will help."

She unscrewed the lid, plunged two fingers into the purplish goo, and began to rub salve over his palm. Bardon poked one big finger in the jar and dabbed the ointment on her head while she continued to work on his other hand. She moved to the welts on his neck as he pulled one of her legs onto his lap and smeared goo onto the small burns covering her calves. Gymn tsked and moved back and forth between them, aiding in their recovery with his special talent for healing.

She swiped her finger across Bardon's throat, then spread the ointment over the edges of the welt. "There. You're done."

"You aren't. Don't these burns hurt?"

"Quite a bit. And they seem to hurt more as time passes. I suppose I was too shocked at first to feel much. When you apply the ointment, it helps." She smiled at him. "I'm trying not to let my mind linger on the pain. Which reminds me." She frowned. "You have some explaining to do. So why don't you try talking your way out of not having told me about these nasty beasties. That should keep my thoughts occupied."

Bardon rubbed the salve onto her big toe where a black dragon had managed to sting her. "Did you kick one of the downed creatures? Their spines secrete poison even after they're dead."

"You can include how you know that interesting piece of information in your general explanation."

"I meant to tell you."

"Seems like you've used that opening line before."

"It's been less than twenty-four hours since I learned of them."

She didn't reply but stared at him, waiting.

"You have pretty toes."

"Nobody has pretty toes. Start talking."

"We had an encounter with these dragon creatures yesterday morning on the training fields."

"Maybe you should just remember it, and I'll peek in on your thoughts."

"Right."

He started with Tieto grumbling and Mikkai directing him through the castle to join the others. Kale followed his memories all the way to the five men sitting around a table with various breakfast treats spread before them.

"While we ate," said Bardon, "a messenger came to tell us that Namee wanted the incident to be kept quiet so as not to alarm his other guests. When you arrived, I thought to tell you but decided to wait until we were alone. Then, I forgot."

He reached for her arm and put the soothing salve on the few spots there.

Kale sighed. "Well, I believe you. It's just like you to forget you had something to tell me." She pulled away from him, sat up straighter, clamped her fists, and put them in her lap. "Bardon, it's one thing to forget to tell me you invited someone to dinner, or you are scheduled to go to council, or someone's wife sent me a message through you. But this...this..."

"I know. All I can say is that I would have remembered, eventually. We were busy from the time we parted from breakfast to the time we went down to the dragon field and left the castle. I thought of telling you on several occasions during the day, but you weren't available. Once we were in the air, it never crossed my mind again until I heard that horrible drone while I pulled in a fish. Then it was too late."

She rested her cheek against his shoulder for a moment. Dibl did a flip on the log and sidestepped toward the end.

Kale sat up. "Oh, no you don't. You stay right there." She frowned at the minor dragons still sitting on the fallen tree trunk, lined up like wooden ducks to be knocked over at the fair. All but Gymn, who aided in administering healing.

"What about you?" Kale pointed a finger at the eight. "Why didn't you tell me? If Mikkai, Tieto, and Filia knew, then the rest of you knew. You can't keep a secret among you. And I am shocked that you would keep a secret from me. Shocked!"

The dragons hung their heads. Greer and Celisse moved as if they had decided it was time to go back to their grazing.

Kale's finger swung around to point at them. "Don't you leave. You knew too, didn't you?"

Bardon took hold of the finger and brought her arm around so he could smear it with purple goo.

"Since when," continued Kale, "do dragons keep secrets from their Dragon Keeper? Am I not trustworthy?" She glowered fiercely. "Am I such an ogre that I can't be confided in?"

Her focus fell on Artross, and she listened. "So Mikkai was so overwhelmed by his experience of being attacked by 'unheard of' dragons that he couldn't speak of it. Traumatized? Humph."

Artross hopped down from the log and walked slowly toward her. Kale continued to voice his thoughts. "All the dragons were appalled that one of your species could be so vile, more like insects than noble dragons.

"Tieto and Filia heard the edict from Namee not to disturb the other guests with the news of the unusual attack. So?"

Artross came to a stop in front of her, placed his foreleg on her knee, and looked up with beseeching eyes. Kale tightened her lips and hardened her heart. At last she released the tension, accepting the explanation from the mottled white dragon.

"So you took that as an excuse not to discuss and not to even think of those—oh, my, Artross. That is not a nice word."

The white dragon scowled. "And when Bardon didn't tell me, you all assumed he thought I shouldn't know of this event"—she hesitated—"because I'd been sick at the ball."

Kale looked at Bardon.

He shrugged. "This is their excuse, not mine."

She gazed down at the dragon and then swept her glance over the others on the log. "I wasn't sick at the ball. I had an upset stomach from the excitement and the rich food. I was not sick!"

The minor dragons nodded their colorful heads and then shuffled off, apparently through with receiving her lecture. Pat pounced on a cricket that Kale had seen the chubby brown dragon eying while he waited for her to finish her tirade. Metta flew to a tree limb and sang with the local birds. Celisse and Greer departed as well.

"Well," Kale said as she released a gust of air.

Bardon took the lid to the jar from where it lay in her lap. "Well, indeed." He screwed on the lid and handed the jar to her. "You're done."

"I am?"

"Yes."

"What are we going to do about all this?"

"I would appreciate it if you would begin by forgiving me for being a dolt."

She grinned and placed her hand on his cheek. The welt had lost some of its flame already. "I do."

"Then you must forgive the dragons for trying to protect you."

She glanced around at her crew, who did not look at all repentant but were busy having fun in their quiet dragon way. "Yes, they meant well."

"And then we go on with our quest. Paladin has given us a charge to find out as much as we can whenever we encounter the Followers."

"And you saw Paladin, when?"

Bardon rolled his eyes and slapped his head in a mock gesture of chagrin. "It was so difficult keeping the ball a surprise, I ended up guarding every thought. I was so worried about spoiling your pleasure in the gala event, I kept my lips buttoned on any number of issues."

Kale sighed. "I think I'm already tired of this adventuring. It does strange things to my husband's honesty."

"We've only just begun."

She waved a dismissive hand at the tent and disheveled camp. "But I enjoy sleeping behind four walls with a roof overhead and the windows closed."

"That can be arranged, lady of mine."

13

A Poor Man's Home

After a day of travel, Bardon and Kale landed in a field near a small settlement on the Hierson River. They unsaddled Greer and Celisse, tucked the gear into a thicket, and walked into town.

Bardon pulled Kale's arm through his and kept her close. Walking right beside him, she was less likely to notice his wincing. The long ride had stiffened his joints.

People lingered in the streets, even at the dinner hour. Small clusters of adults talked earnestly while youngsters darted in and around the crowd.

"Do you think today's market day?" asked Kale.

"There do seem to be a lot of people for such a small village."

"There's the inn." Kale pointed across the street.

Pain shot through Bardon's thighs as he took the two steps down from the wooden sidewalk to the street. He grabbed the wrought-iron handrail to keep from falling.

So much for not telling Kale he hurt. "May I borrow Gymn?"

The green dragon hopped from her shoulder to his without waiting for her reply.

"The stakes?" Kale whispered.

Bardon nodded once. "I believe the poison from the black dragons set it off again. I was feeling fine."

"We'll get you in a comfortable bed for the night. Maybe tomorrow you'll feel better."

Bardon didn't bother to answer but gritted his teeth as they mounted three steps and entered the inn.

Round tables seating four to six customers apiece crowded the room. Air swept in the open windows in gusts that sent the red curtains fluttering.

"Kale, which one of these people is the proprietor?"

Kale looked around the room and then discreetly pointed. "That tumanhofer."

They approached the innkeeper, who was giving three young servants their orders. The gentleman clapped his hands, and the children scattered.

He turned to Bardon and Kale. "May I help you?"

"A room for the night?" asked Bardon.

"I can barely serve you supper. A bed is out of the question. But there's a few folks in town in the habit of renting a room during market days."

Kale looked quickly around. "Is that what all this commotion is about? These men don't look like farmers."

The tumanhofer sneered. "This lot? No, they're not farmers. They call themselves Followers, and they cause a lot of trouble."

"Trouble?" asked Bardon.

"Oh, I don't mean they drink and carouse. They're demanding. They want their food fixed just so, and my wife is accustomed to fixing meals that make your mouth water as soon as you get your first whiff of what's in the pot. But no, they don't like it. They want slop I'd throw to the pigs.

"They fuss over the rooms not being clean. My rooms are clean. But they want everything taken out but the beds and fresh linens brought up as if we hadn't changed the sheets since the last customer.

"And they sit around and whisper. That drives me batty. They hush when I come near as if I wanted to know what their confounded secrets are. And they look down on me and my family. I'd rather have you in my rooms, but I've already filled up."

Bardon studied the groups of mariones and o'rants. "Do they come here often?"

"Once a month. It's too often, but I can't say I don't like their coins. I fill up my coffers and wouldn't have to rent a room any day of the time in between if I didn't want to. But these Followers are trouble, and it's good to have regular folk stay a night or two after I've had my fill of this lot."

He caught a passing child by the back of his collar. "Jahannasamran, take these people to the Buckners or the Peeps first. Take 'em around till you find them a room, then hurry back."

"Yes, Da." Jahannasamran bobbed a bow to his father and then to Bardon and Kale. "If you'll follow me."

"Don't use that word 'follow,' son," the innkeeper grumbled under his breath.

The boy gave him a cheeky grin and trotted to the door with Kale and Bardon behind him. He led them to the outskirts of town on the opposite side of where they had left Celisse and Greer.

The second house admitted them, and the marione housewife gave Jahannasamran two daggarts and a coin for his trouble.

"Come in. Sit down. My name's Elma, and my husband is Garmey, but he's off learning from the visitors."

Kale removed her cape and hung it on a peg. The dragons crept out of their pocket-dens and roosted on shelves, the mantel over the hearth, and sturdy furniture. Bardon and Kale took the wooden seats Elma indicated at her table. The common room held the kitchen, dining area, and a gathering of soft chairs around a fireplace. The home matched Elma's friendly smile.

Elma tiptoed closer to the big chair where Dibl perched. "Aren't you a pretty one?"

Dibl flipped backward, landing on his feet again on the same spot. Giggling rippled from under the kitchen table.

"Are they dangerous?" asked the marione housewife.

"The children under the table?" Kale frowned. "No, I don't think so."

A snort of laughter countered a plaintive inquiry. "Does she mean us?"

A voice piped up. "Can we have one?"

"Your da wouldn't like it, though they do look pretty sitting around. And right at home, not like wild creatures." Elma faced her guests. "Did you have your evening meal yet?" she asked. At Kale's shake of the head, she went on. "I'm not surprised. Your dragons would have put off the inn's guests. Better you eat with us, anyway. These are my young ones, Tallidah and Zepzep."

Two golden-haired young boys peeked out from under the tablecloth. The older crawled out, stood, and presented a bow to both Kale and Bardon.

"My name is Tallidah," he said. "I'm older. Zepzep, get up. Bow. Say your name."

The younger child scooted to his brother's side and hoisted his bottom in the air. Tallidah took his arm and helped him stand. The bow was mostly done with Zepzep's head. "Chipchip," he pronounced with a grin.

Tallidah shook his head, not hiding his disgust. "He's two. I'm four. May we play with your dragons?"

"Will you be gentle?" asked Kale.

They nodded solemnly.

"Then ask your mother if she will permit it."

Elma beamed at her sons and then looked skeptically at the minor dragons. "They don't bite?" she asked.

Kale shook her head. "Not polite little boys."

"Well, that does it, then. My boys don't fit the bill."

"Ma!" The little ones danced on their toes.

"We'll be good," promised Tallidah.

Elma sighed and gave her consent. Bardon watched Kale introduce the dragons as the mother put a meal on the table. His wife sat on the floor and enjoyed the antics of the boys as well as her dragons. He and Kale needed more children in their home. Some of their own would please him fine.

Elma's boys came reluctantly to the table, not willing to leave their new friends just to eat. Kale laughed and lifted each one into their seats. "You must let the dragons rest. Then they'll play with you before bedtime. While you're asleep, the dragons will investigate all your nooks and crannies and eat the bugs that bother your mother."

Elma's meal steamed in the bowls she set on the table. Bardon ate slowly, savoring the wonderful tastes. The broth slid down his throat and warmed him. His jaws began to ache with the chore of chewing the crusty bread, so he concentrated on the tender jimmin chicken and tasty, buttered vegetables. He listened to the lively conversation between the women and children and felt his muscles relaxing. Gymn hadn't left his neck and shoulders since he'd settled on his perch. The healing dragon helped, but not enough.

The back door swung open, and the man of the house entered.

Elma introduced him. "My husband, Garmey." Elma beamed as she nodded toward their guests. "This is Sir Bardon, Garmey, and his wife, Lady Kale."

Bardon stood to shake hands with his host. Garmey eagerly welcomed him to his home. But his demeanor shifted when he turned to the rest of the table. He sent the children to their room along with the dragons, frowned at Gymn, and sat at the head of the table. From that moment on, Elma spoke little and quickly saw to her husband's needs. She filled his plate and cup whenever he raised a finger. Obviously, a signal had been established in their household.

Excited about the meetings that had been held for two days in his village, their host monopolized the conversation.

"I've been accepted to the next level of the Followers," Garmey told them. "I've got a lot to learn. I know that, but they're willing to teach me." He looked at Bardon. "Do you know the things they teach?"

"I am Paladin's knight, sir. I have studied the Tomes all my life."

"Yes, but they's telling me even those at The Hall would benefit from instruction. And I'm going to get all this learning for free without going off and leaving my farm. Then, of course, when I prove myself, when I'm done, they have prepared a place for me to go. A place where I'd be important to the group."

Bardon frowned and chose his words carefully. "A knight knows that his education is never completed. He studies wherever Wulder places him."

Kale put her knife and fork down. "This is true of anyone who wishes to know Wulder and follow His ways."

Garmey nodded in agreement with Bardon but totally ignored Kale's words.

"It's an honor to have you here," he continued with his eyes on Bardon. "The Followers say to deal only with those who honor Paladin, and that brings honor to you. I mean me. I'm going to elevate myself." The marione tapped his chest. "I have aligned myself with the Followers. They will lead me in the path of righteousness." He spoke the last words as if he had memorized them. " 'Course, I can't do it on my own. I never was much good at book-learning, but the Followers are going to help me better myself. Elevate myself."

Kale tilted her head. "If the Followers promote an understanding of Wulder, then the natural outcome of such knowledge is a whole host of virtues."

Again, it was as if she had not spoken.

Garmey offered Bardon more tea. "I've always had a yearning to be a knight, to do big things, go places, and have people look at me like I was something special. Not just a farmer."

Squeals of laughter pierced the calm. The marione looked annoyed and glanced at his wife. Elma rose from the table and touched Kale's arm. "Would you like to help me put the children to bed?"

"Oh yes." She rose eagerly.

Elma picked up the two serving bowls and carried them to the kitchen counter. Kale gathered a handful of cutlery and placed them beside the other dishes to be washed.

As Elma returned to clear more off the table, a burst of gaiety punctuated by a loud cry of "Do it again!" met their ears.

Garmey spoke coldly. "Elma, the boys."

Bardon watched the flicker of hurt in young Elma's eyes, followed by cold anger. She left the disorder and marched out of the room. Kale cast Bardon a puzzled look and followed.

Garmey took another swig of drink and belched loudly. Bardon wondered if he intended for the vulgar sound to follow his wife to the other room.

The temperature in the room stifled Bardon's ability to breathe. The air seemed heavy with the odors that an hour ago had been a pleasant meal.

Bardon stood abruptly. "Come with me, Garmey."

He turned on his heel and left the welcoming home and strode out into the sultry air of a late summer night. Clouds covered the stars, but sheet lightning played high in the sky as if skipping from one matted covering to another.

The knight put his arms behind him, folding them over one another at his waist. Wincing at the stiffness in his shoulders, Bardon relaxed the pull on his sore muscles and waited. He listened with keen ears as the young husband came out behind him.

"You wanted me, sir?" Garmey closed the distance between them with quick steps. "Would you like a smoke? I've 'bacco and pipe."

"Thank you, but I don't smoke." Bardon's quiet voice competed with a platoon of frogs in a nearby pond.

"You're displeased with me in some way." Garmey swallowed and lowered his voice. "I'm a country man, sir. We've never had a knight and his lady in our home before. You won't give a negative report to the Followers, will you?"

"I have nothing to do with these Followers."

Garmey didn't seem to hear him. "Perhaps my wife's cooking wasn't good enough."

"Your wife's dinner was delicious and filling. I appreciate her efforts to make us feel welcome."

"Then?" At a loss for words, Garmey looked down at the ground.

"It is the way you treat your wife that offends me."

Garmey's head jerked up. "Elma? Treat Elma? She's used to our ways. She gets treated right by me. She don't expect nothing else."

Bardon remained silent.

Garmey swallowed again, his Adam's apple bobbing on his thick neck. "Whatcha mean? I didn't hit her, didn't make fun of her food, and I didn't holler at her when the boys made a ruckus in the middle of our meal."

Bardon studied the shorter man. His earnest expression eased the condemnation out of Bardon's heart. The marione truly wanted to better his lot in life. And the way to do that was to implement the principles into his daily life. "You told me you always wanted to be a knight."

He stood straighter. "Yes sir. I know I'd need a lot of training with the sword, and they'd probably want me to learn to read and write, but I could do that. I don't want to, but I'd do it. I'm pretty smart in other ways, and it might just spill over into book-learning."

"The first thing you would have to do is learn to treat your wife like a lady."

"What's that got to do with anything?" Garmey snorted. "Besides, Elma ain't no lady."

"She's your wife?"

"Well, yeah."

"Then she's your lady. You can't elevate yourself without first elevating her."

"She don't expect no special treatment."

"That's very sad, my friend." Bardon walked away, headed for the companionship of Greer and Celisse in the faraway field.

"Wait!" Garmey called after him and scurried to catch up. "I don't get it. What did I do?"

Bardon stopped to look at the man's anxious face. "Many things, little things, but they add up. Let's point to just one as an example."

Garmey nodded, waiting for Bardon's next words with a pained expression on his face.

"You belched."

Garmey blinked, and a slow grin slid across his face. He ducked his head. "Is that all?" He pushed dirt around with the scuffed toe of his boot. "Elma's heard belching all her life."

"Men, when they are enjoying each other's company without the ladies around, often use a cruder set of manners."

Garmey snorted. "I reckon I don't got any manners of any kind. At least that's what my ma always said."

Bardon put his hand on the farmer's shoulder and waited until he looked up. The sober expression in the knight's face must have made the young man realize Bardon's serious attitude. Garmey wiped the grin off his face.

"Garmey, you listened and learned from your father as he talked about farming. I can tell you were a good student by the condition of your fields."

The farmer's gaze swept the surrounding land, and he nodded with pride.

"Listen to what I say about this manners issue. When you use coarse manners in front of your wife, you are saying she is just one of the field hands, one of your buddies down at the tavern, not someone to whom you've pledged your life and love. You treat her with disrespect. Because you esteem her so lightly, why should anyone else honor her or offer her common courtesy?"

Garmey's mouth dropped open, and he stared at Bardon.

Bardon clapped the young man on the shoulder. "Always remember you set the tone in your house. The way you treat those around you will be observed by others, especially your sons. They will know that this is your standard. You set it. You must insist that, in your household, respect is shown to your family members."

Bardon knew he had a bigger stone in this man's field to cast aside than bad manners. "You are in charge of your home, not the Followers."

"You want me to quit the Followers, just when I got to the first level? I'm a seeker, and they say I'm quick. I'll be worthy of the journey before long."

"I've been to their city of Paladise."

Garmey gasped. "That's the name? No one knows the name unless they're several levels up."

"I've been there, Garmey, and it isn't a place you want to go. What you have in these fields, in your home, in your village, are gifts from Wulder. The Followers offer a sham of the real thing. They desire to have power over you.

"That's what these Followers want. They want power. They aren't here to reveal Wulder's power, but to assert their own. Remember this, if someone says they are teaching you to follow Wulder, but also teaching that your worth is only measurable by what you give to them, they are not from Wulder. They only serve themselves."

Garmey put his hands on his head. "I gotta think."

"That's a good idea. While you are thinking, can you stay away from the Followers?"

Garmey frowned.

"Will you stay away from the Followers? Just while you're sorting this out."

"Sure." Garmey dropped his hands to his sides. "Sure, I can do that."

14

Messages

Early the next morning, Kale sat on the floor in the corner of the bedroom. She pulled the talking gateway out of its container and worked with nimble fingers to configure the weave.

The minor dragons chittered quietly as they went about their morning business. Gymn, half-awake, didn't leave his position on Bardon's back as the knight still slept. Several dragons flew in and out of the open window, looking for breakfast or just enjoying being out and about. Pat had risen early. With his stomach full, he stretched out on the windowsill, soaking up the sun.

Kale placed the last thread of the gateway in its proper place and leaned back. Her first message was from her father. He reported all was well in the Midway Castle. Dibl and Metta flew to perch on Kale's shoulders and chirred amazement at the small picture in the portal. Kale's father looked robust, and in the background, her mother strolled back and forth, doing something. Distracted by her mother's activity, Kale almost lost the thread of her father's message.

"What's Mother doing?" she said aloud as if the image in the gateway would hear and respond.

"Oh!" She looked up quickly, hoping Bardon was still sleeping.

He grinned at her from the bed. "I knew you'd like that gateway."

She got up, leaving her father's communication. The picture continued to move, and the uninterrupted words poured into the bedchamber. Gymn left his post and flew through the window, undoubtedly hungry.

Grimacing, Bardon rolled to his side and scooted over to allow her to sit on the edge of the bed.

She sat down gently. "How are you feeling?"

"It's not as bad as it could be." He rearranged the pillow for better support of his neck. "We should ask your father if he knows anything about the black dragons. I'm wondering if they came from the north."

"You said the legend of the monster dragon comes from the Northern Reach."

"Legend, fable, myth. Those weren't fairy tales that attacked my wife."

Kale picked up his hand and began the slow, methodical massage that sometimes eased his pain.

He sighed and relaxed into the mattress. With his eyes closed, he thought out loud about the troubling circumstances they'd uncovered. "Ask him about the Followers, too. From what Sir Dar and the others said, the strongest concentration of these people is in central Amara, and their influence is spreading outward toward the coasts. Your father will know if there are any Followers in his region of the Northern Reach."

"Mmm." Kale worked her fingers over and around his wrist joint. The message from her father ended, and after a few seconds' delay, it began again.

Bardon spoke slowly. "Regidor should have left us a message by now, as well. We should meet up with him and all the others this afternoon. He was to designate a location." He opened his eyes. "This feels good but is wasting time."

"Let me hear what father said at the end of his message, and then I'll change the weave to tell us if Regidor has used the device."

Her father rambled on about various aspects of the dragons she had entrusted to him. None of the news troubled her. In fact, she felt great relief and reassurance as he related each detail of normal daily routine.

By the time she'd reached Bardon's shoulder, the message ran out.

He opened his eyes again and winked at her. "Can I persuade you to get Regidor's message? Please?"

She moved to gather up the talking gateway, and as she suspected, Bardon sat up on the side of the bed.

Kale tsked at him. "You should let me do the other side."

"I'm better. I want to see Regidor."

She set the gateway on the bedside table. "I can't get over the fact that I can move this thing from place to place and it doesn't unravel." She adjusted a strand. "I'm going to leave a message for Father first, since that gateway is already open." She fine-tuned the threads and left a message asking if he knew anything about the Followers and the black dragons. She described both in detail, and when she finished, she couldn't help but compare them as equal threats to the peace of Amara.

Bardon didn't comment on her intuitive leap of understanding. Instead, he urged her again to pick up Regidor's message. She glanced his way and saw lines of fatigue around his mouth. Perhaps on this journey they would find something to keep the stakes at bay.

Her husband dressed as she worked on the weave.

"Hello," Regidor's voice boomed into the room, startling Kale. "I'm leaving the same message to everyone."

His unusual green eyes with long narrow pupils looked steadily out of the portal.

"He looks like he can see us." Kale touched the woven frame. "This is the oddest contraption."

"Today, Gilda and I will be at Danns Crossing at the fork of the North and South Hierson. If you don't join us there, I will leave another message as to where we propose to stop tomorrow evening. Danns Crossing is the only place we will linger, though. Gilda is anxious to reach the north country."

Bardon kissed the top of Kale's head. "I'm going out to talk to Garmey."

"I heard him leave the house earlier."

"He'll be in the barn or in the fields. He's a good farmer."

As Bardon left the room, the dragons slipped out in search of the children. They were greeted with squeals of delight. Bardon reached back to close the door. "I don't think the boys are that happy to see me."

"At their age, would you have wanted to play with a stuffy old knight or playful dragons of almost every color?"

Bardon tilted his head. "Probably I would have wanted to follow the knight, not expecting him to play with me. In fact, I think I did follow the knights around The Hall, but I was a tad older than these sprites." He smiled at her. "Can you be ready to go by the time I get back?"

"After I see you eat breakfast, yes."

"Bossy woman." He closed the door.

Kale lost no time changing into the riding habit she most often wore while traveling. She straightened the covers on the bed, suspecting Elma would wash the linens before someone else rented the room. She picked up the things she had used the night before and tucked them into the hollows of her cape before joining her hostess in the common room.

Dibl had instigated a game of hide-and-seek with the boys. The dragons hid, and just as the boys were about to discover a dragon, the little trickster would jump out and scare the seeker. Tallidah rolled on the floor, laughing and declaring at the same time that the dragons didn't play fair.

"I have something for you," said Elma, wiping her hands on her apron and going to a cabinet. She pulled out a short, squat pot made of fired clay. "It's ointment for your husband's stakes. He has 'em, don't he?"

Kale nodded and took the medicine.

"I thought so. My grandda had 'em. This is the only thing that helped." She reached in her pocket and drew out a worn piece of paper. "Here's the recipe written in my own grandma's hand."

"I have paper." Kale took the brown-edged sheet and sat at the table. "I'll copy it."

"I've got it learned by heart. I don't use the words anymore."

"But you treasure it because of your grandma. I'll write it down, and that way I can ask you questions if I don't understand something."

"You and your husband are so nice. Why is that?"

Kale looked up from her attempt to decipher the faded handwriting. She smiled. "I was just thinking how nice you are to give me this. I think it feels good to offer kindness and have it accepted. We get in the habit of feeling good like that and don't want to stop."

A shadow crossed Elma's face, and she glanced out the window. "Some people don't accept a word of blessing or an act of charity."

"No." Kale wrinkled her brow. "But that's when persistence pays off. All those times when whoever didn't count your offerings as worthy"—she tapped the tabletop with a finger for emphasis—"I think

Wulder counted it three times. Once for doing it, once for not reacting with bitterness, and once for determining to repeat the kindness. You shouldn't be forced by someone else to give up what gives your heart pleasure and Wulder's heart pleasure too."

Elma grinned at her. "Phew! That was quite a mouthful. Is it in those principles from the Tomes that Garmey has been talking about?"

"Yes. Do you read the Tomes?" Kale pulled paper and pen from her cape and began to write out the instructions for the ointment.

"No, no. Garmey don't much like it that I can read, and he can't. He says the Followers are going to teach him to read. For the time being, they tell him a principle and he learns it. And they tell him what it means and he learns that, too."

"And then he teaches it to you and the boys?"

"Oh no. We aren't to learn 'em until he gets up to a higher level. Then we can join him on the path to righteousness."

Kale's hand stilled over the page. "Elma, that isn't right."

"Garmey says it is, and he's the one's been going to the meetings." She put her hands on her hips and looked askance at Kale.

"Elma, Bardon doesn't believe these Followers are following Paladin's instructions."

The marione snorted. "They wouldn't be called Followers if they weren't following."

"That's true, but who are they following?"

"Paladin, of course."

"Not if Paladin doesn't recognize them."

Elma pulled out a chair and sat across the table from Kale. "What do you mean?"

"Suppose many years from now, you wake up in the morning and your husband is away on a trip, but your two sons and a stranger are sitting at the table waiting for the morning meal."

Elma leaned her arms on the table and watched Kale as if she expected a trick from her guest. "So?"

"So the three younger men all call you 'Ma' and all say they're your sons."

"That don't make it so. Only Tallidah and Zepzep are my sons."

"You can tell by looking at them that the third one is not your son?"

"Of course I can. I'm not dimwitted."

"Now a visitor comes by." Kale nodded to the door as if someone had knocked. "He comes in, and the three young men all say they're your sons. And he believes them. He says the stranger looks like one of the family. He's in your house, sitting at your table, and eating your food."

"I'd tell him it ain't so. Only Tallidah and Zepzep are mine."

"Paladin has looked at this group of Followers and has said they are not his. They look like the teachers he sent out, and most of the time, they sound like his teachers. But they are not."

Elma gasped. Again she looked out the window, and her focus seemed to be on someone other than those in the house.

"What's Paladin going to do? Is he going to arrest them? Will they be killed?"

"I don't think those who have been misled will have vengeance rained down upon them. But those who mislead them will suffer as they should."

"My Garmey?" Tears threatened to pool up and run over the young wife's cheeks. "He just wants to better himself. Elevate himself is what he says."

"Could you teach him to read?"

"I've been afraid to suggest it."

"Why don't you teach Tallidah and have Garmey help? He could help play the games we do when we learn our letters."

"He could. It's been a long time. He used to play with the boys, but…" She sighed. "So many meetings."

Elma looked down at her hands and realized she'd picked up the jar of ointment. She held it up. "Just use a little of this on the back of your husband's neck, right where the backbone goes into the skull. If you get it worked into just the right spot, it treats the whole body. Remember, it's not the head that's in trouble. It's where the head connects to the body. Ya gotta be careful to keep that spot healthy."

15

A Meeting in the Woods

Bardon walked beside Kale, trying to evaluate the effects of Elma's ointment. The minor dragons flew about, happy to be going someplace. They chittered incessantly. Bardon tuned out their chatter that he understood all too well with his wife there acting as a conduit.

The morning sun warmed his neck. Kale had rubbed a small circle of sticky substance from Elma's pot into the base of his hairline. No, it couldn't be the sun. The ointment itself must radiate the heat. His neck muscles on both sides felt looser. He rotated his shoulders, bent his elbows, and wiggled his fingers. Each movement cost him a modicum of pain. But the discomfort was nothing like the wretched misery when he moved yesterday, nor like the throbbing around his joints when he remained still.

Kale looked over her shoulder. Bardon did the same and almost cheered that he did so with only a twinge of soreness.

They could no longer see the home of Garmey and Elma. He would have liked to thank the marione housewife once again.

"I hate to leave them," said Kale. "I think they both wanted to learn more about Wulder."

"Since the evil forces withdrew and Paladin made his decree that the populace was to be given the opportunity to learn, many have felt the necessity to return to the beliefs of their ancestors."

"In other words, given the chance, folks want to know."

"Right."

Kale laughed. "Sometimes you still sound like the lehman I met at the hall, using thirty words to say the same thing that could be said in ten."

"And do you know, even then I recognized that my stiff wordiness was contrary to principles?"

"You did?"

"Yes, but I couldn't help myself. I just had to sound important. Young Garmey reminds me of myself in those days."

Kale chuffed, her suppressed snicker blowing softly out her nose. "I don't see any resemblance."

Bardon smiled and walked on.

"Fire." Kale stopped. Her head swiveled as she searched the grass beside the road. "There."

A tendril of smoke curled out of a tangle of weeds. She and Bardon raced to the small fire. Bardon stomped it out while Kale picked up Crispin.

"It's all right. I know you didn't mean to." Her tone of voice changed. "Dibl, come here."

The yellow and orange dragon peeked around the trunk of a tree and then flew to Kale and perched on her shoulder.

"You jumped out and scared him. And when Crispin is startled, he breathes in deep and breathes out fire. Had you, perchance, forgotten this trivial fact?"

A mournful whine emanated from Dibl's throat as he looked down at the red dragon cradled in Kale's arms.

"Saying you're sorry does not help much. Look at the dry grass around here. There could have been a serious brush fire."

"The fire's out," said Bardon. He took Kale's arm and guided her back to the road. "We need to keep moving."

Kale gasped. Bardon's head swung around to see if the fire had somehow rekindled.

"You're better. You're not stiff."

Bardon took a moment to feel his body, really feel it. The breeze pushed his hair away from his face, and that was the strongest sensation among several, the boots on his feet, the rough cloth of his pants, and the softer material of his shirt.

He grabbed Kale, and the two dragons fluttered into the air with a squeal as he scooped her up in a hug and whirled her around.

Laughing, she buried her face in his neck. When he allowed her feet to touch the ground again, she gasped. "Do you think it's Elma's ointment?"

"Maybe." He kissed her soundly. "Race you to Greer and Celisse."

He took off running with Kale hollering, "Wait. Give me a head start."

"No, lady of mine," he yelled back. "Catch me if you can."

The blue water of a lazy river twisted like a ribbon toward the foothills of the northern Morchain Mountain range. Bardon searched the landscape for the point where two rivers came together to make the larger Hierson. Anticipation over this quest surged once more.

He swatted at a tiny feeling of foreboding, not letting it take hold. They'd been in the air for hours, and not a twinge of discomfort had returned. Even Greer felt the difference and kept commenting on how good it was to have a young rider on his back instead of the old man he'd been lugging around.

As they flew over a steeper and longer foothill, Bardon spied the Y made by the northern and southern Hiersons.

He waved to Kale and pointed.

"Finally!" Her voice entered his thoughts. *"I'm sick and tired of this saddle."*

I'm not!

"I'm glad you're feeling so well, but do you have to rub it in? I never could ride as long as you without feeling it in every bone of my body."

At least dragons don't bounce one around like those earth-bound horses. And dragons have better manners. And they know what you're thinking without having to jerk on reins or dig in your heels.

"I know, I know, I know. Horses are not your favorite mode of transportation."

They landed in a clearing between the two rivers and upstream from the crossing. A huge, old building stood on stilts driven into the dry land. In the spring and early summer, the snowmelt flooded the tributaries.

"Looks like we're the first ones here." Bardon walked over to Celisse and caught Kale as she slid down the dragon's side.

"Someone lives here, right?" asked Kale.

"Yes, a family of urohms, the Danns. That's why it's called Danns Crossing."

"Something doesn't feel right, Bardon."

"I feel it, too, or I feel you feeling it."

"This is no time to be funny." Her clothes changed into a costume that would not hinder her movements in a fight. She tinted the form-fitting fabric green and brown.

"Not pink?" Bardon drew his weapon. The blade whispered against the leather of the sheath.

"Not the occasion for pink. Forest colors seem appropriate."

The way she held her hand told him her sword was drawn. "Tell me what you sense."

"There are no urohms in that building. The occupants are bison-becks. Marauders. Five of them. There are more, six more, but they are out scavenging the countryside.

"Bisonbecks without an army. Since the disbandment of Cropper's and Stox's military forces, these men have been at loose ends."

"I thought they sailed overseas looking for mercenary work."

"Many did. And grawligs took themselves into the upper elevations of the mountains rather than mingle with the high races. But some of the bisonbecks who remained weren't really suited to any kind of work, so they became outlaws."

"You're right, Bardon. I have had my head in dragon nurseries for too long."

Bardon felt her presence. The sense of her physical being beside him shifted into the odd bond they had. Part of her had melded with him, and the awareness of her thoughts, emotions, and even her intentions permeated his being. She started to ask him what the plan was and then smiled. She knew.

She sent the minor dragons ahead to cause a distraction. Bardon led Kale to a clump of bushes only a few yards from the steps that rose to the front door of the Danns' house. Loud voices boomed through opened windows. Bardon removed a pouch from his belt and shook the small weapons into his hand, then nodded to Kale. She sent the dragons to do their job.

Nine minor dragons converged upon the house from four directions. They flew into the building through the windows and out the other side. Inside they pelted the marauders with their caustic spit. The bisonbecks exploded in curses. The dragons repeated the maneuver twice, then perched safely in nearby trees.

A loud whack propelled the door open. It swung full force to strike the wall. With shouts of outrage, the five ex-warriors, splattered with splotches of colorful saliva, charged out. Their boots thundered on the old wooden steps.

"Where are they?" roared one, wiping his eyes and swearing with each swipe.

"In the trees," said a second, whose face had not been hit.

"Get them," ordered the first.

The dragons took flight and led the bisonbecks into the woods. Kale and Bardon followed. As soon as the marauders separated, following different dragons, Kale and Bardon chose one to stalk and capture.

Without words, they knew where to position themselves in relation to the bisonbeck's movements. When the circumstances presented a good target, Bardon jumped into plain sight and threw three darts. As the marauder reacted to the attack, Kale came in from behind, threw a net over him, and tightened the binding so he could not escape. Bardon rushed forward and helped her secure her catch to a nearby tree.

Bardon cinched the last knot. "He looks like he's putting up quite a fuss."

The captured bisonbeck fought against his bindings, but even the noisy growls and threats he made did not escape Kale's web.

Kale began forming another net, pulling materials from the hollow in her cape.

The bisonbeck's eyes grew wide as he watched her, and his lips quit moving.

"Can he hear me?" asked Bardon.

"Oh yes."

Bardon bowed to the prisoner. "May I introduce Lady Kale Allerion? I am Sir Bardon."

The captive renewed his squirming. His eyes bulged, and his mouth opened and closed rapidly.

Bardon shook his head. "There's no use in screaming. No one could hear you unless they were inside the web with you."

The man glowered and bared yellowed teeth. He made an unheard remark and then spat. The wet missile hit the mesh and bounced back on him.

"You know, I'm quite sure your comments are not polite at all." He turned to Kale. "He seems to be working himself into quite a state."

"He's probably doubly irritated that his associates aren't coming to the rescue."

"Yes, I'd say he is having a bad day." He winked at Kale. "Ready, lady of mine?"

Kale held up her net and nodded.

"We'll be back," he said to the captive. "And we'll bring your friends to keep you company."

Kale and Bardon set off to capture another bisonbeck. Two fell for the same tactic, but the next one caught sight of them fastening his comrade to a tree. Bardon fought him, keeping him busy while Kale quickly fashioned another web. The dragons swooped in and out of the melee, harassing the ex-warrior. By superior swordsmanship, Bardon avoided killing the marauder. He worked harder as the bisonbeck grew angrier and demonstrated lethal determination to slice Bardon in half with his hefty sword. The opponent's skill grew sloppier, but his blows increased in strength.

The fight moved closer to Kale than Bardon liked. She concentrated on her work and failed to notice. The enemy's weapon swung in a direction that would strike Kale. Bardon stepped forward, blocked the blow, pushing the larger man with his shoulder and his sword. Bardon's blade slipped between the plates of battered armor on the man's chest and straight into his heart.

Kale's hands stopped, and she watched the bisonbeck take his last breath. "I'm done, Bardon."

"A bit late."

Her eyes widened, and she pulled back her arm, positioning the net for a throw. Bardon dropped to his stomach. The web sailed over him and netted the last bisonbeck. She pulled the rope that cinched the trap, and the mesh tightened around the prisoner.

Bardon rolled over on his back, sat up, and sprang to his feet in a move Regidor had taught him. He embraced his wife and kissed her forehead. "Good work. Now, let's get them all in one spot so it's easier to guard them."

"I'm glad we have them all captured. I was running out of material for the webs."

"Now, isn't that good to hear?" The leaves around them rustled. Six burly bisonbecks stepped through the underbrush. Weapons drawn, faces hardened into lines of cold malice, eyes glaring, they didn't look pleased with what they had found.

"You won't be needing a guard for our comrades," said the tallest. "Indeed, we will provide a guard for you."

"Nah," said a bisonbeck wearing a large chain around his neck. A bulky medal hung against his chest. "Just kill 'em. I don't want to be bothered with watching 'em."

"Yeah," muttered another, and the remainder grunted their agreement, their heads nodding with zeal for the task before them.

"Oh, for the discipline we had in the army," the tallest lamented. He lifted a hand and let it fall as he turned. "Do what you want. I'm hungry."

16

REUNION

"You might want to delay killing us," suggested Bardon.

"Why?" asked the one who had first objected to guarding them.

Another marauder took a threatening step toward Bardon. He held his weapon as if he would enjoy the swing that would cost the knight his life. He sneered. "Don't listen to him, Reddig."

"Because," Bardon explained, "unless my wife releases your friends from their bindings, they will die a slow death."

Reddig grunted and walked over to one of the bound men. He slashed his short sword across the weave of the web. The strands did not give. No mark showed at all. He hacked in a frenzy, then backed away to see that his efforts had been to no avail.

He glared at Bardon.

Bardon shrugged. "She's a wizard."

Reddig turned and rushed toward Kale. She took one step back, and where she had been standing, a broad column shimmered. But the bisonbeck did not have time to stop. He ran into the barrier and stuck as if he had been a fly swatted onto a windowpane. His face pressed against the invisible surface, distorting his features. He struggled to get free but could not back up.

The two remaining bisonbecks growled low in their throats, and they circled Kale. Bardon leaned against a tree and crossed his arms.

"Bad idea, fellas," he said as he examined his fingernails.

Kale stood with one hand on her hip and the other resting on the hilt of her invisible sword. From the trees, a raucous call proclaimed the minor dragons had finished their little rest and were tired of sitting around. The nine dragons bombarded the last marauders.

Bardon watched with interest to see if Crispin would be able to actually produce his flame when he wanted to. No, he spit out a stream of scarlet saliva. It burned, of course, but no more than the spit of the other dragons. Each time one of the bisonbecks tried to escape and run into the woods, the flying attackers cut him off and drove him back.

After a few minutes, Bardon and Kale rescued the beleaguered men and tied them up. Kale checked the knots for tightness while Bardon searched for any hidden weapons. He collected a pile.

"I see I'm too late for the entertainment," said a deep voice.

Kale whirled away from her chore and ran into Regidor's arms. "You're here. You sneaked up on me. You're the only one who could."

The green meech dragon squeezed her against his black jacket of superfine cloth. "Gilda, Sir Dar, Sittiponder, Toopka, Lee Ark, Brunstetter, and I seem to have succeeded."

"I was preoccupied."

"Didn't these fellows get the drop on you?"

"Well…"

"You've been too long away from the world. This quest will do you good. Your skills are rusty." He pushed her away. "You aren't covered with blood, are you? This is a new coat."

She laughed, and her uneven curls bounced as she shook her head.

Regidor frowned at the captives. "We found a most unpleasant fellow at Danns Crossing. I assume he belongs with these unsavory characters."

"Indeed," said Bardon. "Do you have a hollow, Regidor, in which to store this bounty of weaponry?"

"I should think the river would be a good cache for this lot." He stepped up beside Bardon and sneered down at the odd assortment of weaponry. "Well, if this junk must be transported to the river, I shall assume the task. It might have been prudent to gather up some of those useful boys you had with you when you quested with Granny Kye."

"The street orphans?"

He nodded with a pained look on his face.

A warmth of affection entered Bardon's heart. No one felt more like a brother than Regidor. "I thought they were beneath your notice?"

"One does notice gnats."

Bardon cocked an eyebrow. "And they did fetch and carry well."

"Yes, there was that."

Kale sat on a log, laughing and holding her sides. "Oh, stop. Please, stop. Both of you."

The men exchanged a glance and shrugged. They strode over and each took one of Kale's arms, lifting her to her feet.

"Sir Dar," announced Regidor, "is fixing a scrumptious meal with the help of Sittiponder and Toopka."

Bardon turned toward the crossing. "I certainly hope Toopka is in charge of buttering the bread and nothing more."

Kale giggled. "She's not very good at that. She bears down with the knife too hard and breaks the bread." A solemn thought transferred from Kale's mind to Bardon's. She turned a worried face to Regidor. "The Dann family. Is there any sign of them?"

"I'm afraid not," said Regidor, matching her somber tone.

Through the trees ahead, they saw a short, square marione marching a hefty bisonbeck in front of him.

"Lee Ark," Kale called a greeting.

The major waved one hand briefly. "The stench from this reprobate disturbed your wife's stomach, Regidor. I propose we tie him to a tree."

"We have just the place," answered the meech. "Not crowded at all."

Bardon squeezed Kale's hand. *You go on and see Gilda. I'll go back with the men.*

"All right, but if there is any talk about the black dragons and the Followers, you are to remember to tell me every word exchanged."

He chortled. *You don't mind if I go with them?*

Kale rolled her eyes. *"Of course not."*

Kale heard the lilting strains of a shepherd's pipe as she approached the old building. Sir Dar sat at one end of the porch with Sittiponder on one side and Toopka on the other. His black lips moved back and forth over the reeds. Metta provided the harmony. Sittiponder's clear tenor joined the melody. Kale slowed her pace to amble her way to a bench by the stairs. There she sat until the song finished.

She jumped up, clapped, and climbed the steps. Toopka ran to throw her arms around Kale. "I've missed you. Sir Dar has fixed delicious food. It's in the oven. Look, Sittiponder came with us."

The young blind tumanhofer stood beside Sir Dar. Kale disengaged Toopka's arms and crossed the wooden porch to embrace Sittiponder. A grin brightened his face as he heard the steps. She kissed the top of his head.

"Ah," said the awkward youngster, "don't get all mushy."

"You've grown," said Kale, trying not to laugh. "And you've gotten persnickety. You didn't used to mind my hugging you."

His cheeks colored, and he ducked his head.

She let him go, unwilling to embarrass him further. "Where's Brunstetter?"

"Off looking for a trace of the urohms who should be living here."

Kale had already searched the area with her talent and knew no living urohm was in the immediate area. Perhaps they had escaped and hidden in the hills or gone to the nearest town. She didn't want to think of what had happened to them if they hadn't fled. "And Gilda?"

"Inside," answered Sittiponder.

"Cleaning," said Toopka in an awed whisper.

"Cleaning? Gilda cleaning?" Kale edged around the others on the steps. She had to see for herself if Gilda was truly cleaning.

Sir Dar nodded. "That's why we're out here. Gilda has her own style of cleaning, and we didn't want to be injured."

"Be careful," Toopka whispered.

A haze of smoke and the acrid odor of something burning hit Kale as she went through the door. She turned back. "Sir Dar, your dinner!"

"My meal is fine. That's Gilda's work you smell."

Kale continued into the room. "Gilda?"

"I'm here." Gilda's throaty voice sounded as if she'd covered her mouth and nose with a handkerchief. "Whatever have you done to your hair, Kale?"

She raised a hand to her unevenly cut hair. "How can you see me? I can't see you through all this smoke."

"Perhaps I have better eyes. Your hair, Kale?"

"Black dragons attacked and scorched my curls. Bardon trimmed it up for me."

"I'll fix it for you once I'm done with this chore."

Kale coughed and waved a hand, initiating a stiff breeze that sent much of the murky air out the open windows. Gilda sat in a bubble with narrowed eyes peering around the room. The protective enclosure surrounding Gilda muffled her words.

"Thank you," Gilda said and gave Kale a halfhearted smile. "I couldn't do that myself from in here, and I certainly wasn't going to sit out there."

She stared at a bench next to the wall, and the whole seat burst into flame.

"Oh!" exclaimed Kale. Then she realized the fire surrounded the wood but did not consume the bench. "Oh," she repeated in a calmer voice. "You're burning off the contamination."

"Bisonbecks!" The fire fizzled and went out. Gilda turned her eyes on a rack of clothing. "Such a stink."

With a whoosh, the hats, coats, and long pants caught fire. In a moment, the room filled with smoke. Kale waved her hand, and the blaze swayed toward the curtains.

"Be careful," demanded Gilda. "I don't want the house to go up in flames."

Kale raised her eyebrows. "Sorry."

The fire went out.

"Now," said Gilda, "you may disperse the smoke."

Kale motioned toward the windows, and the gray tendrils drifted away.

Gilda glared as she surveyed the room. "There! I've purified the entire room. Kale, cover the remnants of that awful odor with something. Choose a spicy fragrance rather than a cloyingly sweet aroma."

"Of course," said Kale but turned to face the other direction so she could first grimace her displeasure at being ordered around. Her expression changed to mischief when she pulled a vial from her hollow pocket and released the bouquet of talcum powder.

"Whatever is that?" Gilda objected in a voice loud and clear.

Kale turned to find the bubble gone, and Gilda standing with her nose scrunched up.

Kale smiled. "It's called baby powder."

"Your idea of a jest?" Gilda waved an arm, and the scent dissipated. She circled her arm above her head, and the room smelled of cloves, ginger, and bridesbark.

"Bardon tells me congratulations are in order."

A smug smile bloomed on Gilda's long exotic face. She strolled to a chair next to the window and sat. "I am, indeed, fortunate." She smoothed the silky material of her long skirt. "What can be a more noteworthy accomplishment than to contribute to the long line of meech dragons?" She shrugged and looked away from Kale. "Of course, all mothers feel that pride of producing one of the next generation and thereby assuring the race will continue. But to be able to increase the meech population. To contribute another to our noble race." Gilda sighed.

Kale stewed over the meech dragon's inordinate pride in her heritage. She narrowed her eyes and almost succumbed to the temptation to use her talent to eavesdrop on the meech's thoughts. As Gilda gazed out the window, did she imagine a long line of prodigy, her prodigy, ready to rule the world, enlighten those less fortunate, and improve society through their noble example? Kale's stomach turned.

Bleh! She needs to memorize a dozen pride-versus-humility principles. I wonder if I could get Bardon to give her a list. No, he wouldn't do it. He'd say I was being prideful, which is true, but I'd never catch up to Gilda.

Gilda turned back with a smile, and Kale banished the uncharitable thoughts lest the astute wizard tune in on her attitude. Evidently, Gilda was too caught up in her own musings.

She awarded Kale a condescending smirk. "You'll understand should you ever be given the opportunity to contribute to your race."

Kale bit her tongue. A new set of uncharitable thoughts refused to be banished.

"You must understand," Gilda purred. "I can't present my egg just anywhere. From what Regidor and I have been able to determine, the meech population has dwindled deplorably. Once we find our colony, we'll have more details, but the refinement of my race and intellectual influence of the meech must not be lost."

"Who are they influencing, Gilda?" Kale interrupted. "They haven't mingled freely with the high races for centuries."

"High races?" Scorn punctuated the two words. She pulled in a deep breath and tilted her chin up. "Regidor and I are accustomed to rubbing shoulders with your high races. We are well equipped to be ambassadors. Our goal is to reintroduce the meech to Amara and guide them into places of influence where their ideas can elevate the general populace."

Elevate? Why did she use the same word that infatuated Garmey?

Kale looked Regidor's wife in the eye. "Gilda, do you know anything about a group of people who call themselves the Followers?"

"Of course not," she said quickly. Too quickly. "The meech dragons are not followers, but leaders." She placed a hand on her abdomen, where Kale could just barely see the bulge that indicated a developing egg.

Gilda's eyes closed, and that satisfied smile crept out to transform her face.

Kale shook her head. *Normally, Gilda can be a bit overbearing. A pregnant Gilda is even more puffed up, and I am not referring to her midriff. If something occurs to deflate her ego, I hope Regidor isn't caught in the blast of hot air.*

17

FACT OR FABLE?

Kale sank into the soft couch and put her feet up on a stool. She rubbed her stomach and sighed deeply.

"Ate too much?" asked Bardon as he handed her a cup and saucer, then sat beside her.

The cushions shifted with his weight.

Kale groaned. "Don't rock the boat."

"Sick?"

"No, you were right the first time. I ate too much. Sir Dar's food is irresistible."

He patted her leg. "That's fine. I worried about you at the ball when you didn't eat."

Sir Dar settled cross-legged on a patterned rug beside an empty hearth. He put his flute to his lips and blew the first tremulous notes of a merry tune. Sittiponder, Toopka, and the minor dragons joined him. Lee Ark and Brunstetter sat in wooden chairs by the table.

"I can't move," said Lee Ark. "Even my grandmother doesn't feed me as well."

Brunstetter laughed. "In my home, this would be the appetizer."

Sir Dar interrupted his song. "Are you still hungry, my friend? I'll fix you something else."

"No, no," Brunstetter wagged his head. "I'm fine. I want to hear your after-dinner music. That is the best part of your cooking."

Regidor and Gilda strolled over to the most elegant piece of furniture in the room, a love seat upholstered in brocade with a green leaf design. Gilda muted the color before sitting down. Now the sofa lent a perfect backdrop to her blue and peach gown.

Kale closed her eyes and let the music lift her spirits and ease the discomfort she felt from a too-delicious dinner eaten too enthusiastically.

"Don't get *too* comfortable," warned Bardon. "Regidor has gotten up and is headed this way."

Kale opened one eye and hoped a one-eyed glare would deter her former mentee. It didn't. He grinned impudently and pulled a chair closer. He sat down, and Kale faced the inevitable. With an effort, she straightened herself against the soft cushions.

Taking a sip of the tea Bardon had given her, she nodded to Regidor. "You have your talking gateway in your hand. Is there a message we should know about?"

"There is a message from your father. His message to me says to tell you that he left a message for you, and I guess I should also pass on the fuss he was making over your not responding."

"I forget to look. Regidor, you'll have to figure out a way for me to know when there's a message waiting." She scooted to the edge of the seat. "I'll have to get the talking gateway out of my cape."

Toopka jumped up from the musical gathering. "I'll get it."

She ran to the moonbeam cape hanging from a hook on the wall but stopped before grabbing it. "What does the talking gateway look like?"

Kale caught Pat's eye and nodded. He flew to Toopka's shoulder.

"Let Pat help," she said. "Then you can carry it over here."

Pat hopped over to the cape and disappeared into the folds.

"Hurry up," said Toopka. She bounced on her toes and fingered the smooth moonbeam material. "Can't you find it? Hurry up."

Pat emerged with the cylinder, carrying it with his front feet. Toopka snatched it and started toward Kale. She stopped, retraced her steps, and said thank you to Pat, before skipping across the room. Pat followed and took up a position on the arm of the couch.

Toopka turned the object around and around in her hands. She studied the flat surface. "Is this where I see the picture? Where do the words come out? Can I leave a message for Taracinabloo?"

Kale extended her hand. "Give the cylinder to me, and I'll show you."

Toopka plopped it in Kale's palm. She clambered into Bardon's lap.

Kale opened the gateway's traveling case.

"You opened it," exclaimed Toopka. "How?"

Bardon settled her more comfortably on his lap. "It doesn't matter, Toopka. You couldn't use the talking device even if you opened it. Only wizards can manipulate the weave of a gateway."

Toopka's face fell into a pitiful mask of disappointment. Kale patted her arm. "It's all right, Toopka. Watch. And I'll let you leave a message for Taracinabloo."

Kale pinched the top of the gateway and pulled the loose loop out of the shell. She placed a thread in the air and shaped the portal into a circle on top of it.

"It's floating," said Toopka. "How did you do that?"

"The same way I float a light orb. Shh! I'm concentrating."

Kale rearranged the threads with greater agility than before. Her fingers learned the patterns more efficiently each time she set the talking gateway into operation.

Toopka edged forward on Bardon's lap. "I see the lights."

Kale twitched a stray strand, and a picture of her father snapped into the center.

Toopka made a satisfied coo.

The image activated. "Hello, Kale. I have a lot to tell you. Did Regidor ever say how long a message we can leave? I don't recall."

Kale glanced up at the meech, and he shook his head.

Her father continued. "Wasting time thinking about it." He rubbed his hand over the top of his head, smoothing down his salt-and-pepper hair. "I have heard of these black dragons you asked about. The first time we heard the legend we were told it was an obscure fable, and most people didn't even know of its existence. But as the years went on, the telling of the tale became more frequent. And now, it seems to be on everyone's lips in our part of the Northern Reach.

"There were also rumors of actual sightings of black dragons swarming across the countryside. But they did no damage. Left no evidence. And disappeared."

He paced away from the portal and jerked around as if he remembered he had to talk to the gateway in order to leave the message.

"Wizard Namee has relayed a message to me for you. You must have Regidor figure out a way one can tell that there is a message inside the gateway when it is closed."

Kale flashed a grin at the meech dragon. "See? I'm not the only one who thinks it's a good idea."

The image of her father pacing caught her attention once more. "Namee's message said the bodies of the slain black dragons turned to dust within twenty-four hours, and the slightest breath of air scattered the remains."

Kale's father raked his fingers through his hair and strode away, messing up the hair he'd recently smoothed, then he returned to the portal.

"I know only rumors and folktales about the black dragons. And I know less than that about these Followers you mentioned. I've discussed this with Librettowit, of course, and he tells the same story of the sleeping beast that I have heard. I believe he sent a copy of the fable to Sir Dar. He'll tell it to you.

"And that brings me to the last point in my message. Librettowit plans to join you in Vendela. He'll take gateways to get there. He says he will be delivering something of importance to you. So, meet him at The Goose and The Gander on the first day of next week."

He stared into the gateway, so that he appeared to be pinning Kale with his eyes. "Be careful. All of you. I fear the enemy is afoot again, and he won't use armies this time in his attempt to destroy Paladin and Amara. 'Do not gather a sheep that howls into the fold of your flock.'"

The gateway's center went blank.

Toopka squirmed in Bardon's lap. "Why would a sheep howl? Sheep go baa. Wolves howl." Her eyes widened. "I get it. The sheep that howls isn't really a sheep at all, is it?"

"Yes, that's right." Kale put her talking gateway back in the case and snapped it shut.

"I didn't get to talk to Taracinabloo."

Kale sighed. "You didn't, did you? And I promised."

"That's all right, Kale. We can do it later. I want Sir Dar to tell the story."

"He and the others are enjoying the music."

Toopka wiggled to the edge of Bardon's lap. "Hey! Everybody likes stories. Sir Dar just needs to know we want to listen to a story now. Just watch."

The doneel child jumped to her feet and ran across the wooden floor. The music stopped.

Sir Dar looked at Toopka from under eyebrows made of long, stiff hairs, one a bit shorter than the other. "If you are going to clomp, you should do so in the rhythm of the song being played."

"Sir Kemry says you have a story to tell us."

Sir Dar tilted his head, then his face brightened, and he picked up a fabric sleeve to put away his instrument. "Yes, I do. One I hadn't heard until I received a scroll from Librettowit. His messenger came just before we left Namee's." He glanced at each occupant of the room. "Do you wish to hear it?"

"Yes." Approval echoed around the room.

Sir Dar stood and waited for his audience to relax in their chosen seats. Regidor returned to Gilda's side. Lee Ark and Brunstetter moved to softer chairs closer to the hearth.

Sir Dar raised a finger in the air to signal he was ready to begin. "It seems a dragon, fierce and dangerous, lived eons ago, but not on our world. He roamed the land of a country not only far across oceans, but far above where birds and dragons fly. What looks like stars to us are sometimes not flaming gases. Light from faraway suns reflects off of worlds made of rock and dirt and water like we see around us here."

He paused and looked solemn. "This dragon's size was that of a mountain. His scales black like coal. His breath reeked of death, and not even the fire that shot through his mouth could disguise the stench of rotten meat between his teeth. The golden color of his eyes held no warmth, but anyone who looked into those oblong orbs saw the beast's intelligence and the shivering coldness of a corrupted soul.

"His name is Mot Angra. Although it is rumored he has had other names in other places. The common belief is that Mot Angra cast his fortune with Pretender and left Wulder at the same time. The tale we know is of a time when he ravaged an entire civilization, burning cities, destroying crops, mutilating animals, and eating people. Naturally, the people of that world under this relentless attack sought an escape.

"They made a gateway and came to us, or so the legend says. The last man came through, bringing an old, sick woman in his arms. The elders moved to close the gateway, but too late. Mot Angra leapt through."

"Here?" demanded Toopka. "Mot Angra came here?"

Sir Dar nodded and looked at her with compassion. "So the story goes, but do not fear. The sick old woman held the answer to controlling the beast. The first thing the woman did was to instruct these people how to put the beast to sleep."

"Why didn't she do this before?" asked Regidor. "While they were still on their world?"

"Because the man who carried her through the gateway had been to several worlds through portals, searching for her. He had only just returned to his world and found it in desolation."

"Is she going to die?" asked Toopka. "I don't like it when people die in stories."

"Yes, she died, but not before she gave the people the knowledge they needed to control the beast, and not before she pleaded with Wulder to one day give someone the instrument to kill the beast."

The girl doneel sighed. "So the bad dragon, Mot Angra, is asleep?"

"Yes, Toopka, asleep with a guard around him made up of the people from the other planet. They feel responsible for bringing him here."

Regidor cleared his throat. "You didn't mention the part about the small black dragons."

Sir Dar looked at the floor. When he raised his eyes, worry darkened his pupils. "Mot Angra sheds his scales. Each scale becomes a dragon."

Bardon leaned forward. "So what is the explanation of these swarms of black dragons being seen now?"

"This phenomenon occurs only when the dragon stirs in his sleep."

Toopka gasped. "Mot Angra is waking up?"

Kale placed a hand on the little girl's back and rubbed. "It's a fable, Toopka." *I hope it's a fable.*

18

In Vendela

Kale tossed her curls, feeling them bounce around her ears. Gilda might be annoying at times, but she came in handy during a fashion crisis. Kale's new hairdo hid the disaster of burnt locks, and she was very grateful not to be walking down the streets of sophisticated Vendela with her hair stuffed under a hat. She tilted her head to view Toopka riding on Bardon's shoulders. "Do you want to go through the market and see if any of your old friends are there?"

Toopka shook her head, vigorously. "There's nobody there I care about."

"Are you sure?"

The doneel craned her neck to look at Sir Dar and Lee Ark behind them. Each held out an arm for Sittiponder to use as guides through the crowded streets of Vendela.

Toopka looked down at Kale. "Yes, I'm sure."

Brunstetter forged ahead of them, making a path in the crowd so the smaller members of their party could pass easily. Toopka had ridden on his shoulder first, but she complained it was too far up to see people's faces.

"Why didn't Regidor and Gilda come with us?" she asked.

Kale shrugged. "Gilda prefers a closed carriage. They had to go the long way around, since only pushcarts and small donkeys are allowed in this part of the town."

Toopka pointed over a stone wall. "Look! There's the dragon field."

With her hands planted in Bardon's dark hair, Toopka rose up on her knees to get a better look. "They aren't there. Our dragons haven't come back."

Bardon grimaced as her knobby knees dug into his neck muscles, and her little fingers tugged tufts of his hair. "We haven't called them, Toopka. Don't worry."

"But some of them were sick. I saw you put smelly liniment on Greer's shoulder. Sir Dar put medicine on Merlander where her skin rubbed off under the saddle."

Sir Dar frowned at the doneel girl. "Merlander has delicate skin. Besides, she likes the attention."

"But where'd they all go, and why have they been gone so long?"

Sir Dar pressed his lips into a thin line. "You are entirely too inquisitive. I believe I've told you to use your eyes instead of your mouth to find out things."

"Is that a principle?"

"No." Bardon laughed. "The principle that would apply is, 'Ask questions of a patient man, for an impatient man will answer to his benefit, not yours.' " He flinched again as Toopka shifted her weight.

Kale patted the doneel's legs. "Sit down now. You're hurting my husband, and I don't like that."

Toopka complied, and Kale straightened the child's yellow, silky shirt that had escaped the waistband of green-dotted pants.

"But where did they go?" asked the little girl.

Bardon grabbed her ankles to stop her from kicking his chest. "Into the mountains and the valleys to the west of Vendela. It is customary for the bigger dragons to socialize there. The minor dragons prefer to remain in Kale's cape. Riding and major dragons enjoy one another's company while they wait for their riders to be done with whatever business has brought them to the capital."

"Will they come back when you call?"

"Yes," Bardon reassured her. "When I think about Greer, he will know it and come to find out why I am bothering him."

Toopka's voice squeaked as she asked her next question. "The dragons all know to go there to see their friends?"

"Yes."

"Will Mot Angra know? Will he go there?"

"Ah, so this is what all the anxiety is about." Bardon squeezed

Toopka's legs, then jiggled them. "No need to worry, tot. If he exists, he's still asleep."

"But—"

Kale put her hand on her husband's arm. "Hush for a moment, Toopka. I need to talk to Bardon. Tieto is excited. He says that one out of every five people we pass has the distorted aura peculiar to those he saw in Namee's castle."

"We'll ask Regidor about it when we get to The Goose and The Gander."

"Do I have an aura? What's my aura look like?"

"A good question, Toopka. I'll ask Tieto."

She asked the question and waited for the reply. "He says your aura is the same as it always is. You have a bright core that looks like it could burst out at any moment, and it is covered with a murky, swirling brown and blue shadow."

Toopka frowned. "Is my aura pretty?"

"Tieto says it's attractive, but unlike most auras."

"I'm unique," bragged the doneel child.

"I agree with that," Kale stated.

Toopka became interested in her surroundings and ceased chattering. When they went through the market, she asked to be let down and walked with her hand clutching Kale's skirt.

At The Goose and The Gander, Brunstetter led them around the side of the inn. His urohm frame didn't fit in the corridor that passed through the building to the tea garden where they would meet Librettowit.

Maye Ghent greeted them. "Welcome to The Goose and The Gander. It's been a long time, my friends. Have we changed much?"

Sir Dar stepped forward, took the marione innkeeper's hand and made a court bow. "Not a bit. The gardens are colorful, the food smells divine, and you, Mistress Ghent, are as gracious and beautiful as ever."

"And you are ever the diplomat." Her pleased expression revealed how much she enjoyed the flattery. "Come, I have a table where you all will be comfortable. The cook has outdone herself today with a delicate pastry layered with nuts and fruit and topped with whipped cream. You must save some room for it." She led them toward a table under a bentleaf tree while she talked. "First, I'll have the servers bring you soup. Do you favor hot tumport, or perhaps cinamacress consommé?"

Kale recognized the soups as dishes Taylaminkadot loved to serve. "Would your cook be a tumanhofer, Mistress Maye?"

"She is, indeed."

Feminine giggles drew Kale's attention. A group of five young maids strolled along one of the garden paths that twisted among clusters of potted flowers. In the center of this bevy of girls, a familiar male marione flashed his white teeth and dimples. His companions fluttered their fans, batted their eyelashes, dipped their heads, and looked utterly idiotic.

There's Holt, she told Bardon, using her talent to direct his eyes to the young man.

"Don't speak to him. We don't want anyone to know we have made his acquaintance."

Do you suppose Holt is the "something" Librettowit is bringing to us?

"Perhaps."

Kale watched in amazement as Holt continued to charm the ladies, leading them to a table shaded by a large umbrella. He carefully seated all the giggling girls and ordered cool drinks.

"You mustn't be seen staring at him, either."

Kale quickly faced Bardon. *I wasn't staring. Staring is rude.*

"You show that much interest in a handsome young man, and I may have to play the jealous husband."

Pooh! She hurried to join the others who had already gathered around the table under the long trailing branches of the tree.

"'Pooh'! Did you say 'pooh'? Kale, sweet lady of mine, I don't think I have ever heard you say 'pooh' before."

Perhaps because you have never said anything so foolish before.

Bardon gallantly separated the natural curtain of drooping limbs, and Kale walked through.

"Librettowit!" She circled the table to give him a hug. "I didn't see you sitting here."

"I'm standing," grumped her librarian. "And you probably didn't see me because you were staring at Holt."

"So you are, and no, I wasn't." She glanced around the table. "Please, be seated."

Chairs scraped over the brick flooring. Bardon let Toopka down and sat on Kale's right, with Toopka and Sittiponder beyond him. Librettowit remained at her left.

She looked at his scowling countenance. He didn't like to travel unless a rare book lured him out of his library.

He caught her staring at him. "I *am* sitting."

"I didn't say you were not."

"And now you're staring at me. When did you become so rude?"

"I'm sorry. I took up rudeness just a short while ago, and I'm not very good at it yet. You'll have to give me pointers from your centuries of experience."

A twinkle came to the old man's eye. "Impertinent."

"Oh, good. That's exactly what I was trying for."

"An ill-mannered wizard. You remind me more of Fenworth each day."

Those at the table laughed, appreciating the humor in Kale's being likened to her mentor, an old bog wizard who enjoyed a constant verbal battle with Librettowit.

Bardon leaned forward to address the tumanhofer. "Please, don't say so. I'd prefer you didn't see her as anything remotely resembling a bog wizard. She wakes me in the middle of the night with miniature fireworks displays going on over the bed. But I'd much rather that than the bog creatures that used to skitter around Fen when he slept."

Several serving maids interrupted their laughter to provide them with drinks and determine what food to bring them. Once these young women left, Sir Dar came to the point.

"Kemry asked us to meet you here, Librettowit. What is this important thing you are delivering?"

"Holt."

Toopka burst into giggles. "Holt can't be important. He's Holt."

"Toopka," said Sir Dar, "the most surprising people come forward to do important things." He looked pointedly at the furry little doneel. "Sometimes even very small people."

Her demeanor changed abruptly. Serious reflection replaced the humor in her big brown eyes. Her smile tightened and thinned and disappeared. She folded her hands in her lap and looked down at them.

The others in the group went on to other topics of conversation, but Kale watched her ward with concern.

Bardon placed his hand over hers. *"You're staring again."*

What was that all about?

Bardon looked thoughtfully at Toopka for a moment. *"I believe our Toopka has a destiny."*

Kale choked down a laugh that sprang to her lips. *I almost echoed Toopka's remark about Holt. She can't have a destiny. She's Toopka!*

"Wulder chooses whom He may."

An arch of light crackled over Kale's head. She jerked out of her reverie and smiled at the others. "Excuse me. I was lost in thought."

Brunstetter put down his tankard. "Don't worry about it, Lady Kale. Again, we are relieved you are not a bog wizard letting lizards and drummerbugs loose on the table."

As the others chuckled and continued their conversation, Kale turned her hand over in Bardon's and squeezed.

Have you ever wondered why Wulder chose us?

"To astound the wise and baffle the learned."

Do you think He's chosen Toopka?

Indubitably.

19

A Secret Meeting

"What do you suppose has delayed Regidor and Gilda?" Brunstetter asked midway through the meal.

Lee Ark glanced around. "My wife would like this place. She'd think it a real treat to bring the children and enjoy the garden, the music, and the food. But not all women like the same things."

Brunstetter nodded. "My family would feel the same as yours." He took a bite of dark bread slathered with butter and bright red jam. He chewed and swallowed. "So you think Gilda took one look at The Goose and The Gander and guided Regidor to a more suitable eating establishment?"

Lee Ark nodded.

"They've missed a fine meal, then."

Kale frowned. Music from three wandering musicians drifted among the chatter of friendly conversation. The mixture of sweet and spicy fragrances from the flowers mingled with the aroma of baked goods and sizzling meats. Not only were the flowers bountiful and gorgeous in their array of colors, but the people also wore their gayest clothing. Kale shook her head. Regidor loved this type of setting. People amused him. Color and music excited his artist's soul. Did Gilda not understand her husband's need to have his senses fed? Regidor thrived on adventure and variety.

It's possible I know him better than his wife does. I bonded with him before he was born. And I am officially still his Dragon Keeper.

When the servants had cleared away the last dish, Maye Ghent approached their arbor under the tree. "There's a private room reserved for you. And the couple who took the room is waiting for you. If you're done with your meal, I'll show you the way."

Sir Dar sprang to his feet and sped around the table to the hostess's side. "One moment, Mistress Ghent." He crooked a finger, indicating he wanted to speak quietly.

She leaned over.

"We'd rather not be obvious, and the procession of us traipsing up the stairway would be quite conspicuous."

"Of course." Maye Ghent nodded with a knowing smile. "If your party would split up? The gentlemen would perhaps like a drink in The Gander? The ladies would like the cool retreat of The Goose?"

Kale pushed her talent past the crowded veranda and gardens to the inside of the inn. She located Regidor immediately and felt Gilda's disgruntled presence beside him.

"Sir Bardon, Toopka, and I can find our own way up."

Maye bent her head. "I shall take Lord Brunstetter up the outside stair. Then I shall come to the door of The Gander and escort the tumanhofers to the room. Last, Lee Ark, if you would give us a moment, then climb to the third floor. I'll meet you at the top of the stairs and show you the way."

Kale, Bardon, and Toopka remained seated as the others dispersed.

"When will it be our turn?" asked Toopka.

"In a minute," answered Bardon.

Kale searched the garden with her talent. "Bardon, Holt is gone."

"Holt's here?" asked Toopka, a grin displacing the impatient expression of only a moment before.

Both adults ignored her.

Bardon twisted in his chair so that he could see a different portion of the gardens. "Can't you locate him?"

"In this crowd, it's difficult. I found Regidor easily enough, since I know him so well."

"Regidor's here?" Toopka stood and hopped on her chair.

Bardon scowled as he, too, looked through the people gathered around tables. "The meeting will not be of any use without Holt."

"Oh no! Not a meeting." Toopka drooped. "Meetings are dull."

Kale got to her feet. "I'll stroll around. Perhaps I'll find him."

"Me, too." Toopka jumped from her seat, but Bardon caught her in midair.

"No, you don't. You're staying with me."

Toopka wiggled. "Why can't I go?"

"Because you're distracting."

Undaunted, the doneel child stood on Bardon's lap and craned her neck back and forth. "I want to see Holt."

"Keep your voice down."

"There he is!"

Bardon pinned the arm and pointing finger to Toopka's side. "If you can't behave, I'm going to hire a nanny and leave you here in Vendela."

"I'm behaving. What did I do?"

Kale sat down. "In the game we're playing, we don't know Holt, and Holt doesn't know us."

"We're playing a game?" Toopka sounded mildly interested, then she scrunched up her face. "You were playing a game, and you didn't tell me. How am I supposed to go by the rules if I don't know the rules and I don't even know we are playing a game?" She pulled her arms out of Bardon's slackened grasp and folded them over her chest. "I don't believe that's fair."

"It wasn't fair," said Kale, standing once more. "I'm sorry. I'll tell you more when we get to the meeting. It's our turn."

"How do you know it's our turn? What about Holt? Is he coming? Does he know when it's his turn?"

Kale reached into her moonbeam cape and pulled out her hand. Nothing appeared to be in her grasp, but she swept her arm over the chattering doneel's head.

"I can run and tell him. I—" Toopka's lips continued to move, her mouth opened and closed, but no sound came out.

Bardon raised his eyebrows.

"I silenced her," Kale answered Bardon's unspoken question.

"Permanently?"

"Hardly."

"One could hope."

"I put an invisible silencing net over her head. We can remove it at any time."

Toopka put her head down on Bardon's shoulder and buried her face in his neck.

Kale patted her back and spoke softly. "I'm going to mindspeak to Holt and tell him we are ready to have our meeting. I'll tell him to come, and I'll tell him where we are going, so he can find us. All right?"

They barely saw the tiny nod of her head.

"All right, then," said Bardon. "Let's go."

He led them to the corridor in the building that passed between the two sides of the inn. The Gander accommodated male guests, and The Goose catered to ladies. In the dark hallway, stairs provided a way to the upper floors.

When he reached the second story, Bardon whispered to Kale. "I didn't know she knew our marione friend."

"She met him once at Sir Dar's."

"Once? Her eagerness made me believe they must be lifelong friends."

"You know what a charmer he can be."

"Oh yes, and especially to the ladies."

They had almost reached the top of the stairs when a commotion erupted below them. They heard the whack of something solid striking another object and a woman's shrill protests.

"You've played with my affections." Whack, whack! "And you've toyed with my sister's heart." Whack, thump, whack! "And you've even led my dear aunt to believe you held her in great esteem." Thump, crash, whack, whack. "You're a two-faced liar, a silken-tongued snake, a..."

"Do you think we should go to the fellow's rescue?" asked Bardon.

"It's Holt," whispered Kale.

"I was afraid it might be."

"Well, then, we can't go to his rescue, can we?"

Bardon sadly shook his head. "No, we don't know him, and he doesn't know us."

Kale clicked her tongue and sighed ruefully. "We are not to be seen together."

"No, we are not." With an overly dramatic sigh, Bardon turned and climbed the last few steps to the third floor. "I hope she doesn't detain him too long. Toopka thinks meetings are boring as it is."

Kale knocked on a door. "Yes, for Toopka's sake, we don't wish to delay the meeting."

"Come in." Regidor's voice welcomed them.

They opened the door to find everyone but Holt convened for their secret gathering.

⟿ 20 ⟾

No More Nonsense

"I've had enough!" Gilda stood and headed across the room. "I'll bring Holt upstairs if only to end this *dreadful* rendezvous in this *loathsome* building without any further *appalling* delays." She opened the door and swept through.

Kale glanced at Bardon and then at Regidor. "Do you want me to go after her?"

A sly grin curled Regidor's thin lips. "She can take care of herself."

"But who is going to take care of Holt?"

Regidor laughed and held out his palm. A golden disk lay on his hand, and an opaque cylinder grew from this base until it stood about twelve inches tall. A dark passage appeared inside, and Kale gasped as she realized she could see the stairwell she, Bardon, and Toopka had just climbed.

"What you're seeing is the scene directly in front of Gilda at this moment. I haven't been able to make it work except at very short distances." Regidor tilted his head. "Listen, you should be able to hear as well as see what goes on."

Gilda rounded the last bend in the stairs. In the cylinder, Holt stood between two furious women with two more people on the outskirts of the melee. Maye Ghent held one of the ladies, and a footman had his arms around the waist of the other. Neither of the irate females seemed inclined to give up their harassment of the golden-headed marione. Even muted, their voices sounded shrill and demanding. Few of the words they spoke came through clearly.

However, Mistress Ghent spoke in loud, sharp tones. "Leave off, now. Let this poor excuse for a man go on his way. You're making a spectacle of yourself and not improving the situation one bit. You can't win with the likes of him."

Gilda's arm came into view, and she grasped Holt by the back of his shirt. No muffling disguised her voice either.

"This is mine," she said and pulled Holt out of the fray. "Thank you for bringing him back. There's no reward for his return, so you might as well be on your way."

A sweep of the walls showed Gilda's turning, and she marched up the stairs, prodding Holt to move more quickly before her. As she reached the top step, the cylinder collapsed, and Regidor slipped it into his coat pocket.

Meech dragon and marione entered through the open doorway. Gilda shut the door, then resumed her seat by Regidor. Holt stood awkwardly in the center of the room.

Kale took pity on him. "Come sit here, Holt. We're about to start our meeting."

As soon as the marione settled, Toopka squirmed out of Bardon's arms, climbed across Kale's lap, and wrapped her arms around Holt's neck. She gestured for Kale to remove the silencing net. Kale shook her head and focused on Lee Ark.

"We've several issues to address." The general crossed his legs, resting his ankle on his knee.

Without his uniform, he looked like a farmer. However, even in this casual posture, he remained a commanding figure. Kale had no doubt who was in charge.

"The first item for our attention is the hordes of black dragons." Lee Ark leaned forward. "For those of you who have not seen them, I'll describe what others have noted. These black dragons are smaller than a lad's fist, about twice the size of a buzz-stinger, and sound like a common bee, but a bit louder. They fly in swarms, breathe fire, apparently live only a few days, and after death, their bodies disintegrate within another twenty-four-hour period."

Brunstetter, Kale, and Bardon nodded.

"They are capable of inflicting a nasty sting from poisoned barbs on their backs. So far we have no reports of a deliberate attack except on our Dragon Keeper, Kale Allerion."

Regidor frowned as he looked at Kale. "Do you know of anything you did that might have provoked the attack?"

"No, but my minor dragons said that a blind rage passed through the swarm, and I was the target for that fury." She took Bardon's hand. "The little dragons had no explanation for the black dragons' hatred, but they said as soon as the menacing creatures were beyond line of sight, the anger dissipated. Tieto's overall assessment of the beasts' intelligence is that they have next to none."

"Instinctive behavior rather than rational," Regidor surmised.

She agreed, as did several others.

Lee Ark stood and moved to the window. He pulled back the curtain, surveyed the view, then returned to the circle. "Rumor has it that the black dragons are connected to an old legend. I have men investigating. Librettowit, here, is in charge of the research."

Librettowit touched two fingers to the brim of his hood, a tumanhofer sign that whatever was assigned would be done.

"Next on our agenda is the problem of the Followers. This is where Holt will be of service to Paladin and Amara."

Holt squirmed slightly under the scrutiny of the others but managed to keep his expression in a noncommittal, neutral mask. Kale wondered at how he could school his face to reflect nothing but bland amiability. She tried to copy him and discovered both her husband and Regidor looking at her strangely.

She mentally stuck her tongue out. Regidor and Bardon exchanged amused glances, then visibly relaxed. A new surge of irritation baited Kale to provoke a quarrel, but she pushed down the temptation. Instead, she returned her attention to Lee Ark, avoiding an exchange of barbs with the men. Regidor continued trying to engage her, but she closed her mind to his banter.

"By Wulder's foresight," said Lee Ark with a touch of irony in his voice, "Holt has already infiltrated a group of Followers near Ianna."

"That's a bit too convenient," said Regidor. "I'd like to hear how this came about." He crossed his arms over his chest.

Lee Ark sat down. "Yes, I'd like to hear the tale from your own lips, Holt."

The marione swept the room with a grimace of annoyance.

"I noticed what they were doing, these Followers. They were duping people into making commitments, giving the elders money, turning over their property to the group." He shrugged. "I'm always interested in a scam, so I decided to take a closer look. The only way to accomplish that was to join them. So I did."

Kale caught herself before saying, "Tut-tut." She cleared her throat. "I thought you'd reformed."

He cast her a slight grin, fully disarming when coupled with dimples and merry blue eyes. "I reform twice a week, Lady Kale. It's good for the soul."

Gilda snickered. "Apparently not any permanent good."

Kale heard the next thought forming in Gilda's mind, but Regidor put his hand on his wife's arm and stopped her before she could scornfully add that none of the high races had shown themselves capable of noble allegiance for any length of time. With her lips pressed firmly together, Gilda turned her eyes away from the members of the gathering and stared out the window.

Lee Ark stood again. "We will receive bulletins from Holt."

"Why?" asked Brunstetter. "Why is he willing to gather information for us?"

"Money problems," answered Holt. "It almost always comes down to money."

Gilda scoffed. "Allegiance bought is soon spent."

Brunstetter ignored the lady meech. "When does he get the money?"

"Each time I deliver a report, I get a pittance. It will take me ten years to earn enough to pay my debts."

"And if you get a better offer?" Brunstetter clenched a fist and spoke through tight lips. "A better offer would turn your loyalty?"

Lee Ark raised a hand. "Holt's definition of pittance is a bit cattywampus. He's being paid handsomely for his information."

Brunstetter scowled. "How does he deliver these reports?"

Holt smiled. "Through a winsome little kimen named Seezle."

Gilda smoothed the material on her sleeve and adjusted the cuff. "At least she will be impervious to your charms."

"You think?" Holt winked, and Gilda pressed her lips together, turning her face away.

"Tell us," said Lee Ark. "What have you already discovered?"

"The Followers prefer to invite members who have property. The elders I first approached were rather cool until they found out about my father's kindia farm and trading business."

He wrinkled his nose. "I've been required to 'sit under' a mentor. At first you are designated a seeker. If you gain acceptance, you become a listener. At that point, listening is about all you are allowed to do. You listen with no questions asked. The next advancement is to repeat, where you may repeat the words you have heard.

"I am presently Listener Holt, so my perception of the repeat level is sketchy. Soon I will donate a sum of money provided by you generous souls, and I will advance. Yes, purity can be bought."

Librettowit grumbled. "Purity's gone down in price. Else, we couldn't afford your uprightness without emptying the coffers in every province."

Holt bobbed his head in cheerful agreement. "You're right there. Now as to what else I know—there's an inner circle called the inquirers. I assume these privileged members may ask questions to lead to higher enlightenment. At the top are the echoes, who repeat not only the formal words but have an ear to the Voice, and so they echo new precepts. Apparently there is only one Voice, and at my level, I'm not allowed to know much about him."

"How do they get followers?" asked Kale. "Why don't people see through the sham?"

Holt's mobile eyebrows arched and fell as a cunning grin captured his lips. "The same as in any con. The Followers make the target feel important. He's one of the few who are worthy of the calling. Then they make promises. Jump through this hoop, and you will be more important, more worthy. Each time you jump through the next hoop, your value in our little community will elevate. In the end you are promised power and glory equal to that of the Voice."

Kale glanced at Gilda when Holt used the word "elevate," but she seemed more interested in the intricate design on the fan she held than the conversation.

"What about Paladin and Wulder?" asked Bardon. "How do they lure Amarans away from our true God and His chosen spokesman?"

"They claim to be the new conduit of Wulder." Holt fidgeted with a button on his jacket, gaze cast down.

Kale longed to enter his mind and find out what he was thinking. *Why would this part of the discussion make him so uncomfortable? Is it because he knows we find such talk of a new conduit to be blasphemy? Or does he himself feel nervous at opposing Wulder's will?*

Holt looked up and spoke with forced boldness. "Paladin showed weakness in the war, and Wulder has chosen the Voice to replace him."

Brunstetter shifted on his chair. The resulting creak assaulted Kale's ears. She cringed.

"If I were a betting man," said the urohm leader, "I would bet that once we get to this Voice and uncover his identity, we will find we've met him before."

Librettowit nodded. "Lord Ire."

"Pretender," said Bardon.

"Another guise," agreed Lee Ark, "and another attempt to overcome Wulder's dominion."

They sat in silence. Kale petitioned Wulder for guidance. As words formed in her mind, she felt Bardon join her with the same binding that caused them to work incredibly as one in a fight. This surprised her, and she felt his surprise resonate with hers. In one accord, they continued to put their concerns before Wulder and request strength for the battle to come. For a moment her spirit felt crowded, and then as if walls around her collapsed, the bond between her and her husband expanded to include Lee Ark, Librettowit, Regidor, and Toopka.

Tears streamed down Kale's face, and she gazed at Toopka, who appeared to be sleeping in Holt's lap. The child glowed. Kale took Bardon's hand, but he, too, had seen.

"What does it mean?" she whispered, and the slight breeze caused by her words entered the hushed atmosphere and dissolved their bond.

Holt's eyes were wide with astonishment, and his cocky demeanor had faded to an expression of wonder. Only Gilda's face remained unchanged, still cold and indifferent.

Those who had participated in the joint petition seemed to shake themselves awake.

"I believe," said Librettowit, "that Wulder has affirmed our purpose."

"Indeed." Lee Ark swept a hand across his face, wiping glistening tear tracks from his rugged cheeks. "If any of you uncover pertinent information on your travels, report. We will add that to our stockpile of facts concerning the Followers."

Librettowit shuffled his feet on the wooden floor under the short bench where he sat. "When will Paladin act?"

"My first answer would be when Wulder directs. My second answer is when Paladin knows for sure he will be capturing the wicked perpetrators of this crime and not the gullible victims."

Brunstetter nodded. "And when we can throw a net over all of them without any slipping out to start more trouble elsewhere."

Lee Ark looked around the room. "Any other questions?"

The gathering remained quiet.

"So," said Lee Ark, "this meeting is adjourned."

Gilda came to her feet. "Adjourned? We haven't discussed the most important business at hand."

Lee Ark raised an eyebrow but said nothing.

"I have an egg to present. The meech colony must be found. No doubt, when we put our case before those learned elite, they will have answers for these minor inconveniences—bah!—Followers and bug-dragons. Finding the meech is synonymous with finding your answers."

Bardon rose from his seat. "I am pledged to give support to the quest for the meech dragon colony."

Lee Ark nodded while Librettowit and Brunstetter looked as if they would object.

Kale probed Bardon's mind and picked up the barest essence of his instructions from Paladin. She stood and took her husband's hand. "I will be questing, as well."

"Fine," said Lee Ark. "We go forth from this room, knowing the path Wulder has put before us. Our duty is to take each step as He makes clear His plan."

"Aye," said Librettowit, "and for once He's letting an old librarian seek knowledge in books instead of on dusty roads among hostile creatures."

"You can come with us," offered Bardon.

Librettowit glared at him. "You had more perspicacity before you developed that confounded sense of humor."

"Perspicacity?" asked Kale.

"Discernment, wisdom, insightfulness to what is appropriate," answered Bardon. "Common sense."

Dibl peeked out of one of Bardon's big coat pockets. The little dragon chirruped and flipped his tail up so that the very tip lay in a curl on his own forehead.

"Bah!" said Librettowit and Gilda in the same breath.

Their eyes turned from the comical dragon and met in a fierce glare.

"If looks could kill…," said Bardon.

Regidor cleared his throat. "We'd have two less members on our side of the battle line."

⟶ 21 ⟵

Go...Be Blessed

The room emptied, leaving Kale, Bardon, and Holt. Sir Dar took Toopka, and Regidor took Gilda, with just about the same degree of coaxing and gentle persuasion.

Bardon pulled his chair around so that he faced Holt. The large circle of comrades had become a small, uncomfortable circle.

Kale eyed her husband's new position. *Holt probably thinks we are going to pounce on him.*

"Why should we do that?"

You don't think you're crowding him a bit?

"I just want to see his face. I would have had to look around you from where I was."

Well, just be gentle with him. He doesn't need someone else telling him what a loser he is.

"Holt? Holt! Are you kidding? Holt has no idea he's a loser."

Yes, he does, Bardon. Be nice.

"While I'm being nice, you find out what Tieto says about his aura."

Kale smiled at his gruff tone. *Yes, Sir Bardon.*

Holt cleared his throat. Kale and Bardon gave him their attention, but not before Kale coaxed Tieto out of her cape and silently requested he look over the colors surrounding the marione. She set him in her lap, where he looked around the room before resting his alert gaze on the blond man.

"So." Holt looked sheepishly at Bardon. "What do you hear from N'Rae?"

"She's happy. She and Granny Kye went back to live with the ropmas that helped raise her. She gave up trying to teach them to read and is now concentrating on hygiene."

Holt pursed his lips. "Sounds like fun." He crossed his legs, then uncrossed them. "And that little mummikun lady, N'Rae's protector?"

Kale kept a tight hold on the grin that was threatening to escape. Holt looked so uncomfortable. "Minneken. Jue Seeno went home."

His head jerked up. "You mean…died, went home, or went home to where she lived before?"

"She went to her home after her duties were completed."

Bardon cleared his throat. "The tower at The Hall contains many gateways. We'll be able to escort you to any location. Where is it the Followers have suggested you perfect your next level?"

"A place called Paladise. Don't laugh. I think it's an atrocious name too."

"I've already heard the term." Bardon allowed the uncomfortable moment to stretch. "I believe Paladise refers to several centers under the Followers' control."

Holt nodded but did not offer any specifics. Again Bardon allowed seconds to tick by in slow, methodical torture. Holt fidgeted and kept his eyes from making direct contact with Bardon or Kale.

What are you doing? Kale asked Bardon.

"Waiting for him to come clean."

About what?

"I don't know, but he seems pretty nervous for someone who just had all his money worries solved."

Tieto rubbed his head against Kale's chin and chirred softly. Holt sat up straighter in his chair.

Bardon tilted his head forward as if intently interested in whatever the marione had to say. Kale caught the flash of a wink in her direction. Her dear husband attempted not to gloat. *"Here it comes."*

"Sir Bardon, Lady Kale." Holt presented both hands, palms up, before him. "I ask you, what further information could I get that would be of any use?" His hands emphasized his words with generous gestures. "There are ten steps at the listener level, and I am on the first rung. There's no way I'm going to be allowed to see anything significant, talk to anyone important, or learn the ins and outs that would profit your investigation."

Bardon clapped a hand on the other man's shoulder. "I gather you are not eager to fulfill your end of the bargain."

Holt shook his head. "These people put a lot of stock in proving just how willing the subject is to be humiliated in order to be elevated. They call it the humble steps."

For the first time, Bardon looked genuinely concerned. "Do you think they're physically abusive? I honestly didn't see any signs of that in the village I visited.

"And where are the children? Huh? Where are the older people?"

Kale nudged Tieto until he rolled over on his back. She ran her fingers over the soft scales of his belly. "Holt, do you have any answers to those questions?"

"No real answers. But I've got ideas. I believe they've taken the younger children to some training center away from the parents. I have a theory on that. If the parents see their children suffering, they're more likely to question the wisdom of the elders. If it's only themselves who have to submit to this ridiculousness, then they allow themselves to be taken in longer. Getting the children back is also another promise, a carrot, to dangle in front of the poor slobs who buy into this messy business. When they are sufficiently knowledgeable to instruct their children, then the families will be reunited."

Kale tried to keep her voice calm. "But you don't believe the older people are off someplace receiving training."

"Not the ones who are so old that they're a bother. Perhaps they're too set in their ways and cause a problem. They won't change their thinking, too indoctrinated with the old school of Wulder knowing everything, and Paladin being an instrument of good. Or maybe it's just that they're too old to be of much physical use in the communities."

"So where are these senior citizens?"

"We're told almost the exact same thing as the explanation of where the tykes are. The old folks are in special training centers where things aren't so hard for them." He cleared his throat and gave a rote answer. " 'They go to a place where the burdens of life are not overwhelming.' "

Kale shook her head. "It sounds like they're taking care of them."

Tieto curled into a ball in her lap, looking like he would doze off. She stroked his sides and the sensitive spot between his ears.

Holt shook his head. "It's not the words the Followers speak, but the way the words are spoken. When the echoes say one day the families will be reunited, and they are referring to the old ones, it sounds like a much more distant time. Like...after death."

Kale reached over and touched Holt's arm. "Are you afraid for your life?"

The marione sat up straighter and pulled back his shoulders. "No! Are you kidding? Most of these people don't have a muscle to hang a basket on. And the mass between their ears is mighty weak, as well. I'll be all right."

"Then why are you so reluctant to go?"

"I fear boredom will kill me." He numbered his complaints by holding up one finger for each count. "No gambling, no flirting, no games of any kind, no music, and no drinks other than water. And as a level one listener, I get to do all the grunge work. And did I tell you the food is awful?"

Holt stood and paced the room. Tieto lifted his head and watched him. The marione stopped in front of Kale and Bardon. "Do you think you could arrange for me to go on the quest? Even putting up with Gilda would be a treat compared to listening to lectures four times a day and scrubbing floors in between."

Kale sat back and giggled. "No, we can't. But, Holt, you do have Seezle to brighten your days."

He harrumphed. "No, she comes to me with her clothes dimmed so as not to be conspicuous." He did another turn around the room, running his fingers through his thick blond hair. "I feel like I've been sentenced to prison."

Bardon winked at Kale. "From what I heard, you were once again a hairbreadth away from time as a worker on one of Paladin's ships."

Holt grinned. "An unfortunate misunderstanding."

"As always." Bardon's face grew serious. "You still haven't told us which Paladise will be blessed with your presence."

"Because I don't know. And this idea of yours, to escort me to my destination, it won't work."

Bardon raised an eyebrow.

"Because they fully intend to escort me there themselves. You don't have to worry about my reneging. Once I enter the transitional house, I couldn't get out of it if I tried."

"We'll just tag along," Bardon assured him. "We'll keep out of sight and only help if we're needed."

"I don't need guardians." Holt crossed to the window and looked out at the scene below. "And then there's the official listener style of walking."

Kale looked at Bardon, who shrugged. "What about the walking? What does that have to do with us making sure you arrive safely at your destination?"

"Nothing! It has more to do with why I don't want to go to my destination." Holt gave up his view of the outside. "Listeners keep their eyes down and their feet on the ground at all times. Shuffle, shuffle, shuffle." He demonstrated with his feet scuffing the wooden floor and his head and shoulders drooped as if carrying a weighty burden. Anger straightened his spine. "It's ludicrous."

He grabbed his backpack and threw it over his shoulder. "Well, let's go. You can take me to the transitional house, though you won't be able to go in."

Kale stood. Tieto fell off her lap but spread his wings quickly enough to fly to a new perch. He chittered a scolding, but Kale didn't heed him. "I'll change our appearance first. Would you like to have two emerlindian friends?"

"Sure." Holt threw himself into the wide chair Brunstetter had occupied. "It doesn't matter."

Kale worked quickly, but now that Holt had decided to get on with his charade, he alternately paced the room or sat in gloomy contemplation. When he stopped to watch Kale transforming herself and Bardon into an emerlindian couple, he fidgeted with the buttons on the front of his vest, combed his hair with his fingers, and produced a raspy, tuneless whistle between his teeth.

Kale dropped her hand from the sash she had formed to belt Bardon's dark tunic. "You're driving me crazy, Holt."

He flashed her a weak imitation of his winning smile. "It's my last chance."

"For a while."

"Yes, of course, that's what I meant."

Kale stared at him.

His jaw worked as if he were biting his tongue. "What are you looking at?"

"You. I'm actually looking inside you to see if this is all an act."

"Well?"

"It's not an act."

"I could have told you that."

"I wouldn't have trusted your words. I wouldn't even trust your seemingly unconscious nervousness, because I know you are a consummate actor. But your agitated thoughts, your accelerated heartbeat, and the way your anxiety alters the way your body functions, you cannot reproduce at will."

Bardon took a hold of the marione by his sleeve. His hand, darkened to the shade of a granny emerlindian, lay in sharp contrast against the fine material of Holt's white shirt.

"We're very different," the knight said. "However, I believe that is only on the surface. You've chosen to make the world believe that your only concern is for Holt Hoddack to have a pleasurable, comfortable good time. But, Holt, I saw you come through time and time again on our last quest."

"To impress N'Rae," he quickly pointed out. "I was just being noble whenever I could to win her good graces. I got it in my head that should we find her father, there would be a reward."

Bardon shook his head. "I don't believe that. I think at the end of our quest, you got in the habit of making right choices. I think you were enjoying being a hero instead of the cad."

"Well, I soon forgot those good habits, now, didn't I?" Holt shrugged his shoulders and moved away a step, effectively disengaging Bardon's touch on his arm. "Being a cad feels more comfortable to me."

He looked Kale over from head to toe. "You look ready to go. You can't take all these dragons. It would be a dead giveaway that you aren't the simple wife of a humble granny."

"They will ride in the moonbeam cape. And the moonbeam cape will be carried as a satchel." She pointed to the floor where a gray carpetbag almost blended into the floor.

"Fine." Holt strode across the room and yanked the door open.

Kale and Bardon followed.

I'm not happy with this, she told her husband as she rushed down the narrow wooden stairs.

"And I'm not worried. I believe Holt is going to surprise us. This is his chance to negate all the mistakes of his youth and finally show what he is made of. What does Tieto say of his colors?"

His aura is in great disharmony. Underneath, there lies a steady rim of green that indicates undeveloped potential. Tieto showed me images of his colors undulating. That was the first time I've seen what Regidor talks about. Fascinating. Really, Bardon, I can't begin to describe it.

"Try, Kale. And walk faster while you do. He'll get away from us."

I could see a murky line wash through his aura like a ripple coming up on the bank of a river. Then the brighter colors diluted the ugly ones.

"What you're basically saying is that he is still untrustworthy."

Yes, but listen to this. Tieto says that a new thread appeared in his aura after we spoke to Wulder in the meeting. And the former colors have been quick to either absorb or repel that new thread.

"A new thread means what?"

Tieto says that the thread is Wulder's.

"So Holt has a new element to deal with. And a mighty influential element it is."

Exactly!

They caught up with Holt outside the three front doors of The Goose and The Gander. Night had come to the city of Vendela. In this part of town, clean, well-lit streets did not see many scoundrels and scalawags. No one feared they might be accosted by a ruffian.

In the light of a street lantern, Kale looked at Holt Hoddack's youthful face. He didn't have the look of a hardhearted conman. But wasn't that why he was so good at wheedling into people's good graces and then taking advantage of their gullibility? What did her husband see in him that she could not? When had Bardon's suspicions and skepticism turned to trust?

Bardon took her elbow as, without a word, Holt strolled away from them. They followed a dozen steps behind.

"I believe," said Bardon quietly, "that Wulder has chosen Holt for this mission."

"First, Toopka has a destiny, and now Holt has a mission." Kale tsked. "Wulder never seems to follow what I would call a logical plan."

"Yet we have enough experience now to look back on the events we have witnessed. From this perspective we are able to see that His design did indeed reflect a superior strategy."

"Yes, but why use people of weak character? The chance of failure is increased a hundredfold."

Bardon quoted, "I saw him fall and did not know / his knees and hands were used to sow / one more seed in Wulder's field / of honor and great deeds."

Kale pulled from what little she had learned of ancient literature. "That's from Poltace, isn't it?"

"No, Barnácee. But you were in the right time period."

Holt turned out of the market streets and into a residential area. His steps slowed.

This neighborhood worked together to present a variety of flowers in ornate boxes and barrels at every corner and at intervals down each block. The night air lifted the sweet scents from flowers hidden in shadows. Kale breathed deeply and thought fondly of her garden at the castle.

Holt paused between two lampposts so that darkness hid his features. Kale and Bardon walked up to him and stopped.

"I have one more thing to tell you," Holt said. "I haven't figured out why yet, but the Followers have a prejudice against all things that fly. They eat the flesh of no bird. Flying insects are loathed. And, most importantly to you, dear Dragon Keeper, they scorn dragons."

"That's an odd custom."

"Everything about them is peculiar, except for the hunger for power you can see if you look for it. I recognize that vice easily enough."

"But these arbitrary likes and dislikes…?"

"Sometimes I think these things are what they use to gauge how firmly they hold power over their members. Sometimes I think their decrees reflect an arrogant attitude of laying down a law just because they can." He took a deep breath. "And sometimes I think that the deviant edicts come from a deep source of evil. The machinations of such a perverse master are beyond what our minds can grasp. Only Wulder is wise enough to untangle their webs."

"Do you really believe that, Holt?" asked Bardon.

"I do."

"Then in the end, you will be all right." Bardon rubbed his chin. "I have one more question for you."

"Make it quick. I'm late as it is."

"When I was in the village of Paladise, I saw a bird carved on each doorstep."

"The Sellaran, an extinct bird they believe will rise again. They don't say how, of course. But these birds were huge, and the Followers hope they will destroy what is left of the dragons."

Kale clenched her fists. "That doesn't make sense at all. The timing is wrong. Since the end of the war, we've had more dragons hatched than in the two hundred years before." She looked at Bardon. "It would have made more sense to try to annihilate them when their numbers were at an all-time low."

"None of what they do makes sense to me. Why single out dragons to abuse them?"

Holt fiddled restlessly with the strap of his backpack. "I don't have time to debate the issue. I must be on my way."

Kale hugged him. "The house you're going to is close, is it not?"

"The next block."

"I did listen to you back at the inn, Holt. I do realize how hard this will be."

He patted her on the back and pushed her away. "Don't worry. I'll be deemed a sterling quality listener. Partly because they think they can get more money out of me, and more importantly, my father's land. They don't want to lose me. And partly because I am as good at a con as they are."

Kale twisted her fingers together. "What if they decide they've made a mistake in bringing you into their fold?"

"The elders always say that their choice of listeners is infallible."

Bardon scoffed. "They never choose someone who will fail?"

"They claim that." Holt looked Bardon in the eye. "No one who has once made the commitment ever returns to a normal life. Their proof is in the fact that no one has ever returned from Paladise."

22

Lessons for Survival

Kale lay on her stomach with her hands folded on the blanket, and her chin resting on her knuckles. "Try again."

Crispin spread his front legs apart and lowered his body until the grass tickled his chin. He set his eyes on the pile of twigs in front of him.

"Make a circle with your mouth," coached Kale.

The red dragon pursed his lips.

"No, like this." Kale puckered as if to whistle. "There has to be a hole for the air to go through." She tooted a shrill note.

Crispin blew, but instead of the stream of fire they hoped for, a thin, reedy whistle issued from his mouth.

"Don't be distressed. We can work through this problem. It's merely frustrating, not the end of the world." She massaged his side with a tiny circular pressure. "You're going to have to analyze where the fire comes from when you flame by accident. That will increase your chances of being able to generate a blaze when you want to. Do you think you can remember to be more aware of what goes on when you hiccup?"

She waited for him to think it over and decide that he could try to be attentive to what was going on in his body. His hesitant tone didn't inspire confidence in his Dragon Keeper.

"Fine." She moved her fingertip from his side to the sensitive area under his front leg, and instead of stroking, she wiggled her nail against his skin.

Crispin collapsed in a fit of giggles. After a minute of writhing under her merciless tickling, he began to gasp. Tiny spurts of fire burst from his mouth. Kale carefully kept her hair, clothes, the blanket, and anything else that would easily scorch out of his range.

"Think, Crispin, where is it coming from?"

The dragon squirmed out of her reach and flopped over on his side, panting. Tiny bursts of flame accompanied each heave. As he rested, they diminished in size.

"Now, Crispin, now!" Kale urged. "Grab that teeny stream of fire. You can do it! Make it big. As big as you can!"

The red dragon hoisted himself to his feet, pulled in a huge lungful of air and blew. The blaze sputtered and went out.

"Wrong advice." Regidor's voice startled Kale.

She rolled over on her back and looked up, shielding her eyes from the morning sun. The meech dragon towered over her.

"I've never breathed fire, Reg. I can only guess how it's done."

"What? Librettowit has no books on the subject?" He offered Kale a hand, and she took it.

"I never thought to ask him." Kale got to her feet and brushed her skirt. "Come, Crispin." The dragon flew to perch on her shoulder. "Could you tell him how it's done, Reg?"

"Certainly."

Kale turned as the heavy fabric of Gilda's dress announced her arrival.

She strode quickly to her husband's side and took his arm. "I thought we'd be ready to go by now."

"Now, my dear, how could we be ready, when you were not here to direct us?" Regidor patted her hand. "Did you enjoy your morning constitutional?"

Gilda scowled at the pile of sticks on the ground beside Kale's blanket. "The fire's not even started for morning tea?" She pointed a long finger. "Is this supposed to be a campfire? Even I can see it's not constructed properly."

"Crispin and I were just about to prepare the fire." Regidor signaled to the minor dragon, and he flew to the meech's head. Gilda stepped away.

Regidor did not comment on her sudden desertion but smiled pleasantly. "Gilda, my love, why don't you make those mouthwatering biscuits that are such a marvel?"

"You know I don't like to cook, especially with no stove. Why couldn't Sir Dar come along? He positively hums with delight over a pot of stew."

"He chose to escort Librettowit to his destination."

"He can't rejoin us soon enough for me. This entire expedition has started out badly. We've had unnecessary delays. We've had children added to our number. I detest these vermin that pass themselves off as minor dragons. How ridiculous! They're nothing but pets. And that brute Brunstetter has come along."

Kale had been briefly offended at the slur against her dragons, but the absurd charge against the noble urohm touched her funny bone. She choked on laughter at the picture of handsome and gallant Brunstetter somehow being touted as a grawlig. Gilda glared at her.

"I'm sorry, Gilda, but you just can't call Lord Brunstetter a brute. Honestly, you can't. He lives in a castle much finer than ours. He rules over a territory in Ordray. His family has been aristocracy for generations. He even dresses far more elegantly than most of Sir Dar's court."

Kale's laughter had bubbled out as she eyed the only other adult female on their quest. Life was going to be very hard if Gilda didn't face some facts. In spite of the danger of ruffling Regidor's pride, Kale decided to continue. "And, Gilda, he is much more genteel in his behavior than you are."

Gilda's mouth dropped open, then snapped shut. She turned her angry eyes from Kale to her husband.

Regidor lifted Crispin from his perch on his bald head. "We fire dragons are going to start the campfire."

He scooped up the small array of sticks with one hand and moved over to the site where a cook fire had been laid the night before.

Gilda tromped over to stand nose to nose with Kale. "You can't have him."

"What?"

"He's mine, and you can't have him."

"What are you talking about?"

Kale's eyes widened as she heard Gilda's teeth grind.

Gilda spoke in a growl. "Don't pretend. I've seen the way you look at him."

"Gilda, I knew him before he hatched. I'm like his mother."

For one second, Kale thought Regidor's wife would spit on her. But Gilda spun away in a flurry of skirts.

Kale turned to Regidor to see if he had taken note of what had just passed between his wife and herself. He seemed oblivious, busy with the fire and coaxing Crispin to set a stick aflame.

Bardon and Brunstetter came trudging through the young woods with fishing poles and two strings of large lake giddinfish.

Their laughter ceased when Bardon looked into Kale's eyes. In a moment, she poured out her confusion without saying a word. Brunstetter remained quiet, obviously aware that something was amiss.

Before Bardon could respond, the minor dragons came from every direction, screeching, squawking, and raising a ruckus.

Kale hissed. "Black dragons coming."

Bardon dropped his pole and fish and ran the distance between him and Kale. "Into shelter for you." He grabbed the blanket from the ground and hustled her toward the closest tent. He lifted the flap and thrust the blanket into her hands. "Wrap up in this for extra protection."

Remembering the stings from before, Kale thought hiding was a good idea. She swathed herself in the heavy material and stretched out on the pallet she'd slept in. With frantic fingers, she made sure every part of her was covered, tucking in the edges of the blanket. A minute passed. She took shallow breaths and tried to ignore the sweat gathering on her back. She wished she were out in the open and seeing what was happening.

Oh, Bardon. This bond between us is so convenient. I'm watching through your eyes.

She heard him chortle. *"Now that you're safe, your little friends have quit raising the alarm. Look, they've taken posts in the trees and are standing guard."*

As Bardon located each of the nine minor dragons, Kale saw them. This region had been burnt by fire dragons back in the war between

Stox and Cropper. None of the trees were over five years old. The dragons looked like big, beautiful blossoms in the young branches.

Where's Gilda?

Bardon's gaze swept the campground. Regidor stood ready with Crispin on his shoulder. Brunstetter had abandoned his morning catch and drawn his sword. Toopka and Sittiponder hung back, remaining near the doorway to the huge tent they shared with the urohm.

"Sittiponder," yelled Bardon, "take Toopka inside and make her stay there."

The blind tumanhofer grabbed the doneel girl's arm before she could slip away and tugged her into the tent.

"Gilda must be in her tent." Bardon paused. *"Do you hear them?"*

A drone reached the camp from beyond the crest of the hill.

I don't think I hear them directly, but I hear you hearing them.

The volume of the buzz increased. The sound produced a quiver along Bardon's skin. Kale reacted with goose bumps.

Bardon, be careful. Remember their stings caused you to have a stakes relapse.

"They only stung me because I was defending you. Hopefully, they'll pass over without even realizing you're here."

Bardon spotted the cloud as it came over the horizon. The swarm approached but looked like it would bypass the camp on the northern side by at least a hundred yards. The hum in the air continued to swell.

"I believe this swarm is bigger than the last one we saw."

I think so too.

"They've changed directions, Kale. They're coming this way."

I see. She squeezed her eyes closed, but the image in her mind reflected what Bardon saw. He watched the ominous cloud come nearer. She shivered.

"They may still go right over us."

The drone increased in pitch to a whine. Bardon winced and covered his ears. They closed in on the camp, circled, and then attacked the tent where Kale hid.

From inside the tent, Kale heard the rapid thuds of the small bodies hitting the canvas. From Bardon's perspective, she saw the beasts regroup to attack again. This time, fiery explosions shot from their tiny mouths. She smelled scorched cloth but knew the tent had not caught on fire. With determined concentration, she added a shield to the weave of the canvas, one she had first seen used by Sir Dar when attacked by grawligs many years before.

Brunstetter and Bardon swung their swords like boys playing stickball. They connected with the tiny targets, and oddly, the black dragons did not turn on their assailants. The beasts continued to focus on Kale. So far they had not penetrated her wizard's armor.

Ha! I'm better prepared, you nasty little beasties. Last time I didn't have time to think. This time I did my thinking beforehand.

Regidor threw fireballs, hitting the creatures above the tent as they recovered from their latest barrage against Kale's frail canvas fortress. The minor dragons flew above and spat into the swarm. Crispin joined his comrades in the air. Kale cheered when she saw a stream of flame burst from the little red dragon's mouth.

The incinerated black dragons fell to the ground. On impact, they burst like delicate china teacups, leaving small piles of ashes instead of evidence of bone and body.

As quickly as it had begun, the attack was over. The straggling remains of the swarm flew off together. Bardon gave the all clear, and Kale climbed out of her cocoon.

Gilda joined them outside the seared tent. "They only attacked Kale?"

Regidor put his arm around his wife's shoulders. "Yes."

"Then perhaps we should send her home."

"What?"

"She attracts trouble. We don't need trouble to hinder our search for the meech colony."

A low growl emanated from Regidor's throat. "She stays."

Gilda tossed her head and strolled back to her tent.

"It's only the future of an entire race you are toying with, my dear husband."

Regidor closed his eyes, sighed deeply, then turned to follow his wife.

23

Into Every Life a Little Rain Must Fall

"Catching up on the news?" Bardon asked Kale as he ducked through the flap of their tent. She sat cross-legged on her pallet with the talking gateway floating in front of her.

"I've heard from Wizard Namee, Librettowit, and Father." She looked up from her work. "I thought I smelled rain when you came in."

"It's breezy, and the clouds have covered the night sky. I'd say the likelihood of showers before morning is strong."

"If we'd brought one of the blue dragons, we'd know for sure."

"When we hear the rain against the canvas, we'll know for sure."

Kale grinned and went back to fiddling with the talking gateway.

Bardon stretched out on a pile of blankets and reveled in the lack of discomfort from stakes. Kale rubbed the ointment Elma had given them into his neck every night. It helped tremendously. As they traveled north, he and Regidor had been doing forms every morning. The exercises had been beyond Bardon's capabilities for many months. Kale joined them most mornings, which left Gilda to cook.

"What are you grinning about?" asked his wife. "You look like a bobbin bird with a stash of worms in his nest."

"I *was* thinking about food, Gilda's food. For someone who dislikes cooking, she sure fixes delectable meals."

"Librettowit says Sir Dar will join us soon."

"More good food. We're going to come back from this quest fatter than when we left."

"Namee says he's coordinating all the information on the Followers for Paladin."

"That's logical. He has the talking gateways, and his castle is centrally located. The Followers' activities have originated in central Amara."

Kale's fingers nimbly worked the threads of the gateway. Bardon's ability to see the contraption was limited. He didn't have a wizard's eye, but as with many things, when he was with his wife, her talent enhanced his abilities.

He concentrated, trying to see more than just vague strands of light. "I know I'd never see that thing if you didn't have your fingers on it."

"You see the pictures, don't you, and hear the words?"

"Oh yes."

"Good, because this one from my father, I particularly want you to hear."

He moved to sit beside her as she finished. The gateway popped once before the image of Sir Kemry appeared.

Bardon scooted closer to Kale so he could see over her shoulder. "Why did it make that noise?"

"I don't know. I must have something out of alignment. I'll ask Regidor later."

Sir Kemry spoke from the portal. "Hello, my lovely."

Bardon chuckled and kissed her cheek. "Obviously, your father is not speaking to me."

"Shh!"

The message continued. "I've had some disturbing news from my friends in the North. The pesky swarms of those dark dragons are spotted almost every day now. They still mind their own business, barreling along until they drop out of sight.

"A farmer witnessed the demise of one of the hordes. He said a thick, black cloud started across his field of corn. The pack skimmed the tops of his plants and seemed to become less dense as it flew. By the time the swarm reached the other side, it had disappeared. He rushed out to examine his crops to see if they'd caused any damage. They hadn't, but he found a trail of their bodies between the rows. The bodies had disintegrated.

"And of more interest to Regidor and Gilda, a meech dragon's body was found on the edge of the Brosnatt Desert where the Callum River goes underground. Apparently died of old age. There's a lot of uncharted territory in that region. They'll want to check into the area."

"They will, indeed," said Bardon.

"Your mother sends her love. Taylaminkadot thinks she's going to have twins. Your dragon Iffit is stealing grain from that farmer—what's-his-name?—down past Orcan's Hollow. I've paid twice for huge dragon-sized suppers. But Iffit promises to behave. He says he misses you, and that makes him hungry."

"Ha!" said Kale. "He's just as hungry when I'm there."

"Take care, my lovely. But enjoy the adventure."

The center popped again, and the image disappeared.

Bardon moved to get up. "Shall we take the message to Regidor?"

Kale flattened the portal and put it in the cylinder. She handed it to Bardon. "I need to groom the little dragons. Would you take Father's message to their tent? He may want to see the others, as well, if he hasn't been contacted. When Regidor opens the talking gateway, ask him if he'll fix that noise."

Bardon leaned over and kissed her forehead. "You're tired, aren't you? We both need this quest to get back in shape."

"The stakes?"

"Not a twinge."

"Good."

"I'll be right back." He pushed the canvas flap aside. "Dark and misting. Artross, will you come with me?"

The gray dragon flew to his shoulder. As soon as they stepped out into the night, Artross began to glow. Mikkai barreled out of the tent and sat on Bardon's other shoulder.

"So you think I need an interpreter, Mikkai?" He listened to his dragon chitter. "Yes, I suppose I do."

Bardon saw Regidor had not yet doused whatever light form he used in the tent. From the position and color, Bardon guessed the meech dragon used floating globes as his light source. Glad that his friend had not retired, Bardon tramped to the other side of the fire. As he and the dragons passed Brunstetter's dark quarters, they heard the urohm snoring and the two youngsters giggling.

Bardon crept over to their side of the tent and said, "Shh!" just as loud as his lungs would let him. Toopka and Sittiponder gasped and let out a peal of laughter. The snickering they made trying to stifle their noise woke Brunstetter. He grumbled something, but the big urohm had a large family and the happy racket of children didn't really disturb him. Bardon heard him snoring again before he went on.

On the other side of the fire, Bardon stopped short. He could call out to Regidor, but instead he eavesdropped a moment. Gilda's strident tone penetrated the cloth walls. Her husband answered each complaint in a stern voice. Without hearing the particulars of the argument, Bardon went back to the blessed peace of his own tent.

"They've gone to bed?" asked Kale as she rubbed oil into Dibl's back and wings.

"It just wasn't a good time."

Kale's eyes flashed to his and immediately away. She would not pry into what he had seen or heard. He could tell her. She probably already knew. But what would be the good of discussing the strife Gilda poured into their lives? He didn't need Tieto to know the meech lady's aura must be jagged and discordant.

The mist thickened, then turned to tiny droplets, soaking the ground with a quiet rain. Bardon helped massage oil into the nine dragons.

"Celisse is calling to me," said Kale, not stopping as she clipped Gymn's tiny toenails.

"Greer, too. They don't quite understand why we would prefer to remain warm and dry."

"I'm willing to go play with them any afternoon when they dance in a warm summer rain. But I'm not joining their antics in the middle of the night."

"Greer says you're chicken."

"Tell him I'm practical." She reached into her medicinal bag and pulled out Elma's ointment.

Bardon laughed. "Are you going to oil me now?"

"Only one tiny spot at the back of your head."

They fell asleep with their pallets pushed together and small dragons piled on top of them.

The drizzle of the rain quieted in the early morning, and when they awoke it was to the unnerving silence of a forest filled with fog. Gray tendrils of mist curled through the slight opening Bardon had left to allow fresh air to circulate through the flaps of the tent.

Bardon got up and pulled on riding pants and a thick shirt before sitting on a camp stool to shove his feet into scuffed black boots.

From where he sat, he peeked out into the gloom. "A hot cup of tea will sure taste good this morning. Crispin, do you think you can start the fire?"

The red dragon stretched and yawned. A burst of flame escaped as he exhaled.

"Come on, then." Bardon ducked through the door. Mikkai followed with Tieto and Crispin. They flew the perimeter of the camp as if checking to see if all was well.

"Greer and the others kept watch, boys." He crouched beside the fire. "Our wood is good and soaked. It's a good thing we put a supply under a tarp."

He retrieved sticks and pieces of old log from the stash and built a campfire.

"Crispin, will you do the honors?"

The small dragon landed beside the ring of rocks. He eyed the organized tangle of tinder and the bigger branches laid across the top.

"Give it a try, old man," said Bardon. "We've got a tinderbox. You don't need to feel as if the world will fall apart if you don't set it ablaze on the first try."

On the third blow, Crispin sent a stream of fire right into the middle of the pile. The flame caught the smaller twigs. Soon the tinder snapped, popped, and shimmered as it turned from brown to orange. The small blaze ignited the logs and continued to lick the wood until the fire permeated Bardon's carefully laid tower.

"Does this mean we won't fly today?"

Bardon turned to see Gilda wrapped in some silken robe that belonged in a fancy castle, not a clearing in the wood.

He gestured to the air around them. "The fog?"

She shivered. "The gray, murky, thick, and silent fog."

"We'll fly, Gilda. First, this vapor may burn off. Second, our dragons will carry us straight up and level off above this ground-hugging cloud. Mikkai can keep us on course even without looking at familiar landmarks. He has a special sense of direction that I've never known to fail."

Gilda sat abruptly on a log they had been using as a seat. "It can't be soon enough for me. This egg is getting larger every day. I don't want to be in the wilderness when it comes."

"That's understandable."

"I don't think you truly do understand. I'm a dragon. When I present an egg, I won't stay to hatch it. I won't even want to. Not then. But now, I care about where I leave it. I want it to be nurtured in a community of meech, not raised by some scurvy specimen from another race." She laughed a mirthless titter, picked up a twig from the ground, and twisted it with her fingers. "Need I tell you that Risto was not a nurturer?"

"No, I can guess as your guardian he was abominable. Cherishing was beyond the scope of his nature."

"I want better for my offspring. Regidor had Kale and Fenworth and Librettowit. You were better off in The Hall than I was."

Bardon opened his mouth to protest, but Gilda plunged on. "At least you were surrounded by your own kind. Whereas I..." She dropped the mangled twig and stepped on it, grinding it into the thin layer of mud. "There was no one I could say was of my kind, no meech. And those enslaved by Risto? Every single soul I came in contact with was either filled with hatred or fear. And I hated and feared them as well."

She thrust her chin forward and glared at Bardon. "I not only want this meech child to know his own kind, I want him to absorb the atmosphere of a meech colony. This child will exude intellect, culture, and refinement. No one will look askance at my offspring."

Her gaze shifted to the fire. Her expression became pensive. Bardon wondered what future she tried to envision in the dancing yellows and reds of the blaze. Apparently, Gilda forgot that Bardon and several dragons listened.

"No one will shun my child," she whispered. "No one."

24

Campfire Tales

Bardon watched Sir Dar's dragon Merlander as the brilliantly colored beast approached. He raised a hand in greeting. The doneel would surely raise the spirits of all those on the quest. Bardon sighed. The group had fallen into a glum state.

He and the others had only been journeying for four days, but something heavy oppressed the country. As they traveled northward, the melancholy became palpable. Bardon tramped through the thigh-high grass to greet Sir Dar. He expected to see the wide smile that typified doneels. Instead, Sir Dar's solemn expression deflated Bardon's hopes for good news.

They sat around in a circle after savoring a meal the doneel diplomat brought with him. He demonstrated a happy demeanor as he heated and served dinner by the campfire. But Bardon detected an underlying distress that his diplomatic mentor fought hard to hide. Finally, after they were settled, Kale demanded a full account.

"It's obvious, Sir Dar, and you're driving me crazy. You are trying *not* to tell us something, or waiting for the right moment." She brushed her curly locks away from her face and looked him in the eye. "My courage is shriveling as I imagine all sorts of bad news. Please, tell us."

Sir Dar sat for a moment, staring at the fire. When he began to speak, he outlined his news in a direct manner, never attempting to gloss over the implications of the events. The most alarming element of his report came last. He revealed the amazing speed with which the Follower faction was expanding throughout the country.

Bardon broke the silence that followed Sir Dar's speech. "It's amazing how quickly evil spreads and how long it takes to gain back the ground with good."

"I don't believe these people just popped up out of nowhere." Sir Dar scratched his chin. "One day the Followers were a rumor. Two weeks later they possess meeting houses in every big city, communes in every province, and even schools for older children. Officials in government are declaring their allegiance to the New Understanding. Businesses and properties have recently changed hands and now belong to the Collective."

He looked around the group and sniffed. "The Collective! Even the name smells of heresy. Wulder has always emphasized the importance of individuals. He's never lumped people together. There's a reason he made seven high races."

"Why?" asked Toopka. Her voice at full volume demanded attention. "Why did Wulder make seven high races?"

Sir Dar frowned at her. "I don't know the reason He did, child. I just know if Wulder chose to make seven high races, He had a good reason for doing so."

Toopka scrunched up her face, then turned to her blind tumanhofer friend next to her.

Sittiponder rocked slightly as he sat cross-legged on the ground. His hand rested on Toopka's arm. "It's called trust, my furry friend. Wulder puts a lot of stock in trust."

The little doneel's shoulders hunched up far enough to touch her cheeks. She let them fall and sighed loudly. "What's that mean?"

"Do you always have to talk so loudly? You rattle the leaves on the trees around us." Sittiponder sighed. "It means He appreciates it when we believe Him."

Toopka clicked her tongue and shook her head. "I believe He made seven high races. I can see them."

"He appreciates it when we believe He has a reason for making seven and not five or six races."

Toopka remained silent.

"Ha! You don't have a question?'

"No." She played with the fringe on the end of her sash.

Sittiponder nodded sagely. "Wulder also appreciates it when you're not constantly questioning whether He's doing things the right way or not."

"So," said Toopka in a quieter tone than she usually used, "if Wulder wanted someone to do something, the someone shouldn't worry about knowing when to do it and how to do it and where to do it and who to do it to and why it has to be done?"

No one answered.

"Well?" Toopka's volume had risen again.

"I'm thinking," said Sittiponder. "You asked a lot of questions in that question."

"As we have seen in our history," said Sir Dar, "Wulder does equip His warriors specifically for the challenges they face."

Brunstetter reached over and put his huge hand on the doneel girl's back. "He provides help in every time of trouble. Sometimes the help comes from a surprising source."

"And that…" Sir Dar clapped his hands together. "That makes our adventures a good deal more entertaining. We cannot predict whom He will use to further His plans."

"You need not worry, Sir Dar," said Gilda. "In the old records Regidor and I have discovered, there are references to the meech holding a vital secret. This mysterious power controls evil. Once we find the meech colony, the destiny of Amara will once more be in safe hands."

Bardon glanced at Regidor, hoping for further details. But his friend wore his most bland expression, and Bardon knew the closed-off attitude well. There would be no explanations from that quarter.

"Would you share with us the extent of your discoveries?" asked Sir Dar. His bright eyes showed interest. His ears perked forward, and his furry hands rested on the elegant cloth covering his knees. He leaned forward, giving Gilda all his attention. "I'm sure all of us are anxious to know more of your ancestry."

The campfire flames caught the resin of a log. Snaps and crackles punctuated the sudden whoosh of sparks shooting into the air. The flare cast a glow on Gilda's exotic features. Bardon caught a glimpse of eagerness in her eyes. The excitement accentuated her fascinating appeal. A moment later, shadows again obscured her beauty. At times, Bardon thought of Regidor's wife as a rare piece of art, lovely to look at and admire, but too peculiar to step out of the frame and be a part of the ordinary world.

Gilda stood and paced, animated by her knowledge. She clasped her hands and addressed the others as if they were an audience in a lecture hall. "The meech probably came from another planet through something similar to a gateway. The only explanation is that Wulder Himself made the portal, and for His reasons, brought what is termed 'the great and the small' by ancient scribes to your land.

"By comparing the three accounts we found, we've concluded that the 'small' are the minneken, who also wisely withdrew from mingling with your seven high races. The legend is that the meech brought knowledge of good and evil, that they controlled evil on their world, and were charged with controlling evil on this world."

Regidor threw a small branch onto the campfire. The disturbance caused another flare up. Red and gold sparks floated up into the dark sky and disappeared.

"The key word in this is 'legend,'" said Regidor. "In all of our searching, we found only three documents. Each was written in the style of folklore."

Gilda started to say something, but Kale jumped in. "Many of the ballads I heard while growing up were history in poetic form. Mistress Meiger always said there is some truth behind the tales woven into the music."

"That's so." Gilda gave Kale a rare look of approval. "Many questions will be answered when we locate the colony."

Sittiponder shivered.

"Are you cold?" asked Toopka. She picked up her gaily striped shawl and put it around his shoulders.

Bardon rose to his feet. The boy's pale face alarmed him. Sittiponder stared with unseeing eyes at the fire, looking distressed. The muscle in his jaw twitched. His lips quivered as if he worked to keep from crying. Kale rose and started forward.

Bardon stepped closer and crouched before Sittiponder. "What is it, lad?"

"The voices have told me to beware."

"I'd forgotten the boy hears voices," said Brunstetter. "We decided they come from kimens, didn't we? Guardians appointed by Wulder?"

"*We* decided," said Sir Dar, "with no real evidence. We never came up with an alternate, logical explanation."

Gilda sat beside her husband. "It's obvious that someone protects him."

"I'm not the one who needs protecting," objected Sittiponder. "I'm supposed to watch after Toopka. She's the one who will face danger."

Gilda rolled her eyes.

Regidor took her hand but addressed the children. "We will all do our best to protect you."

Kale put her arms around the boy. "You're still shivering." She turned to Brunstetter. "It's late. I think they should go to bed."

"Right." Rising with more agility than one would expect from such a large man, the urohm swooped down on both the boy and girl. He tucked each child under one of his huge arms and lugged them off to his tent. Toopka squirmed and giggled, but Sittiponder hung limply without the mock protesting that usually accompanied this bedtime ritual.

Kale bit her lower lip. "I hope nothing's wrong with him."

Gilda took a large breath and let it out slowly. "Nothing is wrong with the child," she said patiently, "that a good night's sleep won't cure."

Kale turned sharply to cast an irritated glare at the meech lady.

Gilda hiked a shoulder and looked down her nose. Before Kale could speak, she snapped, "I am more aware of children now that I carry my own. Those two have vivid imaginations and take an element of truth and stretch it into something that suits their fancy. It's mostly done to gain attention, I presume."

Bardon felt annoyance bubbling in Kale. The rejoinder she formed in her mind had something to do with Gilda taking scraps of legends and stretching her conclusions until the meech colony was the seat of all knowledge and culture. He quickly moved to Kale's side and put an arm around her waist. "I'm tired too. Good night, Sir Dar, Regidor. Pleasant dreams, Gilda."

He turned toward the tent and relaxed when he felt Kale give way to his guidance. A principle came to his mind.

A shield of kind words deflects arrows thrown by the wounded.

"I don't want to pity her."

You don't want to add to Regidor's burdens, either.

Inside the tent, Kale sat down on her pallet and gathered the minor dragons into her lap.

"You know what I think, Bardon?"

"Sometimes."

"Right now I'm thinking I resent the fact that Gilda is going to have a baby. And being a meech dragon, she'll feel a thrill of accomplishment and then no further need to nurture the child."

"It is odd that they deal with offspring in such an inattentive manner. But from what I understand, the child is the concern of each person in the community."

"I don't think I could share my baby with everyone."

"Considering how you felt about letting your father take over your duties with the dragons at home, no, I don't think you would."

Kale sighed heavily. "I don't suppose my ability to share the responsibility of raising a child will be a problem anytime soon."

Bardon sat beside her. Immediately, the dragons spilled over into his lap and began a game of chase, using the two of them as a playing field. "Someday we'll be parents." Bardon dodged Filia as she dashed across Kale's shoulder. He managed to plant a kiss on his wife's cheek before Dibl crash-landed on Bardon's head, digging his claws into his scalp. He winced and shoved the yellowish dragon back into the air. "You, Kale, will be an overprotective mother. I will be an obnoxiously proud father. And all these critters will be guardians and playmates."

Artross jumped onto Bardon's head. Metta challenged him for possession of the prized perch and knocked the glowing white dragon into Bardon's lap.

"Enough!" said the Dragon Keeper's husband. "Settle down and go to bed."

Kale giggled, but Bardon thought her eyes still held a wistful look.

They made plans to visit a town just before they crossed into the Northern Reach. With Mikkai's help, they located a small village on a trade route that would be an adequate resting spot. They also desired to gather more information about the heart condition of the people in the area.

"This has been a rather tame quest, has it not?" said Sir Dar as he dished out stew that evening.

"Be careful what you say," warned Regidor.

"We've had a little rain, but other than that, more than a week of easy travel." Sir Dar sat back on his haunches and dipped his spoon into the savory broth. "But I'll be glad for a meal at a table and a real bed tomorrow night."

Kale put her hand on her heart. "Then why do I feel so tired here? Why am I sad?"

Brunstetter grunted his agreement. "At night my dreams are filled with gloom. And even the children are clearly downhearted. When was the last time we heard Sittiponder sing? Toopka does not chatter from sunrise to sunset."

"Most assuredly, that is not a bad thing," said Gilda.

Kale gave Gilda a sympathetic look. "You've been depressed too."

"I'm with child and tired. Also, the delay in accomplishing our quest is a wretched situation to deal with day after day. I wish Regidor and I had undertaken this journey alone."

"We would not have traveled any faster, my dear." Regidor soothed his wife.

Annoyance flashed across her face, but she did not speak.

Kale and Regidor lifted their faces to the southern sky at the same time.

"Lee Ark is about to join us," announced Regidor. He stood and moved toward the field where the large riding dragons rested.

"He's troubled," said Kale.

"Is he hurt?" asked Toopka.

Kale frowned and searched the shadows by the tent until she spotted her ward. "You're supposed to be in bed."

"I'm not tired, and Sittiponder won't talk to me."

Regidor lifted her to sit on his shoulder and strode toward the meadow. "No, little one. Lee Ark is weary of soul. Perhaps your fuzzy, funny face will chase away his gloom. Let's go greet him."

⟜ 25 ⟝

One More to Quest

"I've hidden my family and sent my troops into the hills to stand ready to fight." Lee Ark strode up the hill, accompanied by Sir Dar, Kale, Bardon, and Regidor with Toopka on his shoulders.

"I almost missed you in this rugged terrain." He gestured to the rock outcroppings and a steep cliff. "My mount sensed the presence of your dragons and guided me here." He continued up the hill without any indication that the strenuous exercise taxed his muscled body. "You know these Followers don't like dragons. More proof of their misguided theology. Is there anything left from your dinner?" asked the marione general. "I'm starved."

"Enough for one serving," answered Sir Dar, puffing a bit from the effort to keep up. "But I'll throw some more biscuits in a pan, and that should fill you up."

"Ah! Sir Dar's biscuits baked over a campfire. That's worth traveling a thousand miles."

"General Lee Ark, I admit you're pushing my curiosity to the limits," said Bardon. "Why are you here? What compelled you to come so far?"

"I'm fleeing the country."

"What?" Kale exploded.

"Yes, I'm a criminal."

Kale let go of Bardon's arm and rounded on Lee Ark. She grabbed the material of his jacket sleeve and stopped him. "Why?"

He shrugged, the pleasant expression on his face never slipping. "Let's see if I can remember it all. Ignoring orders, redirecting delivery of goods requisitioned by the government, arresting an elected dignitary and thus detaining him long enough to miss an important meeting, releasing prisoners destined for the docks to be shipped to penal colonies, and a couple other charges that made absolutely no sense to me. The charges I just listed, I remember doing. There's five or six more that they must have added on for good measure."

Regidor shifted Toopka's position on his neck. "Sounds like you've been quite busy, General. In all that hustle and bustle, it could be that a few minor felonies slipped your mind."

"This has got to be explained," protested Sir Dar.

Lee Ark grimaced. "Before or after the biscuits?"

"During the cooking of the biscuits. And they won't be served until I've heard the tale."

"And," said Toopka, "he won't give you the butter and jam if he thinks you're telling fibs. He does that to me all the time."

"All the time?" Regidor tickled her leg. "I thought you rarely saw Sir Dar."

"I should say every time, then, shouldn't I?" replied the girl in her sauciest tone. "Because I mostly spend *all* my time with Kale and Bardon. But every time I see Sir Dar, he makes biscuits or something else wonderfully delicious, and every time he says I'm not telling the whole truth, and then..." Toopka gave a dramatic sigh. "I don't get the jam."

"Heartless," said Regidor with a sad wag of his head. "Sir Dar, you're heartless, and I never suspected."

"Toopka is a rare artist in the utterance of partial truth and exaggeration. I certainly have not cooked for her every time I've seen her. As one of her guardians, I am only doing my duty in my attempts to break her of these deplorable habits."

Kale still clutched the material of the marione's uniform. She shook the sleeve, and thus his arm, emphatically. "Lee Ark, tell us! Why were you disobeying orders?"

"And committing crimes against the state?" asked Regidor.

The general pried Kale's fingers off his coat. "Because the orders I received obviously did not come from Paladin."

"How could you tell?" asked Toopka.

"The directives I received were contrary to Wulder's principles, little one. Anyone who has read Wulder's Tomes would see the little red flags popping out of the words on the document."

Toopka gasped. "Was it wizard's magic?"

"No, just common sense," answered Lee Ark.

Regidor jostled Toopka as if to throw her off. "She means the flags coming out of the paper."

"They weren't real flags," Lee Ark explained patiently. "They were tiny details that never would have been approved by Wulder, and, therefore, it is unlikely Paladin penned the orders."

"Is Paladin ill again?" asked Kale.

"No, from what I hear, he's as strong as ever and pacing his cell like a caged lion."

"Cell?" Sir Dar glared at Lee Ark. The word echoed off a rock wall in the canyon. "Here's something we know nothing about. Why would our leader be in a cell?"

Regidor raised one of Toopka's legs and pointed it at Lee Ark. "Perhaps Paladin objected to people sending out orders under his name?"

"And those bad people," Toopka exclaimed, bouncing on Regidor's shoulders, "got mad at Paladin for objecting and put him in a cell where they wouldn't have to listen to him."

"Yes," said Lee Ark, "and his own council has been seduced by the Followers."

"Hey, I haven't been seduced," said Bardon. "I'm on that council."

"No, you're not," countered the general. "You're on a quest."

Bardon's hand went to the hilt of his sword. "I can return quickly enough if Kale will find me a gateway. Regidor, shall we go rescue Paladin?"

Lee Ark stopped. "Hold on. That's not among the orders I have for you."

"You have orders for me? From Paladin? How can you be sure?"

"I sent a kimen into Paladin's palace. He spoke to Paladin."

"And what are my orders?"

"Find the meech colony. Find out about this sleeping monster. Find out about the black dragon swarms. And..."

"And?"

"Watch your back." Lee Ark's voice had lost the bantering tone he so often used.

"Is there any reason in particular that I should be watching my back?"

"Yes. The Followers want your property. And they now boldly imprison those who stand in their way."

"Impossible!" cried Sir Dar.

"My mother and father?" Kale tried to suppress the quiver in her voice, but Bardon detected it, along with the rush of fear surging through her body.

"Safe, but not in hiding," answered Lee Ark. "In fact, many people are taking refuge in wizard castles. In the case of your extraordinary abode, there is little the Followers can do to get past so many dragons and two powerful wizards."

The creases in Kale's frown deepened. "Bardon, perhaps we should go home."

"No." Bardon put his arms around his wife. "Paladin obviously has a plan for us in the Northern Reach. Your mother and father are more than capable of handling everything that happens. Wulder has equipped them well."

"I'm going to leave them a message." She broke from his embrace and went to their tent.

Bardon listened for a few more minutes as Lee Ark gave more details of the insurgents' gains. Then he joined Kale. He heard the annoying pop as the gateway became operational.

"Any messages?" he asked.

"One from Namee. I haven't listened to it yet."

The talking gateway creaked and snapped.

Bardon bent at the waist to look over Kale's shoulder. "Anything wrong?"

"I don't think so. There. Now we've caught the message. It was a slippery one."

"Hello, Kale." Wizard Namee looked tired but cheerful. "Such a lot happening in our country. I wanted you to know that your friend Holt ended up in a village called Paladise quite near my castle. Seezle is bringing reports to me, and I have one from Holt especially for you." He picked up a paper from his cluttered desk. "I wrote it down just as Seezle quoted it to me. I think there might be some kind of code involved." He put glasses on. " 'Dearest Kale, whatever have I done to deserve being banished to a village where the women are not allowed to smile? Yours truly, Holt Hoddack.' " He lowered the paper and peered over his glasses. "That's all for now. Be careful, my friend."

Bardon straightened and stretched. "So, do you think Holt put a code in that message?"

Kale burst into laughter. "What do you think?"

"Nope." He grinned. "But I do believe that he thinks he's being punished."

"Guilty conscience," said Kale. "Now I'm going to leave one for Father and Mother. What should I say?"

"Tell them everything is fine, so far. Ask your father if he's been attacked by the black dragons."

"Now, that would prove that everything is not fine. I'd have to tell him I'd been attacked. Twice."

"Then warn him to be careful because you've been attacked twice by the black dragons."

"Then he'll worry."

"I bet he doesn't worry much. Your mother might."

"You're right. He'd say I'm perfectly capable of handling a few temperamental dragons."

Bardon kissed the top of her head. "And so you are."

26

Mysterious Toopka

"Why do we have to walk?" asked Toopka. She kicked the small pebbles in the country road. Grubby stunted plants grew sporadically over the land on either side.

"Pick up your feet." Kale took Toopka's hand. "You're stirring up dust and getting our clothes dirty."

The questing party walked in a loose group. No one, except Toopka, talked much as they traversed the several miles to Arreach. Mikkai assured them that the place existed, a large village, or perhaps a small town, dedicated to the comforts of travelers along the east-west trade route.

Toopka quit scuffling. "All right, but it's not much fun to just walk. Why can't we fly?"

"Because people in this region aren't accustomed to seeing dragons."

Toopka shielded her eyes with her hand and gazed over the scene of rocks, scrub brush, and patches of trees. "What people?"

"Herders live out on these plains, but I was referring to the townspeople. Dragons are scarce here."

"Then we should let them see our dragons. Why aren't we sharing? They could see Greer and Merlander and Celisse and Foremoore. Even Regidor and Gilda ride dragons." She paused, tilting her head. "Why do Regidor and Gilda ride dragons?"

"Regidor explained this to you before."

"When?"

"Years ago."

"Oh! Well, no wonder I don't remember. I was just a baby then."

Kale sighed and wiped sweat from her forehead and neck with a handkerchief that had been clean an hour ago. She stuffed the mucky cloth in a hollow and pulled out another.

"Kale?" Toopka tugged on her cape.

"Oh." She refocused on her ward. "As far as I know, you have never been a little baby. You have always been a child. And as far as I know, you may always be a child."

A breeze flitted by, cooling them and also stirring up tiny dust devils. A hawk called as he tilted his wings in the pale blue sky.

Toopka skipped beside Kale, unconcerned by her guardian's cryptic words. "Why don't Regidor and Gilda fly?"

"Because it would be like you running all day long without ever stopping. Flying all day would wear them out."

"It doesn't wear Greer out when he flies all day."

"Yes, it does. Just ask him. He'll tell you Bardon gains a hundred pounds during the day. He says that he earns his sleep, a big dinner, and a good scale buffing."

"I can't ask him because he won't mindspeak to me. But he lets me polish his scales."

Kale stopped to fasten the front of her cape.

Toopka stuck out her lower lip. "I wish I had a moonbeam cape. Then I would never be too hot or too cold."

"Moonbeam plants are rare, and the cape doesn't really work like that. My hands and face and feet can get very hot or very cold."

They entered a section of the lane where trees on both sides provided shade.

"If I rode in a pocket like the little dragons, I'd be comfortable."

"Why don't you run up to where Brunstetter is? He can carry you on his other shoulder, and Sittiponder will talk to you."

"No, he won't." Toopka's lower lip stuck out further in an exaggerated pout.

"Why not? Have you been aggravating him?"

"He's been aggravating me. He keeps saying I need to get ready to 'bear the life that defeats the foe.'"

Kale raised her eyebrows. "Where did he get that?"

"You know, from the voices."

A stronger gust of wind blew about them. Kale squinted against the grit propelled by the air.

"Yuck!" Toopka spit and sputtered. "I've got to learn to keep my mouth shut."

Kale refrained from making a snide remark. Sometimes the opportunities to tease her furry ward were almost too tempting. Then she remembered how hard it had been to be raised as the village slave, an orphan among strangers.

She put a soft hand on the doneel's head. "Toopka, are you worried about what Sittiponder said? That night at the campfire, he said you were in danger."

Toopka dodged out from under Kale's touch and ran over to the edge of the path to closely inspect a cluster of wild yellow dropsies. The stalks stood up straight, but the blossoms leaned over in a cascade of tiny flowerets, looking as though they were about to fall to the ground.

The doneel sniffed the flowers and hummed her appreciation of the sweet fragrance before she answered Kale. "He can be kind of a worrywart."

"I know, and I thought he might be trying to scare you the littlest bit to make you more cautious." Kale glanced behind at Sir Dar to see if he listened. She could see he took in every word. His ears perked forward, and his eyes never left Toopka.

"I know when to be careful." With stubby fingers, she put a bright flower behind each ear and rejoined Kale in their walk.

"Toopka, I've seen you jump into more than one fight with our foes."

"Only because I am little, and they don't even see me most of the time." She pulled an imaginary sword. "I can run in, poke 'em, and run out before they even know I'm there."

"Well, you run up to Brunstetter and ride with him for a while. I don't want you to be too tired to enjoy yourself when we get to the village."

Toopka scurried away. When she reached Brunstetter, she tugged on his pant leg just above his boot. He plucked her from the road and placed her on his shoulder.

"Sir Dar?"

The doneel quickened his pace to come up beside her. "I heard."

"What do you think? As her guardians, should we be worried?"

"Don't know that worry ever helped a situation. We can be watchful. But if our little Toopka is going to bear a life, she is going to have to mature a great deal."

"I don't think she even realized that expression means to be pregnant."

"Probably not." Sir Dar squinted against the sun as they walked out of the pleasant shade. "I made inquiries about her."

"You did? Why didn't you tell me?"

"I didn't find out enough to tell. She was seen around the market for a few months before you found her. No one knew where she had come from before that."

"She said she'd been in the market for years."

"That's her standard answer. How long have you been living with Kale? For years. How long have you known how to make tea? For years. How long did you know Sittiponder when you lived on the streets of Vendela? For years."

Kale chuckled. "I do recognize that question and answer pattern. Is there anything else you can tell me that you've noticed about Toopka?"

"Oh yes."

Kale looked at him closely when he didn't say anything further. She thought she recognized a lurking twinkle in his eye, but she asked anyway. "What have you noticed?"

"She has atrocious fashion sense for a doneel."

Kale looked at Toopka's pink polka-dot blouse, flowered skirt, and striped bloomers and agreed. "But I've never lost her in a crowd."

Kale watched the little girl bury her fingers in Brunstetter's hair and hold on. She could be affectionate, and she could be very obtuse. "Do you think she feigns her poor memory?"

"Her memories do seem to be sporadic. She may conveniently forget unpleasant things."

"Some time ago, I overheard her telling a servant about a pink castle she had been to. Are there any pink castles in Amara?"

Dar shook his head. "But I've heard of an entire city on the Southern Continent made out of pink stone."

"She's traveled abroad?"

"Or heard stories."

"Where?"

"The marketplace at Vendela. Calm down, Kale. Toopka is just Toopka. A little odd, a little unpredictable, and a little pest. Don't let your imagination run away with you."

Kale gestured toward the blind tumanhofer child. "What about the things Sittiponder said?"

"Another child with an active imagination."

"You think I'm making too much of it, and I think you are taking this situation too lightly."

"I promise to keep an open mind and watch her diligently." Sir Dar performed a court bow, complete with the removal of his hat and the sweep of his arm in front of him. "Will that make you more at ease?"

"Having Paladin here and in the mood to answer questions would put me in a better frame of mind."

"Now, you know asking Paladin to tell you what is going to happen tomorrow, or at any time in the future, is futile."

"I know. He gives those vague answers."

Sir Dar lowered his voice. "All will blend together into a pattern of great beauty."

Kale copied the authoritative tone. "You will be astonished by the end. We shall see magnificent glory with our own eyes."

"The ultimate plan is to bring you home." Sir Dar's eyes shone with contentment. The underlying mischief had flown.

Kale didn't continue the game. "Do you believe it all, Sir Dar?"

"Every word."

27

A Traveler's Warning

The questers marched toward the small trade route village from the southern road. The two children still perched on Brunstetter's shoulders. Kale and Bardon walked on one side of the urohm, and Sir Dar hurried along on the other. The minor dragons had been tucked away in the moonbeam cape. Regidor and Gilda followed, disguised as a wealthy emerlindian couple.

Emerlindians in North Amara were tall. The shadows from Gilda's veils and Regidor's broad-brimmed hat created the dark countenance required. The meech dragons' clothing hid their wings, and the style suggested the couple were city people rather than citizens who preferred the hills and forest. Regidor had devised an illusion to complete their disguise. The bulges that concealed their tails and wings looked more like fashion excesses. He minimized their height so that when a stranger spoke to them, he looked at their chests as if he looked them in the eye. This trick made Regidor chuckle and Gilda indignant. Only another wizard would be able to detect their true image.

Lee Ark brought up the rear. Kale and Gilda had found enough clothing in their hollows to make him look like a servant instead of a general in Paladin's service. However, the soldier just could not remember to slump and shuffle. At the edge of town he picked up a walking stick and leaned on it. That obscured his military posture to some degree.

Bardon noticed the difference between the lane they had just traversed and the highway running east and west. The way they'd come had been little more than a rutted path. The wider crossroad showed signs of much travel, and more importantly, some upkeep. Traffic had ground the fine gravel covering the public road into hard-packed dirt. More tiny rough stones had been spread in the ruts.

Instead of a square, the town center of Arreach formed a circle. Four stone walkways criss-crossed lush green grass so that shoppers could walk the diagonal instead of the lengthy circumference of the lawn. Cobblestone or brick paved the main roads.

Thick clay plastered the wooden structures, and each storefront boasted a different bright hue. Fresh paint indicated that the village prospered. In spite of the harsh winters, this place would be cheerful. Music rang out from several different sources. Contrary to the friendly atmosphere, the villagers greeted them with wary glances.

"Why the suspicion?" asked Brunstetter.

"These people see the same travelers over and over again," answered Sir Dar. "The east-west trade route is popular."

Bardon grunted. "And we are carrying no goods to trade."

"We shall have to win them over with charm," said Toopka from Brunstetter's shoulder.

Kale sent her a warning glance. "You let the official diplomat take care of charming the locals."

Gilda nodded toward an establishment with a sign stating it was the Halfway Pint. "There's the place we want." She made a beeline for the tavern, passing the others in the party. "Sleeping without the cacophony of night insects. Eating bread made in an oven—surely this is the ultimate indicator of civilization."

The rest of the questers followed her imperious figure like courtiers following the queen. She swept through the inn's entryway and took a seat in the dim receiving area. Bardon and Regidor crossed the threshold a moment later. Bardon went to the desk where an o'rant gawked at the invasion of his establishment.

"We require four rooms."

The innkeeper looked over the party, swallowed, and asked, "How long will ye be staying?"

"Just tonight."

"You don't have any baggage?"

"Not much."

The man squinted as he examined the small crowd in his lounge. Toopka and Sittiponder climbed down off their mountain of a ride and stamped their feet as if urging the circulation to return. Quickly, their noise fell into a game with the doneel clomping a pattern and the tumanhofer repeating it.

The landlord's face relaxed as he watched the children's shenanigans. "We don't have anything fancy," he said, "but our rooms are clean."

"Fair enough."

"If your journey takes you west, you ought to wait a day or two till another group comes through. Travelers been having a bit of trouble in the mountains with grawligs. Better to go in a large company."

"Thanks for the advice."

The man behind the counter pushed four keys toward Bardon. "You can eat with us at six, or go down the street to the Keg of Mallow. They serve all evening."

"Thank you again." Bardon picked up the keys. "Do you know anyone who is familiar with the Northern Reach?"

He shook his head. "No one goes there. Nothing to bring back to sell or trade."

"Fine." Bardon turned to the others and signaled for them to follow.

As they started up the stairs, the o'rant called to Bardon. "Come to think of it, there's an old retired schoolteacher who used to say he'd gone north. I can direct you to his house."

"We'll take you up on that, Master…"

"Bandy."

"Master Bandy." Bardon nodded. "I'll be back for the directions as soon as I get my people settled."

At the top of the stairs, they sorted out the rooms. Only one would suit for the urohm, so he and the little ones took the room farthest down the hall. Sir Dar and Lee Ark had the room across from the biggest, and the married couples each had a chamber several doors away from the end. In order to have a meeting, they all crammed into Brunstetter's room.

"I want to go see the schoolteacher," demanded Toopka.

"No," said Gilda. "You would interfere."

The girl put her hands on her hips and glared at the meech lady. "Are you going?"

"No." Gilda sat in a large chair. She removed her hat and veils. The additional disguise contrived by wizardry slipped. Her strong meech dragon features revealed fatigue. "I have no wish to visit the hovel of a retired tutor."

Toopka tapped her foot, her hands still planted as balled fists on her waist. Kale caught the girl's eye. She shook her head slightly at the ornery doneel.

Bardon grinned at the expression on the face of his wife's ward. Kale must have delivered quite a lecture mindspoken with that minuscule shake. His wife's curls had hardly bounced, but the doneel looked chagrined.

Toopka curtsied. "Excuse me for my impertinence, Lady Gilda."

Gilda gave an imperial nod. Irritation boiled in Bardon's veins. He gladly turned his attention to her husband as he took control of the conversation.

Regidor patted his wife on the shoulder. "I shall go visit the schoolteacher, and perhaps Bardon and Lee Ark will join me." He transferred his gaze. "Sir Dar and Brunstetter, if you would visit the places where people congregate in this town? You might glean information from the citizens."

Both men nodded, accepting their assignment.

Regidor smiled at Kale. "And if you, my dear Dragon Keeper, would mingle with the ladies shopping in the various establishments catering to women?"

Kale agreed.

"We can help," exclaimed Toopka, grabbing Sittiponder by the arm. "Don't make us sit in the tavern. Pleeeeease!"

Regidor grimaced at the high-pitched plea. He shook his head as if to get rid of an echo. "I wouldn't think of it, dear one. You shall roam the streets and find out so much information, we shall be astonished."

Only Gilda remained at the inn. In front of the tavern, Bardon kissed his wife good-bye and told Toopka to mind Sittiponder. Toopka stuck her tongue out at her blind tumanhofer friend. Bardon hooted as he watched the surprise on her face. She always forgot that her rude gestures would not cause the expected reaction from him. She fixed a fierce glare upon Bardon for laughing at her and aimed her tongue at him instead. He thwarted any satisfaction she might get by merely turning away.

As they went their separate ways, Bardon matched his pace to the steady stride of Lee Ark and Regidor. He contained his eagerness to hear what this schoolteacher had to say. His companions marched toward their goal without revealing what they might expect from this person.

Each side street left the center of town like a spoke in a wheel. In the dusky light of early evening, the red and white signs naming the lanes stood out under globes of golden radiance. Regidor, Lee Ark, and Bardon turned down the street marked Oben Way, strolled a couple of blocks, and stopped at a house that had a blue door and mumfers, with their crimson blossoms bobbing on tall stalks, lining the walk.

Regidor stepped back, leaving Lee Ark to knock. Footsteps sounded within, and the door creaked open at the hand of a young tumanhofer.

"Come in," he said, standing back. "We've been expecting you. Master Bandy sent word you wanted to talk to Grandda. It's a good thing you've come early. Grandda goes to bed right soon after the sun does."

The tumanhofer gestured toward the sitting area of the small cottage. An elderly man sat by the fire with a shawl over his shoulders and a blanket over his legs. He had a pipe between his teeth, but no smoke curled from the bowl. An old woman sat in a rocker, knitting. A younger woman nodded from the kitchen as she tidied after the evening meal. A man sat in a chair with his suit jacket draped over the back. He rose and extended his hand.

"Welcome. It's a rare treat for Da to have someone come to visit. Most of the villagers are tired of his tales. It'll please him to tell you of his adventures. But you'll have to speak up for him to hear, and he can't see more than shapes now."

He crossed to the elder gentleman and rested his hand on a shoulder covered with wool cloth. "Da, these people have come to ask about your travels in the Northern Reach. Will you give them the time of day, or no?"

The multitude of wrinkles on the man's face shifted into a smile. His wide grin flashed surprisingly good teeth for such an old fellow. He raised his hand, and Lee Ark stepped forward to shake it. He introduced himself. Bardon followed, but Regidor took up a stance in the shadows. The old man tilted his head as if he expected a third handshake but quickly shrugged and motioned for the two to sit.

"My name's Woodkimkalajoss. Do you need a drink, or pie, perhaps? My daughter-in-law makes the best razterberry pie. We had some tonight, and she usually makes two and hides one." He chuckled and winked in the general direction of the younger woman. "We'll persuade her to bring out the one she's got hidden."

Bardon looked at the red-cheeked matron in the kitchen area. She nodded.

Bardon spoke loud enough for the elderly man to hear. "We would much appreciate the pie, Master Woodkimkalajoss. We haven't had our dinner yet, and a delicious bite of pastry will tide us over nicely."

The tumanhofer raised his hand and let it fall on his knee. Bardon took the gesture to be a feeble attempt at enthusiasm. "Got that, sweet girl? Your delicious pastry will be appreciated. Bring out the razterberry and serve it up. I'll have another piece, too, sweet girl. And I bet that growing boy wants another."

The young man who answered the door laughed as he got up. "I'll help you, Ma."

With big mugs of strong, hot tea, and plates full of pie, the guests were too busy to ask questions. But Woodkimkalajoss didn't need any prompting. As he ate, he told his tale of breaking tradition and wandering the lands above the border for years before he settled down and took the position of schoolteacher from his own father.

The room darkened, and no one in the family moved to light the candles. Only the flickering flames from the fireplace cast an orange glow into the room. The mother unobtrusively gathered the empty dishes. The son left, quietly slipping out the front door. The older woman's hands gradually stilled, her head leaned back, and a soft snore rumbled an uncanny backdrop to her husband's words.

He spoke of fierce wild animals, stunning landscapes, occasional scrapes involving both the high and low races, searching for riches, finding satisfaction in simple things, and coming home ready to be content with life in a small town on a trade route.

When the old man's eyes drifted shut and his raspy voice softened to a whisper, Bardon asked, "Did you ever run into a meech dragon in the Northern Reach?"

His eyelids snapped open, and his clouded eyes searched the room. "Aye, I did. And I know you've brought one into my home."

The son and his wife sat up and looked at the man who had remained in the shadows.

"No offense to you, sir," said Woodkimkalajoss. "I can smell you. Meech have a different odor, not unpleasant, but different. I lived in their colony for more than a year."

This time, Regidor straightened in surprise.

The old man nodded. "I'd fallen and would have died, but they brought me in."

Regidor spoke from the shadows. "Can you tell us where to find this colony?"

"You don't want to go there."

Regidor stepped forward. "But I do. I want to find my people."

"They're busy. Best leave 'em alone." Woodkimkalajoss closed his eyes as if to shut off the discussion.

"Busy doing what?" Regidor persisted.

"It's a secret. Just like where they're living is a secret."

"I am one of them." Regidor coated his words with honey. "I am destined to help in whatever is their task."

"Guess not, if you don't know where they are."

A commotion from down the street caught Bardon's attention. He stood. Lee Ark stood as well, and the man of the house crossed to open the door. The noise came from the center of town and approached them. Bardon recognized Toopka's shrill voice raised in alarm. "Get out! Get out! Sittiponder says get out of your homes. Stand in the open."

Her words and ones with a similar message echoed from the streets on either side of Oben Way.

How did she manage to raise such a ruckus? Why are these people believing her?

The urgency in the voices propelled Bardon to pick up the old woman and head for the door. Regidor lifted Woodkimkalajoss, chair and all. He gestured with his head for the man and woman to leave before him. In the center of the street, their neighbors stood. Some of the children and women cried, the men looked puzzled, and no one offered any explanation for why they had responded to a child's summons.

The commands to get out of the buildings subsided. In the distance, Toopka's voice could still be heard, and then that, too, became silent.

For a second, the only sound to reach Bardon's ears was the quiet whimpering from among the small crowd in the street. Then dogs began to bark. Several cats bolted through the streets, screeching off-key.

Bardon's toes tingled, and he realized the ground beneath him vibrated. A woman wailed. A loud crack reverberated from the outskirts of the village. Bardon turned to look in that direction just as the lane buckled. The road rose and fell like a wave on the ocean. Some citizens landed hard on their knees or backs. Children cried. Another undulation tossed everyone off their feet. They crashed down on the broken bricks of the street.

The buildings crumpled, some collapsing in on themselves, others rising up and falling over on the next house. The sound of wooden beams breaking in two, clay crashing as it crumbled, and glass shattering filled the air.

Bardon struggled to keep the old woman in his arms. Her son came to help. He took hold of her from the other side, but the next quake tore him away. Regidor yelled, "Lie down. Quit trying to get up."

The ground shook, then tremored, and then sighed with one last slow movement up and down.

Dust filled the air. People coughed and wheezed. No one spoke at first, then whispers of, "Are you all right?" were barely heard, and finally louder calls rang out as people tried to locate their loved ones—shouts that accompanied their efforts to stand amid the rubble.

Bardon heard the old man's thready voice. "Did I tell you about the time…"

He wouldn't stay to hear this tale. He needed to find Kale.

He tenderly placed the old woman in her son's arms and turned to go. A fit of coughing seized him. The soiled air obstructed his air passages, and he fought to clear them. When the spasm subsided, he drew air in cautiously through his nose. A whiff of something set his nerves on edge.

The first cry frantically rent the air, but panic obscured the word. The second shout came loud and clear.

"Fire!"

⟜ 28 ⟝

Shaken

Kale knelt beside a small o'rant boy with a broken arm. She concentrated to block the child's pain as she and Gymn set the bone gently back into place and began the healing process. Gymn was the only minor dragon she had allowed out of her cape so far. The villagers were shaken enough without having to cope with the unusual sight of nine dragons.

Smoke swirled above their heads. Kale vaguely noted how quietly the people went about moving the weak and injured out of harm's way.

"Are you done yet?" Gilda's plaintive voice pierced Kale's absorption in her task.

"Not quite."

Gilda coughed. "I'm going to the outskirts of town. To the west. The smoke is drifting the other direction."

"As soon as little Dobis here is ready to travel, I'll go with you."

Gilda coughed again. "I'm not waiting."

"You could help someone…"

"Unlike you, Kale, I do not wish to touch these beggars and their filth."

Kale looked away from Dobis. Plaster, dirt, grime, and debris covered Gilda like every other inhabitant of Arreach.

"Have you looked at yourself, Gilda? You couldn't get any filthier."

"I'm not speaking of physical dirt."

Dobis whimpered.

Kale turned away from the female meech, waving her hand in dismissal. "I haven't got time right now to figure out what has put a wrinkle in your world. We'll look for you later on the west side of the village."

Soon the others of the questing party joined Kale in the center of town and then fanned out to places where they would do the most good. They helped put the fires out. Fireplaces, candles, and lanterns had spilled their flames into the collapsed buildings. It took most of the night for the townsfolk to obliterate every spark.

Toopka and Sittiponder located a few people who had not heeded the call to escape the buildings before the collapse. They brought adults to help free them. Brunstetter carried numerous villagers to a field where they set up a hospital tent. Kale and Gymn helped the village apothecary with many of the injuries. Most people thanked them for the aid, but some were in such a state of shock, they numbly accepted help without a word.

The sun thrust thin rays of light through the still-thick air before the questers agreed they could leave the townspeople to their own resources. Bardon tucked his wife's hand in the crook of his arm and pulled her away, telling her she could return to help more after she rested.

As they approached the west side of town, Kale smelled cooking. The odor of sizzling sausages pushed back the scent of destruction. People passed them with plates full of biscuits, breakfast meat, and a pile of thick porridge.

Gilda brandished a stirring spoon at a handful of children. "Find more butter. See if you can locate more unbroken jars of jam."

Kale gasped. "They shouldn't be going into those toppled buildings. What if the debris shifts?"

Gilda cast her a scathing look. "I'm not that foolish. Most of the outlying homes have root cellars. The children are only picking from the holes that broke open. They are 'fishing' with poles I provided. With a little ingenuity, I've manipulated these rods, infusing them with a special attractive power so they pick up the usable items from a safe distance. In all this chaos, my scavengers are the only ones having fun." She waved her hand over the food laid out on makeshift tables. "Come, eat. I know you are tired."

Kale took Bardon's arm. *She amazes me. At times I want to wring her neck. Then she does something like this.*

Bardon rubbed the back of her hand on his arm. *"But she still manages to be irritating as she shows us her generosity."*

We're both tired. Kale's next thought was cut off by her husband's quote.

" 'Words spoken from fatigue resurface like oil on water. They are clearly seen and not easily eradicated.' "

She allowed herself a muffled growl, just to let Bardon know he had struck a nerve. "I was going to say we'd best watch what we say."

"Isn't that what I said?" He blinked with a vacant, innocent air, but Kale suspected he had enough energy left to tease her.

"Bardon, if you quote another principle, I'll kick you."

"You're too tired to kick me."

"Yes. You're right. I am."

"Sit here, and I'll get you a plate."

Kale sank onto the grass among dozens of others who had followed the smell of a good meal. By the time Bardon returned with two plates, she could barely keep her eyes open.

"Where's Toopka?" she asked.

"Sitting with Sir Dar. I think she is avoiding you."

"Why?"

"Eat," commanded Bardon. He watched her take a bite of the sweetened porridge. "Perhaps because she and Sittiponder went screaming through the village last night."

"They're heroes."

"They're children who are worried."

"I want to know how they knew." Kale forced herself to take a bite of biscuit filled with butter and jam before Bardon could bully her again.

"Toopka says she felt the badness coming in her bones. And Sittiponder says the voices said to get out of the houses."

Kale ate without asking the questions that muddled her head. Exhaustion kept her thoughts from stringing together coherently, and she doubted words from her mouth would make any sense. She ate as much as she could and then lay down, as had many of the villagers who had no place but the meadow to sleep. Bardon stretched out as well.

Hours later, Kale became aware of the warmth of the sun on her face. She moved her hand to feel for Bardon and touched fur. Toopka. The child curled between her and her husband. Unwilling to open her eyes, Kale stroked the doneel's arm but otherwise refused to come fully awake. Toopka's tiny hand stole into Kale's and squeezed two fingers. Kale smiled and squeezed back.

"What you did last night was good," she whispered.

"I don't feel so good today."

Kale's eyes popped open, and she gazed into the large brown eyes of her ward. She cupped the child's chin in her hand. "You hurt?"

Instead of a nod, Toopka blinked.

"I ache too." Kale tried to reassure her. "Being tossed in the air and landing hard makes for a lot of bruises and sore muscles."

A tear escaped one of Toopka's eyes. "Will you get Gymn?"

"Of course." Kale opened her cape and called quietly to the healing dragon.

Gymn appeared, took one look at Toopka, and leapt to the child, perching on her chest. He turned about several times.

"What is it, Gymn?" Kale asked.

Gymn chirred low in his throat.

"Toopka, do your lungs hurt? Maybe you inhaled too much smoke."

"Yes." The word wheezed between her thin black lips.

Gymn circled Toopka's head, then crawled down each arm and each leg. He returned to curl up on her chest.

"Gymn says you have lots of bruises, but there is one hard spot near your heart that he is worried about. He'll stay with you until you're more comfortable."

"Did I break my heart?"

Kale smiled and shook her head. "No, darling. Gymn found a small, hard lump like a pebble. Were you eating rocks last night?"

Toopka's weak giggle made Kale's heart ache.

"No," she said, closing her eyes. "We were too busy raising a ruckus."

"Are you hungry?"

A soft snore answered Kale's question.

She left Toopka and Bardon sleeping and went to help with the noonmeal preparations. Sir Dar stood on a wooden block, stirring a pot.

"Did you get some rest?" asked Kale.

"Enough. I sent Gilda away. Pregnant meech dragons are murder to work with in the kitchen." He looked around. "Even when there is no kitchen, per se."

"That is a wise observation. How many pregnant meech dragons have you worked with?"

"One too many." Sir Dar tapped the spoon on the side of the cauldron and then hung it by a leather thong on a nail driven into the side of a makeshift table. "Are you here to help?"

"Yes."

"Would you believe our most abundant food is pnard potatoes?"

"Oh, yum. That should make our feasters happy."

"There is little else to be happy about this day."

Kale surveyed the flattened town, two-thirds of which was scorched as well. "How many lost their lives?"

"None. Isn't that amazing?"

"Toopka and Sittiponder."

"Yes, and whatever force compelled the people to heed the call of two children."

"Look, here come Regidor and Brunstetter. Who are the old tumanhofers they carry?"

"I suspect that is Woodkimkalajoss."

Kale repeated the name slowly. "The old man or the woman?"

"The man."

"Who is he?"

"Someone who has actually been to the meech colony."

Kale's eyebrows shot up. "Really?"

"Were you going to help?"

"Yes."

"Peel potatoes."

"Yes sir!"

Kale sat next to a bushel basket, picked up a knife, and chose the biggest pink potato from the top of the pile. Out of the corner of her eye, she kept note of the progress Brunstetter and Regidor made as they worked their way through the crowd. Soon she realized three other people followed. She thought they might be father, mother, and son. They carried bundles, probably a few possessions scrounged from the wreckage of their home.

Children arrived, carrying fistfuls of greens from the nearby scraggly woods.

"Where's the funny lady?" asked one boy.

Sir Dar plopped a round of bread dough on the baking rock. "Lady Gilda?"

"Maybe. She's got green skin and no eyebrows."

"That would be Lady Gilda." He pinched off another piece of dough and kneaded it into a small ball, flattened it a mite, then placed it next to the other. "She went to rest. Did you bring us feathered chard for our soup? What a tasty addition that will make."

"Will she come back?"

"Probably."

"Does she really have wings under her cape? Is she really a dragon?"

Sir Dar stopped what he was doing and cocked an eyebrow at the inquisitive youth. "Who told you that?"

The lad pursed his lips and looked at the ground.

Another girl stepped around him. "Everyone is saying that it's true. Two meech dragons came to the inn with a bunch of travelers."

"Twenty or thirty," piped up a small marione with big blue eyes. He continued in a hushed voice. "Maybe a secret army."

The child who had been struck dumb by Sir Dar's question nodded and regained his ability to speak. "They came to talk to Woodkimkalajoss. He was me da's teacher in school."

The girl thrust out her chin. "My da says there is no such thing as meech dragons, and if there were, they wouldn't look like the lady. They'd have big teeth and fierce eyes, and they'd growl, not talk like us."

A low growl emanated from above her head. She turned with the others to confront Regidor. He carried the old man in his arms and peered down at the children.

He rolled the ridge above his eyes much like a man would raise and lower eyebrows when teasing a child. He grinned so that his teeth gleamed in the sun. "I disagree with your esteemed father, my dear. Meech dragons do speak."

The children shrieked, dropped their precious contribution to the meal, and fled.

Old man Woodkimkalajoss burst out laughing. All those who had witnessed the interlude joined him.

"Put me down," he cried after a moment. "I've shook my insides until I can't hardly breathe." But he continued to guffaw. "I would like a painting of their faces so I could study 'em up close. I can imagine their big eyes, mouths open like a peep-bird, and all their color draining out until they should have dropped o'er in a faint."

Gilda appeared, apparently out of thin air. "Regidor, you shouldn't have done that. Haven't those children had enough to frighten them over the last twenty-four hours?"

"No, no, missy," said Woodkimkalajoss. "Best thing for them. A real dragon instead of the fears they be imagining. And they'll come to see that this dragon isn't so frightful, while at the same time, those other fears based on the world shaking and their homes falling down, well, those will lose their power o'er them."

"Did you really live in the meech colony?" asked Kale.

"Indeed, I did. Nice folks. Except…"

"Except?"

"They got this secret, and it's best not to meddle with them or their secret."

Gilda squared her shoulders. "You will tell us where they are located."

"I might. I been thinking on it. But then I might not, either. I been asking Wulder, and He ain't giving me a clue as to whether it's nay or yea."

Gilda's hands went to her hips. "It had better be yea, and it had better be soon."

"What are you going to do? Blow my house down?" He wagged his head. "You just be patient, missy. Be patient."

29

Go!

Bardon picked up a stack of small boards and felt a twinge in his back. *Not the stakes. I'm just out of shape. Not used to hard labor.*

The villagers went to work, determined to rebuild the town on the existing foundation, but first the rubble had to be cleared. Bardon loaded wood into a wagon that another crew would assess to see what could be salvaged. Women sorted the usable pieces into piles. Older children, wearing thick gloves, took the shattered boards to the firewood heap.

By late morning, Bardon could feel his muscles protesting hard labor. He dropped his lumber with the rest, then put his hands against the small of his back and leaned against them, stretching his aching muscles from waist to shoulders. When he straightened, he rotated his head, pulling the soreness out of his neck.

Kale approached, stepping carefully, picking her path through the debris, and holding a cloth-wrapped package. His stomach rumbled. He hoped that bundle held food.

"Tired?" she asked as she traversed the last bit of uncleared space, keeping her eyes on where she placed her feet.

"Sore."

Her head snapped up, and she eyed him with worry lining her brow.

"I don't think it's the stakes."

"We haven't been using the ointment."

"We've only missed two nights. Falling onto the mat and sinking into sleep seems more important than ointment at the time."

"Everyone is working themselves to a frazzle." She smiled. "Help is coming."

She unwrapped the cloth and handed him a sandwich.

"Bless you." He leaned against the open tailgate of the wagon and took a big bite. "Who's coming?"

"Regidor and I both left messages with Namee in the talking gateway, and we've received messages from him. He contacted Brunstetter's people, and they have already sent a work party through the nearest regular gateway. It's quite a walk from that point, but they should arrive by evening."

"Then we will probably resume our journey in the morning."

"That will please Gilda." Kale hunched her shoulders and then let them slump. She leaned against the wagon beside Bardon. "Nothing much pleases our dear meech dragon these days." She fished in a pocket and pulled out a corked bottle. "Here. Water from one of the wells."

He took it gratefully. "The villagers have made progress if they've reopened a drinking well."

She nodded.

"Are you all right?"

"Unsettled."

"Why?"

"Gilda is alternately irate that the citizens of Arreach know she's a dragon, and then she shows off. I'll never understand her."

"What did she do now?" He took another big bite of the sandwich. Tomato juice dribbled out the corner of his mouth. He used the back of his hand to wipe the red stain off his chin.

"She lit the cooking fire."

"What's so…" Bardon had a sudden image of Gilda pursing her lips and delicately blowing a stream of fire into a pile of tinder. "Oh!"

"Yes. Oh!" Kale put two fingers to her temple and rubbed. "Of course, the children were delighted. They wanted to know how she did it."

"Did she tell them?"

Kale waved her hand in the air, imitating Gilda. "She said she just opens her mouth and blows."

Bardon dropped his chin to his chest and chuckled. He then raised his eyes to his wife's irritated glare. "That isn't so bad, Kale. It's entertaining for the children, and Gilda gets to be in the spotlight." He shrugged. "The villagers realized in the aftermath of the earthquake that dragons had come among them. Regidor was too busy helping to keep up the pretense, and Gymn came to the rescue. For Regidor and Gilda to continue the charade is really pointless."

"But we agreed to *not* draw attention to ourselves. To travel inconspicuously. That's the whole reason Celisse and the others are so far away. That's why only Gymn has been allowed in the village." She stood as if to pace and then sat back down abruptly. "I sent eight minor dragons out to keep the eight riding dragons company, and she makes a show of her dragon-ness."

"Dragon-ness?"

She gave him a scathing look but didn't respond.

Bardon popped the last of his sandwich into his mouth, wiped his hand on his pant leg, and put his arm around her shoulders. When he finished chewing, he spoke.

"You know, this angst you're feeling may all boil down to a Dragon Keeper being kept away from her dragons. Why don't you go out and visit them?"

"I'm needed here."

"Not so much, anymore." As soon as the words were out of his mouth, Bardon wished he could pull them back. "I meant that you and Gymn have worked hard at the infirmary, and most of the patients are on their feet again."

He studied her face, but his words did not seem to have had much effect. He opened his mind, hoping to catch what she was thinking. Something she had not shared with him troubled her.

"If she tells me one more time," Kale muttered, "that she is carrying a meech egg, I'll explode. Her baby is a meech. Her baby will assure the continuance of a superior race. Her baby will advance her husband's standing in the community. What community? A colony she's never even seen. What if it isn't even out there?"

"It's out there." Bardon stood and brought her to her feet as well. He enveloped her in his arms and kissed her forehead. "Go visit the dragons. Play a little."

Kale stamped her foot. "I'm going to." She stood on tiptoe and kissed his chin. "Don't get into trouble while I'm gone."

He kissed her lips. "I was just about to tell you to stay out of trouble. Seems to me you're the one who has a penchant for falling into awkward situations."

"Well, then." She leaned back and gave him a saucy grin. "If I don't come back by nightfall, you can come rescue me."

Kale had intended to take Toopka and Sittiponder with her, but the two children were more interested in their new friends in the village. Toopka had recovered from her spell, but she still had the hard spot in her chest. Gymn stayed behind as well. He had a patient who still required a healing dragon's care.

Kale kept an eye on the second large hill along the road. After she passed that point, she would call Celisse to come pick her up. That meant Kale would have to ride bareback, but it would save a lot of time.

The earthquake had marred the countryside as well as leveling the small town. Rocks littered the path. Cracks zigzagged from one side of the road to the other and out across the land. Trees leaned at crazy angles, and some had toppled completely. Small, wild creatures hopped and skittered and chased about in the open. Kale brushed several of the animals' minds and discovered they were still disoriented from the upheaval but intent on remaking their homes. A rabbit scampered off, still searching for a safe place to dig a burrow.

"Just like the people in the village. Everyone is determined to start anew."

She ambled along, not in any particular hurry, but enjoying the colors of the fall flowers—rich oranges, bright yellows, and deep reds. A few of the trees bore the markings of chilly nights. High-flying, puffy clouds dotted the azure sky.

Kale topped the first rise and quickened her pace, driven by the urge to be with her dragons. As she came to the low place between the two ridges, she turned aside, following a path that looked as if animals rather than people had worn away the grass. Sheep droppings confirmed her assumption.

She stopped. Why had she left the road? She turned around and, just as quickly, turned back again. She took a deep breath, and as she let it out, a smile lifted her countenance.

"An egg." She marched forward, allowing the pull to direct her steps.

Most of the trail remained intact, but occasionally, Kale scrambled up the slope to avoid a fresh outcropping of rock. Loose gravel and sharp, broken stones made these sections hazardous. The clouds gathered together and darkened. A wind replaced the gentler breezes.

"Great. I'm going to get wet."

She kept tramping along the side of the hill. A light sprinkle fell just long enough to get her thoroughly damp. Ahead of her, a portion of the landscape had cratered. She tried to slow her steps, but the pull strengthened. "This egg is going to be in the middle of that crumbled hole. I just know it is."

Looking down from the edge, Kale decided in the instant before her legs carried her down that she would much rather not retrieve this egg. Of course, she had no choice. The basin looked as big as the village of Arreach. She guessed a cavern had been under the ground and the ceiling caved in.

"This is sure to lead to trouble," she said even as one foot went forward.

Shale sank under her, covering her feet with gritty dirt. She pulled one foot out, shook the debris off her boot, and hurriedly put it down as the other leg sank. Using the same technique she used to form a shield of protection over her, she laid out a clear sheet before her. The invisible board reminded Kale of the baking pans Taylaminkadot used to cook daggarts in the oven.

Standing on the platform, she jiggled each foot, trying to knock off as much of the gravelly bits of hard clay as she could. The shield slipped, carrying her down a few feet before it dumped her on her backside. Her hands shot out behind as she fell and hit the sharp little rocks.

"Ouch!"

She sat up, dusted her palms on her skirt, and inspected the damage. A few cuts seeped dots of blood. "Ooh. Where is Gymn when I need him?"

Reforming the shield, she made it big enough to sit on, and she arranged the configuration directly beneath her so that she rose out of the shifting shale. The urge to reach the egg overrode her natural caution. She thought she might be able to paddle her tiny craft down the hill. Shifting forward in order to dig her fingers into the fine-grained gravel, she realized her mistake. The shield slipped forward like a sled on snow, fast. She grabbed the frame, and her knuckles scraped the rocks.

"Ow!" Snatching her hands back, she concentrated on keeping her balance. For some reason, flying high above the ground on the back of a dragon was less harrowing than this.

The sled skidded across the few level feet at the bottom and started up the opposite incline. The egg was behind Kale now, and the pull to bring her to its side strengthened.

"I will not throw myself off this shield."

Involuntarily, she leaned back. Kale screamed. "No! No! No!"

Her unusual form of transportation slowed, stopped, and began slipping down to the center of the crater once more.

She steeled herself, breathing deeply, muscles tensed, ready to roll off the shield during those few feet of level bottom. The front of the sled swung to the right so that Kale slid sideways. Rocks and gravel cascaded all around, racing her to the foot of the slope.

She squinted her eyes against the dust, wanting to close them, but afraid to. She'd picked up speed again, quickly approaching the base. She had to time this properly. She wrapped her arms around her chest.

"One, two, three!" She threw her weight to one side. The sled flipped up in the air and came down directly on top of her.

Kale curled up in a ball with her hands over her head. She had designed the shield to protect her from the sharp rocks. Her device domed and settled. The loose gravel tumbled against the outside of the shell, piling up until it nearly covered one side.

When the rattle of flowing shale subsided, Kale peeked at her surroundings. Swirling dust blocked her view. She let the shield go, coughing as she stood. She spun around, located the egg, and dug with her hands to uncover it. Had she not been a Dragon Keeper, she doubted she would have recognized the precious object. The egg sitting in her palm looked and felt like a stone, except the smooth surface was in the shape of an ovoid. She tucked it into a pouch woven into her belt with a sigh of relief.

"Now to get out of here."

She placed one hand over her eyes to guard against the glare of the sun and peered up to the rim. She smelled her next problem at the same time she spotted them. Thirty to forty grawligs, with knives drawn and spears raised, ringed the crater. They looked at her as if she were some kind of wild beast.

⟿ 30 ⟿

Unhelpful Grawligs

One grawlig stepped closer to the edge of the crater. The loose gravel gave way, sending a shower of dirt and pebbles into the giant hole. He grunted and pulled back. Leaning from the waist, he glared at Kale with his head tilted.

"What are you?" he yelled.

Kale put her hands on her hips and glared back. "I'm an o'rant."

"No. Not."

The man shook his head emphatically. His matted mane tossed back and forth about his shoulders. "Girl grawlig. What tribe?"

The accusation stunned Kale. The mountain ogres could not possibly mistake her for one of them. She swiped her hair out of her face. Still damp from the rain, tangled locks stuck out from her scalp. She looked down at her clothes caked with mud. Coarse gray clay coated her shoes, legs, skirt, cape, arms, face, and hair.

She looked up again at the crowd above. "I do suppose I look a bit like I'm a grawlig, but honestly, I'm an o'rant."

"No. Face like grawlig."

To her horror they turned and began to walk away. "Wait! Don't go."

Several heads reappeared over the edge of the crater. Brutish faces grinned at her, including the face of their spokesman. He grunted.

"You wouldn't happen to have a rope, would you?"

The grawlig with the impressive conversational skills nodded.

"Would you help me out?"

"Why?"

Kale searched her mind for a reason that would make sense to a grawlig. "I'm a wizard, and I will find something I can do for you."

The spokesman grinned so that all his yellow teeth showed. "You wizard. You get out."

They left too quickly for Kale to make another appeal. She started to sit, saw the shield had fragmented, and pulled it back together. She sat cross-legged on the protective surface and considered her options.

Using her wizard skills, she tested the ground in the huge hole. She needed moisture to form clay steps to the top of the crater. The earlier shower provided enough water, but after experimenting, she decided the process would take too long.

Next she inventoried her pockets and hollows inside her cape. "Who knew I'd need a hundred-foot ladder?" she chided herself.

She drew her knees up and rested her arms on them. She let her head drop forward and relaxed. The sun beat on the back of her neck. "I could do that thing Regidor does where he lifts objects into the air without touching them. Only I'm not good at it. Dropping an apple is one thing, dropping me would be quite another."

A fly buzzed her clay-encrusted head. She waved a hand to shoo it away. "I need help. Bardon is too far away and too busy even if I did reach him."

She focused on Celisse and made a connection with her riding dragon's mind. *Come find me and bring Pat.*

Celisse expressed her concern at this sudden summons.

I'm all right, but very dirty…and very stuck.

She didn't worry about Celisse being able to find her. Their bond assured knowledge of the other's whereabouts over a reasonable distance. However, she didn't like the idea of being down in a hot hole until her rescue party arrived.

Pat will probably take one look at the situation and have a reasonable, obvious solution within seconds. I should try thinking like Pat. She laughed. *Pat is entirely too analytical. I could never think like him. I guess the alternative is to think like me.* No valuable thought sprang to her mind. *I'm a light wizard. What can I do with light to get me out of this trap?*

An idea spread a smile across her face. She stood and put her hands, cupped together, in front of her.

A glowing orb of green light appeared, nestled against her palms. "The point of this endeavor, my little light vines, is to pay attention to my direction. I want you to go up and not wander all over the sides of the slope."

The tendrils pushing out of the light seed didn't hear her voice, but Kale needed the verbal assurance that she could maintain control. Commanding anything to grow along a particular path was tricky. Light plants tended to run wild.

She concentrated, knowing that if even one sprout headed off in the wrong direction, she would soon have an unwieldy mess. The vines of light spilled out of her hands and poured to the floor. Upon coming in contact with the dirt, they bent and started up the basin's unstable walls. They grew in a slithering motion toward the rim of the crater. Leaves popped out every few inches, and the main branches thickened, making a sturdy climbing structure.

Kale kept her eyes on the strip in front of her. She nipped any stray bud that threatened to grow out beyond the swath she designated. In a matter of minutes, she had a network of light vines established from the floor of the crater to the top. She closed her hands over the glowing seed, and the tendrils ceased erupting from the core. The last of the stems dropped to the floor as if cut off. When Kale opened her hands, the orb was gone.

She reformed her dress into trousers. She pushed the sides of her cape behind her so that it hung down her back and out of the way. Then she began to climb. The twisting light vines provided excellent hand- and footholds, except for the fact they were smooth enough to be slippery. More than once Kale caught herself just before sliding back down to the bottom. As she got to the top, she wiped sweat from her brow and panted as though she'd run a mile.

"I've seen you looking better."

"Ack!" Kale lost her footing, screeched again, and scrambled to throw herself over the top edge. "Seezle! You nearly sent me plummeting to the floor of the crater."

"Sorry. I didn't mean to startle you." She scratched at her scalp through flyaway hair. "I've been watching you for quite a while. I thought you'd know I was here." Her lower lip stuck out in a pout. "I wasn't hiding."

"It's all right, Seezle." Kale rested with her arms and legs stretched out and her face to the cloudy sky. Her head came up, and she stared at her tiny friend. "What are you doing here?"

"I came to get you. Actually, I came with the urohms who are going to help with Arreach."

Kale raised up on her elbows and looked around.

Seezle giggled. "They are marching. I moved a little faster." She sprang to her feet and pointed. "And we'd best get out of here, fast!"

Kale followed the line of her finger. The grawligs were clustered around an old barn that stood on a high ridge, several hillsides away. Two jumped up and down, waved their arms, and occasionally stopped to gesture toward Kale and Seezle.

"They probably aren't delighted that I managed to get out of the hole on my own."

Seezle skipped around Kale. "Come on, let's go. You're slow, and I want to get a head start."

Kale pulled herself to her feet and put her hands on her hips. "I don't feel like running."

Seezle quit prancing. "Are you fixing to do some wizardry?"

"Yes."

"Oh, boy!" Seezle plopped down on the grass. "This will be fun."

"Celisse is on her way to pick me up." Kale's fingers worked over her palm as if she toyed with some soft, round object. "We'll just pester these ogres until she gets here."

Seezle cocked her head and watched Kale. "What have you got in your hand?"

"Air."

"What are you doing with it?"

"Smashing it."

"Well, whatever you're planning, you better get it done. The grawligs are coming this way."

The herd of shaggy scoundrels trotted en masse down the slope of the hill. They disappeared in the hollow between the two rises. As their heads appeared at the crest of the next knoll, Kale pitched the airball.

"What's happening?" demanded Seezle.

"The compressed air is expanding. By the time it reaches the grawligs, it will be a substantial wind."

Seezle counted slowly. "One, two, three, four—"

The line of burly mountain men at the front staggered backward, knocking over those behind. Seezle laughed as the attacking force fell over one another, trying to stand and tripping other brutes in the process.

Kale prepared another parcel of air as the grawligs straightened themselves out, reformed their loose line, and came barreling down the hill.

"Will it work again?" asked Seezle. "They are a whole lot closer."

"Yes, it'll work. This one is bigger. And Celisse is almost here."

Kale waited while holding with two hands what looked like a sizable object, even though it could not be seen. She hefted the ball in front of her until the grawligs came over the last rise, then she swung one arm along her side and as far back as she could reach. She rolled the object out of her hand and down the slope toward the approaching enemy as if she were playing peggle-pins.

"I can see it!" Seezle jumped and pointed. "There it goes."

"Seezle, even I can't see it," objected Kale.

"I don't mean I see *it.* I mean I can see where *it* is going. The grass is pushed down. Oh, and the path is getting wider and wider…and oh, boy! Those grawligs haven't got a chance."

"Celisse is here. Come on."

The beat of her wings and the swift rush of air announced the dragon's arrival.

"Just a minute," called Seezle. "I want to see them bowled over."

Kale went to her dragon's neck, patted the shiny scales, and leaned her cheek against the black strip that ran from Celisse's jaw to her shoulder. Pat hopped from his perch between the bigger dragon's ears onto Kale's head.

"Yes, thank you," she told both her friends. "I did get out of my predicament on my own."

The blast of air reached the grawligs and knocked a good many over. The others turned and, with the wind hastening their steps, ran away.

Seezle hopped and skipped and finally came to join Kale.

"What are you doing?" the tiny kimen asked.

Kale busily threaded a strand of light out of a glowing orb in one palm. Pat had an end in his mouth and ran up to the ridges along Celisse's back.

Kale grinned. "I'm discovering all sorts of useful things for these light vines. I'm making a saddle of sorts." She pulled out another length of luminescent ropelike stem. "At least I am making something for us to hold on to."

"I'll help." Seezle took a second, rapidly growing tendril and climbed up Celisse's side.

With several vines wrapped around the big dragon's frame, the travelers were ready. Kale sat at the base of Celisse's neck, wrapping her legs into a tangle of vines and holding on to another. Pat rode in her lap, and Seezle sat forward a bit.

"Where are we going?" asked Seezle.

"I'm on my way to visit the dragons we left in a valley away from Arreach."

Seezle's eyes widened. "You don't plan to spend much time there, do you? Because I was sent to get you."

"What's left of this afternoon." Kale thought how good it would be to see her friends. Then a not-so-pleasant thought disturbed her peace. "Who sent you to get me? Seezle, aren't you supposed to be watching Holt?"

"I was, and that's why I'm here."

"Why?"

"Because Holt's in trouble." She looked over her shoulder at Kale, and her face held an uncharacteristic solemnity. "Namee sent me to get you."

⟶ 31 ⟵

To the Rescue!

Kale chose to wait until they landed before asking any more questions. They covered the distance quickly and set down among the other dragons in a large, sparsely vegetated hallow. Then Kale needed to converse in mindspeaking with the dragons to appease their curiosity. She related what had happened in Arreach and then listened to the dragons' accounts of the world rumbling.

Finally, she and Seezle sat down on a couple of boulders under a scraggly dryfus tree.

"What kind of trouble is Holt in?" Kale asked.

"He's been imprisoned, locked up. I think they threw the key away."

"Why?"

"For kissing an echo's daughter."

"I'm not surprised."

Seezle squirmed on the rock. "He really did a fantastic job of infiltrating their ranks until this girl caught his eye." She sighed. "And I believe he wanted to save her from a life among these fanatics."

"Very noble. Where is he, and do you think we can get him out?"

She nodded vigorously. "Not that it will be easy. He's in a cell in the building that houses the headquarters for the Followers. They don't appear to have any plans to execute him."

"That's a good thing. Maybe we could leave him there for a while."

"But they aren't feeding him."

"What?"

"He gets one cup of water and a piece of bread each day."

"All right, we go rescue him."

Just before dark, Celisse and Greer flew to within half a mile from the outskirts of Arreach. They landed in a wide canyon with steep stratified walls. Lines of different-colored rock lay in layers, making jagged lines as far as they could see. Broken stones littered the floor. Obviously, some of the piles of rock had recently fallen from the cliff face.

I don't know when Bardon will want to leave, Kale told Celisse. *Stay close. And try to keep Greer from being seen as well.*

She paused as her dragon griped about guarding Bardon's older dragon.

It won't be as hard as you think, Celisse. Greer admires you.

Kale chuckled at her dragon's ruffled response. *I think it's perfectly clear what I mean. I mean he thinks you're pretty. Just coax him to do the right thing and discourage him from scaring the townspeople.*

The entire time she and Seezle walked, Kale worked on cleaning her hair, skin, and clothes.

"I'll never feel clean without a bath," she complained.

"You do look better." Seezle giggled. "Now you look like you rolled in a mud puddle instead of looking like you bathed in a mud lake."

"Thanks, I think." Kale eyed the kimen in her sparkling clothes of yellow light. "I don't suppose you have any tricks for cleaning up."

With mischief in her eyes, Seezle patted her mop of unruly hair. "No, but I'm a wizard myself when it comes to styling a becoming hairdo. Want my services?"

Kale laughed. "No, thank you. I have enough trouble with my hair."

Pat fussed as they walked to Arreach. Kale had never been able to put a precise name on Pat's talent. While Gymn was a healing dragon and Metta was a singing dragon, Pat could fix things. If the job was too big for him to fix alone, he understood what the problem was and what should be done. His talent included knowledge of architecture and building expertise. He also calculated anything to do with numbers at lightning speed and did something he called stress analysis. Now he groused that he had not been allowed the pleasure of being at the scene of devastation to help.

Pat rarely expressed agitation of any kind. As he grumbled, Kale realized she had not once considered how useful he'd be in the situation at Arreach.

"I'm truly sorry, Pat. I'm at fault. I never thought how much you would enjoy working on the problems brought about by the earthquake. I forgot how gifted you are in precisely the manner that would aid the townspeople. Would you like to stay with the urohms and assist them?"

Kale sighed her relief when the brown dragon said he was only willing to stay until Kale and Bardon rejoined the quest to find the meech colony.

"Who's going to interpret between the urohms and Pat?" asked Seezle. "I don't think any of the urohms can mindspeak."

"We'll worry about that later."

They saw the urohms in the village before they reached the outskirts. The giant men had set to work as soon as they arrived. The increase in activity impressed Kale as they moved closer. The appearance of outsiders to make their task easier must have energized the citizens. The road that had been littered with debris when she set off at noon was swept clean. People smiled and waved as she and Seezle walked by.

"They seem to be a happy lot," said the kimen.

"They weren't when I left."

"They've got hope now."

"That's right," Kale said. "The horrendous task before them does not seem so daunting. The urohms brought willing hearts and helpful hands to aid these people."

Seezle agreed. "Tackling the impossible is always easier with friends."

Kale followed her bond with Bardon to find him. He sat with the rest of the questing party around a dying cookfire and rose to greet her.

"We've waited to make any final decisions until you arrived. Now that the urohms have arrived we will move on." He kissed her cheek. "Seezle, I am happy to see you, of course, but I fear you bring bad tidings."

Seezle joined the circle and sat beside Sir Dar. "Only that Holt is in trouble." She explained concisely what had occurred and Holt's precarious situation.

Regidor put his hand on Gilda's before she had a chance to speak. "We will continue to the Northern Reach."

Gilda smiled smugly. "We will travel without the riding dragons. It will be good to arrive at our destination unencumbered by the populace of this culture."

Kale pressed her lips together and turned to the next member of the party to proclaim his intentions.

Brunstetter looked around the circle. "I will stay here and supervise the urohms in their reconstruction of the village."

Seezle clapped her hands together. "That settles that problem."

The urohm nobleman frowned at her. "What problem?"

"Pat wants to stay and help, but who would communicate with him? If you are here, you can communicate through Foremoore."

Brunstetter nodded. "Pat's help will be greatly appreciated."

Lee Ark and Sir Dar decided to go with Regidor and Gilda. Kale and Bardon would return with Seezle to rescue Holt.

"What about the children?" asked Kale. "Toopka and Sittiponder will want to go with you, Sir Dar."

The doneel shook his head. "I don't think so. They are enamored with the children here in the village. The game of finding treasures amid the rubble and finding the correct owner has them enthralled."

"Is it safe?"

"Thanks to the poles Gilda devised, it is." Sir Dar stood. "We've had our dinner, but I don't believe you and Seezle have eaten. Let me get you something."

They all turned toward a sudden commotion from the village.

"Under cover for you," Regidor shouted at Kale. "A swarm of those dreaded black dragons is coming."

Kale covered herself with a shield and saw Regidor add a second layer over hers. The clear protective shells muffled the sounds from without. She could see well enough, though. What she saw made her breath catch in her throat.

A moving mass blackened the northern sky. This horde of tiny dragons blanketed the hills as far as one could see from east to west.

Villagers ran ahead of them. Even inside her shelter, Kale could hear screams of terror. Brunstetter ordered his men to direct the crowds into gullies, hollows, and any low-lying areas. Bardon, Gilda, and Regidor stayed beside Kale. Sir Dar and Lee Ark grabbed torches from the back of a wagon. They dunked the point wrapped in heavy cloth into a bucket of kerosene. The general handed one to Bardon. Holding the wooden bases, they poked the soaked tips in the fire. The torches burst into flame.

Kale saw Seezle cover her ears and drop down behind a makeshift table of wooden boxes Sir Dar and Gilda used to prepare food. Her protective shell vibrated with the sound of ten thousand flying dragons. The people around her standing guard scrunched their faces as if in pain. But the look of hatred on Gilda's face hid any discomfort she might feel.

Kale's eyes widened. *Gilda, why didn't you take shelter?*

The meech tossed Kale a glance that would have withered turnips, but she did not answer.

The first dragon hit the invisible shield and fell to the ground, then another and another. Kale lost sight of her comrades outside as a curtain of moving black bodies surrounded her shelter. Despite her confidence in the protective cover withstanding the onslaught, Kale fell to her knees, wrapped her arms around her body, and bent over.

Just outside the shell, the dead and wounded dragons littered the ground until piles of them leaned against the shelter. They varied in size, some no bigger than her thumb and none bigger than the palm of a child. Their skin glistened but did not have individual scales like the dragons Kale knew. The awful creatures looked amazingly fragile. The crumpled bodies of those who had run into the shield had no life at all. Those who were injured rapidly expired. Those blasted by flames from the two meech dragons and those burnt by the torches shriveled up like pieces of paper.

At last, the attack ended as the horde continued on. Both shells dissolved, and Kale stepped into Bardon's arms. The acrid smell of smoke filled her nostrils and burned her lungs. Her eyes watered.

Regidor patted her on the shoulder. "Whatever did you do, my dear, to invoke the wrath of those horrid beasts?"

She shook her head, unable to join him in his light banter.

The villagers arose from their hiding places. In eerie silence they made their way back. Several looked askance at Kale. A few others widened the circle they made around the questers.

Sir Dar twisted his lips in a look of disgust. "They're blaming you for this latest hazard that has come upon them. It's a good time for you to leave."

A burly marione walked slowly by, his eyes narrowed and his lips pressed into a line of anger.

Kale nodded to Sir Dar. "Seezle will show us to the gateway tomorrow. Right now, walking into Paladise, a village of fanatics, doesn't look as dangerous as staying here."

Gilda crossed her arms. "Isn't there a principle about the heat of the fire versus the cold of snow?"

" 'A sensible man,' " said Bardon, " 'does not step out of the snow into the fire.' Or do you mean, 'One does not need to sit in the oven to cook a meal, nor lie in the snow to chill a drink.' " Bardon smiled at the meech lady. "Or there's the one—"

Kale giggled, partly from the inanity of Bardon spouting principles, but mostly from relief. "Enough, Bardon. I think the stepping out of the fire was the one Gilda remembered."

"Ah, but there are perhaps a hundred principles that deal with hot and cold and the danger of any extreme."

Kale tried to concentrate on her husband's voice. She felt odd, as though her body were moving away from itself. "You know, Bardon, I think I'm going to faint." The edges of her vision became black, and the circle tightened, so what she could see became smaller and smaller. "Yes, I am going to faint."

32

Facts of Life

Bardon sat as close to Kale as he could without shoving her off the log they were using as a seat. She still looked pale, but she shoveled in Sir Dar's stew as if she felt fine.

"Do you want me to refill your cup?" he asked.

"I am *really* all right," Kale protested for the fourth time. "I had a very busy day. A new egg, a sand-shifting crater, grawligs, and black dragons, remember? I was hungry. Sir Dar hadn't fed me yet. Inside the shield is very stuffy. I fainted. I'm all right."

She handed him the empty cup. "Yes, thank you. I'd like more tea, but not so much sugar this time."

Bardon joined Gilda at the fire, where a tin kettle kept water warm.

"Is she all right?" asked the meech.

"She says she is."

"I'm glad you're taking her back to a more civilized area. The next part of our trip will be rigorous. Of course, when we join the meech colony, then the hardships will be a forgotten inconvenience."

He poured hot water over tea leaves in a one-cup teapot and set it on the table. "Has Woodkimkalajoss told Regidor the location?"

"Yes. This afternoon." She shrugged. "He didn't want me there. When I saw them talking and came over to see what was going on, he'd already finished." She sipped from her teacup, one salvaged by her band of village children. The handle had broken off during the earthquake, and the saucer didn't match, but they both were china, not ceramic. She pinched her thin lips into a moue. "The old man does not interest me as much as a good cup of tea. I shall be glad when our journey is over. Regidor says it will be no more than six days' travel."

Bardon nodded, wondering exactly what they would find at the end of this quest. He smiled at his friend's wife. "We will join you there as soon as we are able."

In the morning, Kale and Bardon left before the sun shone over the eastern horizon. Greer and Celisse waited for them in the canyon. Bardon didn't mind riding bareback, but Kale took the time to fashion another harness out of light vines. All the minor dragons except Gymn and Pat accompanied them. Just as Celisse beat her wings to rise into the sky, two dark spots appeared, coming quickly.

"Kale, wait," called Bardon. "What are those?"

She put her hand over her eyes, squinting. "Just Gymn and Pat. I wonder why they're coming." She concentrated for a moment. "Ah, they've decided to go with us. Sittiponder has said his voices tell him they will be needed."

"Voices!" Seezle giggled, but Kale and Bardon ignored her.

Instead, Kale mindspoke to her husband. *"If we ask what she means by that, she'll become evasive."*

Right. I don't want to contemplate a slippery Seezle.

Gymn and Pat joined Kale. Seezle directed the larger dragons to a riverside where a grove of dryfus trees hid the gateway. From there they stepped into Wizard Namee's tower.

"A bath," Kale exclaimed. "That's the first thing I want. A real bath."

Seezle laughed and ran ahead. As Bardon and Kale came to the top of the stone steps, the kimen returned with the doneel housekeeper.

"Welcome, Lady Kale, Sir Bardon. I have the same bedchambers you used the night of the ball available for you."

"Thank you, Mistress Orcutt," said Bardon. "We won't be staying long, but we would appreciate a place to clean up. You've heard of the earthquake along the northern border?"

"Yes, a platoon of urohm workers came through the gateways here yesterday." She motioned for them to follow her. "Wizard Namee will want to see you. He'll be sitting down to breakfast in an hour. Will you join him?"

"Yes."

"I have friends to visit before then," said Seezle. "I'll meet you in the dining hall." She zipped away, her clothing leaving a blur of light as she whisked through the corridor.

After bathing and changing clothes, Bardon and Kale descended the grand staircase. Kale gave up on their soiled outfits and pulled new ones from her cape. Her hair hadn't quite cooperated, but Bardon thought his wife looked beautiful, as she always did.

The double doors to the dining hall stood open, and Bardon heard a familiar voice. "Your father is here."

"And Mother!" Kale hurried down the last few marble steps.

Sir Kemry came to kiss her cheeks as soon as they entered the room. "You are carrying a new dragon egg," he said. "Tell us where you found it. I do believe we've uncovered most of the dragons' nests these past five years."

Lady Lyll nudged her husband aside. "I'm more interested in my grandchild."

Kale's eyes popped wide open.

"I thought so!" declared Bardon. The vague uneasiness he'd had about his wife's health disappeared in a flood of joy.

"You thought so?" Kale turned on her husband. "How could you think so? I didn't think so." She turned back to her mother. "I can't be pregnant. I know how pregnant women behave and how they look and all of that. I helped pregnant women keep up with their housework when I was a village slave. And Gilda has been an intense example of pregnant and crotchety."

Lady Lyll cupped her hand around Kale's cheek. "You helped marione women, Kale. You are an o'rant. Our gestation is similar but not the same as a marione's or any of the high races. Each has its own peculiarities. And as for Gilda, well, she has her own row to plow." She clasped Kale's hand. "Come, eat breakfast. Wizard Namee has sent word he shall be late." She tugged her daughter with one hand and waved the other dismissively. "Some matter of business."

Bardon escorted his wife and mother-in-law to the table where Lyll and Sir Kemry had already started their morning meal. Then he went to the sideboard to dish up a heaping plate of food for Kale and a smaller one for himself.

Kale's parents spoke at the same time.

"Tell me about the egg," said Sir Kemry.

"I'm so glad you're going to be a mother," said Lyll.

They tried again and succeeded in overrunning each other's words.

"A minor dragon, of course. Are you going to quicken it?"

"Let's figure out the date the baby will come."

Bardon came to the table with the two plates. He set one in front of Kale and sat down with the other.

"I shall be the impartial third party and decide which topic will get our attention as we eat." He sipped his tea. "I choose the baby."

Lyll rubbed her hands together, a gleam in her eye. "When did you have your first symptom?"

"I haven't had any." She shook her head. "None," declared Kale with a firm voice.

Bardon leaned forward to look around his wife to his mother-in-law. "She began to be a bit grouchy after the new year."

"That's ridiculous," said Kale. "I'd have the baby by now."

"A marione would have the baby by now," said her mother. "A doneel would have the baby by now. But not an o'rant, dear. It's a shame you haven't been around more of your race. But you did have Taylaminkadot in your home when she went through her gestation period."

"She didn't change much. She looked a bit thicker around the middle. I wouldn't have guessed she was pregnant had she not told me."

"Seems to me you know very little about the baby business," her father said.

Kale glared at him. "I know a great deal about dragon babies."

Sir Kemry stirred sugar into his tea and nodded wisely. "Grouchy."

"What does grouchy have to do with anything? I've been tired, so I've been a bit testy. The marione mothers were always jolly, downright giddy at times."

"You're not a marione," her father said before Lyll could reiterate the same notion. "When your mother was pregnant with you, I tiptoed around the castle."

Kale placed her hand on her stomach. "So, how long?"

"That depends," said Lady Lyll.

"Depends on what?"

"It depends on whether you rest and allow your body to take on this new venture. Actually, it is a wee bit more complicated than that. You have to turn from your normal routine so that your system recognizes you are ready for the change in your life."

Kale turned slowly to Bardon. He purposely looked down at his porridge, fishing out a raisin to lift to his lips.

"That's why you insisted on this trip."

Bardon couldn't decide whether Kale's voice held more accusation or wonder. He'd prefer to know more about which way she was likely to go before he added any weight to the discussion.

"How did you know?" she asked calmly.

He felt it was safe to answer. "The kimens who did my treatment for the stakes." He turned to look her full in the face. "I asked them some questions, told them some of the things I observed, and listened to their advice."

"And their advice was?"

"To take you away from your usual workload to a place where we could be together more, and to hold you close and cherish you. They said it was much the way you quickened a dragon egg."

"Why didn't you tell me? Surely this shouldn't be a secret between a husband and wife."

"I wasn't sure that you were truly carrying our child. The whole thing was speculation until I heard your mother say for sure that you're expecting. I didn't want to make you feel like I was disappointed because we haven't had a child yet." He took her hand. "And frankly, when Gilda boasted about her accomplishment in supplying the great egg..." He rolled his eyes.

Kale giggled.

"Well, I didn't want Gilda lording it over you if it turned out I was mistaken."

"Aww." Kale leaned in to kiss his lips.

"And that," said her father, "is the other side of the coin. Grouchy one minute and mushy the next."

Bardon and Kale ignored him.

"Harrumph! I suppose I could go with Bardon to rescue Holt."

They broke off the kiss and turned astonished eyes his way.

"Why?" asked Kale. "I'm going."

Bardon frowned at his father-in-law. "It will be a long time before the baby comes, won't it? Surely she can still travel."

Lady Lyll chuckled. "I wouldn't count on that 'long time.' I'm figuring less than a month."

Kale looked down at her flat stomach. "Impossible."

Her mother smiled. "That baby is fully formed. All he or she needs to do now is put on weight. When he or she is nice and plump, we'll have a grandchild." She took a buttered nordy roll from her own plate and offered it to Kale. "Here, dear. You are going to be mighty hungry from now until then."

33

Visiting Paladise

Kale found it amusing that her father was up in arms, not wanting her to go gallivanting among dangerous people, while her husband had full confidence that she could handle whatever came along. With her hand on her stomach, she smiled, letting the conversation between her parents, her husband, and Wizard Namee drift about her.

A baby. She was going to have a baby. *I am determined not to become odious like Gilda. No smugness. No prideful remarks. No snarking.*

She looked at Bardon and thought of Regidor's saurian countenance. *Not even when it is obvious that our child will be ten times cuter than theirs.* She stifled a giggle. No point in sharing her thoughts with the others. Such words would trample her determination to be a humble mother even before she got started.

Seezle entered with a swish of air and the sound of tiny bells tinkling. Kale tilted her head and squinted to bring the kimen into focus. She moved so fast that when she stopped her clothes blurred for a moment.

"What lovely bells," exclaimed Lady Lyll. "Where did you get them?"

Seezle glided across the hall and offered Wizard Namee a bouquet of slender metal stalks decorated with leaves and clusters of bells like flowers. "A community of kimen make them here in Namee's forest. Fizz made a bunch just for him."

"Thank you, Seezle, and send my regards to Fizz." The silver artwork looked fragile in Wizard Namee's big hand. "I shall give this to Mistress Orcutt before my clumsy fingers bend the stems."

Seezle ran to pull the cord that would summon the housekeeper. Then she flitted across the floor and hopped into a chair.

"You're welcome to breakfast, little one," said Wizard Namee.

"I've eaten. Thank you."

Namee eyed the kimen. His cool eye ran over her flighty appearance as if deciding whether to ask this mistywisp a serious question. He cleared his throat, sat straighter, and frowned. "Do you have something to report? I assume you have visited with whoever took on the duty of caring for Holt."

"That was Fizz's son Ziffle. And the report is good. Holt is alive. We have a route planned to get through Paladise unseen. We can get to the jail cell and out again in ten minutes. The tumanhofer in charge, Glaringtonover, says he's ready, and we should be able to retrieve Holt tonight."

"Tonight?" Kale looked around the table. "What are we going to do all day while we wait?"

Lady Lyll stood and took her daughter's hand. "You and I, my dear, are going to have a little mother-daughter talk. We need to further your education."

"Shall I come?" asked Sir Kemry.

"You," said Lyll over her shoulder, "are not welcome. You may keep Bardon entertained and out of trouble."

Kale and her mother found Namee's conservatory, built onto one of the castle walls facing a small green and a sheer cliff. The glass sides and roof allowed sunshine to bathe an uncountable variety of plants.

Kale saw some she recognized, but most of the exotic foliage were unfamiliar. Damp earth mixed with sweet floral fragrances to create an appealing scent. Stone walkways twined through a jungle of plant life that grew high enough to obstruct the view of other paths. Fountains trickled over rocks. Birds darted between small trees and sang cheerfully in their pleasant circumstances.

The dragons poured out of Kale's pockets in search of an exciting meal. Lady Allerion led Kale to a bench beside a pool with yellow and orange striped fish swimming about.

Lyll examined the pool with uncommon interest.

Kale waited. Dark green, broad-leafed plants surrounded the waterscape. Tiny bright birds hopped among equally colorful blossoms. A charming view, but Kale wanted information from her parent. "Mother?"

Lyll started and laughed. "Oh, I'm sorry, dear. I was lost in memories. I do believe this is the pool by which your father proposed." She sighed with a gentle smile on her lips. "It seems like eons ago."

Kale tipped her head to the side as she asked, "How long is an eon? It might very well have been at least one eon ago."

"Don't be pert. We're here for a serious discussion."

Pulling her grin into a straight line, Kale tried to look sorry. "I apologize."

"Don't sham a contrite spirit, either. I know you have a rampant sense of humor. And you lived with Fenworth on top of that. Who could escape with a normal appreciation for decorum?"

"I believe part of my delight in the absurd was passed on directly from my parents."

Lyll smiled. "Yes. 'The apple falls from the tree, but the worm can't carry it away.'"

Kale tilted her head. "Are you sure you have that one right, Mother? It sounds a bit off kilter."

Her mother waved her hand. "It's neither here nor there. You can ask Bardon if you really must know the exact wording. We have more important things to pursue. Let's talk about babies."

Lady Lyll and Sir Kemry stood beside the gateway as Kale, Bardon, and Seezle prepared to leave.

Sir Kemry paced. "It is not unreasonable to ask her to stay, Lyll."

"She'll be fine." Lyll caught his arm and brought him to an abrupt stop. "You're making me wish I hadn't told you."

"Bah! I would have guessed as soon as the dragons knew."

"That's not guessing when someone relays the knowledge." Lyll frowned. "Why didn't Gymn know?"

Kemry tapped one finger against his chin. "There's a very scientific reason."

"What?" asked Kale and her mother in unison.

"I have no idea what it is, but I know it must exist." The corners of

Sir Kemry's mouth twitched, but he firmed his jaw. His wife wagged a finger at him, and a laugh escaped his lips.

"You see, Mother," said Kale. "A tendency toward levity abounds in this family."

Her father held up a hand. "I'll be serious. Until the baby started growing, he was virtually undetectable. But that does not mean he—"

"Or she," said Lyll.

"—did not exist. There are a lot of things in this world that are present but can only be seen by Wulder's eye."

Kale's chin went up. "I still think Gymn would have told me had he felt a new life within me."

"Perhaps not," said her mother. "Gymn would have detected something abnormal in your body. A baby is perfectly normal. But you have had symptoms."

The strong lines of her father's face showed predominantly as he became serious. He gave Kale a considering look. "And speaking of growing..." His eyes shifted to Lyll. "I remember how quickly that last month went. Your abdomen blew up like a balloon."

"Really, Kemry, that is not a topic for conversation in polite society."

"What's polite about this society? It's just us and the children and Seezle."

Bardon and Kale exchanged a glance with eyebrows raised.

"Speaking of Seezle," said Seezle, "we have to get moving. I have arranged for the others to meet us."

"Others?" asked Bardon.

"Yes. Pardon me if I don't list their names, but we are late already."

"Tumanhofers," said Kemry.

Seezle nodded, and her hair flew around her head. "They've dug a maze of tunnels under Paladise."

Kale kissed Sir Kemry on the cheek. "Don't worry, Father. I'll be fine, and so will the baby. We'll only be gone a few hours."

They stepped through the gateway and entered an oversized, rambling shack lit by a single lightrock sitting on a crude table. The minor dragons flew around the large room examining each nook and cranny.

"Where is everyone?" asked Bardon.

"Down the hole," answered Seezle. She crossed to the side of the room and dropped into an opening in the wooden floor. Her head reappeared. "Come on. They're in the tunnels."

Kale changed into clothes suitable for underground travel. Leggings and a close-fitting tunic would be easier to manage as they navigated dirt-walled hallways.

"Wait here," she told the dragons. "We'll call you if we need you."

Once in the underground passage, Kale made two light orbs and handed one to Bardon. No natural lightrocks dotted the sides and ceiling.

"Hurry, but don't touch the support beams." Seezle urged them on. "The tumanhofers have it rigged to collapse if the wrong people find their work. But do hurry. We're going to miss it."

"Miss what?" asked Bardon.

"Our opportunity."

"I thought we'd be waiting until very late when everyone was asleep."

"No, it would be too easy for the guards to spot you then. We'll move through the town during the march."

"More information, please." Kale reached to grab the kimen to slow her down, but her fingers brushed through the sleeve of Seezle's light garment.

"Five nights a week, the citizens march for an hour. The pattern is set, the pace is kept by the playing of instruments, and the formation is predetermined. The march is organized and fascinating to watch. The real purpose is to empty the houses so they can be searched for contraband."

"Contraband?" asked Kale. "What do you mean?"

"Things they aren't allowed to have. Books, outsiders' clothing, clocks, letters, sugar or salt, lots of things. And the quarters have to meet a standard of tidiness. The Followers put a lot of store in being orderly."

"Do the people know their privacy is invaded?" Bardon asked.

"Oh yes. They earn advancement when they pass a certain number of inspections."

"The echoes must use some excuse for forcing the march."

"Discipline. The Followers are keen on discipline as well."

"Oh, I bet they are," said Bardon.

Seezle turned around to walk backward. She lifted a hand over her head, pointed one finger, and spoke as one in authority. "The march provides exercise of the mind and body. The brisk pace improves circulation and the function of the lungs. The precision drill requires concentration and sharpens the mind."

She turned around to face forward. "I think the citizens enjoy it because they get to hear music, and it's the only time they can move without shuffling."

Kale pushed her unruly hair back from her face. "Will we be able to walk through the town if they're all out doing this march?"

"Sure, easy!" Seezle emphasized her point with a lively skip. "They're in groups of two to eight. You just get behind a group and follow them, then drop out when you reach your destination."

"And how will we know where we're going?"

"You can follow me. They never see me. Kale can mindspeak with me. It'll be all right. These people are pretty confident that what they have established cannot be put asunder. Therefore, they are careless in the most harebrained ways."

Kale heard soft noises of dirt being shoveled.

"Here we are," announced Seezle in a loud whisper.

"About time," said a rough tumanhofer voice. "They've been on the march for fifteen minutes already."

In the crowded space where two tunnels crossed, two men continued to dig while the third tumanhofer handed Kale and Bardon the Followers' standard garb, loose trousers and a tight shirt with the overlay. "We won't be going with you. They only allow o'rants and mariones up there."

Kale sidled up to her husband and smoothed his longish hair over his pointed ears. They exchanged a look, each feeling the other's excitement as they prepared to infiltrate Paladise.

Light from her orb caught a glint in Bardon's eye. Kale resisted the urge to kiss him. *I am so very glad you insisted we go on this quest. Well, not* this *quest…to rescue Holt, but the original quest…to find the meech colony.*

"Does the yellow have any significance?" asked Kale as she pulled the long gown over her head.

"Means you can make a mistake and not get killed for it. You're a novice, and if you make a wrong turn, you'll be prodded with a pole, but not beaten."

"Comforting," said Bardon. "Seezle said this would be easy."

"It will be," said the kimen. "Glaringtonover is a pessimist."

"Follow me," said the pessimist. "You will enter the city through Holt's quarters. It's no longer inspected."

"The floor of the jail cell is stone," explained Seezle before Kale or Bardon asked.

They came to a wooden ladder, and Seezle skimmed up the rungs with ease. She pushed open a trapdoor and slipped out.

"Coast is clear," she whispered a moment later.

Kale hiked the yellow robe up and climbed the ladder. Bardon followed.

No light shone in the bare room, but a glimmer from a lamppost outside prevented total darkness. Seezle glowed a tiny bit, then her light faded to nothing. Kale could no longer see the kimen but heard her merry voice.

"Peek out the window. Watch a couple of groups go by so you can see how they march. It's easy. You'll catch on quickly. When a group passes to the right, we'll sneak out and join their formation."

"They'll see us," objected Kale.

"No, watch," insisted Seezle.

The tune played by a brass ensemble must have been coming from the town center, but it could be heard clearly. The feet of most of the inhabitants of this Paladise tramped in unison, giving a steady beat behind the music, almost like a percussion instrument.

A group of four Followers approached.

Kale gasped. "They're blindfolded."

Marching in step and evenly spaced, they passed with faces pointed straight ahead. With precision, the four turned at the counter, just as another group entered the intersection of the two streets.

"They don't ever collide?" she asked.

"Never," answered Seezle. "The routine never varies, and if they start at exactly the same time and don't vary pace or path, the march proceeds in perfect synchrony."

"I assume you have blindfolds for us," said Bardon.

"Oh yes." Seezle giggled. "Only they aren't exactly blindfolds, because you'll be able to see right through them."

Kale tied Bardon's on, and he did the same for her.

She looked around the room and could see even better than before the cloth covered her eyes. "This has moonbeam thread in it, doesn't it?"

"It does." Seezle opened the door a crack. "Are you ready?"

Kale and Bardon spoke in unison. "Ready."

34

THE BOTTOM DROPS OUT

Seezle, Kale, and Bardon stood inside the door and peered through the crack. The marchers in a unit wore various colors. If they'd had to wait to join a yellow corps, they would've waited a long time. Several groups passed Holt's quarters before one headed in the right direction. Kale and Bardon fell into step behind a group of citizens.

Following Seezle's prompting, they switched groups at different corners, always lining up behind the marchers. Using a convoluted route, they ended up behind the round, white stone building in the center of the village.

Seezle stuck her finger in the keyhole, fiddled a moment with the locking mechanism, then opened the back door.

"No one is here but Holt," she said.

Bardon frowned at the door and then at Seezle. "If you can open a lock like that, why haven't you let Holt out a long time ago?"

"Because there was no way to get him out of the village after I got him out of jail. The village is gated with a wall around it."

"The one I visited had no barricade."

"According to Holt's informants, all the villages will become forts soon." She turned a corner, opened a door, and led them down some wooden steps.

Bardon hurried to follow her, still objecting. "Why couldn't he have walked out in the same manner you walked us in?"

"The tumanhofers weren't ready. Glaringtonover has his own plan for after we rescue Holt."

Kale sensed they were getting closer. Holt's unworried demeanor surprised her. He was more relaxed in these circumstances than when they'd parted ways in Vendela. Fresh air streamed in the shallow, barred window high on the wall of his cell and rushed in a draft past his visitors on the stair.

He came to his feet as they descended the steps.

"Greetings!" He spoke quietly but not in the hushed tones of one afraid of being overheard. "Is tonight to be the great escape?"

Seezle giggled and passed him what appeared to be a wrapped sandwich and a bottle of some drink.

He took them and went to sit on the cot. "Oh, Seezle, you are a true friend." He unwrapped the food and took a big bite. "Umm."

Kale crossed her arms. "And I was afraid you were going to starve to death."

"What?" Holt's charming smile brightened his face. "Seezle wouldn't let that happen to me. And the people of the village... Well, some of them, anyway, are much more generous than the echoes." He shuddered. "Those echoes are mean, like hornets under their guise of tranquility."

"Seezle," said Kale. She gave the kimen a stern look. "You led me to believe this prisoner was on bread and water."

"He is as far as the Followers know." Seezle swung the door open. "We haven't time for a leisurely meal, Holt. We need to get out of here before the end of the march."

He stood, and after taking another bite, he rewrapped the sandwich and put it in a loose pocket. Then he opened the bottle.

Seezle went into the cell. "Here are some fresh clothes."

"Do you have a bathtub hidden away as well?"

She laughed again and danced away from the marione.

"She wasn't carrying anything before," observed Bardon to Kale. *"I suppose she has a hollow in her dress."*

I think each kimen has a hollow. I can remember, even when I was very young and they came to market in River Away, I wondered how they brought their goods for sale.

"You could at least turn around," Holt said, holding up the new clothes to remind them he was about to change.

"Hurry," said Seezle.

"Hurry is your middle name," said Holt.

He grumped but swiftly obeyed. He left the clothes in a pile on the floor. Seezle carefully locked the cell door, and they scurried up the steps. They managed to get back outside in just a few minutes. The kimen relocked the outside door.

She giggled. "The echoes will be stumped in the morning when they find their prisoner missing."

With his voice just above a whisper, Holt answered, "Technically, I wasn't a prisoner. I was receiving special training to bring my will, as well as my heart and mind, under the authority of the leaders."

"Did it work?" asked Bardon.

Holt scoffed as he tied on the fake blindfold provided by Seezle. "Ha! Their first mistake was in assuming they had my heart and mind, so they just needed to work on my will. Their second oversight was the fact that Seezle or one of her friends brought me a meal each night. And rolls and such came sailing through my one poor, unglassed window at different times during the day."

"Here's where we join the parade," warned Seezle. Her light went out, but on the cue she gave Kale, they stepped into the back of a formation as it passed. They made quick progress back to Holt's compact house. Once inside, Seezle eagerly popped down the hole under the trapdoor.

Holt leaned over the underground exit. He saluted. "Thanks, fellows, for digging the escape route. I'm sure you'd agree with me that it seems a waste. All that effort, and I'm the only one to get out of here? Not an efficient use of labor."

Glaringtonover answered. "What do you have in mind, young marione?"

"I suggest we rescue other members of this sect who are trapped and want out."

"And how do we do that?"

"Seezle says you have dug a network of tunnels under Paladise. Why did you do that, good man?"

"I have plans of my own, boy."

"Would it hinder your plans if we used those tunnels to locate and rescue those I have identified as Followers who realize they're following a sham?"

Glaringtonover didn't answer for a moment. "I'm thinking there's no problem in doing a little side job."

"Good!" Holt clapped his hands together and then gestured to Kale. "Ladies first, dear Kale."

When they had all assembled at the bottom of the wooden ladder, Holt pulled out a rough page of pale brown. He unrolled it, revealing a hand-drawn map of Paladise.

"I've marked the houses we need to visit," Holt explained.

"And how are we going to recognize these houses from below?" asked Glaringtonover.

"That's where Kale and Seezle come in. With Seezle following the map on the streets above, Kale will be able to locate her using her talent from below. Seezle stops at a house indicated on the map, and we dig up."

"Sounds like an all-night proposition," one of the other tumanhofers remarked. "How many people are you talking about?"

"The population of Paladise is around six hundred. The people who are too afraid to leave, but want to, number ninety-three."

Glaringtonover frowned at Holt. "Will they come if we knock on their floors in the middle of the night?"

Holt nodded. "If I'm there to reassure them that this is a real escape and not a trap, they'll jump in your hole faster than you can say, 'Followers beware.' "

Bardon smiled at Holt. "You know you're risking not getting out yourself if we get caught."

Holt's serious expression touched Kale's heart. The evidence suggested there was more to the young, rich marione than anyone knew. Bardon was right once more.

"I promised these people I'd help them." Holt glanced around at the others. "Will you help me help them?"

Glaringtonover scratched his beard. "It's lucky for you, when I made my design, I opted for digging under the houses instead of the streets."

Bardon clapped the tumanhofer on the shoulder. "I'd say that was Wulder's providence, not luck."

"Aye," agreed the short, stout man. "Time's awasting. We better get after this job lest the sun catch us in the morning."

The plan worked well, with a few tense moments each time they reached the wooden floor of the houses, knocked loud enough to wake the inhabitants, and then pushed up the boards. Holt told those who responded to pack a few things and come down below, then someone would guide them back to the shack in the woods, using the tumanhofer tunnels.

Holt told them, "Be quick packing and be sure not to touch the wooden supports in the tunnel."

Once the confusion of having someone appear through their floors cleared, the citizens were eager to cooperate. Bardon and the minor dragons escorted the escapees through the maze of tunnels to safety.

Bardon waited by one of the openings. The diggers had moved to the next house.

A man jumped to the tunnel floor, then turned to catch two bundles of belongings from his wife. No one possessed much, since the life they'd led inside the compound was austere. He put these things on the floor and turned to help his wife down.

Bardon picked up one of the packages. "This way," he said.

"You!" exclaimed the husband.

Bardon turned quickly to examine the man's face in the glow of his light orb.

"Garmey?" He looked at the woman. Her lined face looked old. Sympathy flooded him for the young mother he'd met weeks before. Her hollow eyes met his. Deep sadness poured out, and he thought he heard a suppressed sob. "Elma?"

"They took our children," explained Garmey. He put his arm around his wife. "They never told us that before. We wouldn't have agreed to come. On the way to Paladise, they stopped the wagon and moved our boys to another cart, saying they were going to a school. We thought the school would be here, or close by."

Bardon put his hand on the man's back. "We'll find them. We'll get them back."

"Some people here say the children are dead."

Elma turned her face to her husband's shoulder.

Bardon swallowed a protest. "We'll find them. We'll petition Wulder to keep them safe until we come."

He gestured for them to follow and began the long trek out from under Paladise.

The rescuers managed to awaken and evacuate all the people Holt had listed on his map. They huddled in the shack while Bardon and Kale made plans for their next move. Pat checked the gateway to see if it would tolerate such a large group traveling through.

Glaringtonover pulled the curtains over the windows against the dawning sun and anyone who might travel by and see the activity within the shack.

A horn blew in the distance.

Holt grinned at the young lady next to him. "The Followers have discovered something out of place."

She nestled into his side, and he wrapped an arm around her.

Kale's eyes widened as she sought out her husband. *Do you suppose this is the echo's daughter?*

Bardon nodded.

I suppose that means there will be a heated search for her. Will that endanger the rest of these people?

"We shall have to get them to safety quickly."

"What will happen at the sound of that alarm?" asked Kale.

"The citizens are required to assemble on the streets."

Glaringtonover and his men began to chortle, then let loose with loud guffaws.

"What?" asked Holt.

One of the tumanhofers managed to ask a question between his bouts of laughter. "How long does it take them to vacate the houses?"

"Under a minute. Tardiness is not tolerated by the echoes."

Glaringtonover and the other tumanhofers inched their way through the press of people. Lifting a barrel, they revealed it had no bottom, but hid a small coil of rope. Taking hold of the end of the rope, the men braced their feet, and together, tugged.

A creaking reverberated from beneath the shack. The rope yielded, and the men nearly fell over backward. Crashing timbers exploded below, and dust poofed through the cracks in the wooden floor.

"Dominoes," said Glaringtonover with a silly grin plastered on his usually humorless features.

The frame around them shook. Several women shrieked.

"No cause for alarm, ladies," said Glaringtonover.

"What's happening?" asked one of the rescued women.

The tumanhofer leader smiled kindly at her. "The people in the barricaded village are standing in the streets. They're watching the houses collapse in on themselves as the supports in the tunnels tip over and fall, knocking the next timber out of place. There's a special tunnel all the way around Paladise, directly under the wall. That will be the last to sink into the ground."

One of the other tumanhofers draped an arm over his leader's shoulders. "We got tired of sitting around, waiting to free Holt when he got into trouble."

Holt frowned. "Shouldn't that be *if* I got into trouble?"

No one bothered to answer.

"So," continued the tumanhofer leaning on Glaringtonover, "we decided to have a bit of fun." He tilted his head toward his boss. "Our chief engineer came up with a truly amazing plan."

"Inspired," said the two other tumanhofers.

Kale noticed a ruddy tinge come over Glaringtonover's cheeks.

She touched Bardon's arm. *Look! He's blushing.*

"Wonders never cease."

⟞ 35 ⟝

Moving On

Lady Lyll and Sir Kemry reinforced the gateway on one side. Bardon, Kale, and Pat strengthened the other by tightening the threads making up the edges. With the invisible frame fortified to accept the transport of so many individuals, the rescued Followers passed through to Namee's castle. Mistress Orcutt trundled them away to the many bedchambers, offering baths and fresh clothing. After washing to rid themselves of the dirt and grime resulting from their underground escape, they donned normal clothing that had none of the earmarks of the Follower sect's twisted thinking.

In the great hall, Mistress Orcutt spread a hearty breakfast.

"They're so quiet," Bardon commented as he stood with Kale and Lady Lyll at the end of one serving table.

A woman came in through the double doors and stood. She stared as if lost and trying to locate something that made sense.

Bardon went to her, gently guided her to the sideboard, and handed her a plate. "May I get you a drink? Wizard Namee has provided hot tea and cold juice. What would you like?"

"Tea," she whispered.

The woman stood with the empty plate in her hand, and her eyes drifted over the many delicacies on the table. After a moment, Lady Lyll came around to the front and gently took the dish.

"Let me help you." She picked up tongs and began to pile on small squares of light pastries filled with jam and crushed nuts. "Some fruit?" she asked and, when the woman nodded, added cut-up bites of green, yellow, red, and orange melons.

Lady Lyll escorted the woman to a table. Bardon followed with tea.

"What's going on?" Bardon asked as they moved back to the table where Kale served the next victim of the Followers.

"They're dazed. The depth of the persuasion used must have been extreme. Bringing these people under the authority of the echoes damaged the beautiful souls Wulder gave them."

Bardon looked around the room to where nine minor dragons perched, watching the people. The citizens of Paladise were skittish of the tiny creatures. Holt had said dragons had been scorned, and the wary eyes of these guests supported that idea. The friendly dragons held back, confused at the odd reception. Most were unhappy with the situation. "Tieto is as depressed as the Followers are."

"He sees their shattered auras." Lyll patted Bardon's arm. "But Tieto also reports that the dent he saw in Wizard Namee's colors is completely restored. We shall work to see these people rejuvenated. It is not Wulder's desire for them to be in pain."

"What happened to Namee?"

"I can tell you that."

Bardon turned at the sound of the wizard's voice. "I was curious about those Followers. Invited them into my home. There were a number of them present at our ball. Some of their arguments were persuasive. I suppose that was the dent your Tieto saw." He grinned at Bardon and winked at Lyll. "Even an old man can be lead astray."

He sighed. "Fortunately, Wulder sends reminders. When a servant brought me the body of a small dragon, no bigger than a buzz-bird, apprehension niggled at my comfortable tranquility. The servant described the onslaught of the black dragons, and I saw my error."

"How is that, sir?" asked Bardon.

"One tiny creature with a little bit of poison can cause a small wound. But it weakens the body. A horde of the beasts wears down the resistance and ultimately kills."

Namee sighed again and rubbed his hand across his chin. "My curiosity had led me to listen to the Followers, even though I detected a dart of impurity, a prick of untruth, a jab of heresy. Had I continued to entertain their false representation of Wulder, I might have succumbed."

He looked around the room at his solemn and weary guests. "I escaped. They did not. We must give them health, good cheer, and hope."

The wizard wandered off to mingle with his visitors.

"So much sadness," commented Lyll. "I'm glad Namee avoided this downfall. When a leader follows the wrong path, so many people suffer."

Bardon poured a cup of tea and handed it to her. "Mikkai, on the other hand, is delighted."

"Why is that?"

"The destruction of one of the Paladise villages." He poured a cup for himself. "He considers these new cities to be blemishes on the countryside because they are not on his maps."

Lyll laughed, then turned serious eyes toward her son-in-law. "Have you noticed your wife's figure this morning?"

Bardon searched the room and found Kale serving a couple at a far table. Her silhouette showed a slight bulge at her abdomen. He caught his breath.

Lyll giggled. "Yes, that baby is growing."

"Is it safe to take her on the rest of the quest?"

"She will be fine. And traveling and being useful will keep her mind off her discomforts. The last stages of gestation are a bother, but the baby is worth the trouble."

Holt strode into the room, looking debonair in his borrowed clothes. He stopped and scrutinized the many tables. At one, the young lady he sought lifted her hand in a shy wave. He smiled.

"Ladies and gentlemen." He spoke so that all could hear. "I have information as to where your children are being held. I have spoken to Wizard Namee, and we will have warriors from Paladin's army to accompany us. These are soldiers from Paladin's legitimate army, not the counterfeits we saw in Paladise."

Several of the women began to cry.

"Take heart!" said Holt, exuding his most convincing charm. "We go forth this afternoon to retrieve your little ones, and you will have them in your arms by sundown."

At that news, the silence that had held the room dissolved into a mixture of cheers and relieved sobs.

Holt grabbed a plate from the sideboard and began to pile up a bountiful breakfast.

Bardon followed him as he moved down the table. "How do you know where the children are, Holt?" he asked.

Kale approached from the other side in time to hear her husband's question.

The marione chuckled. "How do you think I became acquainted with Mardell, the lovely daughter of the esteemed echo? I prowled through his office in his home nightly, looking for any information I could use. She caught me at it, and I convinced her not to turn me in." He turned and winked at the young woman. "I also discovered she hated everything about the Followers."

Kale took his arm. "The children are alive, then? You're sure?"

"Yes, they're alive." Again, a sober expression stole away Holt's usual carefree facade. "I don't think they're happy. But they are alive."

Kale threw her arms around Holt and kissed his cheek. Her sudden action knocked his plate. Several pastries and a sausage fell back onto the table.

Bardon rescued the tilting dish from Holt's hand. "Go ahead and give her a big hug. She's expecting our first child and gets quite demonstrative with her feelings."

Holt did just that. He embraced Kale and swung her around. Before he put her down on her feet, the lovely Mardell stood waiting. He smoothly let go of Kale and gathered his current beloved into his arms. He kissed her forehead.

"You must meet Kale Allerion, sweet Mardell. She's like a sister, and I just learned she is to have a baby."

Mardell accepted the explanation, and she and Kale sized each other up. Both women smiled and went off together to get better acquainted.

Holt reclaimed his plate and continued picking delicacies from the sideboard.

"You handled that awkward situation with panache," said Bardon. "But your memory for the order of our conversation was not exactly accurate."

Holt poked a small fried mullin into his mouth and merely nodded as his answer.

"One minute, I think you have completely turned from your old habits." Bardon continued to follow the marione down the feast of breakfast items. "Your insistence that we rescue others from Paladise and your concern for the children show a different attitude from the Holt I knew years ago. But then the way you twisted this little incident to avoid trouble reflects a lack of respect for truth."

Holt held up his hand, finished chewing, and swallowed. "I have changed, Bardon. Allow me time to adjust to the things I now deem important. I am not perfect."

Bardon fought the pride that wanted to block his response. A snakelike thought hissed in sympathy. *You come from superior stock. You've served from childhood. You stand in favor with our sovereign. Say no more to this sinner.*

Bardon blocked out the voice he knew was his own. The words did not honor Wulder, and he chose to refuse them. He put a hand on the marione's shoulder. "Forgive me. Yes, you deserve time. And if you need anything from a knight who's been at it a long while and still commits errors, just let me know."

In the afternoon, Holt led a group to storm the halls of a makeshift academy while Kale and her group returned to Arreach.

Sittiponder and Toopka ran out to meet them. But only halfway there, Toopka stopped, bent over, and gasped for breath. Kale, Bardon, and Seezle ran the rest of the way.

Kale scooped the little doneel into her arms. "What's wrong?"

Toopka buried her head in Kale's neck and cried.

"She hurts," said Sittiponder. He grabbed hold of Kale's moonbeam cape. "She's all right a lot of the time, but when she runs, she gets out of breath. And when she's tired, she says her chest hurts. I'm glad you're back. I've been worried. And the voices have no answers to my questions."

Gymn crawled over and around Toopka as Kale held her close. Bardon put his arms around both his wife and the child she held.

Kale looked up into Bardon's face. "Gymn says she has a growth, but it doesn't seem to be the kind that takes over and kills a person." She squeezed the doneel. "Toopka, did you hear that? Gymn says you aren't to worry. This thing is odd, but not life-threatening."

"I know." Her furry head moved up and down against Kale's chin and neck. "I don't like it. I don't want to talk about it." She sniffed and moved so she could peer down at her friend. "Sittiponder, tell Kale what we found."

"A mural!" Sittiponder jumped, his face brightening with a huge smile. "A mural, Lady Kale. In one of the taverns. When the urohms cleared away the rubble, there it was, lying on its back. The wall had fallen outward, and the mural is facing the sky. Toopka described it to me. You've got to come see it."

"Indeed, I do."

"Will you carry me?" asked Toopka.

"I will."

They followed Sittiponder into the village.

"Going to see the mural?" asked one of the urohms as he laid another timber on his pile.

"Yes," called Bardon.

The big man scratched his head. "That's caused quite a stir among the children. The older folks have seen it often enough, but not the young uns. And your two have been telling them all sorts of tales. To be honest, they have my interest too."

He left his work to follow them. By the time they'd traversed the cleared streets in the small town and come to the other side, a whole line of people accompanied them.

Kale and Bardon stopped to examine the wall. Someone had swept away dust and debris. A crack ran from one corner to the opposite side, but the image was still intact.

A hatching egg predominated the drawing. The style was like those of other murals they had seen. But in the others, a group of travelers had been pictured against a landscape. Here, a talon pierced the shell from within, and light streamed out. Mist obscured the trees and mountains in the background.

A hush fell on the crowd as they waited for the visitors' response.

Woodkimkalajoss spoke from among the people. "What is it, Lady Kale? What does the picture mean?"

She shook her head. "It could mean anything. I've never known what the murals mean until later when something happens that seems to be an enactment of the scene. But this could be a fluke and not related at all to our quest. In the paintings we've seen before, there have been people in the picture."

Some of those who had tagged along lost interest and wandered away as Kale and Bardon circled the fallen wall and scrutinized the mural from different angles.

Woodkimkalajoss remained with a few other onlookers. Kale turned to the man. "Do you know who painted this?"

She expected to hear the same story she had heard before: A traveling man who traded his talent for dinner and a place to stay had come and gone years before.

"Don't know his name, but I know where he went."

"Where?"

"North. He was bent on finding that meech colony, just like you. Of course, he never came back. Seems to me that means he found it."

"Why?"

"Cause it's a mite easier to get into that place than to get out." He scowled and looked at the travelers who had been left behind—Kale, Bardon, Sittiponder, and Toopka. "You'd do better to stay here or go back home. But I'm thinking you're probably going to follow those others."

All four nodded. "Yes sir," said Sittiponder. "We are. Toopka's got something grand to do. I want to be there to see it."

36

The Fight's On

The aroma of freshly baked bread lifted Kale from the depths of slumber. She rolled over. A sharp rock reminded her that she was not at home in her comfortable bed. She was on a quest.

Much to Toopka's dismay, Bardon had decided to spend the rest of the day in Arreach and begin the next leg of their trip in the morning. Toopka's dramatic pout had escalated when Seezle announced she would go on ahead. The kimen wanted to reunite with the other kimens trekking north for some undisclosed reason.

Kale shook her head over the natural aloofness and secrecy that characterized kimens and shook her finger at Toopka as the child continued to mope over being left behind.

"Of course, you couldn't go with Seezle, Toopka. What are you thinking? She travels as fast as a breeze, and you would be cranky for a comfortable ride on a dragon's back within minutes."

Kale gladly provided the equipment needed for a campsite out of her moonbeam cape hollows. Bardon set up the tent, and Sittiponder helped Kale prepare an evening meal. The twilight hours had been comfortable, almost normal.

Kale rolled onto her back and placed her elbows on the mat. With her hands across her stomach, she measured the expansion of her waist. Yesterday, her fingertips touched. Today an inch gap lay between the tips of her middle fingers. A baby. Soon. Bardon would be a marvelous father. She'd—

The children!

She sat up on the pallet and reached across the narrow tent to retrieve her talking gateway. The night before, she had checked for a message from Namee about Holt's mission to save the children, but there had been no news. She'd left an image for Namee.

Bardon came in, ducking under the flap.

"Good morning, sleepyhead." He held out a plate of buttered rolls and pastries. "The town baker has his ovens up and running, thanks to the urohm crew and Pat's ingenuity."

Kale tossed him a grin but kept working on opening and aligning the small gateway.

Bardon sat cross-legged beside her and put a muffin in his mouth. "I see you are eager for news."

She nodded. He pinched off a piece of sweet mullin and held it in front of her mouth. She parted her lips, and he poked it in.

"Thanks," she mumbled as she chewed the tasty morsel.

The opening of the gateway snapped twice before clearing.

"I forgot to have Regidor look at this," she complained. "I hope it holds out. I can't see where the error is, but I'm sure he could fix it in a flash."

"Have you had Pat look at it?"

Kale leaned back and stared at her husband. "I never thought to ask him. I've got to remember to use Pat's unique talents, or I'm going to have him permanently miffed at me."

Bardon chortled. "Not as long as he's well fed. He does love to eat."

"So do I." Kale reached for the plate. "Give me another bite."

She retrieved her pastry with the piece missing and took small bites as she fine-tuned the mechanism. "It looks like we have three messages. One from Mother and Father, one from Namee, and one from Regidor."

"Find out about the children first."

Kale plucked a string in the lining of the gateway, and an agitated Namee appeared.

"I'm overrun," he said. "Children everywhere. Oh yes, Holt and his company of warriors were successful in their storming of the fortified academy, but oh my! The children came in and ate and ate and ate. Some have parents retrieved from Paladise on the night Holt escaped. The ones who found no parents to greet them cried and cried and cried. Mistress Orcutt has done wonders in soothing them. Most of these ex-

Followers have nowhere to go. The children with parents could go home, but the parents are reluctant to return. They say their houses are sold or occupied by unforgiving Followers." Namee rubbed his hand across the top of his head. "How can one be a Follower and at the same time be dogmatic and unforgiving? It is a juxtaposition of ideals.

"Holt organized games in the great hall. Not quiet games, mind you. Loud, very loud, and boisterous. I had the servants remove all the statues and art, and, well, all the breakables."

Noises of laughter and shouting came from somewhere beyond the scene depicted in the gateway. Namee closed his eyes, sighed, and opened them. "But they're safe. Some of them show signs of being emotionally damaged, but Mistress Orcutt is mothering them, and I'm sure, with time, they'll be fine."

The image blurred, the gateway issued a series of odd noises, and the middle space closed in on itself.

Bardon frowned. "Was that the end of the message, or did the portal break?"

"I don't know." Kale ran a finger over the rim. "I hope it's not broken. Where are Pat and the others?"

"Out getting breakfast."

The small portal sizzled and popped. Another image came into view. Lady Allerion looked serene, as usual. Sir Kemry sat beside her.

"Kale," said Lyll, "if you get this message before you see the message from Namee, rest assured that what he says in his report is before this message, and we have since then taken many of the children off his hands. If you get this message after you listen to Namee, then you will know what I'm talking about here."

Kemry glanced adoringly at his wife. "Love, I'm not sure what you're talking about, and I've been with you."

She tilted her chin at him, puzzlement clouding her expression. "I'm sure Kale will understand perfectly." She looked again through the portal. "We've come back to your castle, dear. We brought all the children whose parents still remain under the influence of the Followers. Namee and Mistress Orcutt are housing the families while the Follower issue is resolved."

Sir Kemry focused on the talking gateway. "Paladin is taking action. Now, dear, this is hard for me to relate, and I know you will be distressed." He paused.

"What?" Kale sat up straight and peered at the contraption. "Don't you dare zap out on me now, little gateway."

"Does it respond to scolding?" asked Bardon.

"Of course not!"

"Hey! I'm not the wizard in the family. It was a perfectly legitimate question."

"Shh!" Kale adjusted the gateway. "Does Father look sick, or is that just a bad image?"

Sir Kemry's face had definitely paled. "The Followers have issued an execution proclamation against all dragons. There's an enormous bounty. Paladin has declared the Followers' activities to be illegal. There are many counts against them, including embezzlement, child slavery, and murder. He's written a cease and desist order, but the corruption in local governments is making it hard to enforce."

Lyll grasped her husband's hands. "Oh, Kemry, I didn't know this. What can we do to help?"

"First, we are supplying sanctuary. Those being persecuted by the sect can find refuge in the castles of most of Paladin's wizards."

Kale turned to Bardon. "Should we go back?"

Sir Kemry's voice interrupted Bardon as he started to speak.

"I know you children are thinking you should come home and help. But I specifically talked this over with Paladin, and he believes your quest for the meech dragons is merely the task we are able to readily discern. Paladin believes that Wulder is guiding your steps north for a more important mission, one that you will recognize once you arrive. So go, accomplish your goal, whatever Wulder puts before you, and then come home."

The image turned to a haze before fading completely away.

Kale and Bardon sat in silence. Finally, Bardon took in a deep breath and let it out slowly.

"Did you say there was a message from Regidor?"

Kale nodded.

"I'm confused, Bardon."

"So am I."

"Weren't the Followers keeping Paladin sequestered? Not exactly in prison, but restricted so he couldn't act. What has changed?"

"I have no idea. Maybe Regidor will shed some light on the matter."

She changed the threads of the gateway fabric with slow and deliberate movements. As much as she dreaded what might be another disturbing communication, she did not want to break the fragile link they had with others. The configuration took more time than usual. One of the components repeatedly slipped out of place. When she was satisfied with the weave, she tightened the last cord.

The center of the talking gateway blinked white, then gray, then black. Kale pressed her lips together. Regidor's solemn face appeared.

"This trek north is getting to be a bother. I think we've run into every type of adversity imaginable. Gilda complains she is growing mold. It has rained almost every minute since we crossed into the Northern Reach. The nights are frigid. Too often, lightning has kept us on the ground. We are reduced to crawling over ugly terrain when we should be flying. I doubt you will have any trouble catching up to us, my friends.

"Sir Dar and Lee Ark have gone off through a gateway, responding to some urgent message from Librettowit. Gilda and I have battled various creatures, but Lee Ark said before he left that these beasts are only hungry wild animals, nothing genetically developed by the late and unlamented Crim Cropper. Our forces have been scattered, and I don't mind telling you, traveling in the Northern Reach is a bit eerie. I should like some cheery company, so come quickly, will you? We've also encoun—"

The gateway sputtered and collapsed.

"Argh!" Kale lifted the limp strands in her hand, folded them, and put the portal away in its traveling container.

Bardon stood and helped Kale to her feet. "I'll call the others and start packing."

She followed him out of their tent. Heavy, moist air filled her lungs as she stretched the night's kinks out of her back. A flutter in her abdomen surprised her. She grinned and almost called Bardon, but the slight movement did not repeat. Her husband would have to wait a day or two before his hand resting on her stomach could detect the stirring of their child.

She examined the horizon to the north. Black clouds obscured a ridge of mountains. A wind swept over Kale, scuttling dry leaves and scattering dust at her feet.

"The sky doesn't look friendly this morning," she commented to Bardon.

He stood from his chore of loosening the ropes that bound the tent to stakes in the ground. Squinting against the dirt hurled in his face by the stiff breeze, he followed her gaze.

"No, not inviting at all." He put his arm around her shoulders and sang.

"If you follow the road where the merry dells grow,
You'll find a song and a dance as you go.
But the path that is dark with a friend's tale of woe
Will profit you more than you know."

She joined him on the chorus.

"I'd rather go home and sit by my fire,
A good meal and warm bed is my greatest desire,
But a world of ease when I've turned my back on a friend
Is not a world of peace but a black void without end."

Kale sighed. "I've never liked that song."

Bardon hugged her closer. "Surely it is the unpleasant melody that puts you off."

"Surely it is the call to uncomfortable duty."

He kissed her forehead. "After we find the meech colony…"

"We can go home."

"And after we put down the Followers' uprising…"

"We can sit by the fire." Kale sighed again. "One can always hope."

37

Enemies to the Right

A fine mist hung beneath the massive gray clouds, making their flight uncomfortable. Kale pulled her moonbeam cape tighter, not allowing even a wisp of chill air to enter. Toopka and the dragons huddled beneath the warm cloak. Sittiponder and Mikkai rode with Bardon. Kale worried whether the young tumanhofer had enough clothing to protect him from the cold. Like the rest of his race, Sittiponder had a sturdy-looking frame, but she always thought of him as frail. Perhaps because when she first met him, he was a ragged street urchin and undernourished.

Bardon?

"I'm warm enough, and Sittiponder's warm enough. I'm concerned about Celisse and Greer, though."

Celisse says she's all right, but I know cold makes her wings ache.

"Perhaps we should make it a short day."

The hair on the back of Kale's neck stood up. Goose bumps shivered down her arms. This wasn't a chill but something more sinister. She stretched with her mind, trying to locate the source of her subconscious alarm. A buzz.

She peered over Celisse's right shoulder, examining the earth far below. On the ground, a large shadow moved rapidly across the hilly landscape. No sunbeams penetrated the thick clouds. There could be no shadow.

Bardon?

"What? Oh...how far?" He leaned forward to see with his own eyes what he had gathered from her mind.

Kale searched the area for a safe haven. *Do we have time to land?*

"No, they're turning upward now."

The black dragon beasts rushed toward them, closing the gap at an uncanny speed. Kale heard Bardon's interchange with Greer, so she wasn't surprised by his command.

"Into the clouds, Kale. We'll try to lose them."

She pulled the hood over her head and face as they entered the heavy haze. Fear rippled through Celisse, and Kale shuddered. Would this attack be like the others? Would she be the only victim?

I won't have Celisse hurt by these nasty beasties!

Would the dragons and Toopka be in danger because they were inside her cloak? Her moonbeam mantle had protected her many times. Would it do so again?

Wulder, please! Give us a way out.

A thump smacked her solidly between the shoulder blades. Her back sustained another hit. The impact jostled her but caused no pain. Several more tiny dragons thudded against her neck and shoulders, and then the barrage began in earnest. She'd read about people being stoned to death.

The dragon attack forced Kale to bend over so that she lay on Celisse's neck. The saddle horn poked into her midriff, and the bulge in her abdomen reminded her of one more person who could be hurt in this assault. She shifted to protect the child.

Kale heard her riding dragon's frenzied challenge to herself—higher, faster. Celisse demanded more of her body than Kale thought she could give.

Tuned in to her dragon's distress, Kale felt the pain in her dragon's wings and the sting in her lungs as the air grew thinner and colder. The attacking beasts that inadvertently struck Celisse on the underside of her wings left poison wounds. Ice pellets struck the riding dragon's scales. Only those hitting her eyes and nostrils caused enough discomfort to distract the big dragon from the strain in her shoulders.

The black dragons fell back. Celisse continued on for a moment before drifting downward.

Bardon! Celisse's strength is completely drained. We must land.

Kale caressed the dragon's neck. Her fingertips picked up the inner tremor indicating the extent of exhaustion depleting her friend's will. "It's all right. You were magnificent, Celisse. Thank you. Everything will be all right now. Just get us down."

They broke through to clear air, and Kale directed Celisse toward the nearest field.

Bardon!

"We're coming. Sittiponder and I circled to see if we could determine why the dragons cut off their attack."

Why did they?

"They were dropping from the sky. Apparently the cold or thin air killed them."

The thin air hasn't done Celisse any good. Is Greer—?

"Greer is grumbling, but we weren't flying as fast as Celisse. The black dragons hardly seemed to notice us."

Kale and Celisse descended rapidly. The dragon's thoughts became disjointed as exhaustion overcame her. Kale mindspoke a steady stream of encouragement. The dragon stumbled as she landed and fell forward. Kale hung on and jumped from the saddle as soon as the great beast collapsed.

She knelt beside Celisse's head. The dragon gazed at her for a moment, and then her eyes closed.

"Gymn! Gymn!" Kale ripped open the front of her cape. Toopka spilled out. The minor dragons followed in a more orderly fashion. Gymn sat first on Celisse's throat, then wandered slowly down her neck to her chest, taking note of physical signs of distress. He relayed his findings to Kale.

The other dragons stayed on Celisse's shoulder, respectfully waiting for the healing dragon's instructions. Toopka curled over the riding dragon's leg, hugging as much as she could reach with her short arms.

Kale stroked Celisse's cheek as her great ebony and silver head rested in her lap.

"Please be all right. You're strong. You can make it. Don't give up. Gymn and I will heal you."

Greer landed. Bardon, Sittiponder, and Mikkai joined those crowded around the fallen dragon. Bardon crouched beside his wife, and she took his hand.

"Gymn is very worried."

"We'll camp here until she's better."

"Would you build a fire?"

"Certainly. Crispin, come."

Toopka jumped up. "I'll help." She grabbed Sittiponder's hand and pulled him toward the shrubs. Bending over, she picked up a branch and shoved it into the tumanhofer's arms.

"Ouch! Be careful. You poked me."

"Celisse is dying," said Toopka. "We have to build a fire and get her warm."

"No one said she's dying."

"She looks awful, so she's dying." Toopka thrust another stick at him.

He shifted the wood so that it lay in his arms, across his chest. "Looking awful doesn't mean someone's dying."

"You don't know." She put two thick, short branches on his pile.

A leafy twig slapped Sittiponder in the face. He pushed it down with his chin. "You don't know, either."

"She's not dying!" Kale cut into the argument. "Gymn says she's not dying."

Kale removed vials of medicine from her cape and removed the caps. She handed them to the minor dragons.

"Rub this into the poison wounds beneath her wings. Don't get it in your eyes."

The minor dragons scampered to do their part, wiggling under Celisse to reach the spots where she'd been struck by the venomous black dragons.

Kale allowed herself to sink into a healing circle with Gymn and Celisse. Wulder's wonderful presence completed the union. Metta sang as they concentrated on relieving the riding dragon's fatigue and strained muscles.

Bardon prepared a stew and, while it cooked, set up their tent. The minor dragons gathered their meals with less zeal than usual.

"Let's remove her saddle." Bardon's voice startled Kale. She'd fallen asleep. Whenever she engaged in a circle of healing, the wonderment of being connected to Wulder sent a rush of astonishment through her. The flow of energy, as it circled through those close to her and the One she could not see, stirred and soothed at the same time. But that exhilaration settled into a peace, and she often dozed during the process. The circle of healing drained her of energy while reaffirming her devotion to Wulder.

She stood, stretching cautiously to ease the kinks in her muscles. Bardon unbuckled the straps around Celisse's bulky body, and Kale helped pull the saddle from her sleeping dragon friend.

She ran her hand over the smooth, hard scales of Celisse's side. "She'll be all right."

Bardon came back from putting the tack off to the side and embraced Kale. A soft laugh escaped Kale's lips. The roundness of the baby kept her husband a bit farther away than she was used to. He leaned down to kiss her, and the baby kicked. Bardon's eyes widened, and he pulled back.

"Can you mindspeak to that child?" he asked.

"Not yet."

"Well, as soon as you can, inform him—"

"Or her."

"—that you were mine first. I'll share your affections, but there will be some ground rules."

"Yes sir." Kale giggled. "I'll do that."

Within the next half hour, the overcast veil broke up and scuttled off to the south. Afternoon passed into dusk. In the west, trails of vibrant orange and rosy pink floated in a darkening sea of blue. Gold fringed the clouds. The evening star sparkled, inviting the rest of the heavens to bring out their lights.

Kale and Bardon ate while Celisse continued to sleep. Greer stayed closer to the campsite than usual. Soon after everyone turned in for the night, Celisse began to snore.

"Oh, great," said Bardon. "I don't suppose we could get her to roll over."

"You could ask Greer to give her a push," suggested Kale.

Bardon addressed the problem to his dragon friend.

"He says the solution is to move some distance away, and that is exactly what he is doing."

"I know. I heard." She turned over, trying to find a comfortable situation. The baby seemed to have grown just enough that day to make all her usual positions bumpy. "Bardon, could you rub the small of my back?"

Celisse snorted, was silent, then let out a ragged snore that sounded like a farmer knocking down dried cornstalks.

"Seems I'm not going to sleep immediately. I'll be glad to massage your back. Do you want some of my ointment from Elma?"

"No!" She shrugged. "That's for you. For the stakes."

"I may not need it any longer. I only have an occasional twinge."

"As long as you have any twinges, the medicine is exclusively yours. Besides, we don't know if it works on anything but the aches of stakes."

"That rhymed."

"Yes, and Metta could probably dredge up a song about it if she were in here. Why did you tell them to roost in the trees? Are you expecting trouble?"

"Not really. I thought we'd sleep better without the crowd."

Celisse rumbled louder.

Kale rummaged in her cape.

"What are you looking for?" asked Bardon.

"Something to use for earplugs."

The snoring ceased. Kale recognized the sound of Celisse stretching. The dragon flapped her wings twice. Dried grass rustled as the big beast moved. Silence.

"She's gone back to sleep?" whispered Bardon.

"Yes."

"Good, now we can get some sleep."

"Not quite yet."

"Why?"

"Something woke her up."

"Something?"

"I should have said someone."

Bardon sat up. "Is he still there?"

Kale nodded in the dark.

"I should have said some*ones,* plural."

Bardon pushed off the covers and reached for his boots. "Friend or foe?"

"I can't tell. There are too many mixed emotions out there."

Bardon put on his boots and stood. He buckled on his sword. "I'll go ask them."

38

Missing Lights

"Not without me!" Kale wiggled out of the blanket and changed her soft nightgown into leggings and a shirt as she stood. She reached into her pack and apparently came out empty-handed, but Bardon knew she held an invisible sword.

He wanted to tell her to stay in the tent, but that would only anger her. "Are the minor dragons awake? What do they see?"

Moonlight filtered through the slit in the tent canvas. He watched her concentrate. "Pat is awake. He's having a snack. He's not seen anything, but I have him looking and rousing the others." Her frown deepened.

"Filia has spotted something beneath her tree." Kale's face relaxed, and she smiled. "Kimens." She tilted her head.

Bardon felt the tension fall from his shoulders. His muscles relaxed, and he breathed deeply. "I've never heard of unfriendly kimens."

Kale frowned and shook her head.

"What's wrong?"

"Now that Filia has identified the intruders, I can tell where they are and something about their intent." She shook her head again with her face screwed up in frustration. "Such turmoil. They are distraught, every one of them."

"It would be nice if Seezle had hung around."

Kale gasped. "Seezle's one of them! She's among the kimens hovering around our camp."

She pushed past Bardon and dived through the flap. Bardon followed her, still alert but not expecting anything dangerous.

"Seezle," she called. "What is this all about?"

Seezle didn't appear. Bardon and Kale scrutinized the perimeter of the campground. Shadows shifted among the bushes.

"Seezle." Kale's attention focused on one spot. "Come out. What's wrong?"

Seezle's small voice drifted to their ears. "Our lights have gone out."

Kale turned to Bardon. "I saw Seezle and another kimen trapped in a bubble many years ago. While the two slept, their light clothing disappeared. She's probably embarrassed."

Bardon nodded. "Should I close my eyes?"

"There are male kimens here too. We can't all shut our eyes."

Bardon peered into the bushes.

"You're not naked," Kale said bluntly. "Come out."

No response.

"Your underwear is quite modest."

Again no response.

"Seezle, really!"

A bush rattled. Bardon tensed, squinting to catch sight of at least one of their visitors. Only one figure emerged from the undergrowth. Bardon heard Kale's sharp intake of breath. Seezle's tiny, lithe body shivered as she approached. A thin gauzelike cloth stretched over her from ankle to wrist and up to her neck.

Kale sank to her knees. "Come. Maybe I can help."

With Seezle standing in front of her, Kale reached out and spun a thread of light, wrapping it around the kimen's thin shoulders.

"What are you doing?" asked Bardon.

"I'm trying to create a light dress in the same way I grow a luminescent vine."

The string of light looked unsubstantial to Bardon. Kale seemed to be having trouble getting one loop of the thread to join with the next. After repeated attempts, she let go, sitting back to examine the problem.

The glow dimmed to nothing. The dark thread shriveled and fell to the ground.

"Odd," said Kale.

"Disastrous," said Seezle with a sniff. She trembled and wrapped her tiny arms around her chest.

Bardon turned his eyes away. "Kale, do you have something in your hollows we can give them? Handkerchiefs? Material we can cut?"

"Yes, of course." Kale plunged into the tent.

Bardon met Seezle's sad eyes. "How did it happen?"

"We're not sure. We can't—" She broke off and swallowed. "We can't run, either."

Bardon frowned. Kimens moved at an incredible speed. Folklore said they actually flew over the ground. Had Seezle and the others lost their swiftness when running, or was it more than that? Had they lost their ability to fly?

Kale emerged from the tent lugging a bolt of fabric and two pairs of scissors. She sat cross-legged on the ground.

"Can you sew?" Kale asked the kimen.

Seezle shook her head, her eyes on the cloth.

"This won't be as soft as the light you wear, but it'll do for the time being. How many kimens are with you?"

"Thirty-three. I'm number thirty-four."

Bardon sat beside Kale. "What do you want me to do?"

She gave him a large white handkerchief and scissors. "If you cut squares of material, I'll reshape them into clothes for our friends."

She unrolled the bolt of solid blue on the grass. Bardon placed the handkerchief on the corner and cut a strip as wide as the piece. He turned the length and cut off squares. He stacked them next to Kale as she worked, reforming the first plain square into a gathered skirt.

He watched her. "You're going to make these clothes one by one? This will take all night."

"I'll get faster with practice."

"Still…you're going to be tired in the morning."

She didn't respond.

"Why not make a shift instead of two pieces? A skirt and blouse aren't really necessary." He saw her pull out the piece and start again. When she changed her own clothing, she was much more adept. "Wouldn't making one piece save time?"

"They'd look like the Followers. Men and women all dressed in long robes with that ridiculous flap of material hanging down from their necks."

"You could leave off the flap."

"The kimens are *not* going to look like Followers!" She bunched the skirt in her fist, and when she opened her hand, a winsome flower pattern dotted the plain cloth.

Bardon shrugged. He started to object to wasting time in altering the color and pattern of the cloth. Fortunately, he recognized in time that this would be another thing that would irritate Kale greatly if he pursued the subject. His father-in-law had been correct when he said o'rant women were prickly during pregnancy.

As he lined up the next piece to be cut, he admitted he wouldn't be able to talk her out of this, nor did he really want to. Their friends needed help. Then again, with the pregnancy, she tired easily. The day had already been strenuous. He stole a glance at her and saw contentment on her face.

Seezle tried on the skirt. Her small fingers rubbed against the coarse fabric. On an o'rant, or any of the larger races, the material would have been fine. But because of her size, the dainty kimen looked like she'd donned a feed sack.

Seezle's eyes shifted to catch Bardon watching her. He nodded quickly and put a smile on his face. "You'll start a new fashion. We'll call it shabby genteel."

Laughter bubbled from Seezle's small mouth. An echo of giggles could be heard from the bushes surrounding them.

"And we'll rest tomorrow, before going on," continued Bardon. "Celisse will need it."

Kale glanced at him, a knowing look in her eye. *"I'll be exhausted, as well."*

Bardon winked at her. *But we needn't let our kimen friends guess. They're uncomfortable enough imposing on us in their underwear.*

"Exactly, dear husband. You can *be socially sensitive at times."*

Not really. I picked up your concern for making them comfortable.

"Ah, well." She went back to shaping a tunic-type shirt for Seezle

from the square in her hands. *"What are wives for if not to clue in their oblivious husbands to the subtle skills of avoiding embarrassment?"*

Do you want a list? Bardon grinned at her, then winked, before deliberately putting on a mask of mock seriousness. *I wondered before we wed how I would adjust to having someone beside me at all times.*

"Don't you mean 'underfoot,' 'in your hair,' 'nose in your business'?"

Hush. Don't interrupt. Now I wonder how I could function without you.

"You are saying exactly the right things, Bardon."

'A fitting word spoken rightly seals the moment in treasured memory.'

Bardon grinned as Kale squinched her eyes shut.

"You should have stopped while you were ahead," she muttered.

He leaned over and kissed her cheek. "You're going to worry that piece of cloth in your hand until it is nothing more than a kerchief for Seezle's head."

Kale returned her attention to her work. Fashioning the length for a narrow sleeve proved difficult, but at last, she was satisfied.

Seezle lifted her arms, and Kale fit the loose blouse she had just made over the kimen's head. With a couple of tugs, they had the tiny garment in place. Kale adjusted the shoulders with a touch of her fingertip.

"There! That looks neater."

Seezle giggled. "Kimens are not known for looking neat." She twirled in place, and her wispy hair fluttered around her head like a zillion feathers.

Seezle stopped and frowned, her hands smoothing out the rough skirt. "The clothes are nice, Lady Kale, and I thank you. But I'd rather have my light dress. I can't change the color of your cloth, and I can't brighten the day, or become part of the shadows of the scenery." She sighed. "This has never happened before. Do you suppose we're sick?"

Bardon leaned forward. "Have you ever been sick, Seezle?"

"No, never. No one ever has." Her cheeks turned pink. "I mean no kimen ever has."

"We'll do our best to uncover the reason behind your loss. And with Wulder's consent, we will rectify the situation."

Seezle curtsied and whirled away into the bushes.

"Nicely said, Bardon."

Another kimen shyly approached, leaving the cover of a fortaleen bush.

"But keep cutting. We have thirty-three more seminaked kimens to clothe."

39

Enemies Within

For the next three days, the rain fluctuated between a steady drizzle and a downpour. Kale and Bardon erected a second and third tent to accommodate their expanded number. The sodden travelers entertained themselves with songs and games and recitations.

Kale's hastily fashioned new clothes made the kimens clumsy. They blamed the material, not the design, and repeatedly thanked Kale. The kimens laughed at their own awkwardness, and Kale tried to be cheerful about repairing the rips and tears in their clothing.

Finding something different to eat became difficult. Kale could only produce a limited variety of foods from the hollows in her cape. Fortunately, the kimens apparently fixed their own meals or didn't eat. Kale was too busy to seek answers to her many questions about the kimens' way of life.

Greer and Celisse truly rejoiced in the constant rain. The weather provided therapy for Celisse, and she soon threw off the effects of the strenuous ride and the black dragons' poison. The heavy downpour massaged their skin. The light mizzle brought out a frolicking nature, and the two large dragons splashed in the puddles as they played in the grass-covered meadow. The little streams that carried the runoff had smooth rock beds. These delighted the dragons as well.

On the third day, the rain poured down as if from watering cans. Kale and Pat worked on the talking gateway. The apparatus had become more and more unreliable. They had never been able to reconnect with Regidor and Gilda since he had urged them to rejoin their quest. Kale received crackling, interrupted messages from Namee and her parents. But from their topics of conversation, it was clear that none of Kale's posts reached south.

"Have you figured it out?" Bardon asked from the entrance of the tent. He stood dripping, waiting for Kale to dry him out.

She turned from the open portal that showed no spark of life. With concentration, she drew the moisture from Bardon's hair and clothing. A puddle formed at his feet, and she directed a stream to flow out from where he stood at the open flap.

He removed his boots and sat beside her. "Thanks."

"You're welcome."

He gestured to Pat, who was working on the gateway. "So, what's the story?"

"Pat thinks there is a link between the gateway malfunctioning and the kimens losing their lights." She sighed. "And I have another bit of bad news."

His eyes left their inspection of the portal and turned to study Kale. She tried to look nonchalant.

"Well?" he prodded.

"It seems some of my talent involving light is slipping."

He frowned. "And how is this manifesting?"

Bardon's choice of words cracked Kale's apprehension. She giggled. "It 'manifests' by not lasting. Watch."

She held out her palm and produced a light orb. The sphere drifted up into the air, hung motionless for a few seconds, then popped, spraying drops of light much the way a bubble bursting splatters tiny beads of soapy liquid. The shower of sparks cooled and disappeared before landing.

Bardon's face grew impassive, an expression he used when perturbed. "The display is pretty. Perhaps it would entertain Toopka and the dragons. Maybe even the kimens. I hope you have a collection of lightrocks in your hollows."

"I do." But she couldn't bring herself to match the humor that underscored his words. "Have you recognized the depression in me, Bardon?"

"Yes, I've felt it."

"At first, I blamed the melancholy on the pregnancy. I wanted to be home, not here. That seemed logical."

He nodded.

"Then I thought it was the rain. Dreary weather has never bothered me much before, but I thought that, combined with carrying the baby, was responsible for the gloom I feel inside."

"You don't think so now?"

"I think the sadness is due to a lack of light within. I'm a light wizard, and I can't explain it, but my energy, the energy that produces the light, is drained."

"By the baby?" asked Bardon.

She shook her head. "From something outside."

Pat chittered.

Bardon took Kale's hand. "And Pat agrees. Do you feel bad? Ill? Having problems thinking?"

"No." She rested her cheek on his shoulder. "Just sad."

They sat in silence. Pat quit tinkering with the talking gateway and closed it up.

"I don't suppose," said Kale, "that you know a principle for this situation."

"I know a hundred. You know them too."

Kale shifted to a more comfortable position, leaning against her husband. Pat curled up in her lap.

After a while, she spoke again. "Lately, I've been worried about Toopka."

"Because of the growth in her chest? I thought Gymn said it wasn't getting any larger."

"No, because I think she might be the one draining the light."

"Toopka?"

Not only did Bardon's tone tell her he thought the idea was ridiculous, but his feelings flowed right out of him and into her. They swept away the vague uneasiness she had about the young doneel. Toopka fabricated stories. She took advantage of her cuteness and sometimes manipulated those around her. She avoided chores. But she never showed a malicious streak. Stealing light, if the youngster knew how to do it, would be a cruel prank.

"I don't believe she would know how to steal light." Kale squeezed Bardon's hand. "What if she *is* doing it, but doesn't know she is? What if whatever that thing is inside her has something to do with our light fading?"

"On what do you base this, Kale? Be reasonable. You're assigning guilt to comfort yourself."

She sat up. "What do you mean?"

"I mean that it is our nature to pin down a cause for things that happen. If there is no obvious reason, we will grab the next best thing. A theory."

"And a theory is bad?" She twisted a bit to face him. The movement jostled Pat. He grumbled sleepily, then settled himself stretched across her leg.

Bardon looked her square in the eye. "If you act upon a theory as if it were truth, yes."

"I'm not going to do anything to Toopka just because I suspect she might be the root of our problem."

"No, you won't. But mulling those thoughts over in your mind will poison your attitude toward her."

"I don't think so. It's not as if I dwell on Toopka's possible duplicity all the time." She glared at him and noticed the muscle in his jaw harden. "Are we fighting?"

"Discussing."

"Why is this important enough to 'discuss'?"

"Presumptions, conjectures, a mere assumption can lead a whole civilization into the dark."

Kale rolled her eyes. "My wariness toward Toopka is going to lead Amara into wickedness?"

"Your thoughts can lead your heart into darkness. Your attitude can influence those around you."

She started to defend herself, but the bond between them strengthened. She left behind her impulse to prove her position. Bardon's view of her actions sharpened in her own mind to the point she wanted to close her eyes against the vision. Remorse tightened her throat.

She saw the looks she'd given Toopka. She heard the inflection in her voice that wasn't quite approving. She realized that most of the time, those reactions were not to what Toopka had actually done but were rather reactions to the motives Kale assigned to the doneel. She gasped as her heart opened to see her behavior in this objective light.

Bardon rubbed the back of her hand as it rested in his clasp. "Will you do something for me?"

"Of course."

"When one of those doubts against Toopka rises up and demands your attention, repeat the words Granny Noon taught you many years ago."

Kale stared at Bardon. How long had it been since she'd even consciously remembered those words? She spoke them now.

"My thoughts belong to me and Wulder. In Wulder's service, I search for truth. I stand under Wulder's authority."

"You learned those statutes in order to protect yourself from dealing in mindspeaking with evil people."

"I've matured a lot since then." Kale took in a big breath and blew it out slowly, accepting a truth she often skirted around. "And I've learned that sometimes the wickedness of our own insidiously selfish natures is much more damaging than a threat from a foe."

"We learn that again and again," said Bardon.

She nodded. "And again and again and again." She smiled at him, a tender, loving smile. "Why do we have to repeat this lesson?"

"A principle?"

"Yes." She laughed. "Give me a principle."

" 'The mind forgets the dark places in the heart. The heart hides a blemish in shame. The inward eye does not seek any festering. Between the deception of the three, a man thinks he is good.' "

"And Wulder still tries to reach us with the truth. It's amazing that He perseveres with such recalcitrant students."

"Why He does is a mystery, indeed." Bardon scrunched up his forehead. "You never answered me. Why do you think Toopka might be connected to the loss of light?"

"Coincidence."

"Explain."

"We noticed the problems with light about the same time we found out about the growth in Toopka's chest."

"Interesting." Bardon rested his chin on the top of Kale's head. "A coincidence? Maybe not."

Kale sighed. "Did I get a lecture for nothing?"

"A discussion. We had a discussion."

"You had a discussion. I got a lecture."

His head jerked away from resting on hers. She leaned back to look in his eyes.

"I meant it as a discussion, Kale."

She smiled. "I know." She stretched to kiss his lips. "When I'm not comfortable with what I've done, a discussion feels like a lecture. It's not your attitude that needs a change, but mine."

"You do know I love you?"

"Always."

In the morning, birds sang, soft breezes blew, and not one cloud darkened the blue sky. The sun shone with warmth and luster, and the world responded with a clean sparkle. Even the flowering bushes and the smallest animals seemed to abound with enthusiasm. The kimens cheered at the break of day. They sang with all creation and danced among the swaying grasses.

The riding dragons stomped their feet in anticipation of renewing the quest. With everyone helping, they soon broke camp, packed, and took off, flying due north.

They stopped for noonmeal and a rest. Greer groused about all the kimens running back and forth on him while he flew.

"He finds it distracting," Bardon said as he sat with Kale and they ate fruit from a tundra pear tree. "He's not saying so, but I think their little feet tickle him."

"No, he wouldn't admit to something like that. Do you think everyone is warm enough, Bardon? The air is much chillier in the Northern Reach than it is at home. And even colder when we fly."

"You have your moonbeam cape. Anyone who is cold can duck in there."

"Then we have the question of how many kimens can fit in a moonbeam cape. And will they be still? I'll be the one they are distracting."

"We'll fly this afternoon and set down early."

"I've been wondering about Sittiponder's voices."

Bardon surveyed the scene around them. Dibl directed a game of blindman's bluff. Currently, Sittiponder, without a blindfold, was the blind man. He walked directly to three minor dragons, one after another, and caught them. He trapped Toopka and several kimens.

Kale continued. "We've always assumed that his voices were kimens that Wulder assigned to protect him. But if that is so, where are they? Do they still follow him? Did they lose their light clothing? Did they have special light clothing that makes them invisible?"

Bardon held up a hand. "Whoa! I don't know the answers to any of those questions. But I assume the voices still guard and direct him. How else could he find his way in the world as he does?"

Kale watched the game. Now Toopka was the blind man, complete with a blindfold. She approached Sittiponder's back. He deftly stepped aside, and Toopka walked right past him.

Kale tsked. "I saw no kimen warn him that Toopka was about to catch him."

"Neither did I," said Bardon, rising to his feet. "But this is a mystery for another time. We should be off."

They mounted their dragon steeds and took flight as soon as possible. Kale decided the kimens were not likely to get cold, since they were in constant motion.

As they flew over an open plain, they saw a group of black mounds.

What are those? asked Kale.

"Let's fly lower and see."

Dead animals? asked Kale, when they were close enough to see better.

"Dead tundra wolves. Looks like the pack attacked someone or something and didn't survive."

Regidor and Gilda?

"I think so."

The next day they flew over more corpses. A bear at one spot, a large predator cat in another, and three giant boars. Carrion birds picked at the exposed flesh. That night Bardon made sure enough guards were posted throughout the night, and Kale set up a perimeter alarm to ward off prowling beasts.

A mist greeted them in the morning, but the sun burned it off. From the air, they spotted more carcasses. At noonmeal, Bardon and Kale speculated why the animals had attacked.

"It looks like every time Regidor and Gilda landed, they encountered hostile creatures, normal creatures that belong on the plains," Bardon said.

"But surely it isn't normal for them to attack."

"What did Filia say when you asked her?"

"She has little material in that librarylike memory of hers that would shed light on this." Kale drank the rest of her water.

"I heard Mikkai telling the others that we are almost to the place where Woodkimkalajoss said we would find the meech colony. Maybe when we talk to Regidor and Gilda, they can explain what happened." He helped Kale to her feet, hugged her, and then patted her very round belly. "Are you uncomfortable when you ride?"

"No, not very."

He kissed her forehead. "Then I'm afraid it's time to go once more."

On the morning of the fifth day, they passed over a place where someone had camped the night before. At midday, they caught up with their meech friends. In the middle of a circle of slain wild boars, Regidor sat on the ground. He cradled Gilda in his arms. Neither looked up as Greer and Celisse landed.

Kale dropped off her dragon's side and ran to the couple.

"Is she hurt?"

Regidor nodded. "Badly."

He was covered with blood. His sword lay on the ground beside him. The mangled flesh on Gilda's hand and arm looked as though one of the big beasts had tried to drag her off.

Kale took off her cape, and Gymn scrambled out, leaping the short distance to land on Gilda. He crawled over her, finding the worst of the wounds and determining which should be treated first.

As Kale spread out her cape and began assembling the medicines and bandages they would need from the hollows, she remembered how much the meech lady disliked the minor dragons.

It's a good thing for you, Gilda, that Gymn doesn't care whether you like him or not. He'll still do his best to save your life.

Gymn's shrill call alerted them to a gash in Gilda's side, hidden by her wing. Regidor lifted the wing tenderly and revealed a ragged opening probably made by a boar tusk.

Kale spotted something white amid the red. *Is that her rib?* Kale closed her eyes. *Oh, Wulder, help. Please help us help Gilda.*

40

Enemies All Around

Bardon inspected the area, making sure none of the boars would rise up again. Most were dead. He quickly dispatched those who were mortally wounded and suffering. Out of the corner of his eye, he also kept watch over those working to save Gilda's life.

Kale toiled over the open wound, swabbing out the blood and applying a medicine that would keep infection at bay. Gymn scrambled the length of Gilda's body, pausing to heal bruises and scratches. When Kale had the area on Gilda's side cleaned and medicated, he came back to help her.

Bardon gave orders to the kimens and dragons as if they were a military party under his command. They responded well, and he gave them a grim smile. "Thank you, my friends."

Once they began the duties he'd assigned, Bardon returned to Kale to offer his help. Gymn, Regidor, and his wife had everything under control. He wouldn't hinder Kale's concentration but stood by watching and ready to do anything they might need of him.

Regidor still held Gilda, and Bardon assumed he was doing something to keep her asleep. Kale stitched the flesh together under Gymn's watchful eye. The healing dragon knew how the edges should meet on the inside muscle as well as the outer skin. When they were finished and had washed the area once more, Kale covered it with swaths of white cloth.

She pushed back from her patient. "Regidor, will you take my position in the healing circle with Gymn? I've got to clean up."

Regidor barely glanced at her red-stained hands. Blood blotched the front of Kale's dress, but the meech dragon's eyes studied every breath his wife took. His own clothes reflected the savage fight that had played out on this patch of ground. But Kale didn't bother to suggest he clean up. His whole being was engrossed in the recovery of his wife.

Bardon walked beside Kale, carrying the moonbeam cape.

"Were you able to find out what happened here?" she asked.

"Yes, Regidor mindspoke to me while we watched you and Gymn work. He said that he and Gilda have been attacked by wild animals ever since they entered the plains area. They haven't encountered any of the high races. It's as if the countryside has been taken over by savage beasts. Creatures that don't usually run in packs have congregated. Regidor and Gilda have seen fields of slaughtered animals, and the only explanation is these natural loners ganged together but then turned on one another. Of course, that's merely a theory."

He winked at her, but she couldn't muster a smile.

They reached a pool of water bubbling up from the ground. A stream ran off from that point toward the west. Kale knelt beside the sparkling, churning brook. She scrubbed her hands.

"The water's warm," she said, surprise evident in her voice.

"Must be a hot spring."

Kale continued to rub her hands long after any trace of red remained. "I don't understand why Regidor and Gilda didn't just fly away each time they were attacked. And I don't understand why we haven't been plagued with similar attacks."

"The first one, I can answer," said Bardon. "As meech dragons, Regidor and Gilda cannot fly great distances, and, therefore, stop often. If they've been driven back into the air each time they landed, then they were becoming exhausted."

Kale stood, shook water from her hands, and looked down at her dress. "I can't wear this ever again. I'm going to start all over."

Bardon held up the cape. Kale reached into a hollow and pulled out a small cloth bag. She loosened the drawstring and poured dozens of seeds into the palm of her hand. Turning in a circle, she scattered them on the ground. The seeds fell on both banks of the stream. Kale kicked off her shoes and stepped into the water.

Bardon hopped out of the ring of seeds just as the first shoots shot up from the fertile dirt. He thrust the cape into her hands. In one minute, a hedge grew so that she had a leafy bower of complete privacy.

"What's she doing?" asked Toopka, making Bardon jump.

He hadn't heard the youngsters' approach. He chastised himself and gave a quick commander's inspection of the area. No enemies were in sight.

Regidor still tended Gilda. Two of the kimens had joined the healing circle. The other kimens stood guard. Celisse and Greer loitered close by, having finished their chore. The minor dragons, except Gymn, perched on the riding dragons' backs. The doneel girl stood with her tumanhofer friend next to Bardon.

Bardon answered gruffly. "Changing clothes and probably having a good wash."

"In there?" Toopka jumped closer and tried to peek through the leaves. "Why?"

Bardon grabbed her and pulled her back. "So she won't have any spectators."

Sittiponder giggled. "I'm not looking. Kale doesn't have to worry about me."

"Why does she have to go in there?" asked Toopka. "Why doesn't she just make the clothes over into something she wants to wear? Why isn't she doing it like she usually does?"

"You're asking too many questions," said Sittiponder.

"Her clothes are bloody," explained Bardon, although he agreed with the young tumanhofer's opinion. "And she wants to start with a fresh set."

"Is Gilda going to live? Are we still going to look for the meech colony? Why are the animals so ferocious?"

"I believe Gilda will live. Yes, we will still look for the meech colony. And I don't know why the animals are behaving in a manner not in keeping with their normal habits."

"Oh, my!" Kale exclaimed.

Bardon turned back to where his wife hid. "What is it?"

"The egg."

Bardon let go of Toopka and put his fists on his hips. "What egg?"

"The one I found outside of Arreach, after the earthquake."

Toopka stood on tiptoe as if she could see over the thick bushes. "You found it? Where's it been? How come you lost it?"

"I didn't really lose it," Kale called. "I just forgot I had it. I wrapped the egg in a scarf and tied it around my waist."

"Is it going to hatch?" Toopka held her breath while waiting for the answer.

"I would think," said Bardon, staring down at Toopka, "that by this time, you would take an egg-hatching in stride. How many have you seen born?"

Toopka grinned. "Hundreds. But they're all special. Aren't they, Kale?"

"What?" Kale's voice sounded muffled.

"Aren't all eggs special?" Toopka countered by yelling.

"Yes." Kale sounded more normal.

Bardon gently flipped one of Toopka's ears with his fingertip. "Scrambled eggs aren't special."

"Oh, yum!" Toopka scowled. "Why'd you have to say that? Taylaminkadot's scrambled eggs are special."

Sittiponder groaned. "I agree, and we're hungry. In fact, that's why we came to find you in the first place."

Toopka's head bobbed. "We want to roast a boar."

"Wild boar cooked in a pit." Sittiponder licked his lips.

The walls of Kale's makeshift dressing room crackled and separated, allowing her to step through. She wore a brown tunic with tan leggings. "We're not staying here long enough for that."

"Why?" Toopka's tone approached a whine. "We can't go anywhere. Gilda would die if we took her flying on the back of Celisse."

"We are not staying here," Kale repeated more firmly.

"Why?"

"I understand," said Sittiponder.

Toopka wheeled around. She wagged a finger an inch in front of his face. "Don't you side with them."

"It's not siding, Toopka. I figured out why Kale doesn't want to stay.

It smells like a battlefield. Think about it. How could we enjoy delicious roast pork when all we can smell is spilt blood?"

Toopka frowned, sniffed the air, then twisted her frown into a grimace of disgust. "Yuck."

Bardon contorted his face in sympathy. When his mind had been occupied, the smell had been an underlying irritant. Now that he had fully noticed it, he couldn't pretend the odor didn't exist.

"Where are we going to go?" asked Toopka. The whine had taken precedence in her voice. "I sure wish there was a castle or something nearby. Someplace with big beds and lots of food."

Bardon rubbed the silky fur on her head between her soft button ears. "We'll go by foot and find someplace safe and pleasant. Go tell the kimens."

The children ran ahead.

He took Kale's hand and placed it in the crook of his arm. "I assume since you brought up the subject of leaving this place that you and Regidor will be able to figure out some way to transport Gilda."

"Yes. We discussed it while I washed my hands."

"Mindspeaking comes in handy." Bardon surveyed the area once more, looking for any sign of danger. "Do you detect any hostile creatures close by, Kale?"

"No, there's nothing besides rodents and birds. Nothing vicious."

They walked in silence.

"Bardon?"

"Yes?"

"You told Celisse and Greer to take care of the boars' bodies, right?"

"I did."

"Did you tell them to leave one for us?"

"I asked the kimens to carve some meat for our dinner. Seezle said that was a chore kimens did not relish."

"In other words, Seezle said no?"

"Right." Bardon patted her hand. "There's one boar left. I did ask Greer to leave us one. I'll take care of the meat. Will you get Gilda ready to move?"

"We will."

When they walked up to where Regidor still held his wife, tears sprang to Bardon's eyes. He identified with his friend and pictured himself sitting on the ground with Kale's head and shoulder in his lap. A few hard blinks batted the moisture away.

Bardon tapped Regidor on his shoulder, bringing the meech out of his participation in the circle of healing.

"We're going to move to a place more easily defended. Are you ready?"

Regidor nodded. "Kale and I will make Gilda comfortable to travel."

Regidor slipped out from under Gilda. Kale helped him straighten her legs and tuck her arms close to her sides. Then they swaddled her with what looked to Bardon like thick spider webbing. He bent down to touch it, reassuring himself that the loosely woven material was not sticky.

Next, Regidor formed a wooden slab under Gilda with handles at each end. Kale helped pad it. She and Regidor pulled batting from their hollows, shaped it into a long, covered pallet with their hands, and then, using wizardry, shifted the cushion under the patient's prone form. Straps wrapped over Gilda to keep her on the board.

Regidor stood. "We're ready."

He and Bardon lifted the ends of Gilda's stretcher.

Bardon nodded to the small dragon perched on his shoulder. "Mikkai scouted the area and found a hill with large boulders at the top. We should be able to defend that position."

"Did he report any wild animals?"

"Scores of them have moved closer, all prowling in mobs of a dozen or less."

Toopka whimpered and took Sittiponder's hand.

Bardon frowned at them. "You two have got to quit sneaking up on the adults. Eavesdropping is not polite."

Toopka stuck out her lower lip. "I think those wild animals aren't polite either. That scares me."

Kale gathered the child into her arms. "You can sneak up on us because no one thinks you're dangerous. Don't worry. If a wild animal comes close, the dragons, the kimens, everyone will set off an alarm."

"I'd like to be just a little dangerous. Just enough to scare some of those beasts."

Kale lifted Toopka. Bardon watched her shift the small child, and through the bond, he knew Kale felt the inconvenient bulge of her belly interfere with her movements. She hugged the doneel, then looked at her with concern.

"You're smaller. You weigh less. Do you feel all right?"

Toopka rested her head on Kale's shoulder. "Am I in trouble for being smaller?"

"No."

"Then I feel all right." Her eyes closed, and her breathing became slow and regular.

Bardon looked from Kale's worried eyes to Regidor.

Regidor pressed his lips into a grim line. He squinted at the horizon. "I suggest we move. Our problems will not be solved here."

Directed by Mikkai, they began the march. Bardon hoped the short trek would bring them to safer ground. A dozen large scavenger birds circled above. Attracted by blood on the ground, or attracted to wanderers in a lonely land?

41

Toopka's Story

"Get that creature off of me!" Gilda's shrill demand ripped through the quiet of the camp. "Get it off! Get it off!"

Kale dropped her cup and ran to the tent. Gymn flew out the open flap past her. Inside, Gilda sobbed. Regidor sat with his wife.

Let him deal with her. Kale turned and followed her dragon friend.

Toopka ran to Kale and latched on to her leg. "Was it a wild beast? Did one get into her tent? Did Regidor kill it?"

"No." Kale had to stop or trip over. She gently disengaged Toopka's arms and crouched to look her in the eye, careful to balance against the weight of her middle. "Gilda woke up and found Gymn sitting on her."

Toopka tilted her head. "Gymn's good. He's healing her."

"Yes, he is. But Gilda doesn't like minor dragons."

"That's stu—"

"Be careful what you say, Toopka."

"Unreasonable."

"Yes, it is to our way of thinking. I haven't figured out Gilda's way of thinking on this issue."

"She shouldn't be rude to Gymn."

"I agree with you on that point."

Gymn settled on one of the boulders where two kimens stared out into the dark. Kale scooped him up, cuddled him under her chin, and settled into his spot next to the guards.

Toopka pulled on one kimen's pant leg. "Are there monsters out there?"

"No," said the man. "Only confused animals."

"Why are they confused?"

"I don't know, but there is something in our camp they fear. Something that intrigues them but also keeps them away."

Kale shivered. "That would have to be something from our party, because nothing kept the beasts from attacking before we joined with Regidor and Gilda."

Both guards nodded. Kale put Gymn in her lap, and Toopka leaned against the large rock to tiptoe high enough to stroke his green tail.

"Come sit beside me, Toopka." Kale scooted over a smidgen.

One of the kimens boosted the little doneel up onto the rock.

"Is Gymn all right?" Toopka asked as she rubbed the dragon's neck.

"He's fine. He was startled and his feelings were hurt, of course. But he explained to me that Gilda's harsh words come from an injury to her heart that he can't heal." Before the doneel could ask another question, Kale rushed to explain. "Not the physical heart in her chest, but the kind of heart that aches when someone you love goes away."

"I have a heartache," Toopka whispered.

"You do?" Kale put an arm around her little shoulders and pulled her close. "Do you want to tell me about it?"

"Once upon a time there was a beautiful doneel who was going to get married. The man she was going to marry ran a place where children could come and get food and play games and sleep in a bed. One night a robber broke into that place. He scared the children and took a sack of coins and killed the man.

"The next day the doneel came and cried. She told Wulder she would do anything to be His servant, because she no longer wanted to have anything to do with people. Wulder came and touched her here." Toopka pointed to her chest. "Wulder said that He would give her what she wanted, because it was what He wanted too. She would serve Him. She carried a heart for Him, a gift of peace, and a life that slays the enemy. Then Wulder went away, and she didn't cry anymore."

"Were you there when that happened, Toopka?"

She nodded her head and pushed as if she could be absorbed into Kale's body if she snuggled close enough.

Kale rubbed the child's back. "I'm sorry that happened."

Toopka trembled, then shook her head. "One day she will deliver what she carries, and everything will be better."

Seezle came from inside the camp. "Kale, Gilda wants to see you."

Kale left Toopka holding Gymn and followed Seezle back to the tent.

"How is she?" Kale asked.

The little kimen shrugged. "I'm glad she's not my mother."

"I meant how is she feeling."

"She can't sit up yet. But she sipped a little broth made from that pork, and she complained that it was too salty. Regidor took some of the salt out."

Kale pictured the meech dragon stirring the thin soup with one of his long, green fingers. She couldn't think of how a wizard would extract salt.

"He took the salt out?" she asked Seezle. "Did you see him do anything to the broth?"

"Oh yes. He reached in his hollow, pulled out a potato, and diced it very small. Then he cooked it in the soup."

"Oh."

"How would you take the salt out?" the kimen asked.

"Probably the same way. I learned that trick as a child when I helped in the kitchens at River Away."

"I thought you might use a wizard method."

"A potato's as good as any wizard method I know of."

They reached the tent, and Kale entered by herself.

With eyes closed, Gilda lay on her soft stretcher. The makeshift bed sat across wooden boxes to raise it off the floor. The swaddling cloth lay in a heap on the floor, and a soft blanket covered the patient. Regidor stood from the chair situated near Gilda's head and gestured for Kale to have a seat.

Kale moved the seat and took Gilda's cold hand. She held it, cupped between hers. Maybe her warmth would flow into Regidor's wife. Kale watched Gilda's still, pale face. The meech lady radiated beauty. Her state of rest relaxed her taut features, smoothed away the pinched lines between her eyes, and softened the mulish jaw.

Gilda opened her eyes. "Kale?"

"I'm here."

Gilda's fingers tightened around Kale's. "We need to move more quickly. The egg is almost ready to be presented. We've lost so much time."

"We're almost there, Gilda. Don't worry." Kale tried to smile with reassurance. "A few more days—"

"No!" Gilda shook her head. "Not a few more days. Tomorrow."

Kale shot a glance at Regidor. He hunched one shoulder.

"Gilda, I don't know if that is possible."

Kale winced as Gilda clenched her hand. "You're a wizard," Gilda groaned. "Regidor and I are wizards. There's nothing we cannot do."

"There're quite a few things we can't do." Kale wiggled her fingers out of Gilda's clutch. "You need to be reasonable. We'll get you to the meech colony as soon as we can. You need to be healthy enough to travel and arrive there alive."

"If I die, Kale, I want to die among my people. I want to hear the grand orchestra play."

"How do you know they have an orchestra?"

"All meech are talented. Of course there are symphonies and opera and musicales."

"You and Regidor are musical. That doesn't mean all meech are musical. If two out of a hundred meech are musical, then you two might be it as far as musical talent goes."

Gilda ignored her. "I want to see the grand architecture, the paintings, the stylish apparel."

Kale bit her tongue to keep from blasting Gilda's dreams with an alternate scenario. She couldn't help but picture a town full of meech dressed in farm clothes with thick boots on their feet and pitchforks in their hands.

Gilda sighed heavily, closed her eyes, and turned her head away. "I must see home before I die. I must deliver my egg as a hope for the future to my kinsmen."

The urge to chide Gilda's dramatics prickled Kale's tongue. She kept her lips clamped together. *I stand under the authority of Wulder. My thoughts belong to Wulder and me. Oh, Wulder, don't let anything come out of my mouth that will hurt Regidor. Gilda is hard to deal with. I don't want to add to Regidor's problems.* She silently counted to ten. "Is there anything I can get you tonight, Gilda? Would you like a potion to ease the pain?"

Her lips barely moved as she whispered her answer. Kale had to lean over the cot to hear. "Regidor meets all my needs. He provides nourishment and sugar."

Kale stood and sidled up to Regidor. "You're giving her sugar?" she whispered.

"I believe she said 'succor.' I provide nourishment and succor. To succor is to provide help or relief in a difficult or unpleasant situation."

"I know what 'succor' means. It means she's well enough to put on airs. I can quit worrying about her recovery."

Regidor grinned, a twinkle in his eye. "Yes, my dear wife is almost herself again. We will certainly be able to travel tomorrow. She will have to ride with you on Celisse, I think."

"Do you think we can reach the meech colony in just one day?"

"If my calculations are correct, we should be there in time for noonmeal." He gave her a swift hug and looked over her head at his wife. "Thank you for all you've done for Gilda. I know she isn't an easy patient." He squeezed her once more and let her go. "Now off with you. You look tired."

Kale turned toward the tent flap and heard Gilda's gasp. She flew back to Gilda's side and bent to peer in her wide eyes. "What? What's wrong? Did you have a pain? Are you ill?"

"You're pregnant!"

Kale straightened. "Yes. Yes, I am." She glanced at Regidor but got no clue from him as to what horrified his wife. "I guess I haven't seen you since we found out. It was after the earthquake. We saw Mother at Namee's—"

"How could you?" Gilda spoke between clenched teeth. "My child will not share the spotlight with a mere o'rant."

Regidor stepped around Kale and knelt by his wife's head. "One-fourth emerlindian, Gilda. The child has Bardon for the father."

"I don't care if *it* has Paladin for a father. Our child is destined to be a leader."

Regidor stroked her forehead. "I think it is time for you to sleep, dear one. Hush now, close your eyes, remember I love you, and sleep."

Her eyes closed, and she slept. Regidor stood and turned to face Kale.

"What's going on, Reg?" Kale's voice wobbled in spite of her effort to remain calm.

"She's desperate to be someone of importance. She doesn't want to impress the people of your world. She believes the meech are from another world, and she wants to impress them." His shoulders drooped.

Kale said nothing but put her arms around her friend. He pulled her close and squeezed. "I've done all I can, Kale. I don't know what else to do. I think there's something left from the time she spent with Risto. Something in her mind that twists and torments her."

"We'll take her to her people, Regidor. Perhaps they do have the wisdom to replace this obsession with a legitimate hope."

"I want that to be true, Kale. I can't wait to find the colony, and I dread finding disappointment."

Kale stepped away from him. "Tomorrow. We find out tomorrow, and Wulder knows today. Don't despair, Regidor. Wait for tomorrow."

Regidor chucked her chin. "My funny mentor. I outgrew you too quickly, you know. I will wait for tomorrow, Lady Kale. I have no choice."

"I'm not giving you the right words to comfort your heart, am I?"

"No, but you tried. And your trying comforts me more than you can know."

She slipped out the door and turned back once more. "I'm not in charge of tomorrow, Regidor. Thank Wulder, it is in His capable hands."

Regidor chortled. "Kale, I often thank Wulder that you are not in charge of the tomorrows or the todays."

She stomped her foot. "Someone should have taught you manners."

Regidor laughed out loud. "I believe that was one of the things you were in charge of. Go to bed, Kale. Let tomorrow take care of itself, with Wulder's blessing."

Kale trounced off, glad to hear the spirit of fun in Regidor's bantering and dreading that the colony would be filled with meeches of Gilda's temperament. "Nonsense!" she chided herself. "If they are two out of a hundred, what are the chances of the other ninety-eight meeches being duplicates of Regidor or Gilda?"

She strode forward, passing the fire and seeing Bardon talking with Sittiponder near the other tents.

"I'm sure I don't know," she answered herself. "And I'm not going to worry over it."

Bardon looked up and saw her. She forced a smile.

I'll not worry over what we will find tomorrow. Not much.

42

Through a Dark Passage

"If you would let Gymn help, we could completely eliminate the last of this wound." Kale swabbed the red, puckered line that was all that remained of the gash Gilda had received fighting off wild boars.

"No!" Gilda turned her head on the pillow and glared at Kale. "I won't be tended to by a beast! I won't have his dirty feet walking all over me. I don't like the way his kind looks or smells or behaves in that uppity manner as if they were more than lowly animals."

Kale worked to keep her face neutral. She relaxed her mouth, though her lips wanted to squeeze together in a thin, disapproving line. She kept her eyes on Gilda's side, not daring to meet her gaze. Surely the meech would detect sparks of anger, if not bolts of lightning, ready to shoot out of Kale's eyes and zap Gilda. Kale wiped the injury site one more time and applied ointment before securing the bandage.

She stood. "Regidor said you were to ride with me on Celisse."

Gilda's thin lips made a small, wrinkled moue. "Where will the beasts be?"

Kale snatched up her cape and thrust the small jar of ointment into a pocket. "Riding with Bardon." She turned and headed out the tent's opening. "We leave soon. You'd better get dressed."

The brisk morning air hit her in the face. "Phew! I thought I'd strangle a certain someone."

"Who are you talking to?" asked Toopka.

Kale jumped. "No one."

"Bardon says I'm going to ride with him. I came to tell you, so you wouldn't be upset and think I was mad at you or something."

The lack of spunk in Toopka's voice prompted Kale to examine the doneel. "Do you feel all right? You look a little droopy."

"I have a heavy place. Right here." She pointed to exactly the same spot she had touched the night before when she had told Kale her story.

Kale took her hand. "Let's go find Gymn and have him take a look at you."

Gymn assessed the child's condition and told Kale he detected little change. The growth had not increased in size at all, but it appeared to be solidifying. The mass was no bigger than Kale's thumb and probably weighed as much as a dense stone of the same size.

Kale reported the health conditions of Toopka and Gilda to Bardon. He ordered the striking of the camp and divided the passengers between the two riding dragons.

"I can take a dozen kimens," offered Regidor. "They're as light as feathers."

Regidor carried Gilda to Celisse, then flew with her in his arms to settle her in the second seat of the saddle. When Kale mounted, the female meech only made one comment. "Riding backward makes me queasy."

"Tell me if it gets bad, Gilda, and we'll land."

They flew northeast, toward rippling hills. The terrain changed abruptly with deep crevasses zigzagging between sheer rock formations that thrust toward the sky. The tiers of exposed rock varied between rich purples, reds, and a coppery orange. White streaks sometimes ran between the layers. Thick green vegetation hid the bottom of some of the deep canyons, but most of the landscape consisted of towers of rock in fantastic colors.

"Stunning," said Gilda, the first word she had spoken in several hours. "And totally appropriate for the residence of a superior race."

Kale didn't bother to comment. Bardon had signaled their descent. They landed in a broad canyon with a floor strangely vacant of shrubs and boulders.

Regidor examined the area. "Flash floods carry away all but the heaviest objects." He pointed to a boulder as big as a house.

"How long will we rest here?" asked Gilda.

"We aren't resting here," answered Bardon. "We've arrived."

Both women on Celisse's back twisted their necks, examining their surroundings.

"I give up." Kale swung her leg over the saddle and slid to the ground. "I don't see a colony."

Regidor again pointed to the boulder. "Behind that rock, in the canyon wall, we should find a fissure big enough to walk through as if it were a corridor in a palace. At the other end should be the meech colony according to Woodkimkalajoss."

"Help me down," called Gilda. "Regidor, I want to walk."

Kale went to help Bardon remove Greer's saddle while Regidor fetched Gilda from her perch on Celisse's back.

"Why can't we just land in the right place?" asked Toopka. "Why do we have to walk through a mountain?"

"Because," said Bardon, "Woodkimkalajoss said it is difficult to see the settlement from the air. Even from the rim of the valley where he once stood, he had no idea of the colony below. Also, the dragons cannot land in a thicket of trees."

"Is it far?" asked Toopka. "Will it be dark?"

"I'll hold your hand," said Sittiponder.

"I'd still want to see."

"We have lightrocks, Toopka," said Kale. "You can have one of your own to carry."

"What if they don't light? What if they're broken like the kimens' lights and your light?"

"Then we'll use torches," said Regidor. He set Gilda down and then helped Bardon remove Celisse's saddle. Kale took off her cape and pulled out the lightrocks. Toopka rushed to pick out two small ones. Then she traded one for a larger, smooth-sided rock. She bent over, trying to make enough shade to see if the rocks would glow in the dark.

Bardon and Regidor stashed the saddles in a cranny.

"We won't be gone too long, Greer." Bardon stroked the dragon's purple scales along his neck. "Yes, I'll call if we get into trouble, but I don't know exactly how you expect to reach us." Bardon rested his head against his friend's side. "I am well aware that you believe we always find trouble when you aren't around. But I'm not worried. I know you're close. What better rescue team is there than Greer and Celisse?" He leaned away and grinned. "I am not being frivolous, Greer. How can you accuse me? A dragon rescue team is, without a doubt, a pinnacle of practicality."

Bardon joined Kale at the side of the huge boulder. "Is Celisse willing to let you traipse off on an adventure without her?"

"She's acting like a brooding glommytuck. If possible, she'd sweep me into a nest and sit on me."

"Greer is squawking too. I wonder what is making them so nervous."

"I thought it odd as well."

Sittiponder and Toopka returned from inspecting the entrance of the tunnel.

"It stinks," said Toopka.

"Sulfur," said Sittiponder.

Gilda approached, walking with dignity beside Regidor. "A clever way to discourage outsiders from venturing into their territory. Meech would naturally choose a peaceful rather than a violent way of dissuading curious explorers."

Seezle led the kimens to Kale's pile of lightrocks and passed them out. "We'll go first," she said. "We're used to closed-in spaces."

"I'll go next," offered Sittiponder. "The dark doesn't bother me."

"No, you won't," said Toopka. "You said you'd hold my hand, and I'm going to walk between Regidor and Bardon."

"Shall we cease this inane chatter and go?" Gilda tugged at her husband's arm as she moved forward.

"Regidor," said Kale, "are your light orbs working?"

"Not even a flicker." He pointed to Toopka and motioned toward the diminishing pile beside Kale. "Hand me one of those, please."

Toopka clutched the two she held tightly to her chest. "I can't. I can't put these down."

Bardon tossed a lightrock to Regidor, then helped Kale put the remainder back in her cape.

"Hurry up." Toopka danced, hopping from one foot to the other. "They're going to get too far ahead of us."

"We're coming," said Kale as she put on her cape. "What are you going to do about holding Sittiponder's hand?"

"Ooh," Toopka groaned at her dilemma. "Sitti, you're just going to have to hold on to me. Grab my arm and don't let go."

"Aye, aye, sir." The tumanhofer saluted with a silly grin on his face.

Toopka dragged him around the huge rock and into the narrow opening, all the time urging Kale and Bardon to hurry.

Kale wrinkled her nose at the strong odor.

"The lightrocks work," Toopka hollered from the tunnel.

"I never thought they wouldn't," said Bardon.

They stepped farther into the darkness, and the rocks glowed a satisfying bright blue. Kale let out a relieved sigh. "The possibility had crossed my mind."

The trek through the mountain took little time. The crack in the rock made few turns, no rocks littered the floor to trip them, and other than the unpleasant smell, nothing hindered their progress. They stepped out into sunshine filtered through a mass of green leaves. The kimens silently gathered everyone's lightrocks and brought them back to Kale, who stored them in her cape.

"Now what?" asked Toopka. "Where're the meeches?"

"North," said Regidor. "Are you able to make it, my dear? Would you like me to carry you?"

Gilda's chin went up. "I shall make it on my own. Thank you."

"You can carry me," said Toopka, running to his side. "Can I ride on your shoulders?"

Gilda blocked Regidor's movement to pick up the child. "You will not enter the city of your ancestry with that ragtag urchin on your shoulders."

"That's all right," Toopka said, then quickly ran away from the couple, calling over her shoulder. "Bardon will carry me."

Bardon hoisted her up. Kale patted the doneel's leg. "You know, I was going to have Bardon carry me. My back aches, and my legs hurt."

"That's 'cause of your baby," Toopka explained. "But you'd look silly riding up here. You don't want to look silly. That would upset Lady Gilda."

"You're right."

They trudged through the underbrush with the kimens leading. They broke back the heavier limbs and made a path that was easily negotiated. Kale found her steps becoming more labored, but Gilda's gait grew lighter. The minor dragons flitted through the trees. Gilda didn't frown at them or scold them. Not once did she urge them to make themselves scarce. Her attention remained riveted on the path ahead.

Mikkai flew ahead and came back to report that the meech colony was only a few more yards through the thick forest.

"Faster," Gilda prodded the kimen. "We're almost to the city."

When Kale and Bardon broke through the last of the trees and stepped into the clearing, the kimens had spread out to stand in a line against the trees. Toopka whispered in Sittiponder's ear, describing the scene before them.

Gilda leaned heavily against Regidor, moaning, "No, no, no."

The inhabitants of the small village stopped what they were doing and stared at the questing party. Kale blinked in surprise. The houses resembled the homes in Paladise. Simple clay structures with no adornments. Some meech wore long garments of unbleached muslin. Some wore loose trousers below a tighter shirt. Over the under-clothing, each adult donned a narrow sheet of color. A hole in the middle of a length of cloth provided a neck for this panel that hung over the plainer garb. When they'd been in Paladise, she and Bardon had laughingly called this garment a flap.

The village children moved first, breaking out of their frozen surprise and scampering to a parent's side.

One meech strode to meet them. He stopped in front of Regidor, glanced up and down his length as if examining the stranger's unusual clothing, and frowned as he made eye contact.

"What can I do for you?" he asked in a stiff, unwelcoming tone.

"I've come to present my egg," Gilda blurted. "I've come to find the great civilization of meech."

She laughed, and Kale thought she sounded on the edge of hysteria.

Gilda pulled herself together, stood taller, and thrust out her chin. "I might as well have become a Follower. At least *they* are destined to lead. *They* have the initiative to conquer their world, not hide in a dismal canyon." She glared at the man who represented the community. "Where is your city? Your university? Your center of cultural exposition?"

She collapsed against her husband. "Oh, Regidor, get me out of here." She slumped and, had not her husband caught her, would have landed in the dust.

Regidor scooped her into his arms. "May we have a place to rest?"

The meech surveyed their questing party. He took in the line of sober kimen standing in almost complete stillness. The breeze ruffled their clothing, but they scarcely moved to breathe or even blink their serious eyes. He paused to study the little doneel girl holding the blind tumanhofer boy's hand. His eyes briefly rested on Kale's rounded stomach, and his face lost some of its austere disapproval. "Certainly." He gestured to the humble homes. "This way, please."

43

Midnight Discovery

Dim shadows enfolded Kale like cozy blankets. She curled up against Bardon, relishing the peace of this simple home. He slept soundly, snoring softly in the way that always made Kale feel secure. It was good to have a loving husband at her back. His body radiated just enough heat to add to her comfort. A soft mattress eased the ache in her back, and the mistress of the house, Tulanny, had given her an extra pillow to put between her knees. That bit of a wedge gave her hip bones a rest.

Once the meech had recovered from the shock of the questers' intrusion, they had become gracious and hospitable hosts. The questing party had been divided into groups and invited into separate homes. Kale realized that the host for Gilda and Regidor was the colony's physician. She breathed a sigh of relief and asked Wulder to instigate a healing for Gilda's troubled heart.

Kale liked their hostess immediately. The warm-hearted meech was older than most. Her husband had died. Her children, grown and married. Their children, grown and married. Contrary to what Kale had believed, these meech lived in tight family units.

Tulanny talked a steady stream. Both Kale and Bardon were interested in what she said, but their eyelids grew heavy from the day's journey. They couldn't hide their fatigue even with politely covered yawns.

Mistress Tulanny laughed. "Oh goodness, you're tired. And I'm just yammering on, happy as a prentbird to have someone to listen to me. Let me show you to my spare room. I can't call it a guest room, because to be honest, I've never had a guest before. But it was my daughter's room before she married."

After the tent and hard ground of the previous nights, the tidy bedroom had been a welcome sight.

In the light provided by the moon, Kale counted the dragons. Each one had a cushion collected from various rooms of the house. Tulanny had insisted that her little guests be as comfortable as the larger company. She'd lined them up against the wall, but after she left the room, Kale's little friends demonstrated they had ideas of their own. They'd pushed and shoved, tugged and heaved, until the cushions crowded together in a circular mound. She and Bardon had watched them from their bed, giggling at the dragons' antics.

She breathed deeply. The wood furniture, carved from trees found locally, had a peculiar, but pleasant, fragrance. Everything about this colony exuded unpretentious elegance.

Kale relaxed into the comfy bed, closed her eyes, and hoped she'd sleep well. As if by some signal, the baby within began the nightly routine of squirming, turning, kicking, maybe even dancing within the womb. Kale put a hand on her abdomen and mentally crooned a soothing tune to her child. The baby liked the attention and wriggled some more. Kale wiggled a bit herself, trying to get more comfortable. She knew no alternative than to wait it out. The baby would eventually settle down.

Tulanny had served a wonderful concoction made with cheese and a fruit she said the meech had brought from the other world. She had cut the sweet fruit into large chunks, stirred it into the grated cheese, then topped it with butter and cracker crumbs. She called the fruit picklebarrel and the concoction a schop. Tulanny also said she would take Kale and Toopka to the greenhouse where the picklebarrel was grown.

Kale craved another scoop of the sweet and salty dish. The more she thought about it, the more she wanted one more serving. Tulanny's words echoed in her mind. *Make yourself at home. If you need anything, it's yours.*

Kale slipped out of the covers, being careful not to lift the blankets enough to let a cold draft in to wake Bardon. Several of the minor dragons lifted their heads and eyed her. But only one decided to join her for a snack. Pat flew to her shoulder and rode close to her neck.

Light shone through the windows from the moon and two streetlamps. Kale navigated from her room without running into any furniture.

She tiptoed to the kitchen, uncovered the shallow rectangle pan holding the remainder of the pricklebarrel schop, and looked through a cabinet for a bowl.

Lights parading past the front of the house distracted her. She left the kitchen and crept to the large-paned window. A group of six meech men walked together.

"Oh no!" Kale forced her dismay down. She must be silent. She couldn't risk waking Tulanny. *Are they marching like the Followers? No, they're out of step, and certainly not blindfolded. But where are they going? And here comes another group. I'll just follow them.*

She debated whether or not to go for her moonbeam cape. Did she have time before they got too far ahead of her? She crossed to the door and put her hand on the knob. It didn't move.

Locked! How does this thing unlock?

She fiddled with the handle, felt around for a keyhole or a latch. *Nothing! Pat, see what you can do.*

She held him in her hand as he examined the door.

Wizardry? she answered his announcement in her mind. *A wizardry you're not familiar with? How quickly can you—? Oh, well that's not going to do us any good. Surely there's another way out of here.*

Kale surveyed the room. *Look, the windows near the ceiling are open for ventilation. It's only a crack, but I can probably slide it wider. What? Oh!*

She looked down at her very wide girth. *You're right. I can't possibly fit through that opening. Can you go, Pat? Can you follow them and not be seen?*

Pat zoomed across the room and squeezed out of the smaller window. Kale watched but didn't get a glimpse of him.

"Oh, I hope he comes back all right," she whispered. "Maybe I should have sent one of the other dragons. No, Pat will do fine."

"Are you all right, Kale?" Tulanny stood in her nightgown in her bedroom door.

Kale started and turned quickly. She pointed to the kitchen. "You—Your schop was so good. I got a craving for more and couldn't sleep."

The meech hostess smiled and headed for her kitchen. "Let me warm it up for you. And perhaps you'd like some warm milk to help you relax. Are you comfortable in the bed? I know it's hard for you of the high races to carry a baby." She laughed. "Frankly, I think Wulder planned our ordeal more to my way of liking. Of course the egg gets to be a bit much, but then you just present it. And then, oh my, the anticipation. Of course, we choose when the egg will hatch. We have one of the high races quicken the egg. Then the egg hatches. Much more convenient than how Wulder has arranged things for you. But you know Wulder. He does as He does."

Kale followed Tulanny and sat at the table. "Tulanny?"

"Yes?"

"There were men passing the house. I saw two groups."

"Studies."

"Studies?"

"Midnight studies of the Tomes."

"I've never heard of people doing studies in the middle of the night."

"Oh, it's the best time. No children bouncing their balls, rattling their toys, singing, shouting, carrying on. Very quiet. No one comes to call. No one needs help. Everyone is asleep."

"Except those who study?"

"And pregnant o'rants who like my picklebarrel schop."

Kale took the bowl and spoon from Tulanny with a smile and a "thank you." She stretched her talent toward the hostess as she turned to pour a glass of milk from the saucepan on the stove. Kale's mind touched a barrier, and she quietly withdrew.

Why would Tulanny have her mind blocked? Was she holding back information? Was she lying?

Kale tasted the schop and found she'd lost her enthusiasm for the treat. She continued to eat in small bites while Tulanny described the different activities that kept the women of the meech colony busy.

"What is the name of the community?" Kale interrupted. "I don't think I've heard anyone say."

"Bility."

"Is that a meech word?"

"Oh, well, I'm not sure." Tulanny fell into a moment of silence, giving Kale the impression that she fought the urge to keep chattering about the town and its history. The meech gave an exaggerated yawn. "Are you finished, Kale? We really need to get some sleep."

"Yes, Mistress Tulanny." Kale rose and took her dishes to the counter.

"I'll wash those with the breakfast things. You scurry back to bed before you catch cold. Oh, look. I've left a couple of windows undone."

She fetched a pole from the pantry and used it to push the window closed. Then, with a hook at the end, she pulled the latch over into a clasp. The window was locked.

Kale stared at the metal bolt and wondered how Pat would get back in. Tulanny replaced the pole.

Kale smiled at her. "I am tired. Thank you for your hospitality. You're a wonderful hostess."

The meech woman smiled, her sharp teeth gleaming as they caught the light from one of the lampposts.

Kale shivered, glad that she was used to the rather feral-looking smiles Regidor sometimes used to scare his enemies.

Is Tulanny trying to intimidate me?

Kale bobbed her head. "Good night."

"Tuck yourself in, nice and warm. Don't worry about rising early tomorrow. You should rest now. That baby looks ready to come."

Kale murmured an answer and ducked in her room, closed the door, and leaned against it.

Pat! What am I going to do about Pat?

Bardon snorted and turned over, successfully claiming her side of the bed as well as his.

It doesn't matter. How could I sleep?

She tried the window. *Locked! That's just wonderful. What if a fire broke out? How would we save ourselves? By breaking the window.*

Different means of breaking the window flitted through her thoughts. *Don't be silly!* she scolded herself. *You can't break the window.*

She sat down in a wooden rocker and rubbed the side of her abdomen. Her fingers traced over the other bump she carried in a scarf. "You," she whispered.

With a little maneuvering, she was able to shift the egg along the scarf and out through a gap between the buttons on her nightgown. She held the egg in her hand, her fingers rubbing softly over the shell. The egg had changed from a rocklike hardness to a soft, leathery surface that gave under her caress.

"You're ready, aren't you?" She closed her fingers around the egg and rested it against her chest. Leaning back against the wooden slats, she gently rocked.

She dozed, and when she jerked awake, she still held the egg close to her heart, and something rested on her knee. She looked down to discover Pat, sitting up and waiting for her to wake.

"How'd you get in?" She knew before he had a chance to answer. Soot coated his scales. "You came down the chimney. Very clever. What did you find out?"

Kale's eyes widened as she listened to the jumble of words and saw the collage of pictures that poured from Pat's mind. A few seconds into the account, he began to shiver. She scooped up his chubby little brown body with one hand and held him against her right next to the unhatched egg. She soon ceased rocking altogether, then a minute later, rocked hard. When he finished, she slowed the rocker, cooed to him, and stroked his shuddering body.

When she felt calmer, she rose from the rocker and went to sit on the bed beside her husband.

"Bardon, wake up!"

The urgency in her voice reached him immediately. He sat bolt upright. "What's the matter? Is it the baby?"

She shook her head, took a deep breath, and began.

"I was hungry, so I got up and went to the kitchen. Pat went with me. Men were walking by in the street. I was going to follow them, but the door was locked. We're locked in this house, Bardon."

He shifted, pushing the covers away and facing her more directly.

"There was a window open, so Pat followed them. He's just returned. The men went into a cave. They acted as if they were about to begin a ceremony. It reminded Pat of the reading of the Tomes. Only they didn't read the Tomes, they chanted. The words were slurred, but the melody was strong. He said it was not a song to like and hum during the day. But still it held him so he could not move.

"Then a group of men went farther into the mountain. He could smell the fear on their skin. He tried to follow, but something so horrible lurked within that he couldn't get up the courage to follow."

"How does he know what was down there?"

"He doesn't. The men shook with fear as they walked into the tunnel. The men left behind still chanted, but with difficulty. Tears and suppressed sobs interrupted the litany as they intoned the half-words.

"Pat gave me glimpses of the surroundings. Someone had drawn a hideous dragon on the wall of one side of the cave. On the other side was a painting of great beauty. Pat noticed the men avoided looking at either picture. They kept their heads down, staring at the floor, or gazed down the passage into the mountain.

"Then a swarm of those black dragons came out of the same tunnel the men had gone down. They flew directly out of the cave. Pat was able to break away from the enchantment of the song when he realized I might be in danger. But the dragons soared over the forest and disappeared in the opposite direction of the village."

"South," whispered Bardon. "They are going south." He focused on Kale's face. "Do you think the meech are worshiping whatever is deep in the mountain?"

"Pat thought so."

Kale leaned into Bardon, and he responded as she hoped he would. He held her in his strong arms.

They didn't talk for a while. Through the bond, Kale knew her husband was logically sorting through what she had said, what the implications might be, and what course of action might be taken. Even when he contemplated the possibility that Mot Angra lived in the meech ceremonial cave, she did not give way to panic. Her racing pulse calmed under the influence of the steady beat of his heart. His unemotional stream of thoughts counteracted the chaos of her own.

"We must inform Paladin," he said. "I'll discuss this with Regidor and Seezle in the morning."

He got out of bed, took the sleeping Pat from her hand, and placed him in the pile of cushions.

"What is this?" He indicated her clutched fingers as he sat beside her.

"The egg." She opened her hand.

A crack ran from the small end of the egg to the broader end. Smaller fracture lines extended to the sides. A chink had fallen out.

Kale caressed the egg in her open palm. "I feel kind of guilty."

"Did you drop it?"

"No, the dragon is hatching. These breaks mean it will be only minutes before we meet him face to face."

"If you didn't damage the egg, then why do you feel guilt?"

"I've ignored this new life. I've forgotten it for days on end. I don't feel the usual attachment. Even now, when I can feel the thumps of the baby dragon pushing against the shell, I don't feel excited."

The egg twitched in her hand, and another piece of the shell fell out. The gap widened, and a tiny claw stuck out. A nose appeared in the break, followed by an eye peering out. A few more kicks and pushes, and the dragon rolled out of the shell into Kale's palm.

"He's a pretty shade of blue," said Bardon. "What's his name?"

"I think it's a her, and I don't know her name."

Bardon frowned. "Has that ever happened before?"

"No, never."

Kale carefully picked up the bits of shell and moved them away. When she had the area cleared, with plenty of room for the baby to stretch, rub, and roll, she curved a finger to stroke her. The tiny dragon twisted away and hissed.

"This is wrong, Bardon. Everything seems to be wrong. Our lights don't work, Gilda acts demented, we can't tell if the meech are good or bad, black dragons swarm out of the ground, and a baby dragon rejects the Dragon Keeper."

The dragon slinked across Kale's stomach, found the gap in her nightgown, and disappeared inside.

Kale brushed at the soot mark Pat had left on her nightgown. "This is wrong too. I've tried to clean this. It's a very simple wizardry task, but no, the dirt is stubborn and won't let loose."

The bulge under her gown showed where the new dragon had settled.

"She's found the scarf her egg rested in. She's probably seeking security," Kale said, knowing she could only guess at the motives of a dragon she felt no connection with.

"Home and security don't sound so bad," said Bardon.

"We're not home, and there is no security in this world." Kale placed her hand over the baby in her womb. She could feel it push against her palm. She took Bardon's hand and placed it in the same spot. "Our baby wants out."

"I don't suppose he or she is going to wait until this Daddy can purge evil from the world and set up a kingdom of peace and security."

Kale rested her forehead against her husband's. "No, but we didn't come into a perfect world, either."

"We'll do our best to be parents who stay by their child."

"Our parents wanted that and couldn't have it."

"Look around, Kale. What do you see?"

Halfheartedly, she scanned the room. "You, the dragons, furniture, a broken shell."

"And sunlight."

Her eyes lifted to the window. Soft morning light eased away the gloom. She smiled.

Bardon kissed her. "Night always ends. The sun always rises. It's a promise."

She touched his chin, feeling the stubble he would shave away. She knew the principle he referred to. "A promise from Wulder."

44

Confrontation

A knock on the door woke Kale. Someone had opened the window in the bedroom, and several of her dragons sat on the sill. She assumed the others were out eating a breakfast of bugs and small rodents. Bardon's side of the bed was disheveled and empty. The knock sounded again.

Kale forced herself up on one elbow and pushed unruly locks out of her face. Her haircut still didn't look right. Some of the sections burned during the dragon attack were long enough to blend with the others, but she still looked spotty.

"Come in," she called.

Mistress Tulanny's head appeared as she peeked into the room. "Sorry to wake you, Kale, but you're needed. Your little girl is sick."

Kale tossed the covers off and swung her legs over the side of the bed. She ran her fingers through her hair, trying to rake the shaggy mess into a semblance of tidiness. As she rushed to the door, the material of her nightgown thickened, changed form, and became a loose-fitting morning dress with a proper collar and a tie in the back.

"Oh my," said Tulanny. "I bet that comes in handy. That was wizardry, wasn't it? You know we don't have a single wizard left in the colony. Plenty of smart folks, but you know it takes Wulder's touch to make a clever person a wizard."

Kale looked down in surprise at her transformed clothing. "I've been having some trouble with my wizardry. Where's Toopka?"

"She spent the night with Sachael Relk and family. They have a dozen children of all ages, and Mistress Relk said the little doneel had a fine time with her brood last night, but this morning she won't get out of bed."

"Please, show me the way."

They stepped out into the sunshine. Kale called for Gymn with her mind, and he soon joined them.

Kale's heart raced as fast as Tulanny's mouth as she followed her through the street of Bility. Kale didn't care to hear the history of the town or who lived in which house. Tulanny's chatter did help Kale to block some of the more extreme conjectures she came up with to explain Toopka's illness.

They finally reached a house that looked very much like the one she'd just left. Most of the houses looked the same with few variants. This one, however, was less tidy. Toys and children cluttered the front room. The only plump meech Kale had seen answered the door.

"Come in, come in," said Mistress Relk. "She was moaning earlier, but now she's fast asleep."

Sittiponder sat beside a fireplace, looking forlorn.

"Do you know what's wrong, Sittiponder?" Kale asked.

The boy shrugged. "She won't talk to me."

Mistress Relk ushered them to a room filled with bunk beds. The jumble of blankets on each small bed testified to the number of children who slept here. But only one curled up under the covers now. In one of the bottom bunks, the tips of Toopka's brown ears showed over the edge of a blanket.

Gymn flew to Toopka and slipped under the covers. Kale knelt beside the bed. "Toopka?"

When there was no response, she gently pulled back the blanket to expose Toopka's face. The child's eyes remained closed.

Kale stroked her cheeks. "Toopka, wake up."

The doneel's eyelids fluttered.

"That's my girl. Open your eyes. Tell me what's wrong."

Though she didn't open her eyes, Toopka answered in a mumble. "I'm not sick, Kale. I'm tired. I wanna sleep."

Kale moved the covers back some more and revealed Gymn curled on Toopka's chest. He looked up at Kale with sad eyes.

You don't know what it is, Gymn?

The healing dragon relayed his findings. Other than the growth,

Toopka was fine. The growth, however, had solidified completely and separated from the normal tissue surrounding it.

Do you think we should take it out? Kale swallowed. She'd never cut someone open to remove something. She pulled splinters, and on occasion she'd used a knife to open the surface of the skin in order to grasp the sliver of wood. Relief flooded through her when Gymn said he didn't think cutting the growth out was a good idea.

You still don't think that thing is harmful?

Gymn's "no" puzzled Kale, but she didn't press it. When he advised letting the child sleep, Kale kissed Toopka on the forehead. "Sleep tight then, little one, and I will check on you later."

Gymn stayed with Toopka, and after thanking the meech woman for keeping an eye on the doneel, Kale went to search for Bardon. She had not gone far when she saw him coming from the opposite direction. The colorful dragons flew about him as he walked. Children trailed behind Bardon, skipping to keep up with his quick pace.

"Good morning," Bardon said, but his gruff greeting did more to say it was not a good morning than his words.

"What's wrong?" asked Kale.

"We are invited to a special council meeting." He took her hand and turned down the next street.

The children still followed, but now they were engaged in making up a story-song about the beautiful, small dragons.

Kale smiled at them, then turned back to Bardon. "You've been up early, gathering information."

"Exactly." Bardon hustled them down another side street. "And I believe that is why we are being called to this little get-together."

"They certainly aren't used to visitors, but I didn't think they were hostile."

"Here we are." Bardon gestured to a round building of white stone.

Before Kale could react to the similarity to the Followers' headquarters, the ground shook beneath their feet. The children dropped onto their knees, curled forward, and covered their heads.

The tremor lasted only a few seconds, then ceased. The children got up and started to walk away.

"Where are you going?" Kale asked.

One little male meech turned back to say, "Home. We have to tell our families that we're all right. We do it after every shake."

"Do you ever have a big shake?" asked Bardon.

"No sir," the boy said. "My father says the main tremor follows a fault line. The energy releases to the south of us."

"Do you know what that means?" Bardon asked.

The boy grinned. "It means we're safe right now." He waved his hand, then trotted away.

Several men scurried around the corner and almost ran Kale down.

"Sorry," one said. "Oh, you're one of the visitors. I'm Anyeld. This is Ellyk and Laire."

Bardon stepped closer. "I'm Sir Bardon. This is my wife, Lady Kale Allerion."

"So glad to meet you," said Ellyk.

Laire hastily opened the door to the round building. "Please, come in."

Two more gentlemen waited for them in a room sparsely furnished with a large table and chairs. Regidor and Seezle sat in silence in two of the big chairs.

Kale recognized one of the meech gentlemen as the one who had come forward to greet them when they entered the colony. She struggled to remember his name.

He gestured toward empty chairs. "My name is Seslie. Please, be seated."

Bardon shook his hand. "I remember from yesterday."

Kale smiled to herself. At times, Bardon's early training as a diplomat showed up, while her years of living in The Bogs offered her no social graces.

Seslie nodded to Bardon and indicated the other man. "Of course, and this is Karnott."

Bardon dipped his head. "And we met the others just outside the door."

"Then, shall we be seated?" asked Seslie. "We have a lot to cover."

Bardon pulled out a chair next to Regidor for Kale.

"How is Gilda this morning?" she asked.

"Calm," answered Regidor. "For that I am grateful."

All but Seslie sat. When the room was silent, he began.

"Bardon has asked what is in the cave, who do we worship, and why we live in fear."

The men from the meech colony nodded soberly but kept their heads down, their eyes on their folded hands.

"We"—Seslie gestured to the meech at the table—"have decided to answer your questions. First, what is in the cave?"

Laire stood. "The answer to that question is quite simple. Mot Angra. But do you have an inkling of what that means?"

Regidor lifted one eyebrow. "A horrendous, dark dragon whose scales turn into small dragons when they are shed."

Laire sat down again and sighed. "That is all of the legend that remains?"

Bardon, Kale, and Regidor nodded.

"It is not enough to explain the horror of this creature. His size is terrifying. When we escaped our world, Mot Angra followed us."

Regidor held up his hand. "We know nothing of the other world. Would you be kind enough to explain the exodus? We have no records of that event."

"I shall take that task," said Anyeld. "On our world, we had been privileged to know Wulder. We had a special class who studied to know Him and His ways. These were the meech dragons. They passed their insights on to the general public. None of your high races existed on our world, which we called Blaime. Our population consisted of dragons of many forms and minnekens of one form."

Ellyk broke in. "Through gross negligence on our part, Mot Angra was born. We were horrified and quickly subdued the beast. His birth served to bring the people of Blaime to be more attentive to Wulder and his Tomes."

Laire took the story back. "That lasted many centuries, and then... the people became lax again. Mot Angra awoke. During the time of his restraint, he had grown in size. At the time of his second rampage, he was as big as a half dozen of our homes put together. He ravaged the countryside, eating crops, livestock, and the dragons. Each time, after he'd gone berserk, he would sit on a hill, gloating over the devastation. He'd pick his teeth with a claw and belch. He sang songs of his own significance and his exploits."

"He can speak?" asked Kale.

"As well as you or me," answered Laire.

"He's cunning, sly, and devious," said Anyeld.

"Powerful," added Seslie.

"I gather," said Regidor, "that for some reason you are losing control over Mot Angra."

Silence greeted Regidor's comment.

The meech named Karnott stood. This dragon was obviously the oldest of the men there. His wrinkled face bore an expression of deep sadness. "It is our responsibility to keep him under control. It is our fault that he was able to enter your world. Blaime had disintegrated both in its ability to produce food, fuel, and shelter, and in the people's moral commitment to one another. Evil ruled the land. Wulder provided a gateway for those who vowed to turn from wickedness and to honor Him as our Creator. All of the minnekens lined up to enter this new world. Dragons of all sizes followed the smallest of Wulder's thinking races. The meech were last in line, and several of us wished to take the Old Woman of Wust with us. She was the second of Wulder's creation and still lived, choosing to dwell in a peaceful garden hidden by Wulder Himself. From time to time, a representative of those dedicated to knowing more would make the journey to seek her insight. We revered her wisdom and could not see a future without her guidance.

"A young meech named Bellum journeyed to Wust to bring her. His petition to enter the garden was answered, and the hidden entry opened.

"Meanwhile, our people went through the gateway with a handful holding back, waiting for the Old Woman of Wust to come. When Bellum arrived with the woman on his back, she was furious."

Again a heavy, formidable silence filled the room. Karnott sank into his chair as if his part in telling the tale had exhausted him.

Laire spoke up. "The Old Woman of Wust said she was of the old, and Wulder had offered us the new. It would be disastrous to drag part of the old into the new. But the meech argued and pleaded and wasted time."

"Yes, wasted time," echoed several of the gathering.

"Finally, the Old Woman said she refused to go," Laire continued. "And she died. Our men left her body and turned to the gateway. But we had given Mot Angra enough time to find us. We pushed through the portal from our world to yours and watched as the gateway changed in appearance, knowing that Wulder had designed the contraption to collapse in upon itself as soon as the last of us were safely through."

He stopped speaking.

Regidor clasped his hands together and placed them in his lap.

Anyeld cleared his throat as if to speak, but then did not say anything.

Kale looked quickly around the room. The five meech men from the colony all wore expressions of remorse and resignation. Regidor's face had tightened into a mask of controlled anger. Bardon had his look of resolve that she knew so well. He would be planning how to best face this new challenge. Kale wanted out of the meeting. She'd had enough of this drama and wanted to check on Toopka.

Would nobody speak and say the obvious? If they wouldn't, she would. She tried to master her emotions first. Irritation at a past mistake wouldn't help. Impatience for their present humiliation would not help.

She spoke softly. "Mot Angra followed you through the gateway just before it closed."

"Yes," said several while others nodded.

"And you were able to subdue him for a great length of time."

"Yes."

"What is different now? Why is he awakening?"

"We don't know," said Seslie.

"Why did the minnekens leave you?"

"They didn't like the north. Too cold," said Laire.

"They didn't like us," said Anyeld with force. "They couldn't stand us. We had failed to listen to and heed Wulder. We'd brought the terror with us because we thought we'd improve upon Wulder's plan. We were going to add our bit of wisdom by forcing one more person to come with us. Wulder had said the choice was up to the individual. But collectively, our people decided the Old Woman of Wust must come, and we ignored her decision. The minnekens washed their hands of us and left."

Anyeld's pronouncement impressed Kale. This meech would not hide from the truth.

A knock on the door interrupted, and Mistress Tulanny poked her head into the room. Kale's stomach muscles tightened as she waited for the woman to speak.

"Sorry to interrupt," she said, "but Lady Kale is needed. The little doneel girl, Toopka, has disappeared."

45

Into This World

Bardon and Kale hurried after their hostess. The woman took long strides and talked constantly. Kale's breath began to come in short pants.

As they walked, Mistress Tulanny explained how she had discovered the child was missing. "As soon as I realized she wasn't in Sachael Relk's house, I started asking questions of the children playing nearby. Several saw Toopka and Sittiponder heading south. The green dragon was with them."

Kale looked at Bardon. *South? To the tunnel that would take them out of the canyon?*

"Farther south is the cave of Mot Angra."

You don't think Toopka would be curious enough to go explore.

"She doesn't know Mot Angra is deep in the mountain below that cave."

One of the children might have told her.

"I don't think Sittiponder would let her go."

She can be so foolhardy!

Kale's chest contracted into a heavy knot, and she realized how much she loved the exasperating doneel. The intense feeling surprised her on top of the second realization that she had purposely guarded herself from having emotional strings attached to this child.

She repeated a silent plea to Gymn, and frustration hammered her heart when his soothing thoughts did not respond with an assurance that all was under control. *He's too far away. Where could those three have gone off to?* She called to the minor dragons and sent them out as a search team.

She caught up to Tulanny. "I've sent the minor dragons to look for Toopka and Sittiponder. They'll find them."

"Those little beauties are such wonderful creatures. Doesn't it amaze you what Wulder has made?"

"Always."

They walked a few paces, and Bardon spoke. "Mistress Tulanny, you don't seem to be put off by the minor dragons, yet I haven't seen any dragons except the meech here in Bility."

"That's right. They don't like the cold."

Kale and Bardon exchanged a look over the answer they had heard before, recently, but referring to minnekens, not dragons.

"In Amara," said Bardon, "there is a group of people who hate dragons and want to eliminate them."

"Maybe they fear the dragons will become like Mot Angra."

"Other than those in this colony, who among the high races would know about Mot Angra?"

Mistress Tulanny cast a sharp glance at Bardon, lowered her head, and trudged on without a word.

As they turned a corner, they heard a commotion.

Kale hurried her step. "Maybe someone has found Toopka and Sittiponder."

They turned another corner and found a sight they least expected to see. Surrounded by children, Brunstetter, Sir Dar, and Lee Ark tried to answer as many questions as were hurled at them.

"Oh," said Tulanny. "More outsiders. I'll go tell the elders that we have more visitors." The meech matron left in a hurry, heading back to the center of the village.

Sir Dar extracted himself from the young crowd and came to Kale.

She grabbed his sleeve. "Toopka is missing."

"She always shows up."

"No, Sir Dar, this is serious. She's been ill and acting strangely. It's that growth in her chest, the one we discovered at Arreach. It hasn't grown, but Gymn says it's gotten hard." She sniffed and wiped a tear from her cheek. "It's baffled Gymn."

Sir Dar patted her hand. "Calm down, Kale."

Kale took a deep breath. "Where have you been? All sorts of horrible things have been happening."

A grin spread over Sir Dar's face. "We stormed the palace and cleared the Followers out of Paladin's hair."

Kale squeezed his arm. "Is it true Paladin was a prisoner in one of his own cells?"

"Ha! Yes. The Followers told everyone that there had been attempts to assassinate Paladin, so he had been put in a 'safe place' and was conducting business as usual from seclusion." Sir Dar winked. "They didn't realize they spoke a partial truth. Paladin had his own means of communication from the cell, although the Followers meant to cut him off from his people. Paladin coordinated his own escape while they thought he couldn't contact anyone."

"How?" asked Bardon.

"Animals, mostly the castle cat and birds." Sir Dar smiled. "We brought N'Rae in to help receive and send messages through creatures. No one thought to hinder their comings and goings. Paladin continued to collect information and issue orders right under the noses of those hypocrites."

The ground shook, and the children fell into their protective curl. The tremor eased off quickly. Before the children could jump up, Lee Ark and Brunstetter crossed the short distance to join Kale, Bardon, and Sir Dar. The children ignored the newcomers. At some preordained signal that Kale could not discern, they uncovered their heads and rose to their feet. Then they scampered off in various directions without a word.

Lee Ark looked around, his brow furrowed. "Should we prepare for an emergency of some kind?"

Bardon shook his head. "It's the dragon, Mot Angra. The meech colony has sworn to keep the monster under a potent spell. But it has been generations since they first undertook the responsibility, and frankly, they're losing their power over the beast. Each time he attempts to wake up, his great weight can be felt through the earth. He triggered the earthquake we experienced in Arreach."

"And the children?" asked Lee Ark.

Kale suddenly remembered Lee Ark's many children and watching him play with them when she visited his house.

"It's a sort of safety measure, I think," she said. "They protect themselves, then when nothing happens, they report to their parents to assure them that no one was hurt."

Brunstetter surveyed the town, looking over the roofs from his great height. "It doesn't look like an earthquake devastated this place."

"No," said Bardon. "The tremors move along a fault line running south. Very little of the quake is felt here."

"Is it also true," asked Brunstetter, "that the scales of this Mot Angra turn into the black dragons?"

"Yes, and the elders say that when the dragon is fully awake, he can direct where they attack. However, when he stirs in his sleep, they fall off, then fly away with no particular destination."

"Unless they see a Dragon Keeper," put in Kale. "Can we look for Toopka? I am very worried."

"Certainly," said Lee Ark. "We will join the search. Who is already looking, and what area are they covering?"

"I don't know." Kale clasped her hands together, twisting her fingers against one another. "The kimens, the minor dragons, some of the villagers. I don't know how many or where they've gone."

Bardon pointed toward the few children who had already reported to their parents and come back to watch the strangers. "Mistress Tulanny said that some children saw Toopka, Sittiponder, and Gymn heading south."

Lee Ark looked at the woods. The cold nip in the air had decorated the trees with orange, crimson, and gold. "We just came from the south through that path. We didn't see them, so let's concentrate on the western side of the canyon."

Kale, Bardon, Brunstetter, Lee Ark, and Sir Dar lined up along the edge of the woods. Lee Ark gave instructions that they were to march forward, staying within reach of one another.

"Concentrate on the area directly in front of you and at your sides. We'll sweep through the woods until we find them."

Their feet crunched in fallen leaves. The forest smelled of old rain, fresh breezes, and autumn leaves. Occasionally, a small creature, disturbed by their advance, scuttled off through the underbrush.

In fifteen minutes, Kale's legs stung. The muscles across the small of her back burned. Every once in a while a cramp across her abdomen claimed her attention. She kept walking, hoping Bardon would not notice how tired she was. They all called for the children and Gymn.

Through the trees, Tieto flew to meet them, turning somersaults in the air as he twittered joyfully. The minor dragons had found the children, but his excitement tossed the images he tried to send Kale into a whirlwind. She didn't understand much of what he tried to relay. She got the gist of his news. Toopka slept in a hollow. Gymn said she was all right. They must hurry to see the great thing.

They followed him through the trees, going quickly now that they had no fear of overlooking the youngsters. They came to a place where trees parted and gave the sun a chance to shine clear to the forest floor. The kimens and minor dragons had gathered in a circle at the tiny meadow's edge. With them, a smattering of Bility citizens stood in silence.

Toopka lay in a ball among a bed of dry leaves. Sittiponder sat with his back to a tree, his full attention on the sleeping doneel. His pale, wide-eyed expression drew Kale to sit beside him.

"What happened, Sittiponder? Why are you out here?"

"Toopka said Wulder called her to come. And He did." Sittiponder's head did not move. Kale was accustomed to the blind tumanhofer not looking directly at her when he spoke. She took his hand. The other hand held something in a tight fist.

"Tell me what happened."

"We stopped here. Toopka wanted to rest. Then He came. I saw Him, Kale. Not really, though. I saw the light. Most of Him was light, but I saw His hands reach out and touch Toopka.

"Wulder laid her down, and she went right to sleep. He opened her chest. It wasn't bloody or anything, and the light was too bright to see much. He took out an egg and gave it to me to hold. He passed His hand over Toopka, and she was the same as she had been before. Not even her clothes were torn or moved or anything. Wulder pulled His hands back into the light, so I couldn't really see Him anymore, just the light.

"And He spoke to me. He said to keep the egg until she woke up and then give the egg to her. She would know what to do when the time came."

Sittiponder's head tilted forward, and he opened his fist. On his palm lay a small egg, smaller than most bird eggs. Its white shell contained swirls of palest pink and blue.

"It's beautiful," Kale said. She searched for words to describe its uniqueness to the blind child. Toopka usually came up with fantastic descriptions, but she still slept. "Its surface is more like a pearl than an egg. Or maybe, an opal." Frustration stopped Kale. How would the boy know what a pearl or an opal looked like?

"I know." Sittiponder turned his face up to Kale.

She gasped. "Sittiponder, you're looking at me. You're seeing. You… you see me, don't you?"

The boy smiled. "He touched my eyes before He left."

He stood and smiled at the fringe of the small glade where the kimens, meech, and dragons waited. He grinned at Bardon and Brunstetter. He winked at Sir Dar.

The realization that he actually saw them dawned on the spectators. The kimens, with Metta, burst into song and broke from the ring to dance over the brilliantly colored carpet of leaves. The dragons frolicked in the air. Brunstetter picked up Sittiponder and put him on his shoulder. The urohm wove in and out of the trees with the others following in a parade of celebration.

"Hey!" Toopka's loud voice penetrated the commotion. "Hey! What's going on?" She stood where she had been lying, with her fists planted against her hips, and her face twisted up in a scowl.

"Put me down, please," said Sittiponder.

Brunstetter set the tumanhofer on his feet.

Sittiponder ran to Toopka. "This is yours. Wulder took it out of your chest."

He handed her the egg. She took it, but her eyes were on his face. "You…?"

"Yes!"

"That's—" She shook her head, at a loss for words.

Sittiponder grinned, picked her up in his sturdy arms, and twirled her around.

Contentment filled Kale as she watched. Toopka would be all right. Sittiponder could see. Her friends had arrived to help with whatever came up. Paladin was back on his throne.

"Let's go home," she said.

Sittiponder put the doneel down.

"Home? Not yet," said Toopka. "We have to go back to the meech village."

Kale grinned. "Yes, that is what I meant."

Toopka's head tilted to one side, and her eyes looked as if she were seeing something far, far away. "I think I know where my home is."

"You do?"

She nodded her head decisively. "I do. But I can't go there yet. I have work to do."

"What work, Toopka?" asked Bardon.

"Saving the world." She shook her head till her ears bounced. "Someone's gotta do it."

46

War Council

A chill breeze blew through the open window. The crackling flames in the fireplace radiated heat in vain. Only one side of the room held the warmth. In the same official chamber where they had gathered earlier, the meech dragon leaders met with Kale, Bardon, and Seezle. Lee Ark and Sir Dar joined them. Brunstetter sat outside an open window. The mothers of the village had to drag their children away. Not only was the giant fascinating, but he encouraged the youngsters to play.

The impromptu council sat around a huge table with platters of food down the center. The scrumptious meal was largely neglected. The serious prospect of Mot Angra breaking loose dampened their appetites.

The meech leaders' attitude puzzled Bardon. He expected them to dominate the meeting. This was their territory and a problem they knew intimately. Yet they hung back, seemingly unwilling to get started. When the outsider Lee Ark took charge, Bardon sat back in his chair and watched, wondering if part of the colony's problem could be related to a lack of direction.

Lee Ark's military bearing shone through even as he sat in the old wooden chair. "The first thing to consider is whether or not we can stop this beast before he wakes. Can he be killed?"

Laire shook his head. "He can be annoyed greatly by sticking spears into him. He can be made very sick by poisoning his food. The results of that tactic are extremely messy. The last person to cut his throat learned Mot Angra heals quicker than he sheds blood. And that man became Mot Angra's dinner."

Lee Ark considered this for a moment and then asked, "What is it you do to keep him sleeping?"

Anyeld scooted back in his chair and sat straighter. "We never let him get too hungry. He doesn't have a tremendous appetite, just a large animal such as a cow or a mountain sheep each week keeps him satisfied. He never fully wakes to gobble the food. The same with water. He receives ten buckets of water each day in a trough. He's been known to rouse enough to eat one of the carriers bringing the buckets down."

Lee Ark scowled. "Surely, there is something else."

Bardon looked at the five meech men, hoping one would have the answer.

Seslie cleared his throat. "There's the singing."

Ellyk scoffed. "The singing? That's more to keep up the courage of the men who carry down the water or the carcass for Mot Angra's dinner. Few of us even remember what the words mean." Ellyk snorted. "It's not as if our songs are a lullaby."

"What do you sing?" asked Seezle.

"Old relics," answered Seslie. "Songs from the old world in an ancient language."

Seezle's face lit up. "May I hear one?"

"Wait," said Kale. "If this is important, Metta should be here."

Lee Ark nodded, and Kale silently called for the purple minor dragon. A moment later she flew past Brunstetter and in the window. She landed on Kale's shoulder.

Kale got the impression that the minor dragon was flattered to be summoned to an important council meeting.

"I don't understand," said Ellyk. "Why is this minor dragon needed?"

"She's a singing dragon," explained Kale. "She has remarkable talents when it comes to anything pertaining to music, and particularly to songs."

Ellyk's eyes squinted in skepticism, but he didn't say anything else.

Seslie said, "Should I sing?"

The visitors nodded their heads, while his fellow meech dragons looked bored.

In a mellow baritone, Seslie sang,

"O-gitaks to who
Derfor ess soo
Foress mur sees
Indoors forests
Rivers.

Ike awl to who
Der indess
Rest who
Der and sir
Me and set
Me inbraw de
Plae sess."

"Enough," said Ellyk. "The words are nonsense to us now, although I am sure they once meant something. Our parents were diligent to teach them to us."

"Metta?" Kale turned her head, and her cheek rubbed against Metta's outstretched wing.

"What does she say?" asked Lee Ark.

"The song is sacred, but she cannot pull the words out of the meech's memory because these are the only words he knows. She is sure the lyrics are wrong."

Lee Ark addressed the meech. "Are the words written anywhere?"

"It is said," Laire answered, "that in the old world there were books with words from Wulder in them. None of the books came with us through the portal, so generation after generation learned what we could from what our parents remembered."

"Kale," said Bardon, "have Filia and Metta put their heads together. I think what Seslie has sung is a song that is recorded in the middle book of the Tomes. The tune almost sounds like something I should remember. The words tease me like I should recognize them."

Metta landed on his shoulder and trilled notes softly in his ear.

"Yes, that's it. Can you find the words?"

Lee Ark stood. "It is doubtful that our words to a song will be the same as those from another world. But Filia and Metta, I'd appreciate your pursuance of that idea. Gentlemen, I would like to visit the lair of the dragon. It would be good to know if there is some strategic advantage we can gain from the physical setting."

Kale caught Bardon's arm as he started to rise. "I'm going to stay here. Walking through the woods is hard on my back and legs."

He kissed her on the forehead. "Fine, just don't eat all the delicacies while we are away."

"Be careful, Bardon."

"I will."

As Lee Ark led his council toward the cave, Bardon engaged Seslie in conversation. "I'm curious about your history. What did your people do when you first came through the portal?"

"The first order of business was to subdue Mot Angra. Unfortunately, he ate quite a few of our people in those early days. But once Mot Angra's belly is full, he chooses a place to relax. He then acts rather like an intoxicated fool until he drops off to sleep. According to the legend, everyone worked together to move him a short distance into the cave."

"Is there any kind of wizardry that seals him in?"

"We don't have wizards. I suppose we may have had a few in the beginning, but there are no records of any."

"Why is that? Why no records?"

Seslie cleared his throat. "There was the business of gaining control over Mot Angra. Then they had to put up shelters for the coming winter. We brought little with us. We even had to make paper, and you can understand that was not as high a priority as keeping the snow off our heads." He sighed. "And I suppose, if we are to be truthful, no one wanted to put down on paper what blunderheads we had been.

"The other types of dragons were furious with us. As soon as they had contributed to securing Mot Angra, they washed their hands of us and went south. Many meech went south as well, but over the years they have drifted back. We attribute that to the collective dedication to our responsibility. We are peaceful to a fault." He turned to look at Bardon. "I hear Regidor fights…and flies. Remarkable."

"Do you know how Gilda is? We haven't heard, and when Kale asked if she could visit, the matron in charge said that seeing the outsiders would set her off again. I don't really understand what is wrong with her."

"She has presented her egg."

Bardon felt a surge of joy for his friend Regidor and relief for Gilda. "Really? Is she all right? Is the egg…um, is the egg, well, whole? All right? Like it should be?"

Seslie laughed. "They are both fine."

"I was led to believe that the meech have very few eggs and do not cherish the family unit."

Seslie laughed again, obviously more comfortable talking about their culture than their past. "We collect eggs for ten or fifteen years, and then for three years we hatch them out in a spaced pattern. That way the youngsters have playmates, and we can educate them in groups." He chuckled. "Except that Sachael Relk. She's a rebel. She has her eggs whenever she chooses and has them quickened as soon as she can. Why, we'd be overrun with children if all our women took to breeding and hatching the way that woman does." He shook his head and sobered. "You *are* aware that meech mature rapidly?"

"I am."

"Are you aware that our life spans are considerably shorter than yours?"

Bardon caught his breath. "No. No, I was not." He thought of Regidor. "How short?"

"Forty, fifty years." Seslie pushed aside a stray branch. The path to the cave was well worn. "As to our family units? I suppose the rumor that we don't enjoy our families comes purely from not knowing us."

"Is it true you need an outsider to quicken your eggs?"

"Now, that's true enough. A few members of the high races live in this remote territory. We know each of them. They are as odd as you must think we are, and they choose to be reclusive as well. We had a tumanhofer living with us for a number of years."

"Woodkimkalajoss?"

"Yes. Was it he who told you how to find us?"

"I'm afraid so. Reluctantly, but he told."

"I suspect he got suspicious of the tremors. He knew about Mot Angra. I suppose he figured we needed some help. He wasn't very complimentary about how we choose to live."

"Are all of your people content, or do you have more rebels like Sachael Relk?"

Seslie frowned. "Sachael is no harm to anyone, but we did have a man who caused problems. He left us around ten years ago, and no one but Tulanny was sad to see him go."

"Tulanny?"

"He was Tulanny's son. A loudmouth. A persuasive talker. An 'independent thinker' he called himself, but he wanted everyone to line up behind him and follow his new way of doing things. When we didn't fall in line, he got pretty ugly. Meech don't generally yell and holler when we discuss things. His joy was in outshouting anyone who stood up to him. We told him that a bully never got what he wanted and he'd have to learn another way to win people to his side.

"He hated dragons too. He transferred all his fear of Mot Angra into hate for all dragons. He denied his own heritage, separating himself from the reality of his own dragon blood. He talked wildly about what he would do if he could rid this world of dragons. His contention was that the dragons should never have been allowed to pass through Wulder's gateway. But it was Wulder's gateway, and he never seemed to get it through his thick skull that it was up to Wulder who could come through, not up to him.

"He left eventually. I guess he got tired of hearing the same story from us over and over. He couldn't change what we think. I wonder if he found anyone who would listen to him."

A shiver ran down Bardon's spine as he surmised where Tulanny's son may have gone and what he was doing.

"Here we are," whispered Seslie. "Try not to make noise. Mot Angra is restless these days, and we'd just as soon he stay asleep until we come tonight with his offering."

Bardon felt oppression descend upon him as he neared the opening in the rock. The cold, clammy apprehension reminded him of the way they'd felt when the questers first entered the Northern Reach. Now his skin crawled, and he found himself expecting something to leap out at them. He looked at his companions and saw they, too, felt the unnatural atmosphere of dread.

They no sooner stepped inside the cave than the floor shook and grit let loose from the ceiling, showering their heads. A moment later a horde of black dragons flew out of the dark tunnel toward the sunshine. They turned north as soon as they hit the fresh air.

"North!" said several of the men.

"The village," said another.

"Kale," said Bardon and ran up the path he had just descended.

47

New Things

"What are you reading?" Sittiponder stood at Kale's shoulder, examining the book in front of her.

"It's a volume of information on dragons. Leetu Bends gave it to me many years ago." She laughed. "Actually, it was in Granny Noon's library, so I ought to say Granny Noon gave it to me. Leetu thought I would need the information and took it off the shelf and pushed it into my hands. Years later, I asked Granny Noon if she wanted it back."

"And she said no."

"She said, 'I guess not. I didn't know it was missing.' "

Kale examined her young friend. His face lit up upon hearing the story, but he'd already worn an expression of joy. She wondered what it would be like to see the world for the first time. "What have you been doing?"

He grinned. "Looking. I've decided yellow is my favorite color. One of the meech children showed me all sorts of things and told me their names. I'm surprised so many of the birds are tiny. Their songs are so big. I like the way water runs in a brook. The way it moves matches the way it sounds."

Kale turned in her chair and hugged him. "I'm so glad for you, Sittiponder."

"I'm glad for me too."

"Why did you come find me? Do you need something?"

"No, I got cold, so I decided to come inside and watch the fire crackle."

"I don't blame you. I shut the window after Brunstetter left. I couldn't latch it because I didn't want to climb on a chair."

"You couldn't move it with wizardry?"

Kale shook her head. "I tried, but things are off balance around here. The simplest of wizard maneuvers just don't work. No, that's not accurate. Some of my wizardry works and some does not. There's no rhyme or reason as to which manipulation reaps success and which does not." She frowned, thinking. "I've thought maybe it has to do with polarization."

"What?"

She smiled. "Never mind. We'll have to ask Regidor to figure it out." Her smile faded. "Right now he's preoccupied with Gilda."

Kale's own baby felt huge, heavy, cumbersome, and annoyingly active. She tried to reach the baby and met with resistance. How could a baby block mindspeaking? She wanted to sing to it. She wanted to know if it was a he or she. Just that much would be comforting. But this baby lived in silence, not reaching out to its mama. If she continued along this line of thinking, she'd bawl.

She searched her mind for another topic of conversation. "What is Toopka doing?"

"She's playing with the other children. Every once in a while she pulls out the egg and shows it to everyone. She tells them how important it is and that she's going to use the egg to save the world."

"Does she say how she's going to save the world?"

Sittiponder shook his head vigorously. "No."

Kale turned back to the table. "That's actually why I pulled this book out. I'm looking at all the different types of eggs. Some have pictures and some are described. So far I haven't found a match to the one Toopka carries. So, I'm sure it is not a dragon egg, but something else."

A tremor shook the table. The book jiggled toward the edge, and Kale stopped it from falling as she tried to balance on a moving chair. The window popped open, a log fell from the fire, and a picture fell from the wall. Both Kale and Sittiponder grabbed for the platters of food headed for the sides of the table and, consequently, the floor. They managed to shove all the dishes back to safety. The shuddering earth stilled.

"Wow!" said Sittiponder. "That was a big one."

A niggling feeling in the back of her mind brought Kale's head up.

She stared at the window. Something disturbing was just beyond her reach.

"Close the window!" she shouted. She jumped out of the chair, knocking it over. Both she and Sittiponder ran, but the tumanhofer got there first and pushed the two sides of the window into the frame.

"I'm going to boost you up, Sittiponder," said Kale as she grabbed his thighs. A cramp shot across her back, but she ignored it. "You'll be able to reach the latch." She grunted as she shoved. "Why would anyone put their locks at the top where pregnant o'rant wizards cannot possibly reach?"

"Meeches are taller."

"I know that!" snapped Kale. "Oh, I'm sorry, Sittiponder."

The tumanhofer stretched. "Why would anyone put their locks at the top of windows where tumanhofer boys standing on pregnant o'rant wizards cannot possibly reach?"

Kale giggled.

Sittiponder struggled with the metal hook and finally got it to slide into the small notch.

Kale put him down. Her hand went straight to the small of her back. "Ow!" A deep ache coursed across the bottom of her bulging abdomen and settled in to torment her. She wrapped her arms around the pain. "Oh! Oh! Ow!"

Sittiponder took her by the arm and guided her back to the table. "Should I go get someone?"

Kale gasped. "Gymn is coming. So are the others. Oh no, Sitti, the black dragons are coming. That's what I felt. I can feel the buzz now."

"What should I do?"

"Build up the fire so they can't come down the chimney." Kale glanced around the room, trying to find something helpful. "I've got my cape. I'll put up a shield, but I don't know if I can hold my concentration if another contraction hits me."

"Contraction?"

"I think the baby's coming."

Sittiponder stepped back from her as if she had just announced she was carrying the plague.

Kale laughed. "Stir up the fire." She nestled into a corner of the room. Crouching on the floor, it would be easier to maintain a shield if she had less area to cover. The walls would provide part of her protection.

"If they get in," she told Sittiponder, "open the door and run. They won't bother you as long as you leave them alone."

She saw his stoic nod and wondered what he was thinking as he put on another log. She also wondered why she couldn't just penetrate his thick skull and dig out the information she wanted. Everything was harder to do. Was it the labor associated with a coming baby? Was it the closeness of the monstrous evil in the bowels of the earth? Would she be able to hold the shield in place, or would that bit of wizardry slip through her fingers as well?

She heard the distant buzz, the screams of frightened children, and the mixed warnings from her minor dragons. Ducking low, she covered herself with the impenetrable armor. *I hope it holds. Maybe they'll pass right over the village.*

A whack against the windowpane destroyed that flimsy hope. The rat-a-tat-tat against the glass sounded like hail. The new little dragon who hid from her came out of the moonbeam cape. She sat on Kale's shoulder and hissed in the direction of the onslaught.

"It's all right, little girl," cooed Kale. She reached to stroke the blue dragon and got nipped for her concern. Kale jerked her hand back and examined the finger. At least the ill-tempered beast hadn't drawn blood. Kale put the finger in her mouth and sucked away the sharp pain.

She glanced at the window and didn't like the fact that the glass flexed with the impact of each black body. Sittiponder stood between her and the window with a thin log held like a club.

Sittiponder, you are to run. Do you hear me? They won't hurt me. I'm safe. You run. He didn't respond but stood swinging the club, then bouncing it against his palm. Did he not hear her? Could she not even mindspeak? He'd never hear her voice above the droning and the battering of bodies against the glass.

Sittiponder, do you hear me? Great! Now you're deaf instead of blind.

He turned long enough to flash her a cheeky grin.

Kale knew when the villagers rallied to attack the black dragons.

The minor dragons flashed images to Kale of the villagers attacking the black dragons. Her dragons also engaged in the battle, bombarding the smaller beasts from above the swarm. Some of her dragons swooped down and attacked along the flank of the horde. Kale could feel Crispin's excitement as he spat fire at the enemy instead of caustic saliva.

The crash of glass brought her vision back from what others could see to what was happening in this room. Sittiponder swung at the invasion with his clunky stick and managed to hit several of the nasty beasts with each swing. The mass swarmed around him and came directly at Kale. She closed her eyes and concentrated, keeping the shield in place while she listened to the creatures thud against her cover. Too busy with her defense, she didn't have a clue what was happening beyond her small refuge.

She covered her ears, jostling the blue dragon, who bit her wrist. Her concentration flickered, and so did the shield, but she managed to hold it together.

The thudding subsided, then stopped. Kale peeked. Bardon stood in the room with the other questers and a few meech men. She could see the bottom of Brunstetter's legs outside the window. Sir Dar hugged Sittiponder and Lee Ark slapped the boy on the back.

"Come out, Kale," said Bardon, walking toward her. His feet kicked tiny black bodies aside. "It's safe now."

The pain swelling across her abdomen shattered the shield. Kale panted and tried to speak.

Bardon knelt beside her.

"The baby?" he asked.

She nodded.

Tulanny pushed through the crowded room. The blue dragon hissed at the meech as she knelt beside Kale.

Tulanny's eyes widened. "Is this a protector dragon? Is that his talent?"

"Her?" Kale looked askance at the minor dragon who had slid down her arm and stood on her stomach. She shook her head. "No, this is a cranky dragon who has no talent that I know of. She failed to bond."

Tulanny and Bardon helped Kale get to her feet. Tulanny frowned and wrinkled her nose at the dead bodies littering the floor. Then her face cleared, and she stared at Kale.

"These creatures attacked you, didn't they? They were after you."

"Yes." Kale leaned against Bardon. "I really would like to lie down."

"That means," said Tulanny, "that you're not just a wizard with dragons. You're a Dragon Keeper."

Bardon steered Kale through the room. Her friends backed away to make a path.

Kale gritted her teeth. "That's right."

"You're our savior. A Dragon Keeper. It's perfect." Tulanny grinned at the other meech in the room. "Who better to manage that wicked dragon than an experienced Dragon Keeper?"

Kale saw several nods and heard one person's "worth a try."

She had to set them straight.

"Look, I have a tiny blue naughty dragon who bites me. I can't control all dragons."

Tulanny patted her back. "But you can try, Kale. Surely, you could try."

All Kale wanted was a bed, a drink, and some time alone. "I'll think about it," she said, trying not to add a screech as another gripping pain clutched her abdomen. "Right after I have this baby."

48

LIFE AND DEATH

"Oh, I wish Mother were here." Kale panted as Bardon wiped sweat from her face. Gymn sat on her stomach and eyed first her and then the blue dragon that no one had succeeded in chasing away. She sat with her wings outstretched on the pillow next to Kale's head.

Kale huffed. "I wish that confounded dragon would at least flap more often. It cools me off."

Gymn chirruped at the intruder. The blue dragon hissed back.

Bardon picked up a straw fan loaned to him by Tulanny and waved it over Kale's face.

Kale groaned. "I wish Granny Noon were here."

Bardon wiped her face again. "I'm here."

"How many babies have you helped into the world?"

He nodded. "Got your point. Do you want another sip of water?"

"Here she is," announced Tulanny from the doorway.

Sachael Relk stepped into the room, and an enormous weight of anxiety lifted from Kale. But another contraction caught her, and all reason left with the grip of muscles trying to birth the baby.

Sachael gently pushed Bardon to one side and took Kale's hand.

Bardon flinched. "She'll mangle your fingers until you think they're going to sink into each other."

Sachael smiled. "The trick is to give her the palm of your hand to squeeze and keep your fingers free."

"Do you think it'll be much longer?" Bardon asked.

"Son, I just walked through the door. At this point I don't know if it'll be five minutes or five years."

"Years?" gasped Kale.

"Just kidding, young lady." She patted Kale's arm as the contraction eased off. "We'll get you comfortable so the only time you're hurting is when you're working to have that baby. No sense in fidgeting in between times. I'll show your husband how to hold you so he can rub your back exactly where it will do the most good."

Forty-five minutes later, Mistress Relk laid a squirming baby boy on Kale's chest.

"There," said the meech. "He can listen to your heart just like he's been doing for months." The midwife rubbed him with a cloth, listing off his inventory while Kale and Bardon gazed at their new son.

"Two arms and legs. Ten toes. Ten fingers. Two of everything he needs. My, these ears are pointy."

She looked curiously from Kale to Bardon. Bardon grinned and lifted his hair covering his ears.

The baby squalled.

"He's got good lungs," said Tulanny.

Sachael tsked. "That wasn't very original, Tulanny. If you want to be useful, get this nosy dragon out of my way."

"Not me," said the meech. "That beast bites."

The baby's wails turned to soft sobs, then to a coo. The blue dragon crept closer. Bardon reached to keep the creature at a distance from his son. It hissed.

"Just as I thought," said Tulanny. "That's a protector dragon, but she's not protecting you, Kale. She belongs to the baby."

"Oh," whispered Kale. "It's all right, Bardon. Don't move her. I should have known. The dragon bonded to our baby."

The little blue dragon put a wing over the child and looked up to Kale's face.

"Her name is Fly." Kale giggled. "Not the insect kind of Fly, but the act of soaring."

The baby's small fist waved in the air. The blue dragon intercepted a swing and allowed the tiny fingers to latch on to her neck.

Kale laughed again. "Fly has forgiven me for keeping her child trapped inside me. I have risen in her estimation since she can see I've done a fine job of taking care of him so far."

"Well, the dragon has a name," said Tulanny. "What's the boy's name?"

Kale looked at Bardon, and they spoke at the same time. "Penn."

"It's time for Master Penn to have his first meal." Sachael gave Bardon a nudge. "You go tell the men out there what a fine son you have, and in fifteen minutes, you can come back and tell your wife what a fine lady she is. Right now, you're in the way."

Bardon started to object.

Sachael pushed him toward the door. "She needs cleaning up, and she'll appreciate all the pretty things you have to say to her after she's in a fresh gown and has her hair combed. Out."

The midwife closed the door. She turned and smiled at Kale.

"Now, haven't you got the most beautiful boy baby in the whole world?"

Kale sighed contentedly. *Yes, I do.*

For the three days that Kale stayed inside with her husband and baby, Mot Angra slept soundly. Her friends came to see the baby. Brunstetter knelt outside the window and held the baby like a butterfly in his huge palm. Sir Dar said he got the first smile out of Penn. Tulanny said it was a gas pain. Seezle said Penn smiled in his sleep when he dreamed of kimens. The meech community paraded through, offering their congratulations, small trinkets, and tiny bags of potent herbal tea. The fragrance from the teabags gave the room a pleasant air.

Lee Ark showed Kale how to hold the baby with his little tummy on her forearm when he fussed. She already knew to do that from helping marione housewives with their fussy babies. But Lee Ark was so pleased to help, she nodded and smiled and accepted his advice.

Finally, Regidor came to see her. The others cleared out of the room to give them time alone. When Regidor peeked at the baby, tears sprang to his eyes.

"One coming into the world, one going out."

Kale gasped. "Gilda?"

"She's not going to make it, Kale. She doesn't want to."

"Oh, Regidor, I should have sat with her. She probably thinks I don't care."

The meech barely shook his head to disagree. "She didn't want you there. And"—he sighed deeply—"she probably hasn't thought of you once in all the time she's been fading away. All she thinks about is herself, really. Her cosmos is the strange things she has decided are important. I don't believe even I am within that isolated circle."

"How can that be, Regidor? You love her so."

He shrugged and wiggled his hand above the baby.

Penn swung his tiny fist in the air and caught one of Regidor's fingers. Kale tried to absorb the knowledge that Regidor's wife lay dying and he was cooing at her child. It boggled her mind that her sophisticated meech friend cooed at all.

"You're making faces," she said.

"Of course, I'm making faces. That's what you do with an infant."

"How do you know what to do with an infant?"

Regidor looked briefly nonplussed, then he grinned. "I must have read it in a book somewhere during my vast studies of libraries in every city of our fair land."

Kale choked on a laugh. Regidor helped her sit up and thumped her back. Penn started to cry, and Fly zipped across the covers to stand on his little chest. He immediately calmed.

Regidor gave Kale a glass of water when she could hold it, then laughed at her when she spilt it down her front. He mopped her up with a towel.

When Kale could talk, she glared at him. "What are you trying to do? Drown me?"

"Nah, just freshen you up a bit." Regidor eyed the little blue dragon standing protectively on the baby's blanket. "Is this the famous spitfire dragon?"

"This is Fly, Penn's minor dragon."

Regidor laughed and pulled up the stool again to sit beside her bed. "I hear she bites."

"Not so much now that Penn is out where she can see him. Fly really had me stumped, Reg. I couldn't figure out what her problem was."

"And now you know?"

"She was mad at me for keeping her baby prisoner inside my stomach."

Regidor laughed again, his rich, deep laugh. Hearing it made Kale's heart lighter. They bantered over the food and the furniture they'd found in Bility. Then they talked quietly about the history of the town and Mot Angra and, on a note of wonder, what could be Toopka's role in the danger they faced.

"Could it be," Regidor speculated, "that the egg will hatch an equally powerful but good dragon?"

"As far as I can tell, Regidor, it is only shaped like an egg. I'm not convinced that it will hatch into anything. But Toopka has been as happy as any carefree child ever since Wulder removed it from her chest."

"And gave Sittiponder his sight." Sadness fell on Regidor once more.

"What is it, friend?" asked Kale.

"It's been good to sit with you, Kale. For a while I could put away the horror Gilda has brought upon us."

Kale gasped. "What do you mean?"

"Oh, I don't mean us, the community. I mean us, the couple, Gilda and myself. She's taken the precious love we had and tossed it aside. Sometimes I'm so angry, I would like to leave her to her moods and rants and misery.

"I want Gilda to discover joy again. I want her to see her self-destruction. I love her and want to shake her to make her see how her hold on life is riddled with falsehoods, and it is those lies that are killing her. She doesn't listen. She doesn't believe. There is no way I can tie her to a post and keep her from slipping away."

Kale touched his hand. "I think Wulder must feel that way at times." Regidor squinted one eye at her, so she continued. "He has always given us reason to draw near, always fed us truth through word and deed. Yet we, as His people, continue to harbor false expectations, trading a glorious reality for a shabby imitation of truth."

Regidor remained silent, staring off, in his own world of thoughts.

Kale let him wander a bit, then brought him back with a question. "Regidor, what have you been doing while keeping Gilda company?"

"I've been building a gateway."

"You have!"

He nodded and twisted his lips into a puzzled frown. "This gateway has been the hardest thing to construct, and basically, it is an ordinary portal. Not as fancy as the talking gateways."

"Mine quit working."

"So did mine. I think we are too close to that source of power that fuels Mot Angra. The power of his wickedness generates a disturbance to natural laws for miles around."

Kale nodded, although she only partially grasped this concept.

"The animals who attacked Gilda and me as we came closer, I think were driven by the madness of Mot Angra."

"Why you and not us?" Kale nestled her baby closer to her side, marveling at his tiny nose, long dark eyelashes, and pink pursed lips. Fly settled on her shoulder, a perch that gave her a good view of the room.

"Because Mot Angra knows and hates the meech." Regidor slapped his knees. "But the gateway is constructed, complete. It is probably the strongest gateway in the world. I had to reinforce almost every strand to keep each one from slipping out of place."

"Where does it go?"

He chortled. "Where does it not go?" Regidor stood and then bent to kiss Kale's forehead. "I have talked with the others. Seezle is going for help. She will bring back Paladin and every wizard and knight and fighting man loyal to him. The next time Mot Angra stirs, he will face a formidable army of Wulder's people."

Kale looked up at Regidor, a strong warrior himself, whose shoulders drooped with sorrow. "I'm not so sure a big army will defeat our enemy, Regidor."

"This may be true, Kale. But until Wulder reveals another plan, we must be ready."

He left, and Kale continued to muse. She shifted her son to rest on her chest with his head on her shoulder. "One small weapon piercing one vulnerable spot. I think that is what will defeat the foe, Penn."

49

Words Unknown

An influx of warriors, knights, and wizards flooded the meech village, and still, the treacherous dragon slept. On the third day, Paladin arrived. In the evening, he went with the men who would chant in the cave. Some of these men would also deliver food and water to Mot Angra. Bardon and the other warriors tagged along but did not enter the cave. They circled the entrance at a distance and awaited orders from Paladin.

The leader of Amara wore his finest royal garb and on his shoulder sat the purple dragon, Metta, with her head held high. Bardon had been astonished that Paladin requested the minor dragon to accompany him. Paladin had winked and said, "The singing dragon and I are riding on a hunch."

Bardon saw their leader hesitate at the opening. He knew that feeling. The darkness in the cave was not due to lack of light. Bardon felt the oppression even thirty feet away.

Paladin turned and his eyes met Bardon's. *"Come with me."*

Bardon's hand clenched around the hilt of his sword. He wanted to say, "No, thank you. I've been in once, and once is enough." But he bit his tongue and walked quickly to stand at Paladin's side.

Paladin spoke in an undertone. "I want you to tell me if you see or feel anything different from the first time you witnessed this place."

Bardon nodded. He couldn't speak around the lump in his throat. His experience with the cave consisted of his visit plus the secondhand knowledge from Pat, who had followed the men coming here in the middle of the night. The images Pat projected into his mind disturbed him far more than his memories of his own visit.

Paladin looked Bardon in the eye. "A monstrous evil should take your breath away. But breathe, comrade. Wulder gives life and breath.

What the monster has taken away, we shall claim again, for Wulder bequeaths it to us."

The meech men filed into the cave, carrying torches, and lining up in rows. Their chant started with a low hum that crescendoed to the first spoken word. Paladin and Bardon watched from under the beautifully painted wall. Over the heads of the chanters, the black, glistening paint on the opposite wall caught the flickers of torchlight. The fierce dragon in the drawing seemed to flex its muscles. His chest appeared to draw in and out as if panting. Even the great yellowed eyes swept back and forth over the mere mortals at its feet.

"Enough!" shouted Paladin and strode to the front of the men. "Stop and learn the words you were told to sing."

The voices stilled, not at once, but with a staggering that hinted of fear. Afraid to continue, afraid to stop. Most of the men's eyes shifted away from Paladin's strong figure to the gaping black hole at the back of the cavern.

Paladin pointed to a young meech in the front row. "Sing the first line of your chant."

The man cleared his throat and sang huskily, "O-gitaks to who Derfor ess soo."

Paladin opened his mouth and sang the phrase again. "Oh, give thanks to Wulder, for He is good."

The words echoed off the walls. As the phrase bounced from wall to wall, Bardon could see how the individual sounds lost their shape and became distorted from the original. But with Paladin's force of conviction, the first words hung in his heart, and the echoes faded.

Paladin pointed to the next meech. "The second line."

This man sang with more strength. "Foress mur sees indoors forests rivers."

Paladin sang. "For His mercies endure forever and ever."

Metta bounced on Paladin's shoulder as he again pointed.

"Ike awl to who der indess."

Paladin shook his head. "You've moved a word that belongs with this phrase and tacked it to the beginning of the next. The word you sing as rest is really the second part of distress." He threw back his head and intoned, "I call to Wulder in distress."

With the next meech in line, he said, "Sing after 'rest' to the end of this stanza of the chant."

"Who Der and sir me and set me inbraw de Plae sess."

This time Paladin crooned the words with infinite love in his voice, and Metta trilled with him, filling out the fullness of the words. "Wulder answered me and set me in broad places."

He then took the bucket of water from one of the carriers. "Show me where this Mot Angra sleeps." He turned to look at Bardon. "Want to come?"

The words, the real words, of the song had bolstered Bardon's courage. He liked the loud, plaintive notes of "I called to Wulder in distress." And the answer soothed with a reflection of the same melody pattern but in a different key and tone. He hummed "and set me in broad places" as he picked up another bucket and joined Paladin.

Dread of the deeper cavern rippled across Bardon's skin, but the torches shone brighter than he expected. He sang with the men as they incanted "Wulder answered me and set me in broad places" with skill.

Many times, Bardon had received Pat's images of the activities in Mot Angra's cave. The visit to this place had disturbed the little dragon, and he didn't seem to be able to shake the memory. Bardon clearly saw the difference between that evening and this one. Even with the undercurrent of fear and apprehension, Bardon knew this ceremony had more hope infused in the performance.

The air thickened with moisture and a heavy perfume as they descended. The fragrance filled Bardon's nostrils and nearly choked him. The vocalization ceased as the party of men used shallow breathing to keep from absorbing the cloying aroma into their lungs. With the muffling of distance, the group of singers in the entry cave could still be heard.

A nerve-grating noise replaced their pleasant music. The wheeze of a big beast inhaling, then a slight rumble as it exhaled made Bardon aware of the living creature somewhere close by.

They came to a hot cavern. Bardon could only guess at the size of the underground room. Their torches cut through the dense darkness for no more than a few feet in any direction, but his inner sense told him he could walk a great distance before finding the opposite wall.

The meech hurried about their task, moving quietly on the stone floor to positions where they propped the torches in wooden holders. The man with the recently slain deer walked into the dark with two men carrying torches close at his shoulders. Paladin and Bardon followed with their lights lifted to dispense the gloom.

On the floor, a spot smeared with blood marked where the next meal would be placed. Careful to not make a sound, the food-bearer crept closer and gently eased the carcass out of his arms, not letting it drop, but sliding the deer down to rest in front of a black rock.

The rock, however, twitched. Bardon realized he was looking at one nostril of an extremely large beast. The steady in and out of air halted, then started again. The nose quivered. The meech men backed away, pushing Paladin and Bardon away as well.

The rockish form rolled, revealing a slash of mouth. The mouth opened, and gleaming teeth shone in the torchlight. The teeth clicked twice and parted. A thin red tongue slid out, snaking toward the deer carcass. The tip touched the rough fur, tapped down the body until it reached blood, then passed back and forth over the wound. The tongue licked until no more blood caked the fur. The serpentine end wrapped around the corpse and dragged the slain animal toward the mouth, past the lips, over the ridge of teeth, and into the depths of the throat.

A meech signaled by waving a torch in an arc. The men who delivered the deer trudged away from the beast, and those carrying buckets passed them as they went down to pour water into a trough carved in the stone floor. Paladin and Bardon emptied their buckets, then joined the men as they convened at the cavern entrance.

"He didn't chew," Bardon whispered to Paladin.

"Apparently, he swallows his dinner whole." Paladin followed the meech as they retraced their steps to the outer cave. "If his snout is taller than our meech friends, how big do you think his body might be?"

Bardon walked beside his commander for a few moments before he answered, "Big."

Paladin rubbed his jaw. "What do you think his weak points might be?"

"He's so heavy, I wonder if he can fly."

They walked faster as they left Mot Angra behind than when they carried the beast's meal to him.

Bardon puzzled over what little they could see. The feeling of pent-up evil radiated from the beast, but his sluggish manner did not threaten them in the least. However, the meech said the dragon had been known to suddenly awake, grab one of the meech, and then go back to sleep. That prospect unnerved the men who took down Mot Angra's food.

Bardon took a deep breath of the fresh air as they reached the outer chamber. He stopped to survey the scene. The meech faces relaxed, losing their apprehensive expressions.

Paladin strode to face the men. "Mot Angra has a weakness, and we shall find it." He surveyed the solemn crowd. "I would like a few questions answered, please."

Seslie came forward. "Yes sir."

Paladin pointed to the wonderful eruption of color on one wall. The painting depicted a tableau of plants and animals, a blue sky and radiant sun. In one corner, a swirl of beautiful colors exploded from a dark background.

"Who painted this mural here?" asked Paladin. "And what is its meaning?"

"We don't know," said Seslie. "It has always been here."

Paladin pointed to the monstrous black dragon on the opposite wall. "And that?"

Those in the room stirred, and Seslie eagerly answered. "We know of that artist. He lived ten generations ago. He drew Mot Angra so that we would remember why our vigil is important. So we would not forget our purpose."

Paladin nodded sadly. "A mistake has been made." He pointed to the lovely drawing. "This painting was to keep you from forgetting your purpose. You were not to forget the Creator, the One whose glory is seen in living things. I don't know if Wulder drew that for you Himself, or if He commissioned one of your ancestors right after your people came through to this new world."

With a scowl, he turned to examine the dragon's likeness. "Scrub that from the stone. We do not concentrate on evil. When you chant, you focus on the entrance to the evil one's lair. From now on, turn your eyes to the wonders of Wulder. No longer will the treacherous Mot Angra look down on you as you sing of Wulder's greatness. His likeness is not to be allowed here. Even the appearance of evil is forbidden."

Paladin grandly gestured toward the first painting. "Come, men, we are not forsaken. Wulder, who is portrayed in that image, is your Guide and Protector."

The earth trembled, the rocks groaned, and Paladin glared at the hole leading to Mot Angra. "Your time is coming, evil one. Your days are numbered."

—50—

A Surprise

Kale had come to this room for two reasons—to greet her parents and to say goodbye to Gilda. On one side of the small chamber, a curtain separated Gilda's deathbed from the flow of people coming to the expected battle with Mot Angra. The other wall shimmered where Regidor had built a gateway. Kale shifted baby Penn from one shoulder to the other. When she moved him, Fly raced across the back of her neck to sit beside his head.

Holding the edge of Kale's wizard robe, Toopka eyed the furnishings of the room. "Not much here," she said. She tilted her head as she examined the gateway. "Kale, why did Regidor weave the word *hope* in there?"

She pointed to the right side of the portal. Kale looked and squinted and tilted her head at the same angle as Toopka's.

"I don't see a word."

Toopka blew out a puff of air that clearly said Kale was blind. Kale's lips twitched at the girl's impatience.

The surface of the gateway rippled, riveting Kale's attention to the portal. She hoped this time her mother and father would step through. She and Toopka had already greeted several wizards, a knight, and a swordsmith. These people reminded Kale of the grim confrontation approaching. She wanted to share the joy of Penn and forget, for the moment, the battle ahead.

She glanced over her shoulder at the curtain. She'd peeked around the edge when she came in and spoken to Regidor. She'd spoken to Gilda as well but received no response.

"Kale." Her mother stepped through the gateway and embraced her daughter. "Oh, look, isn't he perfect? Let me hold him. Ouch! What in all of Amara was that for?"

Kale stifled a giggle. "Are you hurt?"

Lyll glared at the blue dragon who puffed up her chest. She looked back at her finger. "Just a pinch."

"What's this?" asked Sir Kemry. "A protector dragon? How very convenient. How did you arrange that, my dear? You didn't say you had kept an egg for such a purpose."

"I didn't. I didn't know you could designate a protector."

Kemry and Lyll exchanged a glance. Sir Kemry shook his head woefully. "Another instance where our choice of how our daughter would live has caused her education to be insufficient."

Lyll patted his arm. "We saved her life. She would have had no education at all if Risto had found her and killed her."

Sir Kemry brightened immediately. "That's true." He reached for the baby. "Fly, I'm the grandfather. Behave yourself."

The blue dragon sulked, head down and wings drooping, but she allowed Penn to be transferred to Kemry and then to Lyll. They cooed over the baby, and he obligingly woke up enough to give them an adorable smile with only a little spot of milky drool at one corner.

A piercing scream shattered the calm. Regidor fell back through the curtain, ripping the material from the bar that held it aloft. Gilda stood on the bed, backed into the corner against the wall. With her hands covering her mouth, she continued the high-pitched screech.

Toopka cowered at the foot of the bed, holding something behind her back.

Sir Kemry's eyebrows shot up. "I thought Lady Gilda was within a minute of passing on."

Lady Lyll put a hand over Penn's ear and pressed his head against her shoulder to muffle the other ear.

Regidor scrambled to his feet, Gilda's shriek subsided to a loud moan, and she pointed one shaky finger at Toopka. Gilda's husband lifted her down from the bed, and she cowered in his arms.

"Hmm?" Kale scrutinized the doneel. "Toopka has not done anything particularly naughty in days."

"That's unusual," said Lady Lyll.

"Very," said Kale.

Kemry chortled. "I believe she's broken her good behavior streak."

Kale marched over and crouched beside the trembling child. She schooled her face to be nonthreatening and her voice to be gentle. "What did you do, Toopka?"

Toopka brought her hands out from behind her back. In one rested her egg. "Regidor was asleep."

Now Regidor guided Gilda to sit on the bed. Her thin body trembled in his arms.

"Regidor slept, and what did you do?" prompted Kale.

"Lady Gilda was pretty. She looked sweet and comfortable, but she wasn't breathing."

Kale glanced quickly at the meech lady sitting next to her husband on the side of the bed. Never in all the years she had known Gilda did she ever think the dragon looked "sweet." "And?"

"I touched her lips with my egg."

"Why?"

Toopka's head wobbled back and forth. Her eyes grew bigger. "I don't know."

"The egg burned," gasped Gilda. "My lips burned, and the heat swept through me. The inside of my head held a flame brighter than the sun. My heart contained fire, coals, red hot—" she stopped, closed her eyes, and breathed slowly, evenly, without shuddering. "Wulder spoke to me."

Her eyes popped open, and she searched the corners of the room. Then her eyes fell to her lap. "He told me I was the most foolish of women, and He would show me His Truth. For a moment I entered into a place of perfect peace and all knowledge. I knew the secrets of the universe. I knew the value of each particle created by Wulder. My own being held a darkness, and I was ashamed." With tears running down her cheeks, she looked up at Regidor and placed a hand on his cheek. "Wulder gave me a choice. I could stay in that place, and He would treat me with all the love and dignity that I had never earned, or I could come back and demonstrate to others the grace and mercy He'd revealed to me. I love you, Regidor. Will you take me back?"

Kale guided Toopka away from the couple as they embraced. She and her parents left the room. In the plain common room of the meech household, they gathered around Toopka. She still held out her hand. Kale touched the small egg nestled there.

"Cold," she said.

"Wulder touched Gilda," said Lady Lyll.

"Yes," agreed Sir Kemry, "but it appears He used Toopka and this very small egg."

"Am I in trouble?" asked Toopka.

Kale knelt beside the doneel and wrapped her arms around her. "No, little one. Not at all."

Kale looked up to see Bardon standing in the door.

"I just happened to be passing and decided to stop by to see my son." Grinning, he walked to the cradle, stood gazing at the slumbering cherub, then bent to kiss Penn's fuzzy head. The blond curls looked nothing like Kale's or his hair.

Kale continued sorting small shirts and britches. "Look at all the clothing the meech ladies brought. They love contributing to Penn's wardrobe." Kale stuck her fingers through the seat of one of the garments and laughed. "Of course, I have to stitch the seam where a meech baby's tail would stick out."

Bardon glanced up, smiled, and returned to studying the sleeping child. He spoke softly. "We're making great progress in training the men. Most are seasoned warriors and fall into their roles quite naturally. The younger men are eager and attentive.

"I passed Gilda twice in the streets. Since she insisted on moving out of the gateway chamber, she has mingled on a grand scale." Bardon stroked Penn's cheek with a fingertip.

"Are you trying to wake him?" asked Kale.

"Of course not." Bardon pulled up a chair and sat where he could peer over the edge of the cradle at his son. "Gilda rarely stays in her room, or even in the house. She seems to have decided she is going to meet every meech in the village."

"She came by here this morning."

Bardon looked at her expectantly.

"She was nice." Kale shrugged. "The whole visit was strange. She cooed over Penn. She said her egg was in a building especially designed for keeping the village eggs until the designated years for hatching. She and Regidor are going to choose the first of the three years to have their egg quickened, and she asked me if I would do the honor. Bardon, they're planning to live here."

A tap on the door interrupted Bardon's response.

Sir Dar answered the summons to enter. "Holt is here. He just came through the portal with a surprise."

"What?" asked Kale and Bardon together.

"He's brought us the Followers' Voice."

As they passed through the common room, Kale noticed Tulanny had dropped the knitting she was working on and bolted for the door.

"Am I right in thinking that Tulanny's son is the Voice?" she asked.

"Yes," answered Sir Dar. "He didn't return to his hometown willingly. Holt has gathered quite a group of men who will have to answer to Paladin for their actions."

The ground rumbled beneath their feet.

"That's the first time that has happened in several days." Bardon grabbed Kale's moonbeam cape and covered his wife and son. They waited for a minute, expecting a barrage of the small black dragons.

"Perhaps they went south," suggested Kale after a time.

"Perhaps," said Sir Dar. "Come to the gateway chamber and meet this crowd Holt has brought us."

As they walked through the streets, a lehman caught up with them to report to Bardon.

"Sir!" The young marione saluted. "A horde of black dragons attacked the camp outside the mouth of the cave. The assault was unanticipated, and we have a number of casualties." He stood a little taller, and Kale detected a gleam in his eye. "The entire force against us was slain."

Bardon saluted. "Thank you, Lehman. Continue with your reports."

The marione sped off to find the next officer to whom he should relay his news.

"I don't like this," said Sir Dar.

"I don't either," said Kale. "I don't like them attacking me, but at least the pattern was predictable." She paused. "I was going to send Gymn to help, but he is already on his way. Let's see about Holt, then I'll go to the camp."

A tremor vibrated their feet.

"Small," said Bardon, "but too close to the first one."

They hurried to the house where Regidor had constructed a gateway. With the owners' consent, Paladin now used the building as headquarters.

When they came close to the building, they found Lee Ark dividing the prisoners into manageable groups and assigning different squadrons to be in charge of their confinement. An unusual number of kimens also occupied the grounds, and Kale assumed the small people had aided Holt in his capture of the ringleaders.

Kale leaned close to Bardon and whispered, "I wonder where Holt is."

"I wonder where Tulanny and her son are."

Sir Dar led the way through the crowd and, with a cursory knock, opened a door to a side room. Paladin bade them to enter.

Paladin sat behind his desk. Tulanny sat weeping beside a stoic meech who seemed not to focus on anything in the room. Several men in echo garb stood away from the others.

Holt leaned against the far wall, a sling on one arm and a bandage around his brow. Kale marveled that he cut a dashing, romantic figure, even with the haggard look of a man straight from battle. Regidor's presence surprised her.

Paladin stood when he saw Kale enter with her baby. Regidor scooted a chair from the row against the wall and placed it next to Tulanny. Kale took the seat and reached over to hold Tulanny's hand.

"We have come to a decision," Paladin said as he again sat behind his desk. "The Voice, whose real name is Dander, will be escorted to my palace and kept in the dungeon. Tulanny will accompany him and live in the palace so that she can be near Dander and be assured of his well-being. Holt has brought us a group of echoes. These men will be incarcerated as well. Holt has also managed to detain a group of men not in the inner circle."

He glanced at Holt, and a small smile lifted the corner of his mouth. "I appreciate that you did not bring them along. After we've settled our business with Mot Angra, we'll send council members to interview these Followers individually, and the state of their hearts and minds will be determined. Those whose characters are not hardened in the heretical doctrine will be given a chance to put aside their allegiance to the Voice. With counseling, I'm sure many will see how they were led astray by fancy rhetoric."

Paladin studied Dander's impassive expression. He glanced at Tulanny's miserable countenance, then turned to Regidor and nodded for him to come forward. "Regidor, I put Dander and his mother in your care. Please, escort them through the portal at once. Establish them at my palace and return as soon as possible."

Regidor first opened the door and commandeered several officers. He explained they would be escorting the prisoners to the dungeon. With only the soft sobs of a despairing mother, the room cleared. Paladin's soldiers took the prisoners back through the portal to the palace. Paladin excused himself and left to look over the prisoners being held outside his headquarters. Only Kale, Penn, Fly, Bardon, and Holt remained. Holt came to sit next to Kale.

"May I see him?" he asked. He reached for the blanket and drew back quickly at Fly's hiss.

Kale giggled. "Don't take offense, Holt. We haven't labeled you as a ne'er-do-well who must not associate with our son. Fly treats everyone as if they are too lowly to look at her boy." Kale addressed the guardian. "Holt may hold the baby."

"Wait! I didn't say I wanted to hold him. One peek will be sufficient."

"Oh, that's right. Your arm." Kale looked sympathetic. "Does it hurt much?"

"It's not the arm. I could manage holding a sword if I needed to, but not a baby."

Penn yawned and smacked his lips.

Holt tilted his head and bent a wee bit closer. "He *is* cute."

The room shuddered.

"That's the third quake since I've been here." Holt stood. "Is there a place to clean up? Are there clothes other than these dratted Follower robes?"

"Let's wait just a minute to see if the black dragons come this way." Kale wrapped the blanket closer around Penn and got up. "I'm proud of you, Holt. You've done a good thing."

Holt rubbed his hand across the back of his neck. "I suppose you'll find this hard to believe, and, Bardon, you can laugh at me if you choose, but I enjoyed doing it. Every time I disengaged someone from the Follower's hold, I felt lighter somehow. Strange for me to be operating under no ulterior motive."

Bardon slapped him on the back. "You did have an ulterior motive, my friend."

"No, really," Holt protested. "I wasn't doing it for show. The good Mardell already approved of me."

"I disagree," said Bardon, ignoring Kale's disapproving glare. "The ulterior motive was to clean yourself of guilt for what you finally realized were your nefarious ways. And you were showing yourself that you could do honorable deeds."

Holt frowned. "Well, is that bad?"

"Not in the least. But understand this, Holt. If you died today, you would be accepted into Wulder's other home for us. You don't have to present a list of good deeds. There is no magic number of how many times you have to do the right thing before you are granted admission."

Holt released an exaggerated sigh. "So I can go back to being a lazy bum?"

Bardon laughed. "You don't want to. You enjoy being Wulder's man."

They left the sanctuary of Paladin's office and edged through the crowd. A soldier asked Bardon to come settle a dispute. Kale told him she was going to the camp to see to the injured. Once at the outside door, she and Holt surveyed the skies. No horde appeared over the southern houses. In the street, Holt produced his most charming smile and offered Kale his arm.

A mighty quake rattled the village. Houses shook, windows crashed out of the walls, and fences twisted around the well-manicured lawns. The street beneath Kale and Holt rippled, squeezing pieces of the cobblestone out. The stones flew into the air and thudded where they dropped.

Holt clasped Kale and Penn in his uninjured arm to steady them, but they all fell. The marione pulled Kale around so she fell on top of him and not on the stones. Kale was grateful for the cushion between her and the ground and more grateful that she managed to keep Penn safe in her arms.

In a moment the earth stilled. They stayed where they were for a moment, then sat up. Bardon charged out of headquarters and came to Kale's side.

"Are you hurt?" he asked.

"No," Kale answered.

Fly flew in circles trying to get close enough to examine her child.

Bardon looked at Penn, pulling back the cover. The baby blinked and cooed. Fly landed on Kale's shoulder and leaned as close as she could get to Penn.

Bardon turned to Holt. "You?"

"Fine."

Bardon helped Kale get to her feet, then offered Holt a hand. People began to move around. None of the houses had collapsed. A strange, sweet odor wafted through the streets, getting stronger with each breeze from the south.

Kale sniffed and thought the smell unpleasant. She started to ask Bardon if he knew what it was. A shiver ran down her spine, her flesh reacted with tiny bumps, and she held her breath as if she suddenly felt the presence of a beast of prey.

From above the forest, she heard a steady beat of wings. A roar heralded the approach of a great creature. The bellow paralyzed her with fear. Penn cried. Bardon grabbed her arm and they ran, but Kale had no idea where they could go.

Like a shadow of a cloud racing across the landscape, a huge black dragon sailed across the sky.

51

The Price of Peace

Bardon watched the dragon disappear over the rim of the cliff. Paladin ran out of headquarters and conferred with his commanders, giving orders and pointing in several different directions. Bardon took a step toward Paladin. The men he had been training would need Bardon to lead.

"Kale, you had better seek cover with Penn."

She grabbed his arm. "The people at the cave!"

He looked deeply into her eyes, letting her thoughts mix with his. He kissed her soundly, then touched his son's head with his lips. With his forehead pressed to Kale's, he couldn't say all that was in his heart, but he knew she understood, and that eased the pain of parting. He released her. "Yes, go help at the cave."

She raced off toward the forest path, and he turned on his heel to report to his leader. Holt followed Bardon.

Paladin welcomed them with a grim nod. "Regidor and Gilda have flown to locate Mot Angra. Position your men on the east rim of the canyon for the time being. Kimens will be carrying our messages. Holt, stay with me for now."

Bardon gathered his men and ordered them to muster out with weapons and camping gear.

"I don't know if we'll be back to Bility any time soon."

He led them to the crack in the canyon wall that was the easiest exit to the outside world. Other units gathered there, and Bardon and his men took their turn hiking out single file. From there they doubled back and climbed a stiff slope that brought them to a spot where they could survey the canyon and the plains. From their vantage point, Bardon could see many of the other brigades setting up defense positions.

In the canyon he saw a great crater where the cave had been. The wall with the image of Wulder's creation stood exposed to the sunlight. The opposite wall had crumbled. A deeper pit into the mountain must have been where Mot Angra burst through to the open air. To one side on the canyon floor, warriors struggled to reestablish a camp. The departing dragon had made a passing blow at the men stationed there to guard the entrance of the cave.

What had the monster done? Swiped his tail across the tents? There was no sign of fire. Could Mot Angra not breathe fire? That would be a blessing. *Better not count on a smokeless dragon.* Bardon signaled his minor dragon to come to him.

"Mikkai, survey the area. I'd like to know where our strengths and weaknesses are."

The minor dragon took off and returned four hours later. Bardon sat down and sketched out Mikkai's report, making a credible map of the placement of their troops.

"No Mot Angra?" Bardon puzzled over the whereabouts of such a huge adversary. *Where is he hiding?*

Bardon sent the rolled parchment map to Paladin by a kimen courier. By return messenger he learned Regidor and Gilda had seen nothing of Mot Angra in their flight over the plain.

The sun set. Cook fires sprang up, fragrant with the smell of burning wood and various stews. Chill air crept through the mountain trees and sent tendrils of frost across the plains. The grass crunched as Bardon walked from one fire to the next and spoke to his men.

He stopped last at the rim of the canyon. The design of the houses hid the village lights, but where the dragon had knocked down trees, Bardon could see the camp near the cave.

The remains of the cave. Are you there tonight, Kale? Did you return to the village? Is Penn fussy or quiet? Did you find your parents and Gymn? Are they safe? I'd appreciate having Regidor's wings. I'd fly down and see for myself—

He heard Kale's laughter and turned quickly, but no one stood near his lonely spot.

"I can hear you. And I think the image of you with wings is funny."

You can hear me? I'd think this would be too far, especially with all the trouble you've been having with your wizard skills.

"Troubles with my wizardry have all but vanished. Regidor is back to full steam as well. We've been theorizing all evening as to what caused the dampening of our effectiveness."

How's Penn?

"Adorable. He's so alert! Fly tells me when he's wet or hungry. She's a tyrant and wants her baby attended to immediately. She'll spoil him for sure."

No chance of our spoiling him.

Her delightful laugh rippled through his mind. *"None whatsoever."* She paused. *"I hate the waiting."*

Yes, I'd rather locate Mot Angra and storm his location.

"I'm amazed at what little damage he did on his way out. There are injuries, but very minor. He knocked over trees and tents and left."

Bardon sniffed the air. *I smell him. That nauseating sweet odor. Warn the others! You and the baby get under cover.*

He ran back toward the camp, hearing voices raised in the distance. The men grabbed weapons as they ran to their posts.

The calls to one another didn't sound frantic, as if these men had never faced an enemy of superior strength. But the confusion of an unseen foe of unpredictable action stirred the tension and brewed an uneasy wariness.

"Where is he?"

"At least the moon is full."

"I hear the beat of his wings."

"The smell's getting stronger."

Bardon took his position under a ring of cover with a fire at the center. He prepared his bow, took an arrow from the supply by the fire, and waited.

The camp grew quiet. A great shadow loomed over the grassland. Strong wings steadily beat the air. The beast passed over one of the camps east of Bardon's brigade. Mot Angra shuddered and from his body showered scales.

The mass fell like dead weights, then scattered as the discarded pieces transformed into fighting black dragons. This was the battle Paladin's army had prepared for. What to do with Mot Angra was a mystery. But these dragons, the size of a man's thumb, spat fire and stung. They also died.

The men focused on the swarming foe. Bardon stuck the tip of his arrow into the fire. The end erupted in flame. He straightened, pulled back his bowstring, aimed, and released. His arrow shot into the onslaught of black dragons along with a hundred other burning shafts from this camp alone.

Volley after volley of blazing arrows penetrated the oncoming cloud. The close formation of the beasts' flight acted to the warriors' advantage. The blazes struck and ignited one dragon, and those flying too close were also engulfed in flame. The dragons flew straight into the counterattack, losing three-fourths of their throng before they got within range to do any damage to Paladin's army.

When the remnant of the horde swooped into camp, Bardon and his men picked up torches and swung at the invaders. Whereas in previous attacks the horde had flown on quickly, these beasts circled and struck again and again. The men had counted on this part of the fight to be merely a show of force before the mass flew on. However, they found themselves in earnest combat with beasts so small and quick they were difficult to hit. The knights threw down their clumsy, flaming clubs and drew their swords. As the number of dragons diminished, the men could target those who had picked one man to bombard.

Bardon sighed with relief as he sliced the last one tormenting him. He turned and saw three tiny beasts harassing another warrior. He came from behind and downed one the next time it made a pass. As if to prove the creatures had no ability to rethink strategy in the middle of an engagement, the last two returned in exactly the same pattern as before. The warrior dispatched one, and Bardon eliminated the other.

Small grass fires presented the next immediate problem. The men soaked blankets and beat out the flames where blazing dragons had fallen to the ground. Fortunately, most had burned out before thudding into the undergrowth.

Just as the men's rush of energy generated from battle abated, Mot

Angra appeared again in the sky. A roar from the mighty dragon sent shivers down their backs and put goose flesh on the arms of many hard-ened warriors. The black monster sailed overhead and shook loose a sec-ond barrage of scales.

Weary men picked up their bows.

"Our strategy works, men. Do not lose heart."

Again they fired into the cloud of oncoming dragons. Again they ended the fight in close combat. This time as the men stomped out fires and beat flames into the ground, they picked up fallen arrows. Some were merely stubs and had to be discarded. Others could be used once more.

Mot Angra did not roar as he came back into view. This time the sound resembled a sinister laugh, one that mocked the men who had to struggle with each advance of the enemy. The monster roared with glee as he shook loose another layer of scales.

The men nocked charred shafts onto their ready bows and took aim.

52

Visit with an Old Man

Paladin walked through the camp after the end of the next attack. The men brought back wood for the fire but no arrows. The moon hovered over the horizon and did not give enough light to see the stubs of their spent arrows. Paladin spoke to the men, praising them for their courage and fortitude. He stopped to comfort those wounded, and he walked by the empty quivers before moving on to the next camp.

"Look," said a warrior as he brought an armload of wood to feed their fire. "Look at that!"

A hundred arrows stuck like porcupine quills in each quiver. Pitch filled the pots to overflowing.

Mot Angra roared in the distance, and the worn soldiers laughed.

"Come on, you blistering behemoth. We're ready for you!" yelled one of the men. The warriors around him cheered and fired.

The next attack seemed less frantic than the last, and when Mot Angra passed over again, Bardon knew why. The dragon had run out of scales. The black dragons that attacked right after Paladin passed through the camp had little fire, and their stings only irritated the men's skin slightly. The last foray consisted of tiny buglike creatures. Most dropped from the air in exhaustion before they got to the camp.

In the morning, scouts scoured the countryside and found no trace of Mot Angra. Paladin called for a meeting of his leaders, and Bardon went down to the village.

"It would be best to attack Mot Angra now, while his defenses are low." He hit his fist into the palm of his other hand. "We need a library and a good librarian. Regidor?"

"The gateway can be used to go to Fenworth's library at Bardon's home. And our talking gateways are working again."

"Good. See if you can learn anything about this beast. What is its weakness?"

Regidor nodded, stood, and walked out of the room. Bardon wondered as his meech friend bypassed the room where he'd built the portal and went out the front door. Where was he going first before following Paladin's orders? To see Gilda, Bardon presumed. That would make sense. A smile lifted the corner of his mouth. Gilda was no longer a person to avoid.

Paladin's next instructions could have been issued by any man there. Transport food to the vicinity and move the wounded through the gateway to a more secure location. Replenish the supply of arrows and make ready other weapons. Most importantly, stay alert and patrol the area looking for signs of Mot Angra.

Bardon strode away from headquarters, frustrated and on edge. Filia would go with Regidor through the gateway and help Librettowit search for old lore about the monstrous black dragon. But if the meech had no records, would Librettowit? And hadn't that avenue been exhausted already? Were they reduced to last-ditch efforts to come up with answers?

He passed Regidor, who gave him a cavalier salute. Filia rode on his shoulder.

"On your way to Librettowit's library?" asked Bardon.

Regidor winked. "I have researched all the great libraries of Amara. I've never seen any literature on Mot Angra. I don't expect to find any now."

"Before, you searched for cures for Gilda's condition."

"That's true. Filia and I will dig in the ancient tomes for a bit and then return to aid in a more practical manner."

"May Wulder surprise you, my friend." Bardon returned the casual salute and continued toward his goal.

As he marched through the village, he saw different craftsmen set up to do their work. A row of tents accommodated a number of people making arrows. As a bundle of shafts was ready, a child took the bundle to the open-air blacksmith. After he fitted a metal tip on the ends, the child took the unfinished arrows to the artisan who attached the feathers. Other tents had been erected for the making of additional weapons. New bows, darts, hadwigs, torches, staffs, lances, knives, and swords were all being manufactured for the expected battle.

Anxiety raised a frown on Bardon's face. What good would these types of weapons do against the impenetrable hide of Mot Angra? Knives and swords and poison had not worked before. *Perhaps with his body not covered with scales, we can pierce his skin.*

He passed Toopka dressed in mismatched bright colors and playing a game with the meech children. They had drawn squares in the dirt and hopped from one to another in some kind of order Bardon could not decipher.

Paladin's questions echoed in Bardon's mind. *How long does it take for Mot Angra to grow another set of scales? Was this set the accumulation of centuries? Does he have any other weapons at his disposal? Does he breathe fire? Will he land and fight the warriors on the ground? And where is he?*

Bardon left the village and walked through the forest. He passed the tunnel that led to the outside world. He noted the ease with which he followed the trail through the underbrush of the forest. Many used this old path these days. He paused for quite a while to gaze at the drawing on the exposed wall of the cave. In the sunlight, the vibrant colors shimmered. What type of paint could produce such rich hues? What artist had such skill? Bardon gasped. *It couldn't be!*

He whirled around. No one in sight. He took off down the path to the camp, rushing through the hundred yards, jumping over fallen treetops, knocked down by Mot Angra's departure.

The first meech he saw when he entered the clearing stood talking to Kale. Bardon ran to them.

"Anyeld, what happened to the wandering painter who came here?"

The astonished expression on Kale's face made him pause. He looked into her eyes. *What an absurd idea! But I must know.*

"Maybe not, Bardon. It's worth investigating."

Anyeld's neck stiffened, but his brow furrowed in puzzlement, not in anger. "He lives miles from here, but still in the canyon. He hasn't visited the village in a dozen years. What do you want with him? He's not a friendly sort."

"He may have answers."

Anyeld didn't seem to think that was an absurd notion. "Are you going to visit him?"

"Yes!"

"The fastest way to get there is by boat."

Kale squeaked in surprise. "Boat?"

Bardon bobbed his head. South of the camp a stream of water sprang from a cluster of rocks in the forest. A small river flowed toward Amara from that point, dividing the forest into two unequal parts.

"Do you have someone to take me?"

"I'm going," said Kale.

Anyeld nodded. "Ellyk is the most likely guide."

As Anyeld left to round up Ellyk and rowers for the boat, Bardon felt Kale swoop into his thoughts.

"Oh!" she said aloud and broke into a grin. Then a scowl of concentration pulled on her features. "But how could he be that old? Wouldn't that be older than Fenworth?"

"I don't know, Kale." Bardon hugged her and kissed the little head sticking out of a bundle she wore strapped to her front. "But I'm excited. I think we are going to be surprised by this painter."

"We should learn his name."

"Maybe Ellyk and Anyeld know."

"His name is Kondiganpress," said Ellyk. He paddled the boat with three other meech. The men worked mostly to steer the vessel. The current provided all the power needed to get them downstream. "We should reach his place in an hour."

"Can you tell us anything more about him?" asked Kale.

"He's old. He's humble. He claims his ancestors came from this area. He's traveled a lot. He'll quicken the eggs if we press him to do so. He prefers to be left alone."

When they knocked on the door in midafternoon, Kondiganpress opened it promptly. Short and round, the man looked like he could block a bull from escaping his pen. He wore rough, but clean, clothes, and his long gray hair was braided, including his mustache and beard.

"So, you're Kale," he said with only a slight softening of his expression.

Kale kept her thoughts to herself. *A smile must not visit this tumanhofer's face very often.*

"I've been expecting you."

Kale, Bardon, and Ellyk stepped into the wooden frame house. The rather shabby home stood flush against the wall of the canyon. A double door in the back wall opened into a cave. A door on each side indicated two more rooms in the forefront of the tumanhofer habitat.

Kondiganpress pointed at the baby carried against Kale's chest by a long swath of material tied together in a sling. "Is this the girl?"

"No," said Kale as her eyes roved over the rough, painted walls. Her face appeared on every bare piece of wood. "You were expecting us?"

"Well, I figured I'd meet you someday. And lately, I got the impression you'd be coming here. Your face is the last vision Wulder has given me. And it seems He wants me to get it right, because I've seen it day and night in all sorts of ways. I'm glad you're here. Possibly Wulder will give me a rest now."

"Do you know what my wife's role is in this vision?" Bardon asked.

"Just what you see her doing. Looking on, always watching."

Bardon dragged his eyes away from the walls and spoke to the recluse. "We're in need of information."

"I'll tell you what I can, but I don't have any fresh visions for you other than your wife and the girl. And since this baby isn't the girl, I don't know what I can tell you about that."

"What does this girl look like?" asked Kale.

"Can't tell you much other than she wears dresses and is quick moving. If Wulder wanted me to see more, I would."

"We're interested in the past," Bardon clarified.

Kondiganpress motioned to his chairs. "Have a seat. You might wonder why a man on his own has ten chairs. It's because I'm a painter, not a chair-maker. Every year or so I make a chair. Haven't made a comfortable one yet. A couple of them fell apart. But I do make a good cup of hot brew from a bush that grows in these parts. Sit down, and I'll see if I can find enough cups."

Bardon directed Kale to the most comfortable, sturdy-looking chair. She sat and undid the baby's sling so she could turn him around to sit in her lap. He seemed happy with his surroundings. Fly stood guard on Kale's shoulder, eying everyone in the room with suspicion except her baby's parents.

"Mot Angra is loose," Bardon said.

"I figured as much," Kondiganpress said. "The ground shaking more and more often, then the bigger quake, and then nothing. Wasn't hard to figure out."

Bardon leaned forward. "What can you tell us about the dragon?"

"My family worked a mine here when the gateway opened to another world and poured forth a strange—no offense to you, young man—group of people." Kondiganpress winked at Ellyk. "Large and small, some of the small ones were all colors of the rainbow. The smallest looked like mice, but they spoke and wore clothes after a fashion." The tumanhofer looked in his one cabinet and pulled out five cups. He put them in a sink and proceeded to wash them.

"Of course, that was several generations ago. Seems each generation of Kondiganpress loses some of the talent for painting. I'm poor at my art, indeed, when you compare my splotches to the one on the cave wall up in Arreach. Some say Wulder Himself held my ancestor's hand as he drew what Wulder commanded. I can't compare with that genius. But my family passes down stories better than it passes down the artist gift, so I know a bit from the tales about those times in the distant past."

"Do you have any knowledge that will help us defeat Mot Angra?"

The old man sat in a chair beside his table. He shook his head as he fingered the teapot handle. "The most important piece of information I have for you is from the future, given to me by Wulder."

"What is that?"

"A little girl will carry the only weapon that can defeat this evil. She will carry it into battle."

Kale cleared her throat. She nodded toward an unfinished painting that she could see from her chair. "Behind the door. That silhouette. Why haven't you finished it?"

He rose and shuffled to the cave entrance. "I don't have a clear picture in my head." He closed the door, exposing the short image.

"We could possibly introduce you to the one you are trying to paint," said Kale. "Her name is Toopka."

53

A Definite Clue

They couldn't return. Bardon stomped through the underbrush and fumed over the loss of the boat. He sent Mikkai downstream to search the banks. A quake had disturbed their tea and evidently knocked the boat from its mooring.

He returned to the shack. At his request, Kale set up the talking gateway, and Bardon sat before the contraption. "I can't say that we've gained a lot of knowledge that will help us in our battle against Mot Angra." He spoke to the empty shell of the portal. They hadn't tried it since the disintegration of Kale's abilities had reversed. *Even if this doesn't get through, it's of little consequence. What is the most important thing we've learned? That a silhouette that could be Toopka is the old man's prediction of who will win the day against all evil.*

"Paladin, I'm bringing Kondiganpress with us when we return tomorrow. I've made no sense of his comments, but perhaps you will gain an insight I cannot fathom."

Kondiganpress entertained them all evening with stories of his travels as well as legends of Mot Angra. Bardon noticed a subtle coolness on the part of the tumanhofer toward the meech, but as a host, Kondiganpress offered as much as he was able. Providing some of the ingredients out of her cape's hollows, Kale fixed a dinner that the old artist enjoyed.

The meech set up tents outside the ramshackle house. When Kale and Bardon retired for the night, their familiar tent felt like home. Penn drank his dinner and cooed for his father before drifting off to sleep.

In the morning an excited Mikkai returned to the camp and led Anyeld and Ellyk to recover the boat.

When Kale opened the talking gateway, a message from Regidor waited. "We're back in Bility. Wizard Cam is here, along with most of the other wizards you could name. Be careful in your travels. An influx of dangerous creatures has caused alarm."

"Well, that certainly helped," said Kale as she searched for another message. "Cryptic. I could shake a knot in him. Does he mean quiss and mordakleeps in the waters? Are there snakes or bears or bisonbecks and grawligs? Bah! I won't think of it. His message was designed to upset me."

Bardon rolled up a blanket and added it to a stack they were packing. "I don't think so, Kale. It's just his way. Either the list was too long to go into, or the reports are unsubstantiated, and he doesn't want to guess what might be out there."

Kale gave him a look of disgust. "Was that supposed to comfort me? Ease my stress? Mollify my concerns?"

Bardon scooped up his son and made faces at him. "Mommy is fussing at Daddy. Take note, Penn. This is because Mommy is worried, not because Daddy is a callous rat. She'll do this to you someday. 'From a stew of dismay comes the taste of bitterness.'"

Penn gurgled.

"Just so, we shall, nonetheless, keep our weapons within reach."

Hours later, Bardon stepped off the boat onto a dock near the head of the river. He turned to help Kale out with little Penn. Rowing upstream had been arduous, but Ellyk said trying to make a path through the forest would have taken longer. With Regidor's warning in his mind, Bardon had decided the boat provided a more strategic defense from any approaching wild animals. They encountered nothing out of the ordinary.

Bardon thanked the meech who had taken them on the trip. He took Kale by the elbow and guided Kondiganpress up the trail to the first camp. As soon as they broke through the trees and into the clearing, a small crowd of people, all talking at once, surrounded them.

Sir Kemry waded through and grabbed Bardon's and Kale's arms. "Come with me. I'm sure you can't make heads nor tails of this babble."

He addressed those around him. "Thank you, friends. I'll be sure to give them all the details. Back to your work. Remember, we have no time to waste."

He hurried them and Kondiganpress into the tent where the leaders of Paladin's army gathered. Whatever meeting had taken place recently had adjourned. A few officers studied a map. The substation headquarters was almost deserted.

Lyll circled the cluster of tables to greet them. "Start with the good news, Kem." Lyll bustled over to a small iron stove no bigger than a space heater. A kettle steamed on the flat top.

Kemry ushered them to a table. He noticed Kondiganpress for the first time and thrust his hand forward. "Welcome. I'm Kemry. You must be Kondiganpress, the mural painter."

"That I am."

"Paladin will want to meet you, but first let me fill you in, along with my daughter and son-in-law." He sat down across the table from the others. "The good news is that the riding dragons have begun to arrive from Amara."

Bardon raised an eyebrow. "That's the extent of the good news?"

"Yes." Sir Kemry looked grim. "The riding dragons will be useful in battle and in keeping track of how the battle goes. A view from above is always helpful."

Bardon nodded. "I don't feel Greer anywhere close."

"No. I believe the dragons of the Northern Reach are coming to our aid."

"The bad news," Lyll reminded her husband as she arrived with a tray of tea.

Kemry charged on. "Wicked things are pouring out of the hills, congregating on the plain directly east of us. Grawligs, renegade bisonbecks, schoergs and stinger schoergs, blimmets, and the fiercest of the woodland animals—bears, cats, and boars.

"I guess you could say the good news is that they fight among themselves, killing the weakest. Not good—that leaves the strongest to do whatever evil they've been called to. But even now they are still skirmishing for dominance. We could hope they'll kill one another off and leave only battle-weary foes to face us."

Lyll sat down and took sleeping Penn to rest on her shoulder. "And, of course," she said, "we haven't located Mot Angra. That's a bit of a problem." She looked at the tumanhofer.

"I'm no help to you, milady. I've just come to see the fruition of my vision. I've never seen one come to pass."

The night before, Kale told Kondiganpress about her adventures and how the scenes in his murals had shown up in her life. "I don't understand this mural we saw in Arreach."

The tumanhofer laughed, a self-deprecating sound. "I never understand any of them."

They walked through the woods to Bility and introduced Kondiganpress to Paladin. The two men settled down for a talk in Paladin's strategy room.

Kale caught Bardon's hand. "Let's look for Toopka."

They found Sir Dar sitting on a log and watching a group of five children play. Three meech, Sittiponder, and Toopka had a ball to kick back and forth. The game seemed to be roughly based on the Amaran ribbets.

"I'm trying to analyze how Toopka has changed," Sir Dar said as soon as they sat beside him.

Mikkai flew down the street and landed on Bardon's shoulder.

"This is interesting," he said after deciphering his minor dragon's excited chatter.

Kale stood. "Come, Sir Dar. Mikkai has something to show us on the map."

They raced back to the village headquarters and found Paladin still talking to Kondiganpress.

"Pardon the interruption, sir," said Bardon. "Mikkai has something of importance to show us on the map."

Paladin gestured them toward the table spread with charts. Bardon shuffled through them until he found the one he had drawn with Mikkai's direction. He spread it out, and the minor dragon hopped down and stood on a ridge that made up one of five north of their current location.

"Mikkai has been scouting the area every day," Bardon explained. "He kept going back to this region because there was something peculiar he could not discern. Today, he saw clearly that this ridge has moved."

"Mountains don't move except in earthquakes," said Kondiganpress.

"This mountain apparently got up, turned around, and settled back down."

Paladin smiled. "Like a restless animal in its sleep."

"Like a dragon," said Bardon.

Mikkai chirruped and did a flip, landing again on the ridge.

54

A Walk in the Dark

Bardon stood with a number of Paladin's officers and knights on a rise of land to the south of the battlefield. He surveyed the placement of troops. The light of a few kimen dotted each unit of the regular army. Wizards in their long, flashy robes also stood among those who would fight with sword and arrow. Brunstetter had placed his giant troops in lines among the smaller warriors.

By Paladin's order, his troops faced the sleeping dragon in a horseshoe with the slope of the hills behind them. The first line of soldiers battled creatures prowling in the open fields. As the men approached the area at dawn, the sight and smell of carnage greeted them.

The beasts had slaughtered one another in a frenzy. Only a minor portion of the animals still capable of killing remained. Bisonbecks and grawligs trudged among them, slaughtering the weak and injuring those who attacked. However, former warriors and mountain ogres decreased in numbers steadily as well. An irrational rage pitted them against one another as well as the beasts.

The troops of Paladin's army took their positions and dealt with this wild menagerie. The animals lost interest in one another and attacked the forces of good. When the first line of defense grew weary, a new set of warriors took its place.

"This is unlike any battle I have ever seen," said Paladin. "Our enemies walk up to us as if to request being killed. They don't surrender. They just keep throwing themselves at our weapons."

Brunstetter sat so he was closer in height with the other generals. "It appears to be a campaign without strategy. No one is in charge. No one directs their assaults."

Bardon gripped the hilt of his sword. "Perhaps Mot Angra creates a madness around him that only death can acquit."

Paladin turned to one of his messengers. "Give my order. All men are to keep their thoughts stayed on Wulder. We shall keep this mania from spreading to our troops."

The young marione saluted and ran to deliver the command.

"It will be an easy fight to win," said Lee Ark. "But it feels more like a massacre than a battle against reasoning opponents."

Paladin's eyes swept over the blood-soaked plain. "Keep offering the races capable of logic an opportunity to surrender." He sighed as if his heart broke. "And slay those who attack."

Wizard Cam Ayronn pointed to the dark mountain ridge they now knew to be a dragon in disguise. "The only purpose I can see in this confrontation is that Mot Angra is allowed to sleep without interference. We are busy swatting gnats, albeit big nasty gnats, while the larger threat does what? Grows more scales? Replenishes his strength? Sleeps and dreams of more iniquity?" The lake wizard swung his arm around to indicate the malevolent forces across the plain. He showered water on those around him. "Sorry," he muttered.

Paladin frowned. "I'm sending a squadron of emerlindians to investigate the condition of the dragon's scale armor. For the time being we can only watch and wait."

As the sun reached its zenith, Paladin's men hauled corpses off the battlefield to a huge funeral pyre. The low races were cremated on one pile of wood and the vicious animals on another. The kimens took over the maintenance of both flames. So much blood soaked the wood that it took an effort to keep the blaze hot enough to do the unpleasant job.

By late afternoon, the battlefield held no foes but the wounded. Remarkably, when Paladin's men went out to gather in the injured and provide them care, the remnant of evil persisted. With their last breaths, they fought. Some succeeded in inflicting gashes upon the hands that would aid them. In the end, no prisoners were taken.

At dusk the party of three emerlindians ventured up the side of the sleeping dragon's form. The wizards produced spyglasses through which the reconnaissance team's progress could be followed. They crept to a point where a thrust of a spear would open the jugular vein on a lesser creature.

"No," whispered Bardon as he gazed with one eye through the spyglass. "Don't attempt it." He observed a second man arguing with the first.

All three emerlindians started to descend down the monster's side. Mot Angra raised his head and shook the men off. The dragon's glistening yellow eyes scoured the surroundings. He snatched up one victim, tossed his head back, and swallowed him.

Bardon's fingers clinched around the metal tube in his hand. He ground his teeth and moved the glass to observe Mot Angra's face. Bardon noted the dragon squinted as he searched for more prey.

Could it be that light somehow is our weapon? So far he's only flown at night. He was in that dark dungeonlike cave. Kale first noticed problems producing light when we came closer to Mot Angra. But now the wizards are having no trouble with anything to do with light wizardry. Logic does not seem to be part of this equation.

He watched the two remaining emerlindians crawl slowly toward safety, holding his breath each time their cover became scarce. The sun continued its descent, coloring the sky with rich red, streaks of orange, and a layer of pink disappearing into deep purple in the higher heavens.

Mot Angra raised his upper body on his front legs, stretched his neck, and roared, "You dare to approach me!"

The dry leaves on the autumn trees shook. Some brittle leaves broke off and drifted to earth. The dark dragon heaved his hindquarters to a stand. Sturdy legs stamped the ground as if shaking away all drowsiness. The sky provided a colorful backdrop to the enormous silhouette of Mot Angra. He stretched his wings, then folded them against his body. He bellowed once more and shook. Small, immature scales fell. The ones that hit the stones beneath the dragon clattered. Some flew a short distance and faltered. The dragon laughed.

"Patience," he said in a gravelly voice, "was never my virtue."

He spied movement in the grass and froze as he eyed his quarry. His head darted out, and he seized another of the emerlindians.

Bardon swung his glass around and located the last man. He hid beneath an outcropping of rock. "Just have the nerve to stay there, and you might survive," he advised the man who could not hear him.

The dragon smacked his lips. "Just in case you think I need my scale fliers to do my dirty work—" He roared again and spewed out a stream of fire that blasted the unit of Paladin's army to his right. The men and equipment went up in flames. The nearest unit rushed in to pull survivors toward safety. The line of defense reacted by backing out of range and reforming. As he watched their movements, Mot Angra rumbled with laughter.

The sun sank behind the mountains. The two pyres lit the gory scene. Perhaps the wild creatures had been right in insisting on death rather than face this horror.

Mot Angra took a step forward and devastated another segment of Paladin's army with the torch from his mouth. He sat back then and shook out his wings as if he'd done no more than blow sand off a plate.

Bardon's instructions to his men had been to aim for the tender parts of the dragon's face, his eyes, his nose, inside his ears. *Can they get close enough for even a few lucky strikes?*

The dragon stretched forth his neck and fed on the charred corpses left where they had fallen. He ate loudly, chomping and smacking his lips. With a body dangling from his mouth, he lifted his head and peered across the field.

Bardon turned to see what had caught his attention. Emerging from the line of warriors, a parade of sorts glowed. Dressed again in light, a group of kimens surrounded three figures in the center. Their clothing once again flashed hues of gold and silver.

Bardon lifted his glass to one eye. Toopka marched in the center. Her hands cupped the egglike stone Wulder had plucked from her chest, and she held it in front of her as if she were bringing a present. On one side, Sittiponder, with a face grim and resolute, accompanied her. He had a drawn sword, and the blade either gleamed on its own or reflected the light from the kimens. On the other side, Gilda towered over those around her. She also brandished a long shining sword.

Mot Angra tossed his charred meat in the air, caught it, and swallowed the tidbit. He then tilted his head and examined the approaching company. "Oh, ho! What is this? Do you send me martyrs? I have to warn you, I don't believe in sacrifices to appease my appetite. I shall eat your fools, then ravage the rest of you."

Toopka lifted her chin. "I bring you a gift."

Remarkably, her voice boomed across the land, much as Mot Angra's voice. Was it natural amplification? Bardon twisted his head and saw nothing that would magnify sound such as a backdrop of a solid cliff. Wizard Namee was present. Did he provide this amplification? Or was it Wulder? At the thought of Wulder actively participating in this spectacle, Bardon's heart lifted.

Bardon felt his arm jostled. He looked down to find Kale at his side. Regidor stepped up beside him. Both wore grim expressions. The moon on Kale's face showed her pale complexion. Her expression remained remarkably calm. The paintings on old Kondiganpress's walls came to life as she blinked back a tear. What had the old tumanhofer said? Her duty in this confrontation was to watch.

"A gift?" mocked Mot Angra. "How droll! Do you bring me a golden toothpick to clean your brothers from my molars? Do you bring me a stove in which to cook them? Perhaps a set of cutlery so I may sit at a table and display my manners?"

"It is an egg."

The dragon's booming laughter shook the very earth beneath the feet of Paladin's army. As he guffawed, Toopka and her entourage advanced.

When he drew ragged breaths and again focused on the marching oddity, he wheezed, "You grow dangerously close, little people." He giggled. "And tall madam."

"If you eat the egg willingly, Wulder will relieve you of your heartache, your sorrows, your pain, and give you beauty in return."

"Wulder? Ah, Wulder has offered me similar propositions in the past. If I do this, He will do that. I'll have none of it, little doll. You will be the beauty I devour, and my supposed suffering will continue. It does not bother me much."

The egg in Toopka's hand flashed a bright light at his words.

"You lie," said Toopka. The kimens' clothing lost the subtle yellow and gray of metallic coloring and blazed a white so pure Bardon blinked and squinted to see.

Toopka's voice rang through the dazzling display. "Should you swallow the egg unwillingly, you will die."

Mot Angra turned his face away from the glare. Toopka's small force was now within a hundred yards of the beast.

"You tire me," he growled. "I'll eat you and spit out your egg."

"I don't think it'll be that easy."

Something in the childish tone reminded Bardon of the little girl Toopka weaseling an extra treat out of Taylaminkadot. He took a step forward, but both Kale and Regidor grabbed his arms.

"She must do this," Kale whispered. "I finally recognize what I should have seen long ago. The egg is the light of this world, Truth."

The dragon roared. Flame singed the air. His pointed incisors glimmered in the light of both death fires and a child's hope. He gnashed his teeth and swung his head over the approaching force twice. On the third swing he opened his maw and snatched as many of the party as he could.

The watching crowd gasped. Most of the kimens had fallen, their light clothing extinguished.

Toopka, Sittiponder, and Gilda were gone.

Mot Angra stomped his feet, howled with his chin pointed to the stars, and steamed from his nostrils, his mouth, his ears, and even his eyes.

Bardon put his arm around Kale as tears streamed down his face. He looked at Regidor's expression and felt his resignation to accept Wulder's will. A flash of anger seared Bardon's heart but quickly lost its heat. *I cannot quote Your principles day in and day out and not trust Your hand to bring forth Your best for us. But it is hard, Wulder. It is hard.*

The beast's next scream, a keening yowl, made everyone cover their ears. Silence followed. Mot Angra's black skin let off a vapor smelling of the sweetness that threatened to close their throats. Paladin ordered his men to place a cloth over the lower half of their faces. The instruction rippled through the units. Some saw their comrades with the white handkerchief from a distance and followed suit.

Labored breathing broke the quiet. The great beast crumpled to the ground as his legs gave out. He rolled on his side and struggled to pull air in and push it out. His skin continued to steam and then to disintegrate. Much as the scale fliers' bodies turned to powder after death, the evil dragon turned from a solid mass to a mound of dark dust. Not even a rib curved into the air above the vestiges of the vile monster.

The wind picked up and blew the sickening odor away and dispersed the remains of Mot Angra. As the hill diminished, several lumps could be seen in the residue. The lumps moved and walked out of the dragon's dirt.

A cheer went up among the forces of Paladin as the warriors realized the three sent by Wulder had survived.

Kale squeezed Bardon's arm so hard he thought it would bruise. "They're alive. Our champions have lived through death."

Bardon blinked back new tears as Regidor left his side, running down the slope toward his wife.

Thinking of the many tranquil images of Kale's face at the old tumanhofer's home, Bardon asked, "Did you know this is the way it would end?"

She pressed her face against his chest. "This is what I hoped for." She leaned back and gazed into his eyes.

Their thoughts mingled. Penn, home, too many dragons to count. Bardon kissed her forehead. "Soon, lady of mine. Soon we can take Penn home."

The roar of the crowd claimed their attention. Two urohms hoisted Toopka and Sittiponder into the air and placed them on their shoulders. Regidor and Gilda walked arm in arm behind them. An impromptu parade of clapping, cheering soldiers streamed behind the heroes as they progressed toward the hill where Paladin stood waiting. The kimens danced among them.

Music broke out. First indistinct and disjointed, but as more of the crowd joined in, the most popular of Wulder's marching songs echoed throughout the throng. Those who did not wield an instrument sang gustily. When the surge of revelers reached the top, Paladin joined in the celebration, leading them on toward the camp.

It took hours for the joy to expel its last breath in a sigh of contentment and relief. The camp settled down, many of the warriors making the trek to the canyon and the village of Bility.

Bardon looked around the campfire where those he knew best had settled. Paladin gestured to Toopka, and the small doneel came to stand before him.

"You've done well, my little friend."

She nodded.

"Tell me how you came to lead the march that destroyed Mot Angra."

"You mean why did the others go with me?"

"Yes."

"They're all bigger than me, sir. I couldn't really tell them what to do. And when they said they were coming, too, well, I kind of liked the idea of not going by myself. I knew because Wulder told me that I needed to get that egg into Mot Angra. But He never said I had to go alone."

Paladin crooked a finger, and Sittiponder approached.

"Why did you decide to stand by Toopka's side?"

"I could see it was my place. Wulder gave me my sight, and I knew He wouldn't have done that right before this big thing was going to happen unless He wanted me to be right there to watch after Toopka."

"Gilda?"

The stately meech disengaged herself from her husband's arm and came forward. "I went as a representative of the meech." She looked down at the ground. "Not because we have so much to offer this world, but because this world has offered us refuge." She lifted her face and looked Paladin directly in the eye. "Before Toopka brought me back with the touch of that egg to my lips, I stood in a place where truth is vivid. To my sorrow, I can't remember everything revealed to me there. But the promise that I would one day return stays with me."

Paladin took her hand and kissed it.

Toopka tugged on his sleeve. "It was pretty when the kimen joined us, wasn't it?"

Paladin scooped her into his arms. "It was spectacular."

Epilogue

Kale nodded to the far end of the palatial room where Bardon stood, talking with several men. "Do you think Paladin is looking fat?"

Her mother's peal of laughter caught the attention of everyone in the room.

"Mother," Kale whispered, "don't say anything outrageous." She handed her mother a tiny baby wrapped in pink and took the one in blue.

Lyll smiled at those in attendance and held up her granddaughter as if showing off a prize. Two minor dragons switched places, one following the girl babe to Lyll's shoulder, the other leapt to Kale's back, then peered down at the nursing baby boy.

Lyll shooed the protector dragon to one side and proceeded to thump the babe's little back. "You are the one who's outrageous. Fat?" Her eyes examined the tallest man in the group with Bardon. "He's certainly filled out some. Comfortably content, not fat, dear. We became accustomed to his looking wan and gaunt. Now he is healthy, robust."

Paladin looked up and caught Lyll's eye. She smiled and nodded. He responded in kind and went back to his conversation.

"Speaking of robust and healthy," said Lady Lyll, "where is Penn? It's his third birthday. You'd think he'd be in the middle of things."

Kale looked around. "There's no food here." She let her mind reach out. "Fly says he's following a servant carrying a platter of daggarts."

A side door opened, and a line of uniformed maids bustled in and placed refreshments on a long table covered with a brightly patterned cloth.

"There he is," said his proud grandmother.

"Where?"

"He just ducked under the table."

In a minute the servants departed, leaving behind a scrumptious array of food. As soon as the door whisked shut, a little hand appeared, reaching from beneath the tablecloth and patting the serving space.

"Penn!" Kale whispered in exasperation.

Lyll just laughed.

The hand located a plate and pulled it closer to the edge. Fingers stretched and found a brown, crunchy daggart. Fly landed on the wrist of the thief and nipped her boy. Penn dropped his treasure and withdrew his hand. Fly flew under the table, and Kale heard her scold.

Lyll sighed. "Does Penn like being a big brother?"

Kale nodded with a rueful grin. "He says babies should come one at a time. Our babies' hair is too black. Their eyes are too blue. They smell bad sometimes. They won't play, and they don't talk. Yet he absolutely adores them. He is glad they came for his big birthday party."

"Is there something special he wants?" Grandma had a gleam in her eye.

"He wants to see his Uncle Regidor and Aunt Gilda and, of course, Toopka and Uncle Dar."

"Regidor visits frequently, does he not?"

"Yes, but Sir Dar does not. He felt the wanderlust and took Toopka to tour the world. They've been gone quite a long time."

"They've promised to come?"

Kale nodded. "I'm going to sneak Penn a treat before he knocks something off the table or strangles Fly."

She put the sleeping boy in the wide cradle and scooted over to the table.

"Come out, Penn."

Sheepishly, her older son emerged. He made an awkward attempt to straighten his party clothes. Kale helped him tuck his shirt in.

"Do you want a daggart?"

"Yes, please."

"All right. Next time, ask." She picked up a small plate and, using tongs, selected several small treats.

"Who's that, Mommy?"

"Where?"

"With Uncle Dar."

Kale turned to the door where Sir Dar stood with a very winsome young lady doneel. "Oh my, she is pretty. I believe your uncle Dar is, at long last, caught."

"He's caught?"

"You can see it in his eye."

"He's got something caught in his eye?"

More interested in analyzing the affection between the two newcomers to the party, Kale responded to her inquisitive son without much thought. "He's enamored."

"Armored?"

Kale put the plate on the table. "Let's go meet Uncle Dar's lady-love."

She took one of Penn's hands, but not before the other one had reached back and snatched one of the daggarts.

Kale hurried across the room. "Sir Dar!" She leaned over to kiss him in her favorite spot of soft fur between his ears. "Who is your friend?"

The lady giggled, and the familiar sound shocked Kale. "Toopka?"

The doneel bobbed her lovely head. "It's me."

"How did you grow up in two years?"

"Two and a half since we saw you last, although I've really been grown for a year now."

"I don't understand." Kale gasped. "You're the woman in the story you told us. I assumed you were one of the children who witnessed the tragedy."

"I was that woman. Wulder gave me a gift to carry in my heart and made me a child. The more time passed, the hazier my memory became of what actually happened."

"You didn't know what you carried next to your heart?"

"I knew He'd given me a gift, and I thought I had lost it."

Paladin came from across the room, knelt before Toopka, and kissed both her cheeks. "I am glad to see you well."

He stood and shook hands with Sir Dar. "I see you are content."

"Content," Kale's mother whispered in her mind. *"Content seems to be the word of the hour."*

It's a lovely word, Mother.

"Yes, I agree. The Tomes say, 'Content as I am is far superior to content as I was or content as I am to be.'"

Bardon and Sir Kemry approached and greeted the old friends.

Bardon smiled down at the couple. "I hardly recognized you, Toopka."

She giggled.

He pointed a finger at her. "That I recognize."

Sir Kemry harrumphed. "I finally get to ask my question." All eyes turned toward him. "Toopka, when did you know what to do with that egg?"

She shook her head. "I never really knew. But as if my steps were ordered, I just kept walking. Sittiponder went with me, but then, he always did. When we got closer to the battlefield, he pulled out his sword. But his old one had been replaced with a gleaming blade. Then kimens collected around me, and I still didn't know where we were going. But I could hear Wulder's voice. 'Go. Do not fear. I go before you. I will open the evil one's mouth and destroy him.'"

Several of the women who pressed near oohed at that statement.

"Then Gilda came to walk with me, and she's so big, I thought everything would be all right.

"I heard Wulder laugh. He said, 'Her size makes you confident? Child, you should see Your Creator in all His glory. Size?' Then He laughed again, and I felt warm and safe.

"When we reached Mot Angra and he spoke, I opened my mouth and words came out. I was very surprised when he swallowed us. But inside the darkness, a fresh breeze blew. I could hear singing, and I held Gilda's and Sittiponder's hands. Then the darkness fell away like a mist settling on the ground."

Her eyes opened in earnestness. "I'd do it again. It was so peaceful." She frowned. "But I think it was wise not to tell me ahead of time what I was expected to do."

Sir Dar took her hand, raised it to his lips, and kissed it. "Wulder is wise."

"Did you come for my birthday party?" asked Penn.

"Yes." Toopka beamed at him.

"Here." Penn thrust out his hand, offering a daggart with the top licked and one bite gone. "For you. You had a hard time getting here."

Toopka pulled him into her arms and squeezed him. "We all have a hard time on our journey, Penn. But Wulder gets us to the destination."

"Is He coming too?" He looked over his shoulder at the banquet table. "Does He eat a lot? You said He was big."

"He gives more than He takes. It's the way He is."

Glossary

Amara (ä´-mä-rä)
Continent surrounded by ocean on three sides.

anvilhead snake
A long, thin snake whose outsized head is supported by thick neck muscles.

bisonbecks (bī´-sen-beks)
Most intelligent of the seven low races. They comprise most of Risto's army.

bobbin bird
A small thrush.

bridesbark
The dried root of a deciduous tree with aromatic bark.

buzz-stinger
Similar to our bumblebee.

chukkajoop (chuk´-kuh-joop)
A favorite o'rant stew made from beets, onions, and carrots.

cinamacress
A perennial water plant with peppery-flavored leaves and stems.

daggarts (dag´-garts)
A baked treat, a small crunch cake.

doneels (dō´-neelz)
One of the seven high races. These people are furry with bulging eyes, thin black lips, and ears at the top and front of their skulls. A flap of skin covers the ears and twitches, responding to the doneel's mood. They are small in stature, rarely over three feet tall. Generally are musical and given to wearing flamboyant clothing.

dryfus tree
A small spiny tree.

echo
A leader in the Follower movement.

emerlindians (ē´-mer-lin´-dee-inz)
One of the seven high races, emerlindians are born pale with white hair and pale gray eyes. As they age, they darken. One group of emer-

lindians are slight in stature, the tallest being five feet. Another distinct group are between six and six and a half feet tall.

Followers
A sect of people purporting to follow Wulder more closely than the average citizen.

forms
A regimented set of exercises.

giddinfish
A freshwater food and game fish; usually has a streamlined, speckled body with small scales.

glommytucks (glŏm´-me-tŭks)
Large aquatic birds with a long slender neck and shorter, rounder bills than ducks. Lay large clutches of eggs and are wonderful birds for roasting.

gotza fruit
Edible fruit from a spiny-stemmed cactus.

granny emerlindian
Grannies are male or female, said to be five hundred years old or older, and have darkened to a brown complexion with dark brown hair and eyes.

grawligs (graw´-ligz)
One of seven low races, mountain ogres.

heatherhens
Chickenlike birds having brown plumage with speckled breasts and short tails.

jimmin (jĭm-mĭn)
Any young animal used for meat. We would say veal, lamb, or spring chicken.

kimens (kĭm´-enz)
The smallest of the seven high races. Kimens are elusive, tiny, and fast. Under two feet tall.

kindias (kin´-dee-uhz)
Large land mammals noted for speed, strength, and endurance. Kindias are exceptionally adapted to traveling long distances with great efficiency and to surviving on a diet of nutrient-poor, high-fiber grasses. The shoulders are a foot or more taller than the hindquarters, giving the animal a slanted back.

kitawahdo
Tumanhofer bean soup.

lightrocks
Any of the quartzlike rocks giving off a glow.

listener
One of the levels of the Followers.

mariones (mer´-ē-ownz)
One of the seven high races. Mariones are excellent farmers and warriors. They are short and broad, usually muscle-bound rather than corpulent.

meech dragon
The most intelligent of the dragons, capable of speech.

minnekens
A small, mysterious race living in isolation on the Isle of Kye.

moonbeam plant
A three- to four-foot plant having large shiny leaves and round flowers resembling a full moon. The stems are fibrous and used for making invisible cloth.

mumfers
Flowers with small, densely clustered petals.

mullins (mŭl´-lĭnz)
Fried doughnut sticks.

o'rants
One of the high races. Five to six feet tall.

parnot (pâr´-nŏt)
Green fruit like a pear.

peggle-pins
Targets in the game peggledy pin.

pnard potatoes (puh-nard´)
Starchy, edible tuber with pale pink flesh.

pricklebarrel
A large fruit with juicy yellow flesh, a thick prickly brown skin, and a sprout of tough pointed leaves at the top.

razterberry (ras´-ter-bâr-ee)
Small red berries that grow in clusters somewhat like grapes on the sides of mountains. The vines are useful for climbing.

repeat
One of the levels of the Followers.

ribbets (rib´-bits)
Ball game played between two teams, similar to soccer.

schop
A casserole made from pricklebarrel fruit and cheese.

seeker
One of the levels of the Followers.

Sellaran
An extinct bird that legend says was instrumental in the rebellion of Pretender.

stakes
A disease that leaves the victim stiff for weeks after the fever has passed and can recur when the patient becomes overtired. For children, the symptoms pass. In adults, the side effects can last ten to twenty years.

trang-a-nog tree (trăng´-uh-nŏg)
A tree with smooth, olive green bark.

tumanhofers (too´-mun-hoff-erz)
One of the seven high races. Short, squat, powerful fighters, though for the most part, they prefer to use their great intellect.

tumport
An infusion of root herbs served hot.

tundra pear tree
An odd tree whose fruit is juicy considering the arid land it grows on.

urohms (ū-rōmz´)
Largest of the seven high races. Gentle giants, well proportioned and very intelligent.

watch
A unit of dragons (like gaggle of geese).

wild yellow dropsies
A wildflower. The stem is long, the flower heavy, and therefore the blossom bows.

1

A View from a Tree

Beccaroon cocked his head, ruffled his neck feathers, and stretched, allowing his crimson wings to spread. The branch beneath him sank and rose again, responding to his weight. Moist, hot air penetrated his finery, and he held his wings away from his brilliant blue sides.

"Too hot for company," he muttered, rocking back and forth from one four-toed scaly foot to the other on a limb of the sacktrass tree. The leaves shimmered as the motion rippled along the branch. "Where is that girl?"

His yellow head swiveled almost completely around. He peered with one eye down the overgrown path and then scoped out every inch within his range of vision, twisting his neck slowly.

A brief morning shower had penetrated the canopy above and rinsed the waxy leaves. A few remaining drops glistened where thin shafts of tropical sun touched the dark green foliage. On the broot vine, flowers the size of plates lifted their fiery red petals, begging the thumb-sized bees to come drink before the weight of nectar broke off the blooms.

Beccaroon flew to a perch on a gnarly branch. He sipped from a broot blossom and ran his black tongue over the edges of his beak. A sudden breeze shook loose a sprinkle of leftover raindrops. Beccaroon shook his tail feathers and blinked. When the disturbance settled, he cocked his head and listened.

"Ah! She's coming." He preened his soft green breast and waited, giving a show of patience he didn't feel. His head jerked up as he detected someone walking with the girl.

"Awk!" The sound exploded from his throat. He flew into a roost far above the forest floor, where he couldn't be seen from the ground and watched the approach of the girl placed under his guardianship.

Tipper strolled along the path below, wearing a flowing, golden gown over her tall, lean body. She'd put her long blond hair in a fancy braid that started at the crown of her head. A golden chain hung from each of her pointed ears. And she'd decorated her pointed facial features with subdued colors—blue for her eyelids, rose for her lips, and a shimmering yellow on her cheeks. Beccaroon sighed. His girl was lovely.

The bushes along the path behind her rustled. Beccaroon's tongue clucked against his beak in disapproval. Hanner trudged after Tipper, leading a donkey hitched to a cart. The man's shaggy hair, tied with a string at the back of his neck, hung oily and limp. Food and drink stained the front of his leather jerkin, and his boots wore mud instead of a shine. The parrot caught a whiff of the o'rant from where he perched. The young man should carry the fragrance of citrus, but his overstrong odor reminded Beccaroon of rotten fruit.

A tree full of monkeys broke out in outraged chatter. Tipper, when alone, walked amid the animals' habitat without causing alarm.

"Smart monkeys," said Beccaroon. "You recognize a ninny-napconder when you see one." He used the cover of the monkeys' rabble-rousing to glide to another tree, where he could hide at a lower level. He had an idea where Tipper would lead Hanner.

"Here it is," said the pretty emerlindian. She pulled vines from a clump, revealing a gray statue beneath. "My father named this one *Vegetable Garden.*"

Hanner pulled off more vines as he made his way slowly around the four-foot statue. "*Vegetable Garden*? Mistress Tipper, are you sure you have the right one? This is a statue of a boy reading a book. He's not even chewing a carrot while he sits here."

"Father used to say reading a good book was nourishment."

Hanner scratched his head, shrugged his shoulders, and went to fetch the donkey and cart. Tipper's head tilted back, and her blue eyes looked up into the trees. Her gaze roamed over the exact spot Beccaroon used as a hidden roost. Not by the blink of an eyelash did she betray whether or not she had seen him. Hanner returned.

Tipper spread out a blanket in the cart after Hanner maneuvered it next to the statue, then helped him lift the stone boy into the back. Hanner grunted a lot, and Tipper scolded.

"Careful… Don't break his arm… Too many vines still around the base."

They got the statue loaded, and Tipper tucked the blanket over and around it. She then gave Hanner a pouch of coins.

"This is for your usual fee for delivering. I couldn't put any extra in for traveling expenses. I'm sure you'll be reimbursed by our buyer."

He grunted and slipped the money inside his jerkin.

Tipper clasped her hands together. "Be careful. And give Master Dodderbanoster my regards."

He tipped his hat and climbed aboard the cart. "I always am. And I always do."

She stood in the path until the creak of the cart wheels could no longer be heard.

Beccaroon swooped down and sat on a thick branch wrapped with a leafless green creeper. The vine looked too much like a snake, so he hopped to another limb.

"Was that wise?" he asked.

"I don't think so either, Bec, but what else can I do? I only sell the artwork as a last resort when we need quite a bit of cash. The well needs re-digging." Tipper pulled a tight face, looking like she'd swallowed nasty medicine. "We've sold almost everything in the house. Mother sees them in the market and buys them back. Sometimes I get a better price for a piece the second time I sell it, and sometimes not."

Beccaroon swayed back and forth on his feet, shaking his head. "She never catches on?"

"Never." Tipper giggled. "She shows remarkably consistent taste. When she spots something that was once ours, she buys it, brings it home, shows it off to me, and tells me she has always wanted something just like it. And she never notices pictures gone from the walls, rugs missing in rooms, chairs, tables, vases, candlesticks gone. I used to rearrange things to disguise a hole in the décor, but there's no need."

The sigh that followed her explanation held no joy. Tipper looked around. "There never is a place to sit in this forest when one wants to plop down and have a good cry."

"You're not the type to cry. I'll walk you home." Beccaroon hopped down to the path.

His head came up to her waist. She immediately put her dainty hand on his topknot and smoothed the creamy plumes back.

"You're the best of friends. Keeping this secret would be unbearable if I didn't have you to confide in."

Beccaroon clicked his tongue. "No flattery, or I shall fly away."

They moseyed back the direction Tipper had come, opposite from the way Hanner had departed.

Beccaroon tsked. "I don't like that greasy fellow."

"I know." Tipper gently twisted the longest feather from the center of Bec's crest around her forefinger.

The grand parrot jerked his head away and gave her his sternest glare. She was his girl, but he still wouldn't let her take liberties. She didn't seem to notice he was disgruntled, and that further blackened his mood.

"Hanner is all right, Bec. He takes the statues to Dodderbanoster. Dodderbanoster takes them to cities beyond my reach and gets a fair price for them. Sometimes I think the pouch Hanner brings back is way too full."

Beccaroon clicked his tongue. "Your father is a master artist. His work is worth a mighty price."

"Hanner says sometimes Dodderbanoster sells them to a dealer who takes them even farther away to thriving districts. Wealthy patrons bid to own a Verrin Schope work of art." She held back a leafy branch so Beccaroon could strut by with ease. "Late at night when I sit in my window and think, I hope that Papa will see one of his sculptures or paintings in a market in some far away metropolis.

"I imagine the scene. He exclaims with shock. He turns red and sputters and shakes his fists. In fact, he's so angry, he comes straight home and yells loud and long at his daughter who dares to sell his masterpieces."

Beccaroon rolled his shoulders, causing his wings to tilt out, then settle against his sides. "What of your mother? Does she ever mention your father's absence?"

"No, why should she? He's been gone for years, but she still sees him. She talks to him every night after his workday is done. Promenades through the garden with him. Pours his tea, and just the other evening, I heard her fussing at him for not giving enough money to the parish."

"I suppose she dipped in the household funds to make up for his neglect."

Tipper sighed. "Yes, she did."

They went on a ways in silence.

Tipper picked a bloom, savored its spicy odor, then placed it behind one pointed ear. "Mother has an idea in her head."

"For anyone else, the head is a splendid place to keep an idea. For your mother, she should just let them go."

"She's determined to visit her sister." Tipper raised her eyebrows so that the upside-down V was even more pronounced. "She'll go, if she manages to pack her long list of necessities. Some of the items are quite unreasonable."

Beccaroon snatched a nut from an open shell on the ground. He played the small nugget over his tongue, enjoying its sweetness, then swallowed. "And you? Is she taking you?"

"No, I'm to stay here and make sure Papa is comfortable and remembers to go to bed at night instead of working till all hours in his studio."

"I don't like you being alone in that house."

"I don't either."

"Of course, there are the servants."

"Only two now."

Beccaroon ruffled his feathers, starting at the tuft on top of his head, fluffing the ruff of his neck, proceeding down his back, and ending with a great shake of his magnificent tail.

"It seems I will have to move into the house."

"Oh, Bec. I was hoping you'd say that."